MW01113432

And I Remember

And I Remember

S. MARSHALL KENT

ARCHWAY
PUBLISHING

Copyright © 2022 S. Marshall Kent.

All rights reserved. No part of this book may be used or reproduced by any means,
graphic, electronic, or mechanical, including photocopying, recording, taping or by
any information storage retrieval system without the written permission of the author
except in the case of brief quotations embodied in critical articles and reviews.

This is a work of fiction. All of the characters, names, incidents,
organizations, and dialogue in this novel are either the products
of the author's imagination or are used fictitiously.

Archway Publishing books may be ordered through booksellers or by contacting:

Archway Publishing
1663 Liberty Drive
Bloomington, IN 47403
www.archwaypublishing.com
844-669-3957

Because of the dynamic nature of the Internet, any web addresses or
links contained in this book may have changed since publication and
may no longer be valid. The views expressed in this work are solely those
of the author and do not necessarily reflect the views of the publisher,
and the publisher hereby disclaims any responsibility for them.

Any people depicted in stock imagery provided by Getty Images are
models, and such images are being used for illustrative purposes only.
Certain stock imagery © Getty Images.

ISBN: 978-1-4808-6720-8 (sc)
ISBN: 978-1-4808-6719-2 (e)

Library of Congress Control Number: 2018909809

Print information available on the last page.

Archway Publishing rev. date: 09/12/2022

Contents

BOOK 11

BOOK 111

A New Beginning

Introduction

Some stories grow in our mind and seem to last forever. They almost haunt you...until...finally you do something about them. This is just one of those stories. It has been brewing in my imagination for years and itching to come out.

It is written as a trilogy because that is how it grew. This is the first time it is being written. Why did it take so long to write? Because: life, love, family and work happened leaving little time for much else.

Bear with me this is not a story about scenery or settings. It is about people, events and the lives they lead along the way, coupled with their thoughts, fears, frustrations, insecurities, and pain. Their challenge was to focus on the realities before them, while unlocking their biases, as they developed good communication and loving relationships unconditionally.

Those that faced those challenges for the sake of love and family learned to accept, understand, forgive, and concur their own demons or misinformation, while learning to love unconditionally. There are those however—as there always seems to be-that wallowed rigidly in their own thinking and biases and unfortunately suffered the consequences.

About The Author

"AND I REMEMBER"

This is S. Marshall Kent's first published book; and it comes in the form of a trilogy. "As a storyteller, I find myself a late bloomer. Retired, my desire to expose the years of thought and compelling stories now seek "Life." My imagination glistens at the thought of seeing my stories written but yields to concern over the "History" of verses and the edification of style. Critics could rightly identify my literary artistry lacks the structure of successful writers of today.

"Yet, we are all "style changers" in one way or another. I seek not to "misguide" my thoughts into complete conformity. Therefore, I ask that the inequities of background, settings and place be forgiven and the reader grasp at the heart within the story."

The book attempts to personify the value of continual communication, understanding, forgiveness and unconditional love and commitment to the point of surrender, peace and bonding.

It delves into the spirit, hearts and minds of the complicated Wilson Family for four generations. This family personifies the journey of human fears, emotions and the continual changing of traditional values.

There is an attempt to put the reader in a position of sideline coaching and routing for one or the other of the characters. The characters are put into the emotional sides of ever emotion.

An attempt is made for the reader to recognize some of the situations, dialogue, results, and mistakes as a way of relationship awareness. The events strive to reveal the inner strength of those who are resourceful, perseverant, understanding, and forgiving as they seek and find family harmony.

The names, characters, events, locations are derived from my growing imagination. I write with a penname primarily to escape the wrath of those more prolific in this craft who could argue I dare encroach on their perfection by attempting to engage in it. With your indulgence, I shall continue to master my style.

Before World War 11

Michael Wilson was a shy young man filled with a love of life that was unchallenged. Michael had many dreams for his and Nora's future together as husband and wife. Nora Wallace fulfilled his every dream.

When Michael returned from serving in the army during World War 11 those dreams developed a glitch. What he lived through while in Germany brought Michael in front of a reality that changed him. When home, in time, those changes would soon become apparent.

The love of "life" Michael enjoyed before the war was now shaded-by the experiences he observed in the war, and they eroded his thinking. Coming home Michael would struggle with marriage, family, discipline and loyalty.

In Germany, Michael witnessed the senseless killing of men, women and children; the destruction of property, the suffering and needless mutilation of humans, without compassion as Hitler and his men attempted the genocide of a human race and much more.

The enthusiasm Michael enjoyed about life, prior to serving in the war, was no longer part of his make-up. His experiences in Germany changed his personality, disposition, and his temperament along with his ability to trust. He faced a sad reality about: life, people, power, loyalty, the love of country, and even the ability to trust.

Michael was now a man filled with heartache, fear, and disenchantment with people—harboring a staunch demand for respect, obedience, and control.

But wait… I am getting ahead of myself

BOOK 1

Chapter 1

Michael, Nora and World War 11

This is a love story about the lives of two high school sweet-hearts Nora Wallace and Michael Wilson. It is about their journey through life together that began on the very first day they met and smiled at each other on the stairs of Clayton High School. Both were entering the ninth grade at the time.

Michael was shy. Nora was outgoing. Her smile broke the ice as she said *"Hi, I am Nora Wilson what's your name?"* The two found themselves in many of the same classes and even in the same lunchroom. It did not take long, and their love grew all through high school. The love birds planned on being married shortly after graduation. They would settle down in Clayton to stay near the family.

Their plans were interrupted by the devastation of World War 11 and the need for young men to fight and right the wrongs that occurred at Pearl Harbor. These men were fighting for freedom, liberty, and the pursuit of happiness and to send a message to those that tampered with the lives of United State Citizens that we would not be deterred from our revenge. Nothing (and no one) was ever going to put the United States down.

Michael, his father-Kevin Wilson, and sister, Rita all lived together in a modest home in Clayton. They, Nora Wallace and her Aunt Lilly Bing were the primary reasons that Michael and Nora decided to stay in Clayton. Family was most important.

The only family Nora Wallace had was her maternal Aunt, and Godmother Lilly Bing. When Nora's parents died Lilly adopted Nora.

Michael Wilson was a strong young man six foot four inches tall with a wide jaw and thick sandy brown hair. A formidable figure of a man with deep brown eyes, long lashes, a strong sturdy stance.

Michael was a gentle natured man acutely aware of his strength. He graduated from high school, with honors. Michael played some sports in high school, but they were not his passion or love.

Michael Wilson was a family man who loved being with his sister Rita, and his father. The family often stayed home together just talking, playing cards, watching television or playing board games. Later as Michael and Nora fell in love and planned to marry, she and her aunt Lilly Bing became part of their family.

Michael's father, Kevin Wilson, was in the insurance business for twelve years before the war began. Michael and his father shared the dream of one day working together. The war was going to delay that dream for a while; but Michael assured his father that when he returned from the war their dream would eventually become a reality.

Chapter 2

Falling in Love Kevin & Mary Jo Wilson

Kevin Wilson and Mary Jo Brook met at "Anthony's Barber Shop." She and her mother were there to clean the barber shop.

Kevin and his father were in the shop. Kevin just finished getting a haircut. As they were leaving his father bumped into Mary Jo's mother almost knocking her down. While his father was apologizing the kids just looked at each other. Shy Mary Jo thought **Kevin was handsome.** She looked into his eyes but turned away quickly as she felt a blush coming on.

Kevin was twelve years old at the time and Mary Jo was ten years old. Kevin was taken back by how pretty she was, with her big smile. Her eyes seemed to sparkle as she looked at him. He never forgot that day. He felt something inside drawing him to her immediately.

Kevin's parents were poor. They lived in a small one-bedroom apartment. Kevin was sleeping with his younger brother on a sofa bed in the living room. The two boys did not own three changes of clothes between them.

Kevin was fifteen years of age when he left home. He found a job cleaning at a local garage. Across the street from the garage, was a rooming house "For Men Only." It was a clean place to live. The rooming house charged $1.50 a week for a sleeping room without services. They changed the sheets every two weeks. Kevin moved in and felt safe there.

The bathroom, for his room, was just down the hall and shared with six other boarders. Four days a week the rooming house provided a bagged dinner at an extra cost of $2.00. The dinner consisted of a slice of bread, half of a baked potato and a small piece of meat; pot roast, meat-loaf, or chicken; a napkin was also in the bag. Eventually, he made friends with the cook; and every so often, if he could afford a bagged dinner, an extra piece of bread was in his bag.

Kevin soon realized that his job did not pay a lot of money. Two weeks later he found a second job at the shop next to the garage, where he was working, at night. He was hired to clean all the building's offices and bath-rooms. There were four offices in the building.

From the garage where Kevin worked, he often saw Mary Jo walking to school. Greeting her, he asked her name, and reminded her of their meeting at the barber shop. In time, Mary Jo began leaving home early giving them more time to be together. That was how the two of them stayed in touch and eventually fell in love and found themselves wanting to marry. Kevin Wilson was seventeen years old when he asked Mary Jo to be his wife; Mary Jo was three months shy of being fifteen years old.

Mary Jo's family was extremely poor, and they were not close. She was the only girl of four children. Her father tended bar for a living and spent much of his time drunk or drinking. Her mother cleaned houses and businesses to supplement their income. Mary Jo was five years older than her next sibling and twelve years older from the last child. She was forced to clean with her mother from the age of seven.

When Mary Jo told her father of Kevin's marriage proposal; her father stared at her for a moment and then said, *"Why not? It would be one less mouth to feed, and less noise around here."*

Kevin and Mary Jo's wedding would not be fancy. Nothing really mattered to them, they were in love and wanted to be together and married.

Mary Jo was aware that Kevin did not earn a lot of money. Kevin knew from their past conversations that Mary Jo wanted to be married by a priest. He began working extra hours at both jobs to have the money to for the wedding. Then he asked Father Joel to marry them.

Working at the garage, Kevin was able to renew his acquaintance with Father Joel. The two men originally met a few years earlier when Kevin attended a Christmas Mass at St. Ann's Church with his mother. The rectory, where father lived, was just across the street from the garage where Kevin now worked. They saw each other often and became close friends chalking up several conversations about life, government control and eventually about love, and marriage.

Father Joel liked Kevin and wanted to help him. He met Mary Jo several times and understood their circumstances. So, when Kevin asked Father Joel to marry them, he agreed. At that time, age was not an issue—in fact -very often young people married. Father Joel knew the couple would not have many possessions-let along money to begin married life. He wanted to give their marriage a head start. He requested the ladies of St. Ann's Church Guild to provide a small "wedding reception" for Kevin and Mary Jo-in the basement of the church-after the wedding service. The ladies agreed.

The day Kevin and Mary Jo were getting married, Mary Jo's mother was ill, and her father was too drunk to understand, or even care, that his daughter was getting married.

Kevin's parents previously moved from their apartment to a new neighborhood across town; Kevin still did not know where they moved too or how to contact them. So, no one from either Kevin's or Mary Jo's family came to the wedding.

Mary Jo did not own a fancy dress let alone money for a wedding dress. She was married wearing a brown shirt-waist dress, without a slip, two sizes too big, and a pair of Buster Brown shoes without socks.

Kevin was married wearing a pair of wool gray pants and a striped green shirt. He wore a pair of shoes that his father gave him when he left home. The shoes were big and fit best if worn with two pair of socks. Each of them had only one or two extra items of clothing besides the clothes they were wearing –at the time they were married.

Father Joel married them in the Chapel at St. Ann's Church. After the service, he invited the couple to join him in the basement of the church. Five ladies from the church guild "congratulated" the couple on getting married. Father announced that through the kindness of the women from the church guild a small "Wedding Reception" has been prepared in their honor. The ladies served coffee, tea, small sandwiches of peanut butter and jelly, and a few cookies. There were a few "gifts" for them through the courtesy of some members of the church congregation.

The gifts consisted of a used electric hot plate, a wool blanket, two sheets, two dishes: two pans-a soup pan and a fry pan. Friends of Father Joel donated $2.00 in cash; and two silverware settings with two water glasses. Another family provided a small end table with two chairs.

Women were not allowed in the rooming house where Kevin lived. He asked a friend to locate a temporary place for them to live. Keven's friend located a room above a garage. There was no stove, ice box, heat or water in the room; but there was electricity and one light bulb hung from the ceiling. The room was for rent for seventy-five cents for that week. The owner said they could stay there just one week. As a wedding gift, the owners invited the couple to a "wedding dinner" consisting of each having beans over bread and a baked apple for dessert and tea.

The first night after they were married, they slept on the floor in the room above the garage snuggled in their large warm wool blanket. The owner of the garage left them several disposable cans that acted as their toilet and some old newspaper.

The day after they were married, they located a thrift shop and purchased a mattress and two pillows for $1.50. They carried the items to the garage. Kevin talked the owner of the garage into letting them live there for two months; while they found another place to live. While the owner agreed, their rent was now $2.75 a month.

The couple lived on a can of soup and a slice of bread each-daily. They heated the soup on their hot plate.

Mary Jo began looking for work immediately. Kevin left both of his jobs. Two business owners, with buildings next door to each other, hired Kevin to clean their offices and their grounds after hours.

Mary Jo found a part time job at Rick's Diner. She began washing dishes and mopping floors three nights a week. The owner of the diner had a daughter around Mary Jo's age. He felt sorry for her –so young- and already married. To help Mary Jo, he allowed one of his waitresses to teach her "How" to wait on tables one hour a day. Mary Jo was not paid for that hour; but she was good with the customers and they liked her.

Mary Jo was a quick learner. The owner of Rick's only wanted her part time and so far not as a waitress-only to clean. Mary Jo was determined to get another job and anxious to earn more money.

Two weeks later, she located a second job, working at a place called "Diamonds" Restaurant. She told the owner she had waitressing "experience." Her hours at Diamonds were 6AM – 1 PM five days a week. Diamonds was a small restaurant purchased six months earlier, by an Italian man from Naples, Mr. Salvatore Tambina. The restaurant currently seated forty customers. There was a small storeroom in the back. Mr. T, as he liked being called, planned on completing the renovation of the storeroom for additional customer seating, within three months. He needed a waitress for the morning rush five days a week, and eventually three afternoons a week for the lunch crowd. Once the back room was opened there would be a total seating for seventy-five customers. Mary Jo was a great waitress from day one. Mr. T promised her more hours as soon as the second seating was opened.

When the owner of Rick's Diner learned that Mary Jo was working at another restaurant as a waitress-he fired her.

After learning that Mary Jo was fired from Rick's Diner; Mr. T hired her full time. Mr. & Mrs. T did not have any children, and they fell in love with Mary Jo right from the day she came in looking for a job. She worked from opening through lunch three days a week: and lunch until close three days a week. When she worked through close, she worked with Mrs. Angela Tambina. Customers called Mrs. T- "Angie."

Angie told Mary Jo she had to know all the ingredients of everything cooked; Mrs. T asked her to "taste" everything made; in this way she could answer customer's questions.

Both Mr. and Mrs. T and Mrs. T's mother (Millie) did all the cooking. Millie began teaching Mary Jo how to prepare everything on the menu-just in case they needed help and to prepare for a larger group once the additional room was completed.

Kevin and Mary Jo continued to dream and save most of their income. Their first dream was to have apartment with; a real kitchen, a living room, a stand-alone bedroom and bathroom. Their goal, and most important dream, was to have a house of their own. Neither one of their families, or anyone they knew, owned a house of their own.

Two months after working at "Diamonds" Mary Jo met Mr. Lester. He was a regular customer and liked talking with Mary Jo. She reminded him of his daughter Megan.

Megan was going to school in Buffalo New York, studying to become a teacher and living with Mr. Lester's mother.

Mr. Lester owned a one room cottage that was "For Rent." The cottage had a full bathroom including a tub and sink, a full kitchen with sink and cabinets. The Kitchen area opened into a sitting area that doubled as a bedroom with a small sofa opening into a bed. There was a small space heater that made the place comfortable on cold nights.

Mr. Lester offered the place to them. The moment Kevin and Mary Jo walked in they loved the place. The room was quaint and with the heater ready for winter. The cottage was close to the bus stop and stores for shopping. It gave them a warm feeling. Taking a bus or shopping would be limited as the increase in their rent cut into their budget. Despite the high rent-this was a step in the right direction to fulfill their dreams. Mr. Lester gave them a break on their rent. It would now be $8.75 a month. They lived there for eight months. Mr. Lester also found Mary Jo a weekend job cleaning a small business office.

A girlfriend, Debbie Hacker, from Mary Jo's grammar school, came into Diamonds restaurant. The girls renewed their friendship. Debbie wanted to help Kevin and Mary Jo locate a "real" apartment. She asked her dad for help. Two months later Debbie's father located a vacant third-floor walk-up apartment on Spring Street a few blocks further down from the cottage. The apartment had: a full bathroom, a separate bedroom, and a large kitchen with a dining area, a small stove and an ice box.

The rent was $10.25 per month. The bus stop was close by but, with the increase in rent, would not be used too often.

This was a "real" apartment and the kids rented it. The people that moved from the flat left a coffee pot, some cups, a deck of playing cards, some sheets, pillowcases, and some tea towels. Mary Jo washed the sheets in the tub. They still had the used mattress and pillows from the thrift shop, along with the table and chairs and the other items they received as wedding gifts. The couple lived frugally, putting the mattress on the floor. They would look for a bed frame later. One month after they moved into the apartment while walking down Spring Street, heading to work, they noticed someone discarding an old two cushion sofa; they asked the owner for permission to take the sofa.

The owner of the sofa said: *"He would not allow them to have the sofa unless they gave him seventy-five cents."* Kevin asked the man *"Why charge them if he was throwing the sofa out?"* The man answered *"Because it is my experience that young people do not appreciate having things unless they pay for them. So, I want you to pay for the sofa."*

Kevin asked the man if he would take fifty-five cents for the sofa. The man agreed. Kevin helped the man put the sofa back into his garage. They needed to figure a way to move the sofa to their apartment.

The negations took a long time, and the kids were late for work; the nice man agreed to drive them to where they worked. They accepted and thanked him for his kindness.

On Saturday they returned to pick up the sofa. Without a car or truck the two of them carried the sofa – one at each end – carefully, stopping to rest often- down Spring Street to their apartment.

Walking with the sofa was not as hard as carrying it up to their third -floor apartment. But this was their first sofa—and their first real apartment. When the job was completed—the two of them sat on their sofa—looked at each other—and burst into laughter. They knew that having furniture in their apartment meant they had arrived at beginning to establish a home.

With a place for people to sit, the first thing they planned on doing was to invite Debbie Hacker and her sister Ann over for an evening of rummy and coffee.

Two years later Kevin and Mary Jo were still in the same third-floor walk- up apartment still dreaming of owning a home-one day.

Every week, like clockwork, on their way home from work they stopped at the Clayton National Saving Bank to make their deposit.

Chapter 3

A House

Kevin Wilson and Donald Cameron had been friends for two years. The two men met-when Donald was doing some construction work at one of the restaurants where Kevin was employed.

Donald and his wife, Candy wanted to move to California. They believed California was the land of the future, bustling with opportunities just waiting to be tapped. They wanted to live a comfortable life in a warm climate and not freeze in winter. He and Candy were confident they could live nicely without heating bills to pay or purchasing snow equipment. They surmised they could even save money by planting a garden and growing their own food. This was their driving force in wanting to move to California. Donald worked construction for the last five years and hated being laid off every winter.

Donald and Candy owned a house on Rogers Road in Clayton. They purchased it two years earlier. The house had approximately 950 square feet of living area sitting on a 35 x 110 lot that was fenced. There was one small bedroom, a living room, kitchen and dining area, full bath, a utility room and a full un-finished full attic and basement. The house had many possibilities needing work and money.

Donald had ideas but, in the time, they lived there he did not repair or update the house in any way. The only reason he and Candy were able to purchase the house was because: it had an "assumable" bank mortgage; Mrs. Dorm, the original owner of the house wanted to sell and move into an apartment. Candy's parents gave them all the funds necessary for the transaction.

An "assumable mortgage" means:
If someone wants to purchase a house—from an owner-who wants to sell-the buyer (the persons that want to buy the house) gives the owner an amount of money-in cash-to cover the difference between what the owner (s) wants to sell, called the "Sale Price," of the current mortgage balance at the time the transaction closes.

This amount (the difference between the sale price and the mortgage balance) is called the owners "equity."

When the seller (s) agrees to the amount (the money to be received in cash) and the sale price-a deal is made.

Legal papers are drawn-up by an attorney and signed by all parties (the seller and the buyer) to solidify their agreement.

The papers identify the sale price, and that the buyer (s) is assuming the balance of the current mortgage and giving the seller the difference between the two amounts at the time the sale closes.

Finalizing the transaction, requires the buyer to pay: <u>A bank a fee-to put his (and/or her) name (s) as new owner(s) on the balance of the mortgage; the buyer also</u>

pays the transfer of ownership tax known as a "state tax." This also records (there may be an additional fee) the new owner or owners. When all the fees and tax payments are made, the buyer (s) may move into the home. Once the buyer moves in- the next order of business is to obtain "home-owner's insurance."

Mrs. Dorm and Candy's mother had been friends for many years. She watched Candy grow up and went to her wedding. When the house was too much to handle, she decided to help the "kids" own a home.

Mr. and Mrs. Dorm had been married many years and loved each other very much. When Mr. Dorm died, he provided for her with sufficient funds, to keep her comfortable for the rest of her life, in his will.

She agreed to accept $500 in cash (equity) to sell the house (sale price) to Candy and her husband; **if she had the legal assurance of being released from owner-ship of the house and the responsibility for the mortgage.** Candy and Donald agreed to the purchase; Mrs. Dorm's attorney drew-up the papers. When they were all signed and recorded -with all fees and taxes paid- Donald and Candy became owners of the home. Living in the home –they purchased the needed home-owner's insurance.

Nothing ever stays the same and people change.

Donald and Candy decided to sell the house; they wanted to move to California. Donald knew Kevin and Mary Jo's dream was to one-day own a home.

Since Donald and Candy purchased the house by assuming the mortgage; Donald felt that would be how he would sell it to Kevin and Mary Jo; thereby, making their dream come true. Their banker identified the mortgage was still assumable. Donald felt this would be a "win/win" for both families.

Candy was anxious to move. She and Donald were caring for Candy's niece Ellen who was in the second grade. Ellen's mother was Candy's sister. After her back surgery, her husband was not able to care for his wife and their child—while also working.

They asked Candy to allow Ellen to live with them for a year until her mother was able to get back on her feet. Ellen's parents felt it would be a good experience for the child. And they agreed to compensate Donald for the additional expense.

Donald and Candy felt it would be a good experience for them as well as a little extra money in their pockets. Ellen loved Candy and Donald. She was excited about the idea of moving in with them. Ellen slept on a cot in the utility room for the entire school year.

The more Donald and Candy thought about moving-the more they felt that taking Ellen back to her parents in California in August -would be the perfect time to move.

Donald decided to "work on" Kevin while Ellen was in school- with the idea of "selling the house to him" by the time they were ready to leave. Donald needed the money to drive to California. So, he began talking to Kevin.

He explained to Kevin that *"All he had to do was to pay him $900 and assume the mortgage payments at the Bank. It was just that simple."*

He surmised that: **If Kevin wanted a house badly enough, he would find the money to take over the mortgage.**

Kevin knew Donald very well; he also knew Candy's parents and Mrs. Dorm. He was fully aware of the entire transaction that took place when Donald purchased Mrs. Dorm's house.

He figured the $900 Donald was asking would provide him a large profit for doing nothing to the property to either maintain it or enhance its value. Kevin turned down the "opportunity." But Donald was determined to push Kevin.

In February, after lowering his offer to $685, he mentioned to Kevin: *"The monthly mortgage payment was $33.86 a month with taxes and government insurance."*

Kevin could not think of a way to have enough money to pay for the monthly mortgage; or pay Donald; let along have money left over to pay for everything else necessary when owning a home. He turned the "offer" down again.

Kevin and Mary Jo were saving money all along now they tried to figure out a way to save even more. They both worked in restaurants. Mr. T gave Mary Jo all her meals at the restaurant "Free" from the time she began working there. She was already working a second job cleaning a business office.

Mary Jo asked Mrs. T to hire her to clean their restaurant on the nights she was off. Angela agreed. It was a help because Angela and her mother usually cleaned the restaurant themselves on those nights.

One of Kevin's jobs was cleaning a restaurant in the basement of a department store. The manager agreed to let Kevin bus tables during lunch three days a week and give him all the day's left-over cooked food. Kevin and Mary Jo only kept oatmeal and milk in the apartment.

By the end of March, Donald was becoming more anxious to sell. He changed the offer to $590 over the mortgage if they could do it by the first of July.

Kevin and Mary Jo did not have that much money saved and they could not borrow from anyone. This was another opportunity they would just have to turn down.

In April, Donald tried again changing his offer. His new offer reduced the amount to $545.

Donald said he would accept half the money up front and allow Kevin to pay the difference at the rate of $20 per month until the balance was paid in full.

Donald was not happy when they turned this offer down. They were leaving for California no later than August 1ˢᵗ. Candy wanted to be near her sister in California. Donald's friend in California had recently finished building an apartment above his garage. He told Donald that if they came to California, he would let them live in that apartment "rent free" for three months until they could find a job. Donald figured that living "rent free" would help him with selling his house to Kevin and Mary Jo.

Ellen's parents were ready to have her back and time was getting short. He and Candy were arguing as they needed some cash for the trip. Donald was determined to work out a deal with Kevin to buy his house, no matter what; he was not going to take "no" for an answer.

Meanwhile, Kevin and Mary Jo were excited at the idea of owning a home. They really wanted to buy the house. Kevin was gambling that Donald would reduce the price more as time got closer to August. Fate was knocking at their door-it was thrilling. They also knew that this opportunity needed to be viewed carefully.

The end of May, Donald was desperate. He approached Kevin with an offer he could not refuse. He changed the amount due in cash to $400 over the mortgage with just $100 down and $20 per month until the $400 was paid in full. When it was paid, Mrs. Dorm's attorney would finalize the sale.

For Kevin and Mary Jo, there was no choice they decided to take the offer. They needed to figure out how to pay $20 a month to Donald along with everything else like the mortgage, insurance, gas bills, electric, water, and just the normal maintenance of owning a home; never mind food, clothing, or bus transportation in the winter.

Owning a home was exciting, invigorating and truly frightening -a double-edge sword. But it was an answer to their prayers.

Kevin and Mary Jo had saved a little over $200 to date. Mary Jo was worried and told Kevin. He told her not to worry it just made wrinkles and solved nothing. Kevin agreed to the deal. Now, they needed to figure out: how to physically make the move as the house was located four blocks away from their apartment.

They did not own a car and no one they knew had a truck they could borrow. Neither one knew how to drive anyway. When they moved into the apartment, they made friends with a neighbor. Kevin called him. He had a wheelbarrow and agreed to loan it to them.

Kevin was determined to walk their belongings four long blocks to their new home with the wheelbarrow; he felt with the wheelbarrow-it would take four trips! Figuring there would be two trips carrying the shopping bags they saved, for their personal belongings and small stuff.

**As luck would have it, they were
in for some surprises**

It rained the day of they moved. It took six exhausting trips with the wheelbarrow to get some items to the house, but the wheelbarrow was too small for the sofa. They wrapped the sofa in a blanket and began to walk with one on each end to their house. A nice lady saw them and felt sorry for them. She lent them a large tarp to put over the sofa. She said they could return it when they walked by on their way to work.

The tarp saved the sofa from the rain.

Chapter 4

Making It Work

Kevin and Mary Jo moved into the house, fifteen minutes before Donald and Candy left for California. Candy told Mary Jo that she left the monthly bills on the kitchen counter.

There was no time for discussion; Donald said:

"Our new address is on the cover of the bill folder; that is where you are to send the $20 monthly until the balance of the down payment of $400 is paid." And with that said they accepted Kevin's $125 in cash and gave Kevin a receipt. Next, they both Kevin and Mary Jo needed to sign some papers. Once the papers were signed Donald, Candy and Ellen walked out the door.

Kevin and Mary Jo sat at the table and reviewed the bills for the house. They were flabbergasted. This was the first time Kevin had some doubt about accepting Donald's offer. The cost of home ownership was a real surprise.

Kevin was not sure how they would be able to handle the house, let alone purchase food, pay the gas bill, water, and electric bills or travel back and forth to work in the winter. The house was much further from their jobs and walk would be difficult, tiring and time consuming during the winter.

Still, they had gone through with the purchase and signed the papers. The woman at the bank told them they would need something called "homeowners' insurance." Mary Jo upset looking at the bills and thinking about the homeowner's insurance. She began to cry and said:
"Kevin, there is no way we can meet all these expenses. I am worried. We still need to purchase the insurance. We really could lose this h" Kevin interrupted *"I promise you; Mary Jo I will figure this out. We will have this house forever! What do I always say about worrying—it will add wrinkles? Your face is fine just the way it is. Trust your husband; I will not let you down."*

Mark Row was a regular customer at one of the restaurants where Kevin cleaned, and he sold insurance. He would often come in late after his visiting customers.

He and Kevin talked frequently and over time they had become friends. Kevin approached Mark for the "homeowner's insurance" they needed.

Mark Row liked both Mary Jo and Kevin he was able to provide them the kind of insurance that permitted monthly installment payments instead of a lump sum.

Kevin was very appreciative. He then confided: *"Mark, I may have bit off more than I expected with the house. Mary Jo is worried- of course she is a worrier. Even though we are going to set up a budget tonight; we really do need a hope and a prayer to make this work."*

Their budget left nothing for food, transportation, clothes, or repairs. The house was further away from their work and in the winter it would be difficult. But they were determined to make it work. They concluded that walking to work even in the winter was healthy and just part of the deal of owning a home.

The next week they stopped at a thrift store and purchased two more wool blankets. With the blankets, they planned on keeping the temperature in the house down to sixty-five degrees.

Searching the house, they found an old toolbox in the attic. There was a hammer, several screw drivers, nails and some clips, for hanging pictures.

Candy had said: *"I have already packed what will fit in the truck. You can keep whatever we left behind. There are a number of boxes around the house and in the basement and attic."*

They located a toolbox that Cheryl's father gave Donald as a Christmas gift—still wrapped—never opened. They decided to check out the rest of the stuff at another time.

The first week of September Mark Row spoke to Kevin about his working in the insurance business. Row saw it as an opportunity for both men. He was tired of all the late nights. Selling insurance dictated home visits, and Mark found himself traveling six days a week. By now, Mark had been in the insurance business for fifteen years. He managed the business alone. It was to his benefit to hire Kevin and let the younger man do the leg work.

Mark felt that with him as Kevin's teacher he could easily learn the business in six months. His success would bring about an expansion of the business while helping Kevin and Mary Jo. He felt Kevin had all the qualities to make an excellent insurance salesman.

Mark Row was forty-five years old with sandy-brown hair and large hazel eyes. At five-foot-nine inches tall, he walked with a slight limp due to an accident years ago.

Mark enticed Kevin by mentioning the money he would make. He said *"Look Kevin, you will have every penny of your current salaries from both your jobs; plus, I will pay all your transportation costs and the insurance test expenses; I will give you an extra $30 per month while you learn. You get to pay the bank, and Donald with a few dollars left over. Think this over Kevin, Mary Jo stops worrying, and you become a great husband and salesman."*

Kevin discussed it with Mary Jo and then accepted the offer. Mark was delighted. Mark offered Kevin a 66/34 commission split on any new business Kevin brought in during his training period. Mark also agreed to give Kevin a six month draw against commissions after he passed his licensing test.

Kevin took the offer as the bills for the house were coming faster than he had imagined. He kept his weekend job cleaning at the restaurants as a fallback position; they needed the money.

Mary Jo had no doubt that Kevin would be successful. This was a real opportunity for him. His job would put him into the "Professional" category. She was a bit concerned that; when Kevin was successful, he would look down on her as not being educated enough for him. Kevin assured her: *"Listen my worrier; you are the love of my life-forever and ever!"*

A week after joining Mark, Kevin went to the library and took out a book titled "The Art of Salesmanship." Kevin was an avid learner and Mark was a great teacher. Kevin passed the insurance test in four months. When Kevin passed, he quit his night jobs. Mark Row and his wife, Karina were best friends of the Wilsons by now. They took the couple out to dinner to celebrate Kevin's passing the test.

Mary Jo was expanding her culinary abilities as Karina was giving her pointers on French cooking, along with pointers on decorating, makeup and dress.

In less than a year, Kevin was selling insurance on his own. When Mark and Karina were over for an evening of playing cards; while sitting at the table Kevin mentioned that the living room was drab and that they needed to "dress" up the house some. Mark said he had some left-over cream beige paint from painting the offices and he offered it to Kevin. Karina suggested some artificial flowers.

Mark and Karina were invited to dinner on Saturday. The men decided that would be a good time to paint the living room. Mark offered to bring over the paint and help. Karina purchased the artificial flowers for Mary Jo. The women decided this would be a good time for them to shop while the men painted.

Shopping proved successful. The ladies returned with a pair of curtains for the back door, a tablecloth for the kitchen, and a bookshelf. The new paint job looked beautiful, and the flowers gave the room a festive look.

Everyone felt the day "well done" as they enjoyed baked chicken, stuffed potatoes, and home-made apple pie Mary Jo prepared.

A year later Mary Jo was still working her two jobs and Kevin was a top salesman selling insurance. They were now able to handle all their bills and have a flexible budget.

But nothing in life ever remains the same.

Just as they were feeling comfortable with the house and the bills, Mary Jo's father came to visit. He said Mary Jo's *"Mother was ill, and the mid-wife, Mrs. Rita Arcana, said she was going to die soon."*

Mary Jo decided to visit her mother thinking: **"How could Mrs. Arcana know that my mother was going to die? My mother is only forty-five years old.**

Mary Jo remembered the night her mother saw her father coming out of her bedroom. Mary Jo was crying, and her father was drunk and closing his pants. Her mother yelled and asked her husband, "What did you do? What did you do? She is just a little girl."

They argued and her drunk father began hitting her mother repeatedly in the stomach. Mary Jo cried and tried to help her mother, but her father slapped her so hard she fell to the floor and passed out. Her father always hit her mother where there would not be any visible marks. No one ever spoke of that night again.

Mary Jo wondered if all her father's regular hitting caused her mother damage and this pain

What happened to her that night when her father came into her room was something Mary Jo would never tell Kevin or **anyone**! Only Mary Jo, her parents and God knew.

A few days after her father's visit Mary Jo went to visit her mother. Her mother was in bed, thin and in pain barely able to talk. Her mother asked, *"If Kevin ever hits her."* *"Never"* she answered. *"Good"* she said. *"Promise me, that you would leave him if he ever does hit you? Promise me!"* Mary Jo promised. Her mother could not talk long; she was in pain. Mary Jo left crying.

Three weeks later Mary Jo's mother passed away.

Her father came to their house again for help to bury her mother. *"After all,"* he said, *"You two own a house-why should I pay anything?"*

That night Mary Jo spoke to Kevin asking his help with the burial cost. The wooden coffin was $55, and the plot was $80. There would not be a wake, or any embalming-her mother would be placed in a "bag." Kevin paid the total cost to bury her mother. Mary Jo knew her father would never give them any of the money back. Kevin said it really did not matter.

With the genuine kindness Kevin showed, Mary Jo fell deeply in love with Kevin. She was so proud of the man she married. She knew Kevin would never hurt her or lie to her-that he would always be good to her and take care of her. She trusted him completely.

She was willing to do everything and anything she could to make her husband proud of her and a happy man. Mary Jo made that her goal in their marriage.

Chapter 5

The Family Grows

The first six months after Kevin was licensed, he brought in as much money as Mark–in a year. Mark agreed to split commissions 50/50. Kevin and Mary Jo were overjoyed.

It was just about that time; Mary Jo was feeling out of sorts and tired. She mentioned it to Karina who made an appointment for Mary Jo to see her doctor. It was the first time Mary Jo had ever been to a doctor and she was not sure she would ever return. She decided not to tell Kevin what the doctor had to do that day. But, at the end of the appointment she learned they were going to have a baby.

The doctor suggested Mary Jo delivers their baby at the hospital. They did not own a car or drive; and the hospital was too far and would be too expensive.

When Kevin came home, she told him about the baby. They both felt that she should be a stay-at-home mother and wife. But how would they manage? Who would deliver the baby?

With a baby coming, Kevin and Mark re-negotiated their commission arrangement. Kevin was a natural go getter bringing in more business than Mark dreamed. Their new commission was now 55/45. But there was a change. Mark had been paying Kevin's transportation to his clients. Now Kevin would pay his own transportation costs. Eventually, Kevin said they would own a car on day but for now that would have to wait a while.

The doctor felt the baby would arrive in May. This gave them seven months to plan. Karina began showing Mary Jo how to make calls and appointments for Kevin. In this way when she was no longer working, she could, set up his appointments, and keep his schedule and records.

Since her mother's death Mrs. Arcana visited Diamonds often to see Mary Jo. On her last visit she told Mary Jo *"Your father has a girlfriend. They are getting married and moving to Ohio."*

Mary Jo was stunned and asked about her siblings. *"I understand they are all out of the house on their own now. Too bad they were all so young."* Mrs. Arcana said. As for her father, Mary Jo had no love lost.

Mrs. Arcana noticed that Mary Jo was pregnant. She mentioned living only one bus away, and if Mary Jo decided not to go to the hospital, she would be available to help. Mary Jo invited her to their home for tea on Friday.

From that day on Mrs. Arcana became a regular visitor helping Mary Jo prepare for the baby.

Mary Jo wanted to learn enough to one-day pass the high school equivalency test. She was a fast learner but needed help learning to read and write better. Mrs. Arcana brought over books for Mary Jo to read, and helped her with writing, spelling and math.

She gave Mary Jo her first journal and told her to begin writing in it as a "memory" of all they had been through.

As the time for the baby grew close, Mary Jo asked Kevin *"If they had a girl would it be okay to name her "Rita Ann after Mrs. Arcana."* He agreed. She then asked: *"If the baby is a boy would you want "Kevin Junior?"*

"No," he said. *"I would like Michael" after my father."* Mary Jo agreed.

When Mary Jo went into labor, Kevin called Mrs. Arcana. She came as soon as she received the call. Eighteen hours after Mrs. Arcana arrived at the house "Rita Ann" was born. The baby was beautiful.

By the time Rita Ann was a month-old Mary Jo was keeping Kevin's records, making all his calls, setting up appointment. They were working together as a team.

This team spirit developed into a charmed life as now Kevin was really making a lot of money.

The Family Continues To Grow

Two years after Rita was born, Michael joined the family. Mrs. Arcana had left Clayton by then and her sister Violet helped Mary Jo deliver Michael. Kevin was ecstatic-a boy to continue the name. Mark gave Kevin a five per cent bonus from his earnings every year from then on.

Happiness and success lasted nine years. During that time, the couple earned enough to pay off the mortgage on the house, do many repairs. They were living comfortably with two children, and they were the envy of everyone that knew them.

Life has many twists and turns

Kevin was a great salesman with a tremendous following. He was now getting a 70/30 split on all the business he brought to the firm. Mary Jo continued setting up Kevin's appointments and keeping his files.

When both children were in school, one of Kevin's clients offered Mary Jo a part time job of two days a week four hours a day. The money was great; she had the time and could work from home while the children were in school- she was able to do it all.

Kevin reluctantly agreed. He had become used to having her around so he could stop for lunch or have her change appointments. His clients all loved her, and she handled all questions without a problem.

Mary Jo loved her work and was able to make and record his appointments, handle all the records, keep the house and children in check. She handled it all easily.

The couple really had arrived –they had enough money to take the children out for dinner to the Swiss Chalet a couple of times a month.

They purchased beds for the children; and by the time Rita was five years old Kevin finished a bedroom for her by adding a window, door and small closet to the utility room. Later he cut the attic in half making a bedroom for Michael keeping the other half as the children's "Office." He installed lights and a desk for each of the children to do their schoolwork or play some board games.

Life was peaceful, the kids were good and smart in school. Kevin and Mary Jo were still very much in love. Both dreamed that their children would finish high school one day and even go to a college.

Chapter 6

Mary Jo

While in the shower, Mary Jo found a small round ball on her left breast. "**What could it be**?" The family rarely needed a doctor, but Mary Jo decided she should make an appointment.

Since she was a new patient, she had to wait two months for an appointment. It was a long two months. The stress of waiting caused her to lose about six pounds from her already ever so small frame.

During the appointment, the doctor asked Mary Jo to permit some tests. Cost was a factor she asked the doctor to do only the most important tests. When the tests results were in the doctor asked Mary Jo to come into the office. **Cancer** was and is a terrible disease. When the doctor told Mary Jo his diagnosis of her condition, she cried. The doctor said: "*The cancer has spread and there is little that could be done at this time; however, that said, there are some new methods I am willing to try.*"

Mary Jo needed to talk with Kevin. When he came home, she told him what the doctor said. They cried together that night and made love. They held on to each other tightly the rest of the night.

Mary Jo had one of the first cases of infiltrating breast cancer in Clayton. Even the removal of her breasts did not help or change the situation. It took her life in four-long-painful years. Kevin was with her all time-he never left her. He worked when she slept.

Mark Row helped him with some of his calls. And at the end Kevin was at her side. He took Mary Jo to the hospital when they tried radiation but to no avail. She was sick and cried often as she was wasting away. Kevin was always there holding her hand. And every day just as before the cancer he told her he loved her.

Cancer and death took Mary Jo from her loving family. Michael and his sister, Rita were devastated by their mother's death. Rita Wilson was close to her mother.

During her sickness, Mary Jo continued to teach Rita as much as she could about caring for the family, knowing full well that after her death Rita would become the "lady" of the house.

Chapter 7

Things Change

Rita Ann Wilson was five feet three inches tall and weighed about one-hundred pounds soaking wet. She had curly dark brown hair and big brown eyes. She was just fourteen years old when her mother died. Rita did all the housework, cooking, cleaning and shopping.

Michael was twelve years old when Mary Jo died. Before her death he helped his father with the work outside; but when Mary Jo died it was all left to him.

When Mary Jo Wilson was ill, Kevin never complained or showed signs of weakening to Mary Jo, the children or to Mark.

After Mary Jo's death Kevin became a basket case. In shock, he was not able to cope. For weeks, he sat in a chair crying. He ate little and never went into the bed. He slept in a chair in the living room. He was a lonely, broken man.

Mark did not realize the deep depression Kevin would be going through after her death. The last time Kevin took Mary Jo to the hospital; she kissed the children and told them she loved them. Then she asked them to "Take *care of their father.*" It was as if she knew she would not be returning.

Going to the cemetery to find her final resting place was so traumatic for Kevin that Mark knew he had to go with him. When they found the plot where both, would be buried Kevin knelt on the ground and cried. Mark's wife Karina stayed with Rita and Michael as often as she could when Mary Jo was ill; and, even for a year after she was buried.

Mary Jo's treatments changed her looks drastically. She did not want their children's final image of her to be one in the casket. Kevin placed a picture of Mary Jo on top of the closed casket. Many of Kevin's clients and friends came to the funeral and remarked how beautiful she looked in that picture. Mark and Karina helped the children handle the stress of the funeral.

Mary Jo died in the Hospital. Her struggle changed Kevin. He was not himself. His patience had been worn thin, along with his zest and zeal for life. His nerves and emotions had been so tested that he lost his reason for living.

The children tried to help him regain himself, but he was just out of it.

As time passed, Kevin was slowly able to get a hold of the situation. His children watched him suffer and truly felt his pain. Unfortunately, Keven never realized that his children also suffered a lot of pain, with losing their mother and their father's lack of interest in life. It was like losing both parents at one time. The children were fortunate to have Mark, Karina and each other. They talked out some of their issues.

Mark also made sure there was enough money for food and the household bills.

In time to survive and return to productivity; Kevin went back to selling insurance. He paid Kelly-Mark's sister- to make his appointments and handle his files.

Time and loneliness where Kevin's enemies and he took his frustrations out on Michael. *"Just once,"* Kevin said, *"I will show you Michael how to handle paying the household bills."* He taught Michael how to write a check; clip the receipt to the bill and have the envelope ready for his review. If Kevin agreed with the bill, and liked how the check was written, he would sign the check. Once the check was signed it was Michael's job to place the signed check and the original bill in an envelope, stamp it, and walk it to the post office on his way to school.

Kevin would not listen to any excuses. If the penmanship was sloppy, Michael saw the check ripped up. Kevin often told his children *"What you two do reflects on me; and I do not want to be embarrassed! Do you both understand?"*

Michael enjoyed helping his dad. He witnessed his father's respect and love for Mary Jo; while understanding the strain his father had been under, for years, with his Mother's illness and death. His father's love for Mary Jo gave Michael an example for not only being a good man; but, also for being a good husband as well.

Michael took his responsibilities very seriously. He set up a filing system for the household bills and receipts so if Kevin ever needed to be sure a bill was paid-he had the evidence.

Everything was kept for his father's review-even the reconciling of the bank statements.

As the years passed after Mary Jo's death, the kids became Kevin's life. Eventually, everything he did was for them. The family established a routine for shopping, holidays, and having some fun together. Much of their free time was spent together. They played card games, board games, went for walks together, and out to dinner as a family. Kevin pushed his children to do well in school and low and behold both were excellent students.

Rita Wilson graduated from high school at seventeen years old. Kevin was proud of his daughter, and he purchased a Kodak camera to memorialize her graduation day. The three celebrated the day at the Swiss Chalet Restaurant. It was the first time they had been there without Mary Jo.

Rita was not sure her father was financially able to permit her to attend college. She turned down a date for the senior prom because she would not ask her father for money for a dress. She was not comfortable asking for anything. She knew that Mary Jo's illness took all the money her parents had in the bank

She had plans of her own; the first was to learn "customer service." She found a job at a small shoe store located off Main Street. The owners of the store, Mr. and Mrs. Laden agreed to teach her the business of sales.

Rita's work hours were 1-6 PM Monday, Wednesday and Thursday; and 9 AM -2PM Friday and Saturday. The Laden's lived upstairs in a rented apartment. Mrs. Laden handled the store when Rita was not there; she was also the bookkeeper.

Rita was hired-to give Mrs. Laden more time with the children. The position was only temporary, as the building's lease expired November 1st. At that time, the Laden's planned to close the shop and leave Clayton returning to Mrs. Laden's family located in Tonawanda New York.

Rita eventually planned to apply for a job at "Taylor's Fashion Boutique." It was an "Up-scale ladies dress shop. Salesladies applying, with customer service experience, received ten cents more an hour. They were the first to be placed on a "commission plus basis" in the most expensive departments; and the first to be moved "up" for promotion as department heads.

It was a good plan, and it would have worked; except the war changed everything; and money was tight all over.

With the advent of the war many women, including Mrs. Laden, became a Red Cross Volunteer. Mrs. Laden would often talk about her experiences at the Red Cross while she was at the store. She thought it her "civic duty" to suggest that Rita become a Red Cross Volunteer.

Off from work and bored one day, Rita applied at the Red Cross. After her interview, Rita received a call from the personnel office. The lady made no mention of a volunteer position-instead, she was offered a full-time job. The personnel lady went into detail, telling Rita all about the position. Rita felt this was an opportunity to learn about health care and people. She accepted the position and agreed to attend the ten-week training.

She was lucky the Red Cross training was from 8 AM until Noon on Tuesdays and 6 PM to 9 PM three days a week. With those unusual hours, it meant Rita could keep her job at the shoe store and still do the training. The Red Cross inspired her to think about college. She began to daydream about the future, and her options.

Her dreams led her to think about continuing her education **"I wonder what would my future "hold: if I were able to get a college education? Money being the key factor; would identify my educational options.**"

Helping people gave Rita a good feeling inside. Being a nurse sounded nice but there are many different fields in medicine to explore. Research was needed to make a reasonable determination as to a future career. She put it out of her mind for now.

There was a war going on and while that was happening, she had the ability to save money and take, all the training the Red Cross had to offer. The training was "Free," and there was no pressure. It would look good on a resume.

The job at the Red Cross was hard, stressful work. Most people working there were volunteers. She was fortunate to have a paying position -that included free training. Still, she needed to think of her future, and right now she could barely make ends meet.

She decided to search for another position. Once in the city, she applied to all the department stores for a position. One store had a sign out: "Hiring." Rita applied and secured an interview on the spot. She received a call from their personnel offering her a part-time job three days a week, Friday, Saturday, and Monday. One of the benefits offered was a five percent discount on all purchases. She immediately accepted the position.

Rita noticed Kevin was home more these days. Unusual for someone in the Insurance Business. Insurance is a service business 24/7. Hesitant to question her father; she reasoned that the war-most likely- put damper on spending. Many people did not have extra funds to purchase insurance.

Everyone seemed to suffer during this time. Kevin Wilson was not able to keep his insurance position. The commissions he and Mark earned were insufficient to support two families-Mark's and his.

Consequently, Kevin found a job at the local grocery Store. It was a clean place to work, and the people were very friendly. Kevin needed a job that paid a regular salary. This grocery store was only one bus ride away-super convenient.

Michael was going to graduate High School at the end of June. Kevin felt Michael would get a job and contribute just like Rita. Rita was contributing fifty percent of her income.

Kevin knew Mary Jo was smiling down on him for keeping his promise—both of their children would soon be high school graduates! He hoped Rita would find a nice young man and marry.

He felt confident that Michael's girl-friend Nora would make him a lovely wife one day. **It was as if his job and struggle to be a good father was over—except for the war.**

Chapter 8

Michael

Kevin Wilson loved his children deeply. They were his life. Now the country was at war—and it frightened him. It brought back his old fears to the point that his body trembled. Death is so real and final.

"Lord, I have a son. I beg You to keep my son and all the young men of this country safe. Please Lord, <u>End</u> this terrible war."

It was on a Monday afternoon when the registered letter from the draft board came in for Michael. Kevin face dropped. His fears of Michael being drafted into the war were now a reality. Michael would now be taken to join those fighting in the war, far from home, and in constant danger of being killed.

The possibility of losing Michael brought back the fear of what he went through with Mary Jo, and the despair he lived with for so long, with her Breast Cancer and eventual death.

Just two weeks earlier, Kevin received notice that his parents died in an apartment fire. Now he was facing the reality, and possibility, of losing his only son. He was beside himself trying to stay calm.

**"Lord, enough is enough—Please
PLE ASE DO NOT TAKE MY SON!**

Kevin put the letter from the draft board on the hall table. When Rita came home, she saw the registered letter and began to cry. Kevin noticed her tears and gave her a hug. *"We must be strong for Michael. He cannot go to war thinking we do not expect to see him again. We must pray for his safe return and write him often keeping things positive in all our letters. Okay? God will bring him back to us and we will all be together again."* *"I understand"* Rita said.

When Michael arrived home, Kevin asked him if they could sit together for a few minutes in the living room and talk. Michael agreed. The two men discussed their feelings about the war and the responsibility of every citizen to help protect the United States, its freedoms, values, land and most important of all its people and our democracy.

Kevin spoke of the many dangers of the war. He mentioned how a lack of trust from one country to the next, was changing the world.

"We trust people from other countries, not to revolt against any other country; that everyone would compromise and seek peace. In this way, all the peoples of the world would have a good life. But sometime people have fears, and fears seem to mount at times. Things happen and egos increase, as does the desire to save face. A loss of desire to compromise many times leads to war." He said: *"I have a fear not just for your physical safety Michael, but also for the mental and emotional health of all the soldiers-serving in the war. The visions of destruction, the killings and the deaths, have a way of infiltrating a person's thinking and changing their lives."*

It was then he told Michael that a letter from the draft board arrived. He asked him to stay mentally strong and safe. Father and son loved each other and hugged. Kevin gave Michael the letter.

Rita was in the kitchen listening when Michael read the letter she came into the room. She told her brother: *"Michael you are an integral part of this family. We would be lost without you. Please take care of yourself. I love you."* They proceeded to a group hug. Michael graduated from high school two weeks earlier hardly gave him enough time to get a job. The letter identified that Michael was to report for a physical in five days and be ready for immediate deployment.

Kevin and Rita knew that five days would go by very quickly. Michael called Nora. As he told her of the letter from the draft board her tears just seemed to flow. *"I will write Michael and pray. Please come back to all of us?"* Nora said. *"I promise"* Michael said.

Three days passed and Kevin was getting more stressed about the fear of losing his son. Then, Michael walked in with his army uniform. He looked so handsome that Kevin took a picture as his eyes were filled with tears. He was proud, frightened and sick to his stomach all at the same time.

When Rita saw her brother, she ran over to him and gave him a hug and kiss. As she kissed him, and said: *"Michael, I love you, please take care of yourself and come back to us."* The three of them just looked at each other and hugged each other tightly—all of them were now crying.

\It was a custom during the war; when a "soldier" was called to fight—that a Candle be placed in a front window. There would be a small American flag under it. Next to the candle would be a picture of the soldier. One night a week, at a designated time, the candle would be lit for one hour.

It would be a signal to the neighbors that the soldier (son, father, brother) was "OK." If it were not lit—and the picture turned down-prayers would be offered by everyone that knew the family. The turned down picture and unlit candle meant the soldier was captured, injured, or lost somehow.

If a black cloth was put over the top of the picture and the candle un-lit- it signaled that "The light of their life was gone forever" and the family was in morning.

Kevin put a candle with an American flag under it in the front window for Michael. It would be there until Michael came home from the war.

Rita cried as she saw her brother packing his things. He was getting ready to leave in the morning. She would miss him. Rita planned to light a candle at St. Ann's every Friday for Michael's safe return home.

The night before he was to leave Michael proposed to Nora. He did not have money for an engagement ring, so he gave her his class ring. Michael shoveled snow and cleaned yards for the entire neighborhood to buy that class ring. When he gave it to Nora, he promised that upon his return he would give her an engagement ring and a wedding ring. Nora promised to wait for him and write because *"She was his girl forever."*

Kevin and Rita knew about Michael's plans to marry Nora. They too loved her and felt good about the marriage. They also loved Nora's Aunt Lilly from that very first Christmas Dinner they shared together when the kids were sophomores in high school. Lilly's special gift to all of them was a stuffed Turkey with homemade cranberry sauce. Rita made mashed potatoes and a home-made pumpkin pie. It was the first of many such days to come over the next two years as Lilly entrenched them all in her fabulous home cooking and funny stories.

Both Rita and Kevin feared they would lose that "family" feeling once again when Michael was gone. Little did they know what was to happen next in their lives?

Life has many twists and turns.

Kevin and Rita promised Michael they would stay connected with Nora. They felt Lilly and Nora were "part of their family now." Michael felt comforted hearing that they would still see Nora and Lilly.

With Michael leaving, his parents both dead, Kevin thought he should try to locate his brother. He learned from the school that his brother, enlisted in the army shortly after their parents died.

A wife dead, a son and brother in the war fighting for their lives, and parents both dead in a fire.

HOW MUCH MORE CAN A MAN STAND?

Kevin's thoughts were a constant source of pain.

After learning that his brother enlisted, Kevin-put the only picture he had of his brother, attached to a spot in the frame of his son's picture. Now both pictures would be in the window, with a small candle near them.

Chapter 9

Nora

Nora Wallace was five feet two inches tall with a natural blush face and fare skin, golden brown hair and big brown eyes. If Nora weighed 100 pound soaking wet-something must have been in the towel she was holding, or the scale was broken.

Since her sophomore year in high school, she and Lilly enjoyed many visits to the Wilson home. Michael invited them on numerous occasions for a dinner or picnics.

Everyone at school knew the kids would marry; it was inevitable they were so much in love.

With the world at war many young men in their class did not wait for the draft and just enlisted—leaving school.

Nora and Michael did not pay much attention to the war in the beginning. They were deeply in love and never thought anything would separate them.

Nora often daydreamed about the day she and Michael met on their first day of high school. Both seemed to be walking into the building at the same time. Nora's eyes caught Michael's and she could not stop looking at him. She began the conversation with *"Hi I'm Nora. What is your name?"* Michael was shy but her beautiful smile broke the ice.

It was a cinch from then on. I do not think either of them knew what hit them. They were in many of the same classes, even having the same lunch period in the same lunchroom.

By their sophomore year they were going steady, and they were together at every school event. There never seemed to be a lag for conversation as the two of them really enjoyed being together.

By their senior year they were together most evenings and weekends—as both worked part time at the "Dollar Diner" on Filmore Ave. They would take the same bus to and from work and insisted on the same working hours.

Nora's parents were killed in a train accident when she was eight years old. Her parents were traveling to visit one of her father's business customers. On the way back from the trip the train derailed and one of the cars hit another car—about ninety people were hurt- thirty seriously.

Both Nora's parents and five others died, they were the ones in the front car when it hit the other car. Nora was being cared for by her aunt while her parents went on the trip. After their death Lilly adopted Nora. Nora's mother Gladys Day was Lilly's older sister and the most logical person to care for Nora after the accident since there was no other family on either side.

Lilly Bing was an elementary teacher five feet five inches tall in her late twenties at the time of the adoption. Lilly loved teaching the first grade. She had big brown eyes and long auburn hair. She was not married and never dated.

The rumor around town was Lilly had fallen in love with a Navy fellow when she was quite young and when he jilted her no one else ever seemed to interest her. No one knew for sure if it was true or if it was just a rumor. Lilly always lived with her parents, except for about a year when she and Gladys went to Illinois to help their mother's parents, who were both ill.

When her grandparents died, they left Lilly's parents enough money to purchase the house they were living in. Lilly inherited that home when her parents died. That is the same house where she and Nora still live.

Gladys gave her portion of the home to Lilly when she got married. Nora was an only child and lived with her parents in a trailer at the time of their death.

A friend of Nora's father sold him the trailer when he and Gladys they got married for $1000. They were going to live there until they saved enough money to purchase a home. But it was a big trailer, and they were only paying fifteen dollars per month lot rent.

It was cheap living -the rent included both heat and water hook-ups. Their original plan expanded to save enough money to purchase a car.

Nora's father was a salesman; her mother stayed home and quit her part time job after Nora was born. Even with a small car his salesman's job did not bring in much money. The trailer was cheap and a comfortable place to live there was no rush to move, even with the baby.

When Nora's parents died Lilly sold the trailer, with most of the furniture for $1205. Lilly put the money from the sale of the trailer and the $31.60 Nora's parents had saved into a Trust for Nora at the Clayton National Bank. In time with interest, Lilly hoped the money would be helpful for either college and or a wedding for Nora.

Lilly loved the thought of having a "daughter," even if it did happen from something tragic. Lilly was also Nora's Godmother. They bonded immediately and saw each other a great deal before the accident. Lilly's adoption was a logical evolution to the tragedy. Nora was incredibly happy living with Lilly they were not just family but best friends. They went shopping together, cooked dinner together every evening. Both were avid readers going to the library together every month. Every couple of months they hit on new bookstore to see what was on sale and even exchange some of their purchased books.

Eight bookcases in the house were filled and Nora knew about every story. Among her early reading were stories of entrepreneurs like Madam Curie and Ben Franklin. Lilly wanted to develop Nora's brain and expand her thinking as far as possible.

Lilly loved Michael from the first time Nora brought him home to meet her. With their influence Michael now became an avid reader. He would borrow some of their books to be able to converse with them about some of the stories. He was comfortable and fit in as family with the two of them. He was there for dinner at least once a week and joined in as they played monopoly.

Lilly was always teaching. She would check Nora's homework daily and slowly made house rules. She made sure Nora understood about the war, the value of an education, and gently imparted some of life's values to the child. Michael helped Nora with the yard work and took out their garbage on Thursdays. Lilly thought Michael was a good match for Nora—but in the back of her mind she still hoped Nora would go to college.

She knew Michael had no interest-let alone money for college even though he was very smart. But she prayed

Nora would get an Associate Degree if not a bachelor's degree.

She thought Nora was a natural teacher and at times she would present the idea to her. But Nora was very much in love with Michael. All Nora wanted was to be with Michael, be his wife, have his children, take care of him, and love him. Needless to say, when Michael was drafted and left for the war—everything changed.

With Michael away Nora and Rita had more of an opportunity to develop their friendship. It also gave Lilly a chance at enticing Nora to further her education.

Nora and Rita began seeing each other on a regular basis and talking on the telephone. Sometimes on Saturday mornings the three ladies would entice Kevin to all having breakfast together. After high school Nora found a job at the same grocery store where Kevin was now working. Kevin was overjoyed when he and Nora were able to ride the bus together one day a week as their hours matched.

The money Lilly had put in the bank for Nora had really grown. Lilly told Nora she did not have to work full time. It took about a month after Michael left for Lilly to convince Nora to enroll at the University of Clayton for the fall semester.

Lilly said, "*If she did not like school she would agree to her quitting at any time.*" Nora loved where she was working. She loved the people and working in customer service was something she could grow into for years to come.

Nora made the deal with Lilly. Luckily, Nora's excellent high school grades gave her the opportunity to receive a partial scholarship. Lilly agreed not to push her if she really, wanted to quit.

The grocery where Nora worked offered employees a real opportunity if they were going to school and had good grades. They would pay a small percentage of the tuition cost; and arrange their work schedules around the times the employee had to be in class.

This made college even more affordable and available. Nora kept Rita informed every step of the way saying, *"It was just to see if I would like it."*

Rita was excited for Nora she thought about the possibility of going to college herself-but she knew money was tight. She never really discussed this with her father.

Rita was fine with working and saving money for now. It would give her experience and the opportunity to find out what she would really like to do.

Each month Kevin put a little money in the bank for his children. He never told either of them –it was for an emergency.

Chapter 10

Opportunity Knocks

One evening Rita came home exhausted from listening to Nora "ranting" about her going to college and loving every moment. Kevin watched as his daughter just sat on the sofa, staring at the ceiling dreaming. Noticing the tears in her eyes he sat down next to her. They talked about her dreams and her future. Kevin saw the longing in Rita's eyes when she spoke of Nora going to college.

She told him about the "deal" Nora and Lilly made about attending college. Kevin never realized his daughter wanted to continue her education. He asked about the type of things she liked. Rita had not given it much thought. But she could see herself pursuing something in the medical field. Kevin promised to check into the cost of college.

He asked her if she liked nursing. She remembered a place in Triton called "Care Medical Center." It was supposed to be affiliated with Foster Hospital. Rita was not sure about nursing but decided she would review all the requirements after her father had some information about the cost.

Days went by and Kevin never mentioned anything about the school. Rita concluded he must have forgotten or decided the cost was out of the question.

Rita knew Kevin needed help financially. She was giving him half of her paycheck. It was difficult for Kevin to keep-up with all the house-hold expenses after losing his insurance position.

She was aware that the medical and funeral costs for Mary Jo left him without any reserve funds.

Rita decided not to pursue school. She had a decent job. She was learning how to sell; and there was still the job at the Red Cross after her training.

"Everything will happen when the time is right all she needed was faith.*" She thought.*

One day while working at the shoe store Rita met Mr. and Mrs. Roger Phillips. They came into the store wanting new shoes for Mr. Phillips and a pair of slippers for Mrs. Phillips.

She was surprised to learn that Mr. Phillips just accepted the position of training instructor at the Red Cross.

The three of them hit it off from the start. Mrs. Phillips was very personable and kind. Mr. Phillips was a budding comedian. Rita's heart shinned through as she sold them their shoes.

Mrs. Phillips was teasing her husband about some of his choices. They made Rita laugh. Mr. Phillips teased both right back. Mrs. Phillips was very fussy about her husband's shoes. She wanted him to look very strait laced and professional. Mr. Phillips, on the other hand loved the rugged look.

Rita sold both slippers and each a pair of shoes. Mrs. Phillips liked to wear healed slippers around the house. Mr. Phillips liked slippers that had warm lining.

Their conversation soon moved to the Red Cross and the training class. Mr. Phillips was sure his new class would be no problem for Rita. Even though Rita had just completed her ten-week training, his new class would extend that training. Mr. Phillips was quite impressed with Rita. He offered her the opportunity to continue her training in his class. This was an opportunity she could not pass up. She accepted and thanked him for the invitation.

Mr. Phillips was so impressed with Rita he thought that when the training class was over, he would offer her a position working for him as an intern at the University of Clayton.

He needed permission from Mr. Parker his supervisor, to hire Rita, but that once he met her there would be no problem. Mr. Parker also needed an intern. He was the head of all interns at the university and the two men knew each other quite well.

Mr. Phillips planned on having Rita and Mr. Parker casually "bump" into each other—often. He decided it would be a good fit for Parker—in time to hire Rita to help him.

Mr. Phillips waited for the last class of her training and then, he asked Rita if she could meet him at his office on the university campus that next afternoon. She agreed.

He hoped the campus environment would add to his offer making an internship position more appealing.

Walking on the college campus immediately ignited Rita's imagination; the students looked; so professional, important, and serious. She closed her eyes and made a wish to someday-somehow to attend college. Then she proceeded to Mr. Phillips's office.

After they exchanged pleasantries, Mr. Phillips asked Rita if she would consider working for him in a part-time paid position on Campus. Rita was hesitant she was employed by the shoe store and the department store, and soon for the Red Cross.

Mr. Phillips knew all Rita's jobs. He knew the shoe store ended in two weeks; and he knew about her position at the Red Cross, so before their meeting he decided to work that out. Mr. Phillips met with Rita's supervisor at the Red Cross; and explained the opportunity he was providing Rita. Her supervisor agreed to Rita working part-time at the Red Cross until she completed her internship with Mr. Phillips.

Mr. Phillips's made Rita an offer in such a way that she could work for him and the Red Cross. Her total working hours being employed at both places would be forty hours a week.

The decision was up to her. All she had to do was say "Yes." Rita needed time to think this was a great opportunity. She asked Mr. Phillips if she could talk it over with her father. Phillips agreed. She stated she would get back to him in a week. Phillips felt this gave her too much time to think, so to sweeten his offer, before she left his office he said: *"By the way, Rita, did I mention that under the school's policy you would have the opportunity to take two courses per semester free at the university's evening division? You would be working for a full–time instructor, so there would be no cost to attend classes!"*

She could go to college and there would be no cost! It would be at night and it would add to her time away from home. But she would be in college! Rita's head was spinning. She still wanted to talk to her dad.

Mr. Phillips really needed someone full time, but the budget availability did not permit offering a full-time salaried position to interns. The courses were his "carrot, and Rita knew as soon as he mentioned the opportunity, she could not turn down the position.

Mr. Phillips added there would be no cost for books. He said they could work something out so she would have whatever book she needed.

Books free! Courses free!
It Is Truly a Gift… FROM GOD!

In the future, when the university permitted full time interns, he would entice her with the opportunity to attend courses each semester, as part of her full-time salary. This would be no problem because free education was offered to all full-time interns. Instructors received a discount on the course study for full-time interns; Mr.

Phillips thought that paying the discount would be cheaper than paying Rita a full-time salary.

Rita was excited. She told Mr. Phillips that she would meet him back at his office in a half hour. He agreed. She left Mr. Phillips office and telephoned her father. When she told him of the offer, he told her: *"This is the opportunity of a lifetime and there was no way you should pass it up."* Rita went back to Mr. Phillip's office and accepted the position.

Kevin heard back from the nursing school. He was heartbroken. All the money he saved would not be enough to put Rita through even one year of nursing school. When he received her call, it was as if God had heard his prayers.

That night Rita and Kevin celebrated with a special spice cake that Kevin purchased and brought home from the store.

Rita called Nora and told her of the good news. On her way home she decided to let the people at the department store know she was leaving. They felt disappointed but agreed school was more important.

Nora and Lilly were happy for Rita. Everyone felt war was terrible, but, somehow because of it, their lives had taken a turn for a better future. Rita and Nora were becoming more like sisters every day. There were so happy to be going to be at the same university. Even though Rita's classes were at night, the two of them, devised a way to meet at the cafeteria and have a coffee together. They chatted on the telephone often.

Working part-time at the Red Cross gave Rita more time for her studies. Everything was moving along perfectly.

Rita was permitted to use the employee discount at the department store. She purchased her presents for the holidays carefully. She was saving money to give Nora and Michael a special wedding gift. It was a nice Christmas that year. Lilly invited Kevin and Rita to her house for Christmas dinner. Everything was so perfect that holiday except for the fact that Michael was not there

Rita was sure she wanted to finish college-she was just not sure what she wanted to do after. She loved being at the school and helping wherever possible.

The change in Rita's employment put a financial strain on Kevin. He began looking for a part-time job. When his boss at the grocery store learned Kevin needed a part-time job, he offered him ten additional hours of over-time every two weeks. Kevin was surprised the overtime made a big difference.

As the second semester rolled around Rita began putting in more time for Mr. Phillips. Rita loved being at the university-just being on campus was invigorating. She wrote Michael of her opportunity. He was happy for her.

Little did either of the girls know, but Michael was concerned about how their education would make him feel once he got home. Since Rita was also a college girl-he wondered if, where, and how would he fit in; and if he and Rita would still be as close. His thoughts did not have time to expand the war kept him on his toes

Over the next year, both girls continued to attended college. Both decided to become teachers. Nora wanted elementary school. Rita loved teaching high school Science.

Nora instinctively knew how Michael would feel about her getting her degree. She wrote him often about how she was looking forward to his coming home and spending their lives together. She sent him a copy of her class schedule hoping to put to rest his fear of a romance with another.

Michael's perspectives on life were changing. The effects of war were not good. His letters stopped being regular, they sounded different. When a letter did arrive it really took Nora back, he wrote of the men that died and how their families must be suffering.

It was a concern. Nora did not know for sure how to address some of his statements. Nora knew she loved Michael and attributed the sound of his letters to stress. **"The war was obviously keeping him busy and getting mail out had to be difficult. Not to mention that to stay alive- in a war zone was not the easiest place to write."** She thought.

There were times when she was alone in her room, she would let her mind wonder and considered the possibility of their relationship not materializing.

She dismissed it immediately as just nonsense. She knew that Michael loved her, and she loved him. She remembered the night Michael proposed; their kisses were leading them to going to a much further show of their love and affection. Even though she was ready for Michael's love, he stopped. He assured her, his love for her would never hurt her. He said that the uncertainly of war was not going to persuade him to destroy what would be a beautiful honeymoon and future. She knew that was true love. She just knew things would work out for them.

Rita spoke to Nora about how much she enjoyed working for Mr. Phillips. He introduced her to just about every professor at the college telling them all what a great "find" he had in her abilities. It really did boost her confidence.

Mr. Phillips had the opportunity to introduced Rita to Mrs. Parker. The two women really "hit it off" became instant friends. Mr. Parker was the "Man of the hour" he really made things happen for young people at the university. Mrs. Parker knew he also needed an assistant, but money was tight for his department as well.

Everyone was affected by the war in one way or the other. Mrs. Parker knew Rita was truly a person she wanted to help any way possible. She persuaded her husband to work with Mr. Phillips about sharing Rita's time. She knew it would be more economical for the men to share Rita's time adding just a few more hours to her schedule.

Mrs. Parker knew it would also be a feather in their caps if Rita was to complete her degree while working for the two men. The clincher to it all was the fact that both men would have the benefit of an excellent assistant at minimum cost.

Phillips knew this would happen-just as he planned. A deal was struck in no time, adding eleven hours to Rita's schedule meant she would be for the two men for a total of forty-two hours a week. It was the opportunity of a lifetime; being a full-time intern meant she could be a full-time student at a highly accredited university-free!

It would now mean leaving the Red Cross. Rita felt badly about and all the free training they provided. Still, she needed to be sure there was time for her to study, and do a good job working for two men who were helping her get an education and finding all her books.

Never underestimate the power of a woman.

Rita met with Mr. Phillips and Mr. Parker, discussing working for both. The two men agreed to adjust their schedules so Rita could go to school full time and still work for both men at the university. As a "full timer" she could take as many courses as she could handle each semester whether in the day or in the evening. Mr. Parker was an administrator at the college and would do anything to help a student who really wanted an education.

Rita was a terrific intern. Attending classes all year around-day and evening at times-was not the best situation. At first College was quite an adjustment as high school work was nothing compared to what college professors expected. She breezed through English and loved her Math. But some things needed a bit more attention. She was at an advantage with Mr. Phillips he helped her on the things she needed a bit of tutoring to understand.

Rita was a great student with a photographic memory. Rita's grade point average each semester was 3.7 out of 4.

God had really taken care of Rita; now she wanted his help bringing Michael home. She desperately wanted her family together again.

Kevin was overjoyed with the advantages Rita was offered and her ability to handle her workload with two professors.

His life had begun to change around that time as well. It was time for him to move on. Many years have passed since Mary Jo's death.

Chapter 11

Kevin and Betty Hewett

Kevin never told Rita, but he met a woman while working at the grocery store. Betty Hewett was her name. Betty worked in the accounting department. Kevin worked in produce. They began dating after Kevin was there for six months.

They saw each other several evenings a week mostly while Rita was at school. Betty worked for the grocery store for ten years. She never dated anyone before. In fact, Betty never even had a boyfriend or dated—before Kevin. She just always lived with her mother and never went out.

But Kevin and Betty were falling in love, and their time was coming. There was a glitch in their relationship that needed to be worked out. Betty had a hard time with her mother if she ever disobeyed. Sheltered for most of her life this was the first venture out of her mother's "orders" that Betty had ever tried.

Consequently, her relationship with Kevin was a secret.

Kevin too was keeping a secret. He wanted to tell his daughter, and the whole world, just how happy he was with Betty. But he wondered if Rita would approve his taking another wife. He knew both Rita and Michael loved their mother very much. Kevin had been alone for several years; he was waiting for the right time to bring his relationship up to Rita about Betty, but it never was **the right time.**

With Christmas six weeks away, he wanted to ask Betty to marry him. He hoped to give her a ring on Christmas Day.

On the Friday just before Thanksgiving, Kevin and Betty went to the local picture show for their evening out. Kevin was under the impression Rita would be at work or school; that was how he always calculated his available time to see Betty over the last two years.

Of all things, Mr. Parker and his wife planned on going to that very same show on that very same Friday. Instead, the pregnant Mrs. Parker gave birth to a baby girl at 5 PM on the Tuesday evening before. Consequently, Mr. Parker, had two paid for tickets for the same picture show that Kevin and Betty were going to see that evening.

Parker offered his tickets to Rita. Going to picture shows was something Rita loved. Two free tickets—were great, because that meant she would have the opportunity to invite Nora. The ladies decided to put studies aside and see the show.

The two girlfriends arrived at the picture show-just seconds after Kevin and Betty were seated. Not many people went to the theater during the war. As Rita and Nora walked down the aisle-they saw Kevin turn and help Betty off with her coat. Rita eyes met with her father's.

Kevin said, *"Oh My God Rita, I did not want you to find out like this."* While beginning to shake, he said *"This lovely lady is Betty Hewett. We have been seeing each other for quite a while."*

Unbeknown to Kevin, Rita had secretly been praying that her father would one day fall in love again. She knew that her father loved her mother-but Mary Jo had been gone from his life for years. He was lonely and still young man. When she saw the look on her father's face, it showed how worried he was about this introduction

Rita knew that look well but loved her father. Rita said, *"That's fine, Hi Betty, I am Rita, Kevin's daughter and this is Nora-my best friend and soon to be my sister-in-law—would you excuse us so we could take the seats next to you-then we could all sit together."*

Kevin was shocked at how matter-of-fact Rita's response to this introduction went. For the entire movie Kevin was unable to concentrate. He was more concerned about what to do after the show, on things would work out when he and Rita were home and alone.

His stomach was showing signs of his concern he was tied in knots he was sweating. He excused himself and went to the men's room. He prayed as he washed his hands and face that the evening would go well. He returned not knowing what the picture was about or what they would do after the show.

When the show was over Kevin's mind was still wondering **"What to do?" How should he handle leaving**

the theater? Kevin's stomach identified that worry, fear and anxiety were all his as he was not ready for Rita's questions of Betty or of him. He did not want her to find out about Betty in this way. He planned on telling her in a calm fashion.

After the movie ended, they all began walking up the isle to leave. Kevin nervously turned and invited everyone to the diner for a hot drink. He hoped there would be some pleasant conversation, and maybe he would really see how the women interacted face-to-face.

Betty Hewett was nine years younger than Kevin and very well preserved. She and her aged mother lived just five blocks from where Rita and Kevin had their house. How strange the two never met before.

They all walked to the restaurant in silence and then all sat in a booth. Kevin ordered a coffee, a tea and two hot chocolates. Betty took notice that she and Rita had almost the same color hair, eyes and were almost the same height. Both girls noticed it as well. Betty wondered what Kevin's wife Mary Jo looked like. She thought Rita could pass for her daughter. There was no doubt in either Rita or Nora's minds –as they observed the interaction, between Kevin and Betty—they were obviously in love.

The clincher came when Kevin said Betty was "**Wonderful**" that really gave it all away.

As they were served their drinks, Rita, being bluntly bold and desperately wanting to see her father happy blurted out: *"So Dad, when is the date?"* *"Wh-what?*

What date Rita" Kevin stuttered; he was stunned at his daughter's acceptance but felt it was a bit presumptuous. After all, she had no idea if this was his first date with Betty or not. He did not mention anything about being in love. At first, he acted like he did not hear her question and he passed the sugar to Betty.

Rita knew Kevin had not dated since Mary Jo's death. Therefore, this lady had to be someone special; and it was obvious they were in love. Kevin surmised that Rita must have been joking. Still, he thought maybe it is one of those woman's intuition things or something.

Then Rita said, *"You two love each other, right?"* Again, Kevin did not answer. Betty just looked at him and put her eyes down and cracked a small smile. Kevin's relationship with Betty appeared to be out in the open and obviously Rita approved. But Kevin was not sure the restaurant was the time or place to discuss such a private thing.

Again, Rita asked, *"Do you two love each other?"* Kevin looked at Betty and then he looked at his daughter-his eyes gave him away. Rita then said, *"I see the answer is yes so when is the wedding?"* Kevin felt pressured; **He did not think it was the best time to ask Betty that "all important question." He had hoped to do it on a romantic evening alone.**

Then in an instant, he changed his mind. He decided to do it in front of Rita and Nora and hoped that would make it special.

Unfortunately, special was not what Betty needed. She needed time to prepare herself for marriage; and there were other issues that needed to be dealt with before she felt free to make a commitment. Kevin did not think that far ahead he just let his emotions fill him. It seemed Rita was ok with him marrying again; so now the time had to be right—all he needed was the nerve.

Kevin turned his head toward Betty slowly he took her hand in his and held it ever so gently. The two looked at each other for a moment and their eyes gave their love away. Then, Kevin's voice a bit horse began: *"Betty this may not be the most romantic place or the best way of saying I love you, but you know I do."* His pause was unbearable for Rita—and Betty was not sure what was to come. He continued *"Betty, I think I fell in love with you the first time I saw you—and my daughter is right—I want and need to ask you something very special."* There was another almost unbearable pause again.

Kevin did not suspect the impact of what was coming. Betty tried to hold his words off and she said *"I know you love me Kevin and I love you. Girls lets drink up it is getting late."* Kevin got up the nerve to continue *"Betty-I do not want to drink up- I want you to"* he stopped and then stuttered as he began again *"lel let me change that-I want to spend the rest of my life with you Betty—Betty will you do me the honor me of marrying me and being my wife?"*

Finally, it was out and both Rita and Nora were overjoyed. The girls watched Betty's face-they could see love but there was not the immediate response or reaction they had hoped. Betty took her time. They all waited with anticipation for Betty's answer.

All three were now looking at Betty. Waiting, hoping and searching for some response or reaction. As Betty took her time, she looked at her cup and twirled it—her eyes were facing downward toward her cup and then she looked at the girls; finally, after what seemed like an eternity she said *"Kevin,"* and then she paused.

Rita felt they both seemed to have long pauses in common. Betty began again *"Kevin, I have my mother to think of, she has only me. I love you—you know that—I think I fell in love with you the first time you came over to my desk looking for a stapler—but I do not know what to do?"* Kevin and Rita spoke in unison: *"Say YES!!!!"*

Betty continued *"Kevin, I have never loved anyone before ...you really are my first love... I do love you very much. I am happy when we are together and (*she hesitated*) I would hate to lose you."*

Betty's eyes filled with tears as she looked at Kevin, she paused again her eyes traveling back at Rita and then again at Kevin finally she screamed: *"Yes! Yes! Yes, Kevin, I will marry you! We will have to work it out somehow!! But YES, I love you Kevin Wilson and I want to spend the rest of my days being your wife!"* Rita and

Nora jumped up and hugged them as Kevin and Betty were now both in tears.

The two girls left the restaurant first so Kevin could take Betty home. As they were leaving Betty said to Rita *"You are a very good and loving daughter-I would be honored to have you as my friend let alone my daughter."*

Rita answered *"I will love having you as part of my family. Welcome!"* Both girls were happy for the loving couple. They walked slowly to the bus stop neither girl saying a word. The bus came on time and the girls were silent most of the way.

Nora could not stand the silence she had waited as long as she could and finally said *"How are you really feeling Rita about all this...I mean your father getting married?"* Rita said *"They seemed to be like two love birds happy with each other. I have not seen my father so happy in years. He was not only happy he was acting so young-like he was a kid again with excitement."*

She continued *"This marriage will create some changes in my life."* *"What kind of changes?"* Nora asked. Rita continued *"When they marry, I will need to find a place of my own. As a newly married couple they should have a house to themselves without a "spy" around."*

It was obvious to Nora that this was a mixed blessing. Rita continued *"After all I am 21 years old —many single girls have a place of their own."*

Nora knew a single girl in an apartment would be frowned upon let alone expensive. Nora had the solution and said, *"Why don't you move in with Lilly and me? We have two extra bedrooms, and it is a big house I bet Lilly would just love the idea of having two daughters living with her."* Rita thought the idea was great, but she was not sure the Lilly would agree. The girls decided to discuss the matter with Lilly when they knew all the wedding plans.

By the time Kevin got home Rita was asleep. She left a note on his bedroom door with a big sign: *"Congratulations—it is about time!"* Kevin was over-joyed at Rita's attitude about his marring again. He knew she loved her mother very much and no one could really replace Mary Jo in Rita's heart.

He also knew the position Betty would take-with Rita would be friends. He decided not to fight it and-just enjoy the gift he was receiving from his daughter.

He loved Betty and she loved him and now they were going to get married. He was excited. Kevin planned on taking Betty to the jeweler in the morning letting her pick out an engagement ring. He would send a letter to Michael telling him all about Betty later. He was sure Michael would not object to his marring again after all Michael was in love with Nora and men do understand how love behaves. As he fell off to sleep, he thought that tomorrow will begin a special day for his family.

Christmas still six weeks away, Rita thought about their family tradition. Since Mary Jo's death, after Christmas Mass, when they came home, Kevin would cook breakfast for the three of them. After breakfast they would gather around the tree and open their gifts together laughing and joking. Rita and Kevin kept the tradition going even through Michael was gone.

Rita surmised that this Christmas would probably now include Betty and her mother—things seem to always be changing but Rita decided no point in making an issue of anything on Christmas morning.

The next morning Kevin and Betty went out for breakfast and then visited a local jeweler. When Kevin returned home, he told Rita that Betty had picked simple ring with one stone to be joined with a gold band. He chose a matching band for himself. The jeweler was happy to take the wedding ring he had when he married Mary Jo in for trade, so his cost was nominal. Rita knew that Mary Jo's rings were saved for her.

Kevin seemed relieved and happy, but the rest of the day he was strangely per-occupied. He seemed to stay that way for about three weeks. Rita thought it was something mental such as planning their future and a wedding. Maybe even how to take care of a new wife and a mother-in-law.

Rita was hoping Kevin would let her in on some of his or Betty's plans. Even discussing some of the little things; but no such conversation was forthcoming. When the fourth week past, with no mention of the wedding or Betty; Rita could not hold her tongue any longer. *"Dad"* she began *"Is there something we could discuss?* Kevin appeared disturbed. Rita continued *"I have not seen Betty since the movie and well Christmas will be here soon. Do you have plans for Betty to join us on Christmas?"*

Kevin looked at his daughter as love and tears filled his eyes. *"Rita, I have no idea what we will do for Christmas."* Rita said nothing but she felt her father's heartache and pain. Kevin looked at his daughter as tears filled his eyes. *"Rita, Betty's mother has kept her quite busy these last few weeks. She was not happy with the idea of Betty getting married."* Rita said nothing but she felt her father's heartache and pain.

Later Rita called Nora and told her that there was some possible change in plans, but that Betty was having a problem with her mother accepting the idea of her getting married. Nora though it silly at Betty's age to have her mother object.

Meanwhile, Betty's mother was livid:

"How dare you, have I taught you nothing? A widower-it won't take him long and he will compare you to HER!

There is no need for you to marry.

What is to become of ME?

What kind of daughter have you be-come? You sneak around dating and lie to your mother? Is that how I raised you!

There will be no marriage—

DO YOU HEAR ME!"

Chapter 12

A Wedding

On Christmas Day, Betty did not join them at Mass. Kevin said Betty's mother was ill. After mass, Kevin and Rita went straight home; when they arrived; Kevin pulled an envelope from his pocket and gave it to Rita.

"What is this dad?" "It is a bank book Rita. Since your mother died, I saved a little money for you just in case...well it is not a lot...but it is time to give it to you, especially since, I hope to be getting married soon." Kevin said.

The bank book was in Rita's name and had a balance of $268.56. *"Wow Dad, are you sure you want me to have this just now? It is a lot of money; you may need this for you and Betty." Rita commented*

"There is another paper in the envelope" he said. *"What is it Dad?" Rita said. "It is the deed to this house*

Rita. I put the house in yours and Michael's names after your mother died-as protections for you and Michael– should anything happen to me."

"I do not understand Dad" Rita said.

Kevin explained: *"Betty will not leave her mother. If I am to marry Betty I have to agree to move into her mother's home. If I do not agree, the wedding is off."*

"Oh Dad, I am so sorry." Rita's eyes were filled with tears.

"Don't worry honey. That house is paid for and it will be Betty's one day. Her mother is up in years and not too well. I understand the situation and I am OK with it. When Betty's mother dies, she will sell that house and we will move. Then we can purchase a house together."

"But Dad" Rita protested *"Shouldn't you sell this house now that you are getting married? Then you and Betty could put the money from the two houses together?"*

Rita was concerned that her father would not have enough money to match Betty's. But that did not seem to be a concern for Kevin. *"Things will be fine honey, do not worry."* and with that Kevin left to go to pick up Betty for their Breakfast together. The traditional Christmas breakfast they enjoyed for so many years before the war, did not happen, and they did not open any gifts.

Kevin agreed to meet Rita at Lilly's later in the day for dinner. Betty would not be joining them. Rita would spend most of the day alone.

It was a long lonely difficult day. She did not want to impose herself on Nora and Lilly –by going over too early—after all—they had their tradition as well. Rita tried to think of how to spend her time until she would need to dress for their Christmas dinner. The first thing she thought of was how lonely life was going to be living alone.

Kevin mentioned that they were hoping for a wedding on January 2nd. Rita felt that since Kevin gave her the deed to the house, he must be planning on moving out just after the wedding. Rita never really thought about living in a house alone. Now, she will be waiting and planning for the day when Michael would be coming home from the war. Suddenly thoughts of painting, changing the curtains and adding some small touches to the house to make it "her own" **Wow, she thought what a wonderful opportunity for self-express**ion!

Kevin said they would be getting married, so things must have changed. He said, *"they would be married by a justice of the peace; because they wanted their lives together to begin "simply."*

A justice of the peace wedding is about as simple as it gets. Rita, Nora and Lilly would be the only invitees as Kevin said Betty's mother was not really well enough to attend.

Nora told Lilly all about the proposal and the engagement of Kevin and Betty. The ladies all were excited and waiting to see Kevin later in the day to hear the plans while enjoying Christmas dinner.

Mid-afternoon, Kevin called and offered his apologies; he would not be able to attend dinner, he would be at Betty's most of the day. His call just missed Rita at her house because she arrived at Nora's about ten minutes after his call to them.

They were all disappointed. Rita was the most upset. **She surmised their family would change after her father married, and that would take some getting used to; but really it has changed before a new family has been created. I will just have to adjust because it will not be long and both Kevin and Michael (when he comes home from the war) will all be married.**

Rita was feeling sad thinking "**I will be really alone.**"

Christmas dinner with Nora and Lilly was fantastic as usual. The ladies played rummy after dinner and opened their gifts. Rita arrived home about 10 PM.

Getting ready for bed Rita heard the front door open then close. Kevin was home. Judging from the way he looked when she entered the room—it was obvious his Christmas did not turn out well. His demeanor was noticeably sad, and he looked drained.

Rita's excitement for the day waned. The look on Kevin's face prompted her to ask, "*If he was alright.*"

His response was *"I am alright."*

Something was really wrong; his face, and tone of voice did not match his words. This was Christmas day-and their gifts were still all under the tree—unopened. Kevin did not want to open anything. He did not give her any explanation-he just kissed her forehead and went to his room.

Rita sat looking at the tree she had spent so much time decorating. It was beautiful. There were gifts under the tree: for Michael, Kevin, Rita and Betty. She left all gifts under the tree; but she put Michael's gift in his bedroom closet.

Tears rolled down her face-as she thought:

"What has happened to us? We do not seem to be a family anymore-Michael being gone and Betty's coming in—just changed us all? I want our traditions back. I want Michael. I want us to be happy again. I want…"

Rita lay on her bed crying uncontrollably. It was as if her body was telling her something was changing from her previously "happy life." She was not sure if those changes were for the best or …

She tossed and turned; her mind running through tons of scenarios. It took hours before she fell asleep.

Chapter 13

Nothing Stays the Same

In the morning, Rita went into the Kitchen to make coffee when Kevin came in. He looked glum. He told Rita that *"Betty's mother was emphatically against the marriage. Betty and I argued, and I left the house with Betty crying. There is not going to be a wedding on January second. Betty agreed to speak with her mother about a later date."* Rita felt sorry for her father and Betty-what a predicament he had with Betty's mother.

After breakfast Kevin suggested they exchange their presents. Rita purchased a pair of slippers and a robe for her father. Kevin gave her a 14 Karat yellow gold cross necklace. The cross was beautiful. This was her very first gold piece and she gave Kevin a hug and kiss. *"I will treasure it always Dad"* she said. Kevin loved seeing her happy and smiling.

Kevin said he would: *"Like it if the two of them could stay home together this New Year's Eve."* Rita did not have any other plans, so she agreed and offered to prepare a special meal.

On New Year's Eve at midnight Kevin just kissed her and went to bed. Rita cried all night.

On New Year's morning she called Nora and Lilly to wish them a Happy Safe New Year. Kevin had invited Lilly and Nora to join him and Rita for an early dinner at the Swiss Chalet-Kevin's treat. When dinner was over, they all went to Lilly's for home-made carrot cake.

It was a pleasant, quiet day; but still troubling because Kevin was obviously stressed. Everyone walked on eggs not to ask questions. Rita knew her father was terribly upset and disappointed.

Chapter 14

What To Do Next

Rita thought that the next romantic time for a wedding would be on Valentine Day. She mentioned it to Kevin -he responded with "*We will see.*"

The month of January went by quickly. Rita was so busy with school she forgot about wedding plans. But when Valentine Day passed, and there was still no mention of a wedding, there did not seem to be words to express how sad Rita felt for her father.

Kevin received a package a couple of days after Valentine's Day. It was Betty's engagement ring with a letter. Kevin sat in his chair for about three hours looking at the ring, never opening the letter.

He put the un-opened letter with the ring in his desk drawer and retired to his room. He without saying anything to Rita. The look on his face said it all.

The next morning, Kevin was up early, and he left the house without a word. When he returned, he told Rita he had just quit grocery store and would be looking for another job.

He had the newspaper under his arm and retired to his bedroom. Rita went off to school wondering how they were going to live if Kevin did not find a job soon.

It took-just a week after he resigned from the grocery store; for him to be hired at the City Steel Plant. The job was more money and Kevin wanted to be away from Betty and all the memories that were now tormenting him.

Kevin and Betty seemed so much in love; Kevin never spoke of Betty again. But Rita could see how much he missed her. When home, he read the paper, had supper and just went to bed.

As the New Year continued Rita and her father went back to the life they lived previously.

Betty's Christmas gift would stay in the top shelf of the entrance closet. One day Rita noted that it was put to the back of the shelf so it could not be seen.

Rita thought she would give it some time and then she would donate it to a charity. She said a prayer that night—that if her father at Betty were destined to be to-gether—please don't let their- getting back together take long; and if they are not meant to be together' please help my father find someone to love.

Chapter 15

Time and Love

Rita wrote Michael hoping he would have some sympathy for their father's situation. She mentioned how their father's disappointment was affecting him; describing how he and Betty really seemed to be in love. She likened his sadness to the time when their mother had passed away. Her letter was long and caring.

Michael answer was short and to the point. He wrote *"It probably was for the best. After all it is not as if Dad really needed Betty-he was doing fine on his own."*

Rita thought: **"Michael's response was selfish, cold and uncaring-their father was a lonely man and he needed someone to love. Their mother had been gone many years. But because he was in a war zone-she decided not to disagree with him via the mail."**

By spring Rita noticed Kevin was not looking well. He was pale and had lost some weight. She tried talking with him about all the extra shifts he was taking-but he refused to discuss it. She was becoming really concerned and began cooking more soups and stews hoping the different options would entice his appetite-to no avail. He rarely smiled or joked-let alone watched television with her. He spent most of his time alone in his room.

Kevin purchased a used car for $300. He insisted Rita and he take driving lessons. They took six lessons, and both passed the driving test. What a difference having a car made—it was great not to have to take a bus on rainy or snowing days.

Kevin was able to sleep an extra hour in the morning and came home an hour earlier.

If Rita was so inclined, and she was a couple of times a week—she would drive Kevin to work and pick him up keeping—the car all to herself for a few hours. When she did pick him up from work, she tried to start a conversation. But Kevin just wanted to get home, have dinner, read the paper and go to his room. Rita was feeling lonely herself.

Chapter 16

The War Ends

Then it came—it was on the radio- the announcer was loud, as he said it a number of times with joy and

gladness in his words and tone—"the War—the War is OVER! It is Finally over – people! The war is over! The war is over!"

People were dancing in the streets. School children were given the day off. People all over were walking out of their jobs, and their buildings gathering in the streets hugging each other sharing the joy. It was as if they were in a holiday spirit.

The soldiers would be coming home-no more would die—no more families would suffer, no more weddings postponed, or letters from the draft board. Families could get together now without sorrow or fear there would that—knock on the door telling them they would be without a loved one. It is over! The war is over.

The war had taken three years and two months away from Michael and Nora. But now, Michael would be coming home! Nora knew there would be a wedding! Nora's dream to marry Michael was going to come true.

Except

Nora knew Michael would have issues and difficult feelings coming home to not just her as a teacher, but Rita as well, both college graduates. Michael will be coming home with a few things being different. His father is no longer an insurance salesman. He is now working for the steel plant. Mine and Rita's schedules are different now that we are teaching school. His father is not the same after separating from Betty-he seems sad and lonely.

Lilly was right; Nora loved school; she carried an unbelievable load most semesters while maintaining a B+ grade in every course. Nora finished college early and never stopped thinking about Michael. College boys would call and try to date her, but no one even had a chance to win her over. She focused only on her studies and her job at the grocery.

Nora was excited and hopeful that with the war behind them they would be able to build a life together. She was in love, and she wanted to marry Michael as soon as he was home. She asked Rita to be her maid of honor. She was sure that when she married Michael they would live happily ever after.

Her dream was to marry Michael—take care of him and be the mother of their children and be happy. It was a Cinderella story "living happily ever after." **But dreams have a way of not necessarily always coming out the way they were planned.**

Michael left home a young man-filled with dreams and hopes; he comes back a soldier-who has seen death and had to fight to stay alive; always looking over his shoulder. He will need to get used to peace – and being home again.

Of course, even with the war over there are those families, and young women who must find a way to muster up the strength, grace and self-reliance to continue in the world having the best possible life—they could be—cause—their man was not coming home. They will suffer for years with only memories of what was and what could have been. Pictures and memories will fill their hearts as the move along rebuilding their lives.

Chapter 17

Time Heals

Michael's plane arrived two-weeks before Easter. Nora, Rita and Kevin were all at the airport in anticipation of seeing Michael. As the plane landed their anxiety was heightened –then they saw Michael step off the plane.

Everyone immediately noticed something different, their eyes went back and forth to each other. Their minds confused "**Who is this man? His face is Michael's but...there was something different. He lost a lot of weight. H**is *hair is different—there is gray in his hair!*" *His eyes are void of any expression—and his smile—it looks hard and ridged.*"

Michael's last letters had changed. They were very matter of fact, short and distant. They lacked a certain flair that Nora loved. In fact, it was almost as if someone else was writing his letters. He did not mention that he loved her or anything about his and Nora's future.

Rita and Kevin just looked at each other. Their eyes said it all. The effect of War has been hard for Michael. <u>Where was the young man full of life and smiling all the time?</u>

Nora could not put her finger on the reason; or just how to express what she felt, but she too felt the war had taken its toll on him. He his whole stature, and appearance was changed. At that point-she wondered if he still loved her-or if she could love the man that returned from the war.

On the way back to the house, Michael announced, in the car, that, he wanted to wait six months before he and Nora married. Everyone was a bit stunned. Nora said, *"That is no problem"* Kevin and Rita just listened. Michael said he: *"Wanted time to unwind, find a job and just rest."* Nora agreed.

In Nora's mind she thought: **"I need time to determine if I could have feelings for the man that came home from the war. I wonder if the man that came back from the war is the man, I loved all my high school years?"** It appears they were going to need time to understand what direction they were going-in life. They each needed to re-discover each other—if there was really—should be—a wedding. They needed to be confident about their love for each other and determine if they wanted a future together.

Michael told Nora he loved her. But his hug was very different-less warm and inviting. As he said the words "I love you" his tone and demeanor seemed somewhere else-detached—like they were just words.

A few days later, Nora and Michael tentatively agreed on an October wedding. Michael wanted just a simple church ceremony. Nora mentioned that she had friends she wanted to invite; Michael said he would not be comfortable with a crowd. They agreed to inviting fifteen to twenty people to the wedding.

Normally in the past the two families would go to church together. But this Easter was different. Michael refused to attend the Easter Sunday service. He refused to eat breakfast or to go over to Nora's for supper. He just wanted to stay home and in his room. This was what he had done since he came home. He slept most of the day; saying he was tired and just out of sorts.

On Easter Sunday, he did not come down for breakfast or lunch. Kevin and Rita went to Nora's for dinner and made his apologies.

Finally, at 8 PM Michael came down to the kitchen for something to eat. Rita made some lunch and put it in the ice box to keep.

Michael looked at Rita with a blank stare *"What did you have for dinner?"* he asked. *"Dad and I went to Nora's and had her famous pot roast with all the trimmings and strawberry short cake for dessert. I made you a grilled cheese sandwich with some pickles."*

Nothing else was said; Michael just took his jacket and walked out the door. Michael left and walked to "Miss Kelly's Diner" two blocks away. There he ordered coffee and some mashed potatoes with fresh cooked spinach. The bill came to ninety-five cents; he left the girl a dime tip.

Before Michael was served the waitress asked if he was *"One of those "soldier boys" that just came home?"* When he said that he was—she doubled his order and did not charge him for the extra-large order. Michael ate everything on the plate. He has been wishing for a hot dish for quite a while.

When he arrived home, Kevin was waiting for him. *"I am so happy son that you were able to rest this whole week. Could we sit down for a few minutes; I would like to talk with you about something."*
Kevin explained that he was never going back in the insurance business or in the grocery business. He told his son that there was *"A good salary offered to those that worked at the steel plant and it offered many good opportunities."*

He suggested Michael apply for a position the next morning. Kevin explained that he felt his *"Applying early would give you a head start from other soldiers that would like to relax for a month or more before looking for a position. Will you come with me to the plant tomorrow morning son and meet Mr. What's his name in personnel?"*

Kevin did not like that his son was sleeping so much he felt it was a kind of depression that was not healthy. He did not like how Michael treated his sister or Nora since he returned home. The tone of his voice was demanding and demeaning. He also felt that Michael was his responsibility, and he was not going to let him think he could just sit around the house doing nothing and just wallowing in thought and sleeping. The war was over, it was now time to get back to living and working putting it all behind him. Kevin was fearful that if the effects of the war lingered much longer in Michael's conscience, productivity would lack, and emotional stabilization would be difficult to recapture.

The prayer of serenity says it all.

Kevin hoped that his working at the plant would help Michael get a position there. If it did help, then they would be able to go to work together just like they always planned. Kevin explained to Michael that he made an appointment for him to meet the head of personnel the next day. He asked Michael to please come to work with him in the morning.

Michael loved and understood his father's intentions and did not want to disappoint him and shatter his hopes of the two of them working together. Then he said *"Sure Dad, what time do we leave?*

Kevin said *"Thank you son, now that the war is over it is time to get it behind you. This will be a good start. We leave at 5:30 AM"* Michael replied, *"No problem Dad and thank you."*

At 5:30 AM the two men left for the plant in Kevin's car. Michael went directly to Personnel. He met Mr. Howard.

There was no doubt that Kevin being a current employee helped Michael being offered a job. In fact, for the referral Kevin would receive $5.00 in his next pay envelop.

Michael was with Mr. Howard one hour, and at the end he was hired and offered many options, he chose the strip mill coal mine. It was one of the hardest places to work hot, grueling shoveling coal all day-but the salary was the highest and Michael thought **"it might just give him the medicine he needed to re-focus."**

It was nice of Mr. Howard to arrange for Michael to have the same shift as Kevin for a while. The men could travel together to and from work. Traveling together would give Kevin a chance to learn about his sons' experiences in the war and help bring him back-from those horrible experiences.

Later that week Kevin heard from the war department. His brother never made it past Normandy. His brother's dog tag and wallet were being sent to him by the war department along with some paperwork for him to sign. His body would be buried in Arlington Cemetery.

Chapter 18

Things Are Coming Together

The next two months went by quickly but by June 15th, Nora was getting anxious about the wedding. She and Michael appeared to be still in love.

Lilly was making the simple dresses for the wedding. Rita chose a caramel-colored material and Nora wanted an off white. Rita designed both dresses and was overjoyed at Lilly's talent for using and cutting the newspaper as a pattern for the dresses.

Rita's dress had three-quarter sleeves, and a round neck. The dress stopped two inches below her knee. The back of the dress was cut into a "*V*" with pearl buttons covering the zipper.

Nora wanted long sleeves. Rita designed the dress with lace coming up from the waist and crossing at the breast resting on each shoulder and the lace extending to the wrist in the front and to a "V" in the back. Under the lace front covering her breasts would be white silk. The back of the dress was a continuation of the lace and silk that closed with a zipper. The floor length dress had a slight gather at the waist.

Lilly took silk to frame the top of the lace and added pearls dropping three each inch until the center. Lilly purchased enough pearls to make herself a necklace. Nora and Rita needed shoes. They waited for the Sales. No luck in several places, so they finally went to

"Shoeprints." It was a long way to go but it was worth the trip. They loved their pumps, and they were on sale "buy one get 50% off the second pair. Everything was now set Nora and Rita.

While Lilly was purchasing the pearls, she found a set of three tier pans that would be perfect to use for a wedding cake. She decided to make some small sandwiches and offer a fruit dish after church reception along with some punch. The last thing needed for the wedding was for Michael and Kevin to have a suit to wear. There was little money for suits-both men found black suits at the local thrift.

Michael was willing to do everything Nora said but Michael's heart was not in the excitement of a wedding. It was Nora now that initiated their kissing. Michael participated but it seemed half-heartedly. There were times Nora felt that Michael was in a different world-more viewing than participating.

Michael proclaimed his love for Nora; but he was no longer that young romantic boy who could hug or kiss her all the time. Time was getting short and now October was six weeks away. One of the teachers Nora worked with asked about their honeymoon plans. Nora was evasive but the teacher mentioned a place in Niagara Falls. Nora and Michael never spoke about a honeymoon. She decided they would not have the money; but she felt there was no harm in mentioning the place to Michael.

The last Saturday in August was sunny and beautiful, Michael and Nora went for a leisurely walk in the park. Cautiously she explained to Michael that a friend mentioned a place in Niagara Falls for a honeymoon. Michael said he would "think on it" but that money was tight.

While in the park Michael asked Nora if they could sit for a minute and talk about her college days and her new job. As he began asking questions… Nora interrupted *"Michael Wilson, I told you-before you left-that I was your girl—didn't you believe me? Not one fellow interested me-you are the love of my life!"* Michael laughed he put his arms around her and kissed her passionately. *"I guess, I am the luckiest man in the world. Honey, many of the men received letters that…*Nora interrupted again *"Michael Wilson, I love you. I have loved you since the day we first met, and I always will." "Honey, I just needed to hear it from you. I did not want you to marry me just because you promised before I left. I need to ask you something, but I think am afraid to ask. I never spoke about this, but I need to know—*What is it Michael *"would you be marrying me just because you promised before I left?"*

"Oh Michael, you are the man I want to spend the rest of my life with. No- one else interests me and that will never change." Michael felt that a weight was lifted from his shoulders. This time he smiled from ear to ear and even looked like his old self again. "OH, Nora you have just lifted a worry from me-I love you so much I could

never stand to lose you but many of the men received letters just before departing and it was the kind that hinted that it would not be the same when they arrived home—if you know what I mean?" "Oh, Michael, I love you now-maybe more than ever. All I want is to be your wife, have your children, and take care of you for the rest of my life." Nora said.

From then on things changed. Michael began singing to her "*I love you now and forever.*" He was "tuned in" to wedding plans, making jokes, and kissing Nora often. Nora knew they were going to be "alright."

The couple went to an old pawn shop to purchase their wedding bands. The jeweler sold them to the couple or $25.00 each.

Nora saved enough money to purchase a small gift for Michael. It was a wristwatch-she planned on giving it to him shortly after the wedding ceremony.

Michael had a surprise of his own for Nora. While in Germany, he purchased a small diamond engagement ring from a farmer who needed money. It cost him three month's pay in US dollars.

It was supposed to be an antique. He was not sure of the size of the diamond or anything, he just liked the ring.

When he went to the pawn broker to pick up their wedding rings, he asked the man to size the diamond ring to the size of Nora's wedding band. The man was shocked. He told Michael it was a half Karat diamond, perfectly set and a quality diamond. He promised to size the ring, and have it fit in nicely with the wedding band they just purchased.

The man was stunned when Michael told him what he paid for the ring. The pawn broker told him that the ring was worth much more.

Michael wanted to surprise Nora at the wedding ceremony and give her the ring when they were exchanging rings. He thought he had it all figured out.

Michael began thinking about a honeymoon in Niagara Falls. That Sunday "The Town Cryer" had information on places in Niagara Falls with articles, pictures, and information about the number of honeymoon spots in the falls. Each place had a toll-free number to call for information.

Michael found one he liked and called the number and inquired about a honeymoon package. This one had a real special offer it identified: "<u>If a couple traveled on their wedding night and stayed three nights: their wedding night would be free, and the hotel would provide a free "Greyhound" bus ticket to the hotel; with a fifty percent fair discount ticket to return home from the hotel. The hotel also offered a bridal sweet with flowers, wine and a basket of fruit in the room along with three free breakfasts.</u>"

Michael thought it would be a perfect gift for Nora. He booked the place for the honeymoon. Now he needed to decide when to give her the Honeymoon information.

He picked up the brochure and decided to give it to her, with a copy of their itinerary, at the Labor Day family picnic. The jeweler agreed to have the engagement ring ready in time. Everything was finally coming together.

The family's Labor Day picnic was perfect as usual. Lilly made her famous fried chicken with hot corn on the grill. Nora made a potato salad and coleslaw; Michael made his famous pork and beans with sausage and bacon; Rita made a stuffed angel food cake filled with strawberries and blueberries covered in whipped cream. Everyone was enjoying a cup of coffee and a piece of cake when Michael stood up and announced: *"You all know Nora is the love of my life, there is something, I have not done, but what every girl should remember. I want to do it now. Please bear with me:*

Then he went over to where Nora was sitting and gave her his hand and signaled her to stand. Once Nora was standing, he went on one knee and said: "Nora, *I love you more than life itself. If you will marry me-from this day forward I promise to love you, care for you, and try to make you happy every day of our lives together."* *"Oh Michael, you know I love you and of course I will marry you."* Nora answered she almost thought it was a joke. But Michael turned to the family and said *"She is MINE! And this will prove it to you and the world.* With that he handed her a box with ring and sai*d "I purchased this ring for you when I was in Germany. I give it to you* now with my heart, and my love forever." Nora said the ring was "a beautiful ring and I love it!"

Everything went as Michael planned, and Nora was overjoyed. She showed everyone the ring and they admired it. When Nora was finished showing everyone her ring Michael said, "There is more." Michael handed Nora an envelope. Inside the envelope was a letter of confirmation for the honeymoon suite, the bus tickets, and a copy of the article from the newspaper and an itinerary.

Michael loved seeing Nora happy. Then Nora realized that Michael had completed all the plans for their honeymoon in Niagara Falls.

"Oh my God! Oh my God! Oh-Oh—a beautiful ring and a honeymoon all with the man I love—life is wonderful, and I am so happy! "She grabbed Michael hugging and kissing him crying. Kevin said, "That's my boy-always prepared."

It was a great day and as she got into bed, she looked at her ring and marveled- **"it is truly beautiful"** she thought. Then she began to read about their honeymoon plans. She loved Michael very much-and his words would remain forever in her heart.

Michael left that evening feeling particularly good. He loved surprising Nora and seeing her happy-he really loved her very much. He made a promise to himself-that he would try to live up to the standards that his father personified with his mom.

The Tuesday before the wedding, Nora went shopping with Rita. Rita had a special gift for Nora, she wanted to be sure she liked it and it fit before giving it to her. The ladies went to Taylor's Fashion Boutique were Rita had something put on "hold" in the lingerie department. When they arrived, the salesgirl brought out the item-and gave the box to Nora.

In it was a white long silk, empire waist nightgown with matching coat—absolutely beautiful. Nora tried it on, and she looked lovely in it.

Rita wanted their first night together as husband and wife to be a romantic and hoped Michael would be stunned seeing Nora in the nightgown. This gift was perfect, and Nora thanked her, hugged her and told her she loved her and the lingerie.

They stopped at the shoe section and purchased some slippers to match. Nora wears a size six and the saleslady said they only had one size 6 and it was on sale at 75% off. It was their lucky day

Nora wanted to get a few other things and they shopped for another hour. There was a great restaurant called "The Waldorf" and they stopped there for lunch. The ladies did not arrive back at the house until four o'clock, Michael was there and reminded Nora—they had an early dinner date. **Oops!**

Chapter 19

New Lives Together

The wedding took place at St Mary's Chapel. Eighteen guests attended the ceremony.

After the service everyone went to Lilly's for lunch; consisting of specially made sandwiches with salad with seasoned chicken on top and homemade Caesar dressing. The homemade wedding cake was three layers; one vanilla, second chocolate and last tier marble cake. Fresh raspberry cream filling enhanced the flavor in the middle with butter frosting- it was delicious! Coffee and tea were offered to top it off. Everything was planned and went off like a clock.

By 6:30 PM the bride and groom had changed clothes and were on a bus to Niagara Falls for a honeymoon. They arrived at the hotel at 8:45 PM.

Sometimes the excitement and planning of an event is more rewarding than the actual event.

Nora was young, beautiful and was hoping for passionate romantic evening.

Unfortunately, life is not a Cinderella story.

The hotel lobby was beautiful. Their room had a double bed, and there was a large bouquet of flowers on the small table, two glasses of wine, a basket with two apples, several small pastries and some chocolate candies.

Once their luggage was in the room: Michael wanted to walk around the falls. He enjoyed how it was all lit up at night.

They left their suitcases unopened in the room and left the hotel. In a minute they began viewing all the festivities around the falls. They walked around the streets for about an hour and a half then returned to the hotel. Stopping to try some of the home-made fudge and noticed some of the unusual restaurants.

When back at the hotel Nora changed into her new lingerie. When she opened the door to lay on the bed. Michael stood up and looked at Nora he said, *"You are a picture of loveliness, you are my heart and soul."* As he kissed her Michael said, *"I will always love you, Nora."*

His kisses were tender and held her ever so gently. He felt completely devoted to her. It was then their love became as passionate and as beautiful as Nora dreamed.

They slept in each other's arms and in the morning, they made love again and showered together.

Nora felt safe and loved being in Michael's arms. She was devoted to making him happy. She never wanted to be away from him again.

She knew this really was God's plan because she could trust Michael with her life.

Breakfast was included with the room and the honeymooners just made it down before serving closed. It was a literal feast-one of those "all you can eat things."

There was: coffee, tea, milk, bacon, eggs, sausage, cereal, pancakes, waffles and French toast, apples, bananas, fresh squeezed juice, and a huge tray of numerous delicious pastries.

The waiter mentioned they were permitted to take anything back to their room that they could carry. He was just bringing out cinnamon pastries. After such a huge breakfast they were full. But since only breakfast was included with their package, they decided to take two sandwiches filled with sausage and cheese for lunch along, a cinnamon pastry each and a banana and an orange. This way they would limit their spending.

At this time Nora decided to check over the hotel lobby. There were several large, beautiful gold-based planters filled with flowers; Oriental rugs enhanced the hardwood floors and leather furniture, and brass trim was everywhere along with leather chairs for people to sit down and rest. It was very impressive.

The streets in the falls were so inviting –lit up with tons of little shops. They were excited and ventured out to check every street and shop.

They looked around most of the day. About 5:30 PM they started to get hungry. They found a place called "Mama Lena's Italian" restaurant. The couple enjoyed "A Dinner for two special-for $5.99." It consisted of a big dish of spaghetti with two meat balls, a basket of garlic bread, a glass of homemade wine plus a cannoli each for dessert.

They really enjoyed the meal and the Italian music that was played.

Before returning to the hotel, they again observed the beautiful lights that decorated the falls at night. When they returned to the hotel, they made love and fell asleep.

Michael woke up first, he brushed his teeth and washed his hands; the movement in the room woke up Nora. It was 3 AM but neither of cared, they made love again and held each other tightly. Nora felt "settled" in his love. They missed breakfast but remembered the sandwiches and other food they had saved from the day before. They ate the sandwiches in their room. They talked about their dreams for their future together. Then once again they walked around the falls streets looking at all the shops. There was an area that they felt missed the night before and so they went there first. They walked around holding hands and kissing often. They passed a small curio shop where Michael saw a small broach in the window. It was a perfect cameo and he purchased it for Nora

About 4 PM they began to get hungry. Since they did not have any lunch and missed that big breakfast; they decided to return to "Mama Lena's." At "Mama Lena's" they split the special of the house it was a huge dish of tripe with a dish of spaghetti on the side, a lettuce salad, a glass of wine and a dish of gelato $4.99. The restaurant charged them an extra $.50 for splitting a meal. Having been there the night before they knew the size of their meals would be more than enough for the two of them.

Michael admitted to loving Italian food. Nora enjoyed the food, but she loved the desserts and the homemade wine best. Michael asked Nora to have Italian food often. Nora promised to learn to make some of the things he enjoyed.

The bus back to Clayton came soon enough. When they were home, it was not long when the humdrum of everyday life took over. Before the wedding Michael moved his things in to Lilly's house. He felt living with Lilly, after they married, would be best for all involved.

Rita and Kevin continued to live in the house where Michael grew up; even though that house was now half Michael's. If Kevin was single, the kids felt it was his house.

In September Lilly decided to take some time off from teaching. Lilly was a great cook and she just wanted to do the things she never really had time for in the past. She was offered the opportunity to some substitute teaching instead of taking on a full load. It sounded terrific. The school had no problem with her taking a hiatus as long as they could have some of her time.

Michael and Nora planned to relieve some of the financial burden from Lilly. The house was paid for; the expenses Lilly allowed them would be minimal, just taxes and insurance and some of the maintenance.

Nora began teaching the second grade that September at St. Gabriel's School. She was the only lay teacher at the school and everyone parent, teacher, student and the priest all loved her. She was always helpful, had great lessons prepared, on time and willing to help any child.

In December Nora came home excited. One of the parents mentioned that they were going to sell their old car. They were purchasing a brand-new Chevy.

They offered Nora their old car at a very reasonable price, letting her pay them for the car monthly. Michael was against it *"We have no debts you are going to put us in the poor house; the bus works, and my dad drives me whenever he can. We just can't begin buying things —especially a car when we have responsibilities here."* Michael protested.

It took about two hours for Nora to win him over to her way of thinking. The car cost four hundred dollars. Nora would put eighty-five dollars down and pay the man twenty-five dollars a month until paid.

If Michael said yes Nora agreed, they would not drive the car until it was paid in full. Nora wanted the car for the winters.

It gets quite cold in the winter and waiting for the bus Nora always froze. She also thought it would make Michael's life easier as well; especially if she could take him to work when he worked the swing shift. This way he did not have to rely on his father. She could also pick him up on her way home from school.

Lilly surprised them both. She wanted to contribute two-hundred dollars toward the car. She called it her wedding gift to them.

Her logic was they were now picking up the taxes and insurance on the house; if they agreed to take her to the new grocery store on Meyer St. every other Saturday; and to the doctor, when needed, it would be a great deal.

That night Michael called Kevin and told him about the car. Michael was attempting to complain. Kevin decided it was the time to give Michael his share of the money that he had saved for him. Michael had no knowledge that his father had saved any money for him.

Michael's money grew to two-hundred seventy-nine dollars and fifty-seven cents. Kevin said it was a belated wedding gift.

The money from Lilly and Kevin would give Michael and Nora enough for the car and help pay their insurance. It was a real surprise and welcome.

The car was completely paid for when it was turned over to Nora and Michael. Michael admitted that the car was certainly comfortable.

Gasoline was expensive they only drove to the doctor, the grocery and, back and forth to each other's work. It beats walking in the snow and waiting on the corner for a bus. It would be a great help bringing the Xmas tree home.

Chapter 20

A Scare

One night, Lilly's was feeling ill. She was in and out of the bathroom walking around the house unable to sleep. Nora heard her and offered to make her some tea. Lilly said she needed to go to the doctor. Her pulse was rapid, and she did not look well.

In the morning Nora called Dr. Shaffer, he agreed to see Lilly that afternoon and perform some tests. On the drive to the doctor, Lilly told Nora that she had met with Mr. Frank two weeks earlier. Mr. Frank was an attorney. He was the attorney that arranged for Nora to be adopted by Lilly after her parents died.

"Why did you want to see him?" Nora asked.
"Why to make my will of course. I think we should always be prepared." Lilly answered.

She continued, *"Nora I leave everything I have or own to you. You will inherit the house and everything in it and anything I have in the bank. The house is in reasonable shape-and it will be yours someday. It will help you and Michael not to incur any debt as well."*

Nora knew that Lilly had no other family but, she was in shock just the same. Lilly reached over, touched and kissed Nora's hand *"We never know what God has planned for us, so I want to plan your future while I am young and able to do it for you."* Nora thanked her and told her she loved her very much.

Dr. Schaffer called with Lilly's test results a couple of days later. Lilly's tests identified a kidney stone. She would have to take some medicine plus she needed to rest. It is a good thing she was not teaching full time because if the stone did not pass, she could need surgery.

Nora took over more of the housework and did all the laundry. Lilly shopped with Nora and they cooked together most times. The kidney stone brought to light just how fast things could happen.

Nora told Michael of her conversation with Lilly and her eventually being given the house. Michael was always helping with the maintenance; but now he took a serious interest in upgrading and keeping the house and grounds in excellent condition. He began painting some of the rooms.

Lilly was a great cook-Nora never took a serious interest in cooking in the past. But now, she would focus on understanding how Lilly did things. Lilly was a gourmet-using wine, stuffing, spices and sauces. She did something to a potato she called "<u>dressing it</u>" it was perfect, but she baked it two or more times. Her deserts were to die for.

Nora decided it was her turn to learn from the best cook ever. The next five months seemed to be running smoothly. The three of them were into a routine that helped prepare for Thanksgiving, and Christmas, both went off without a problem with Kevin and Rita joining.

No one went overboard on spending this year-they set a limit on each other —and stuck to it! But as the holidays approached it was easy for everyone to see that Kevin was still sad. He really loved and missed Betty it was a year since they had seen each other. Still stubborn, hurt, and resentful he would do nothing about it-not even a telephone call.

Then the last week of June, eighteen months since Kevin and Betty seen each other, Rita noticed in the newspaper that Betty's mother passed away. Nora and Rita went to the wake together. Betty was happy to see them. She talked about how much she still loved and missed Kevin. She looked drawn, thin and sad as the time apart was hard for her too.

Rita told Kevin about Betty's mother's funeral, but he just sat in his chair. Kevin did not go to the wake or the funeral. He did not call Betty or send a card. Rita told Nora that Kevin "*Would not discuss his relationship with Betty. It is like he just closed his mind to her and nothing-not even a change in circumstances could change it.*"

Betty's mother was buried on the last Friday in June. A week after the burial, Rita and Kevin were sitting in the living room talking about planting a garden next year when the doorbell rang. Kevin went to the door, and when he opened it, there was Betty standing at the door. Kevin spoke,

"I have nothing to say to you—you made your de-cision a longtime ago." Betty tried to reason with Kevin, but he just closed the door.

The doorbell continued to ring. Rita walked over and opened the door. Kevin had returned to his chair. Once the door was opened, Betty walked right into the house and over to where Kevin was sitting.

"Listen you stubborn mule-I am going to say this like it or not." She continued: *"My father just left us, he got up one morning and left for work—can you hear me? And neither one of us-mom or I-ever saw or heard from him again.*

You think that did not leave an impression on both of us? My mom was pregnant at the time and lost the child. She had to beg for money to be able to keep the house and feed us. When I was old enough to go to kin-dergarten, she worked at the cheese factor. Not having money for a bus, my mother walked one mile winter and summer to the factory. At first, she worked part-time, but when, I was in school all-day she went to work full time."

Kevin got up from his chair he began walking out of the living room. *"Come back here"* Betty shouted as she was following him. *"In the early days, the church kept us alive with food and charity. My mom would clean the church to pay back the debt. Neither of us had any friends. When I was old enough to work, I worked taking out garbage for the butcher.*

It was his wife who taught me to sew. I was taking in sewing at twelve years old. No one ever really helped us. Are you listening Kevin?

I understood my mother and I loved her. She was not always right in her ways-but I loved her, and I understood her.

I know things did not happen the way either of us would have liked" Betty was quite upset and began crying. *"But I love you Kevin Wilson, I have never stopped loving you. If you do not understand why and how things had to be this way—then be lonely, be sad, and the two of us can go to our graves dreaming about what could have been. Do you hear me?"*

She was screaming at the top of her lungs as she walked over to Kevin and but her arms around his neck. *"Are you going to throw me back-leave me again-or are you going to allow both of us the happiness we deserve?"*

She was shaking, crying as their eyes met-but Kevin's showed no compassion. He lifted his arms and with his hands removed her arms from his neck as he asked her *"Are you finished because I am?"*

As he spoke Betty looked at him-her tears stopped-she put her head down and backed up a little. She turned and without a word began to walk toward the door. Her steps were small and her head down.

As she passed Rita she said, *"I will love him till I am in my grave-which is where he seems to want to push Me."* and with that she opened the door and walked out.

Just then Rita turned to her father crying she said *"Are you just going to let love and happiness walk out the door a second time—what is it your stupid pride—you are acting like an immature child you ...you... suck! Dad admit it you love that woman...I hate seeing you both like this-see what being so stubborn has gotten you. You are lonely and you know you love her. You talk about love-well what is loving someone if it is not showing compassion, understanding and most of all offering forgiveness to each other. Two people who love each other must know that the most important thing of all is working together to resolve all issues.!"*

OMG Kevin never heard his daughter speak to him in such a manner before. He just looked at her and he did not move. His eyes were burning with anger **"How dare she talk to me like that-I am her father! Where is her respect?"**

With Betty gone Rita turned to her father again and this time in disgust she said: ***"You are pitiful, here this lady loves you-and by the way-You love her as well!***

You are stubborn, stupid, resentful, unforgiving and cruel. You are willing to throw her and her love all away-because your feelings were hurt!

Your pride could not accept what she was forced to deal to handle. Unconditional love is accepting the other person for good or bad, loving them, accepting them, and the differences between them. God puts

people in a check and balance situation- but-no you will wallow in that pride of yours.

I hope it keeps you company because you will be ALONE! This is it for me I am leaving this house right now this minute. Do you hear me? Dad-I am leaving and you! If her love means nothing to you – then mine can't mean much! I am not sure you are you capable of loving either one of us...just yourself?

You are a self-centered, selfish, egotistical man and I cannot...no I will not subject myself to such stupidity or ego any further."

Rita stomped up to her room packed a bag with as many clothes as she could fit into the small suitcase and walked downstairs.

She saw her father still sitting in his chair staring at the wall. *"Do you see me Dad? I am packed—I am leaving and -You are now going to be alone—and you will probably be that way until you die. Michael is married and has his own life and home. I say again, you are acting stubborn, un-forgiving and selfish. I ask you now—Is your pride going to stop you from saying anything to me? I am leaving you do you understand?*

After a few minutes of her father just looking at her, she said: **"How could you let love pass you by? How could you be so cruel to Betty? And to me? I am your flesh and blood. Are you just going to—let me—leave? Look at you—why can you not say- I want you, I love you or I need you?**

Will you just let us both leave? Dad is this avoidance what you are going to do to me? Will your pride and stubbornness put me out of your life as well? Do you think acknowledging needing someone as being a wimp?

Do you think that to love someone and yield to them is being a wimp?

Well, when you give to another person your trust, your honest feelings, all your emotions-with genuine compromise you do that -for the sake of the most important things in the world—and when you can do that—you gain respect, love and family.

What? What motivates this indifference you seem to have? This cavalier attitude of yours? Do you not need love? Don't you miss love?

Tell me Dad, because once I am out of that door it will be—to hell with you!

Dad—Dad I am begging you to talk with me, -do not throw away our love.

Dad, bending, and forgiving, and growing together are part of real love. Something you cannot— no will not—do. What a shame, you are acting like a child."

The more she spoke the more Kevin became angry.

Dad you never acted like this with my Mom. You loved her deeply and everyone saw and marveled at that love. You always had her back, and bent it for her often you knew how to love then Dad, what happened?

Michael and I marveled at your, caring, respect, and devotion; You, were the real example of true unconditional love then.

Stop this Dad face the stupidity of this situation. If you do not you are an idiot and will never be my hero again.

Kevin never moved, but his thoughts were **"they all leave me one way or another-so what is the difference."**

Rita stalled a bit more:

"Look Dad, do you see what I have in my hand" it is a suitcase, and I am packed. Dad, I am going out that door. You are a man filled with ego and pride; I am begging you Dad-tell me you love and need-me? Kevin just closed his eyes.

Rita walked out the door crying, slamming it behind her. She realized she had not considered where she would go. But, in a second, she thought of a perfect place.

She went over to Betty's house and knocked on the door. Betty opened the door and saw Rita there with her suitcase in hand, crying. Betty was overjoyed.

Rita tried to speak but all she could say was *"I left him can I... I?"* *"Stay here-of course you could stay here Rita"* Betty said.

The two women talked most of the night-they were waiting-hoping- praying-for Kevin to come knocking at the door begging their forgiveness and telling both that he loved them. But that did not happen.

A couple of days went by and Rita left a note in Kevin's mailbox. She asked him to forward her mail. It was obvious to him that it was Betty's house.

Two weeks went by-and no sign of Kevin. The two weeks became three and then four.

By the end of the fifth week the women decided that he would never show up. They were getting along very well.

Rita offered to pay Betty something for room and board. But Betty would not take money for rent it was her house, she would have lived in it and would have paid for it alone. The ladies agreed to just alternate paying for food. Betty's decision was a bit kinder and more generous than Rita expected. She was also falling in love with Betty-she was like the mother that was taken from her at such a young age.

By the end of the sixth week the ladies had settled into a routine. They were great friends and seemed to just complement each other's personality.

A lady at the grocery store thought they were mother and daughter they looked so much alike.

They laughed together a lot. They went to the picture show, and even out to dinner together.

Neither of them was aware of Kevin's loneliness nor his pain. Kevin would not tell anyone what he felt-he knew he could go to Michael-but he did not want to burden him.

Two days after Rita the house left Kevin began drinking and drinking and drinking. By the second week he was purchasing two bottles of scotch every Friday night on his way home from work. He would finish the entire two bottles over the weekend. Sundays he would try to sober up-with a bit of food.

These days Michael was going back and forth to work with Nora; he never even suspected his father had a problem. He also rarely called him on the telephone he spent much of his free time mowing the lawn and taking care of cleaning out the basement of years of unused stuff.

Michael had an opportunity to get some extra hours at the strip mill coal mine and Kevin was in another building.
The way the men communicated was with notes in their locker room. Michael did not even know that Rita had left.

Kevin paid two boys in the neighborhood to mow the lawn and he would pay them every two weeks.

Chapter 21

What Now?

Rita stopped at the house early on a Saturday morning. She left the house in such a rush and she always needed something. This time she needed a special dress.

When she walked in, she found Kevin on the kitchen floor, drunk and out cold—his left hand was bleeding from a cut.

Rita went to the phone and called Betty. When Betty arrived, the two women managed to get Kevin upstairs. Took off his shoes and put him on the bed. Rita went downstairs and began making black coffee, while Betty stayed with Kevin and cleaned his hand from the cut. She was very gentle as she bandaged it.

When Kevin came to, he would not drink the coffee he just argued with the two women, still drunk. So, they "picked him up, each with an arm over one of their shoulders, and they put him in to the shower stall—clothes and all—turning on the cold water.

The women left the bathroom with Kevin sitting on the floor of the shower and the cold water running on him. It took him a few minutes to come to is senses.

Kevin undressed himself, tossed his wet clothes aside, and began to shower.

When Betty returned and heard the shower still going, she thought Kevin was still sitting on the floor, so she opened the bathroom shower door.

Kevin was naked. He immediately grabbed a towel from the rack. Betty ripped it quickly out of his hands. *"See what your stubbornness has done for you-you have become a drunk!*

You are naked with nothing and no one to care for you. You have become a pitiful person, and you are going to spend the rest of your life alone. You are stupid. You lost it all because you have been and are a stubborn fool!"

The shower was still running as Kevin grabbed hold of Betty. He twisted her so her back was supported by the shower wall. He began kissing her. He was holding her in his arms. She did not put up a struggle.

She wanted his kisses—his love – she missed him very much. They were both dripping wet as his body showed her how much he wanted her.

As he was kissing her, he began taking off her clothes his hands moving ever so gently everywhere and love just could not be stopped. Before long-they were in a passionate embrace both naked and showing their love for each other.

Rita returned to the bedroom, heard the shower and she peaked in through the open part of the door. She saw them through the bedroom mirror, both in the shower and realized it would be better for her to wait downstairs.

About an hour later both Betty and Kevin both emerged into the kitchen wearing robes drying their hair.

Kevin declared *"I have to make an honest woman of her and marry her before she claims I took unfair advantage of her."* And with that declaration Betty stated that *"They would get a marriage license on Monday morning without delay."* They all laughed and agreed.

Betty dressed in some of Rita's clothes from her closet and both the ladies left the house. Kevin agreed to be at Betty's for dinner later in the day.

After dinner, Rita went to a picture show to let the love birds have the house all to themselves. She did not want to call Nora or ask her to go to the picture show. In fact, she had not seen much of Nora since she and Michael married so Rita went to the show alone.

It was 9:30 PM when she arrived back at Betty's. She found the love birds in a passionate embrace in the living room. *"Ok you guys—you will be married soon enough."* Kevin left giving both ladies a hug and kiss.

On Monday morning Betty and Kevin received their marriage license.

Rita call Nora and Michael to tell them of the news and all of them were excited.

The wedding took place on the next Thursday afternoon by the Justice of the Peace. They went back to Lilly's where she had had prepared a small lunch. After lunch they enjoyed a small angel food cake with blackberries and whipping cream.

Rita moved back into the old homestead the night before the wedding. Kevin moved into Betty's house.

When Kevin left Rita realized that this would be her house alone now. She felt confident Kevin and Betty would be happy from now on. Kevin promised never to get drunk again.

As she looked around the house, she was mentally calculating the cost of paint, curtains, and flowers. This is my opportunity to develop some decorating skills.

Chapter 22

New Emotions

With school now closed for the summer, and both Kevin and Michael married,

Rita decided she needed a project. It was time to re-decorate the house! She would change curtains, move the furniture around, add some plants, and paint.

Everything would be done with minimal cost, and she would have the choice of colors and how it should look. Rita also thought about getting a part time job for the summer at one of the downtown shops on Main St or maybe even returning to the one she was at prior to going to college.

On Saturday morning as she was getting ready to catch the Main Street bus the telephone rang.

It was Mr. Parker inquiring about her plans for the summer. Before she had a chance to answer his question he added *"Because I have a job for you, if you would consider it."*

Rita agreed to meet Mr. Parker at his office at the university, Monday at 9 AM. All weekend long she was trying to think of what kind or type of job she was going to be offered.

Monday came, and Mr. Parker was waiting for her. As soon as she arrived, Monica, his secretary told her to *"just go in.* to the office"

The two met and talked for over an hour. Mr. Parker wanted Rita to write a workbook for his next semester classes.

As a university hire Rita would do all the research, and provide the answer key, to Mr. Parker for his classes in "Political History."

It would not be a fun job-but the university would publish it for internal use, and she would receive the credit as "Author."

Rita felt not only was it a great opportunity, but she owed it to Mr. Parker for all the help he gave her getting an education.

Parker agreed to pay her for four hours every day, Monday through Friday for eight weeks. He forgot how resourceful Rita could be. She finished in six weeks. The workbook was over eighty pages with an answer key and an index.

Mr. Parker made some minor changes and sent it to the printer. He liked it so much that he agreed to pay her for the full eight weeks and give her a small bonus.

He invited her to his home on the last Sunday in August and asked her to attend a service at the Methodist Church. His best friend's son was to be the new pastor and would be giving his first service.

Parker and his wife were having a little reception later in the afternoon after the service. He wanted Rita to be part of that reception. She accepted the invitation. Never having been to a Methodist Church before she thought it would be a learning experience. Since Rita had two weeks before the party, she decided to concentrate on her original plan of redecorating the house. She purchased some material to make curtains for the kitchen and a tablecloth.

Two Weeks Later

When she arrived at the church, there was a young sandy blond-haired fellow with hazel eyes standing in the pulpit.

He was young, quite tall and very handsome with a terrific smile and eyes that just made you feel you wanted to know him. To Rita's surprise, he was the minister. She felt something strange come over her –her stomach seemed tied in knots. She wanted to run out of the church for some unexplained reason. This was a new emotion. Rita had never experienced it in the past.

Nevertheless, she stayed and listened to his sermon.

He spoke about love. Specifically, on how it changes people, allowing them to grow, and how if they work at their relationship, they become a better person.

"True love in a relationship, initiates the acceptance of the differences in personalities, experiences, values, traditions, fears, all the while teaching forgiveness, patience, tolerance, and eventually yielding to unconditional love. He concluded by saying that *"giving unconditionally in love actually brings people closer to God."*

As the young pastor spoke about love, Rita was drawn to his eyes. Indeed, their eyes met a couple of times. Rita would immediately look away. There was something compelling about this man. She controlled herself and then she realized she was attracted to him. He seemed so relaxed—so aware of everyone and their attention. He had the whole congregation mesmerized and captivated with his sermon on love and his handsome smile.

It is customary in the Methodist, faith for the minister to stand at the entrance of the church and greet everyone-coming in and going out. Rita decided she was not going to pass where he was standing when she left. These were feelings she needed to explore before meeting him.

When the sermon was over, she began to leave the side entrance when suddenly she felt a hand on her shoulder.

"Hi, I am Mathew Blitz, did you enjoy today's sermon?" he said extending his hand to her. *"Yes"* Rita could feel her face blush as her stomach was still tied in knots. As she shacks his hand thinking **"Does he want me to say something but what? Why do I feel like this**?*" "You speak very well Mr.-ah Reverend Blitz"* and he interrupted *"Please call me Mathew."* and just then Mr. Parker walked over and said *"Hay you two—enough chatter- we have a reception to attend. Rita, may we give you a lift?"*

Rita's mind was racing- again. For some reason, she could not explain, she did not want to go to the reception. She felt uncomfortable being attracted to Mathew. She said no to the offer of a lift. *"Will we see you soon Rita? I am counting on you being there."* Parker said.

Now an answer was needed but Rita did not know what to say. She began with, *"Well, I have so many things going on today and—**she hesitated**—planned on—**she hesitated** again her mind searching for what to say as— she noticed the look on both Mr. Parker's face and Mathews. She continued *"I can make it if you do not mind my getting there a bit late."*

Parker then said, *"Please Rita, I am counting on you I want to introduce the "writer" of my workbook to others and do some boasting. Please do not disappoint me. There are a number of people I would like you to meet."*

Just then Mathew added *"It would be so nice to find out what it is like to work for Mr. Parker—you are coming even if late—right Miss?"* Parker said, *"This is my author Rita Wilson"* There appeared no way out for Rita she had to be there. *"Yes, I am Rita Wilson"* she replied as she still hesitated *"I will be there but-but a bit late."*

With that assurance they exchanged pleasantries, and all went their separate ways.

Rita had no rational explanation or understanding for her emotions or uneasiness. She simply had never been so attracted to anyone like this before. She reasoned, **"It must be just a fluke of my imagination. Still, he is very handsome and has quite a stature-very tall and his eyes are compelling." Enough she told herself. This is silly.**

She decided to be an hour late arriving at Mr. Parker's house. When Rita arrived Mrs. Parker, answered the door. She aged well over the years. There was a bit of gray beginning in her hair and after five pregnancies she had gained a little weight, but she looked beautiful and was as always very poised. Mrs. Parker missed seeing Rita.

During her college days Rita was a frequent visitor at the Parker home. She was happy that Rita could make the party. The ladies kissed and walked into the living room.

There were about forty people still mulling around the house the invitation said 1-3PM.

Mr. Phillips was there with his wife and several other people from both the church and the university.

As Rita turned to walk over to the refreshment table Mathew approached her. *"Well, you finally got here"* he said. *"We all thought you would never get here. Tell me all about yourself Rita? Mr. Parker says you are the best assistant ever?"*

Rita was a bit startled. *"Excuse me"* she said, as if she did not understand Mathew's sudden familiarity and question.

Just as she was about to answer with a smart remark an attractive young woman came up next to Mathew and said: *"Well, you must be the famous Rita that Edward Parker has been talking about? We would all like to have a word with you. Tell us how was it working with the master? We hear he is a slave driver, and you are a wizard. What was it like helping him by writing his new workbook? Hi, I am Catherine, Mathew's wife."* She said extending her hand to shake hands with Rita.

Rita felt the tension immediately leave her. He was already married. She was safe—but safe from what she did not know.

Mathew was about six foot one or two inches tall and weighed about two hundred, or so, pounds. They looked like a happy couple. She saw their eyes meet several times.

They exchanged pleasantries with Rita, and she offered a few quips about working for Mr. Parker. She soon moved along to meet and talk with others still at the party.

As the reception ended, Rita was leaving, she thought *"how much she enjoyed being there and meeting everyone."*

Leaving the party, she shuck hands with Mr. Parker and gave Mrs. Parker a big hug.

Just then she heard her name. Mathew called out to her. *"Oh, Rita, I wonder if you could assist me with something?"* he said. She turned and answered, *"Yes, what did you have in mind?"* she hesitated to wait and hear *"Well, I am contemplating writing a pamphlet for teenagers on values and virtues and we hoped to persuade you to give me a hand?"* Mathew said.

Rita did not know what to say then Mathew added *"The church will pay you, but they are not quite as rich as Mr. Parker's university, I figure we could be finished in about two weeks—what do you say?"* Stunned Rita said, *"Let me think about it Mathew, I have so many things of my own to handle this summer."* Rita replied. Mathew coached *"I promise to let you make your own hours, Catherine and I really need some guidance."*

When Rita heard that Catherine would be involved, she felt better about the offer and said *"Ok, let me check my schedule. I will call you in a couple of days to set a date to discuss what you had in mind."*

On the way home Rita reviewed the events of the day; along with the strange and unexplainable feelings she had over seeing this Mathew Blitz. She was not sure if she was frightened of him or liked him or what created this feeling.

Three days later she called the residence of Rev. Blitz and Catherine answered. *"Hi this is Rita Wilson, how are you, Catherine?" "I am fine thank you we have been waiting to hear from you."* Catherine said. *"You have? I am sorry it took me a while to get my schedule open."*

Rita felt relieved, **"obviously Catherine knew of Mathew's offer and since she used the words "we" she felt most likely Catherine would be involved."**

"Yes" she continued, *"I understand you have been persuaded to assist my husband in writing a pamphlet for teenagers on values and virtues for young people. Is that correct?"* Catherine continued: *"This should really be for kids from about ten to eighteen years of age-not just teenagers. What Mathew hopes to do is instill in them a proper respect along with values while providing resources available for all kinds of self-help. Are you able to assist us?"* Again, the term **"us"** was a relief to Rita. She felt silly for having been so skeptical about Mathew's request for assistance. Catherine asked:
"Would Thursday afternoon be ok to begin learning what you are expecting to be included in the pamphlet? "That would be fine," Rita answered.

"Mathew has an opening -on Thursday he can meet you at the rectory at noon. Is that, ok?" Catherine said.

Rita did not feel that she wanted to meet Mathew alone still being uncertain about her feelings.

She mentioned to Catherine: *"That would be fine;"* she continued *"However, I would like you to be there. It is always good to have different perspectives; and a woman's ideas add a different tone when speaking to young people. Would that be, something you would be able to do?"*

"Certainly" said Catherine, *"Michael does not usually ask me to join him when writing his pamphlets, but I would love to have my thoughts considered, we will see you Thursday."*

Rita hung up the receiver and felt relieved. She put the meeting out of her mind for now.

Thursday came soon enough, and it was time to meet with Mathew Blitz and Catherine.

When Rita arrived at the rectory, she was a bit surprised Catherine was not there. Mathew said that something had come up and extended her apology.

He was very businesslike, discussing what he expected and what he was thinking for the pamphlet. Rita asked a few questions took a few notes and agreed to review his outline and get back to him.

As Mathew handed her his notes, Rita's eyes noticed an appointment on his desk:

"Attorney Appointment Friday at 1PM."

The work that Mathew asked her to do was not at all difficult. But her curiosity was piqued, and for some reason she was interested in knowing more about his appointment on Friday.

Rita finished writing the pamphlet and the graphics in two weeks. She called the rectory to let the minister know.

This time a strange lady answered the telephone. *"No, Mrs. Blitz is out of town. She is in California visiting her mother-but Mr. Blitz is here."*

Mathew came to the phone; he was excited to hear that Rita finished. They made an appointment to meet in the next morning at his office.

Rita's mind began working overtime again. It was stupid she kept asking herself **"Why do I have *these strange feelings? Am I afraid of the reverend? Or am I afraid of me?"*** She did not like that he acted too friendly so quickly. But try as she could, she could not find anything wrong with that; he is a minister.

She arrived about fifteen minutes before the scheduled appointment time. When she opened the door to the rectory's front hall there was Mr. Parker. He was standing in the hallway. *"Is there something the matter, Mr. Parker?"* she asked.

"No, my dear I am just here on business." A moment later Reverend Blitz came into the hallway; *"Ah, Rita, thank you for coming and for working so quickly"* Mathew said. *"Won't you come in, and have a seat, Rita."*

As soon as she was seated, she gave him the envelope. He made a gesture that identified the envelope was heavy and he just laughed. *"I will read it this evening may I call you with any questions I might have?"* He was in control of the situation.

Mathew then sat on the corner of his desk, he looked at Rita. *"How are you, Rita?"* he asked. *"Fine thank you,"* Rita answered. *"Good, good, I am happy to hear that."* *"Did you have any problem doing this?* He asked. *"No"* Rita answered. *"Great, I will give you a call after I review it alright?"* Rita felt a bit odd—all her concerns about the man seemed unwarranted. It was as if he wanted to cut this meeting short *"That will be fine reverend"* she answered. And, with that he stood up signaling to Rita that their meeting was over extending is hand to shake hers.

Mathew asked if she had calculated the total hours she worked on the pamphlet. Rita stated that a sheet with the hours was placed in the envelope. He assured her a check would come within a couple of days to pay her for her services. He said, *"Thank you again"* and with that Rita left.

All the way home, Rita felt puzzled. She wondered what was going on with her mind and stomach. Why was Mr. Parker there? Why did Catherine go to California? Why do I get so upset being near him?

The rest of her day went by quickly. She was putting up curtains in the kitchen after supper when the doorbell rang. "I wonder who this could be at 7PM."

She opened the door and there stood Mathew Blitz *"I am sorry to just barge in like this, but I was at Mrs. Murphy's. I wanted you to know that I am being called away. May I come in?"* With that statement Rita opened the door wider and Mathew walked in. *"I am leaving for California in the morning; I will be gone for a while. The parsonage secretary will be sending you a check; you should receive it in a couple of days. The pamphlet is perfect thank you. It is exactly what I had in mind"* Rita was still shocked to see him at her front door. All she could say was *"Ok-that will be fine."*

Mathew continued to walk from the entrance into the living area as he was talking. Rita closed the door.

He continued, *"Catherine and I have some things to work on. It is a long story. For now, this is what is happening: Mr. Kohl will be the new minister. He will be calling you. I have given him the pamphlet. I am confident he will want to contact you to add some of his thoughts to it. I have given him your telephone number. Is that alright with you?"*

"That will be fine" Rita said.

And just as quickly as he appeared, Mathew walked toward the door and began to open it to leave.

"I want to thank you for your assistance Rita. It has been a pleasure to meet you."

Rita did not know how to respond. She felt shocked. He just arrived as the new pastor, and now he is leaving.

Before anything else could be said, he bid Rita goodbye, and he was out the door.

He was always a complete gentleman. She really felt silly for all her mixed emotions.

After Mathew left, Rita phoned Mr. Parker. *"What is going on? Mathew was at Mrs. Murphy's; and he stopped-here. He said he was leaving town. He said he and his wife were working on something."*

Mr. Parker hesitated and then said, *"They have had a difficult marriage. I do not have all the particulars. But Mathew feels if they could end up in a divorce. If that eventually happens, he would not continue as a minister. I cannot say much more."*

After a few more pleasantries, they ended their conversation.

Sometimes it is hard to read people or get involved with their personal problems. This was one of those times.

*　*　*　*　*

Rita was invited to Lilly's for dinner. She wanted to spend the afternoon making a new dessert: Blackberry Crumb Bars to bring over to Lilly's.

When she arrived at Lilly's, she learned Nora had prepared her first pot roast dinner.

It was delicious. Rita and Nora both hoped someday to cook as well as Lilly. Rita only made simple things.

Despite her desire to enhance her culinary skills, she first wanted to redecorate her house, living alone—food was not a priority just yet.

There were many "free" Cookbook offers on canned food labels –she decided to order a few for herself. When one arrived, she found herself eager to try it out.

After supper, Lilly decided to go to bed early. Michael went to work on something in his shop.

It seemed the right time for Nora and Rita to have a little "girl talk."

Nora began: *"Rita, since Michael and I were married, he has had nightmares. Even though it may not be too noticeable to others, his attitude and behavior has at times concerned me. While he is obviously able to handle work, and his responsibilities at home; something has been fighting him-and now me at times. He will not talk about the dreams."*

Nora felt confident and presented her thoughts *"I feel it was something that happened during the war that bothered Michael or was difficult to accept."* She said: *"I had hoped time would take the war and its terrible killing out of his mind; but how long would it take? What do you think I should do?"*

Rita tried to change the subject. **She did not understand these things or know how to advise Nora. This was her brother's wife, her best friend asking for some in-sight.**

How could she say that—she too, thought Michael was different since returning from serving in the war? She did not have any answers and when something like this happens—the only thing one can do is—change the subject.

She told Nora to "*Just love him and be patient.*"

That was all she could think of to say.

Once again, she began talking about redecorating the house.

Nora was relentless and needed some direction; she was more concerned about Michael. She wanted to discuss how her concerns were obviously becoming an issue for her and their marriage. She was searching for advice.

She continued: "*Michael exhibits strange almost "indifferent" emotions and behavior toward me at times-like he wants to be detached from me-and yet- claims he loves me. It is difficult. When I talk about issues at school, he "turns me off."*

His usual sentence when it comes to my school concerns-he says, "I just do not understand what you are talking about." Rita I am frightened-I feel there is little between us now. His feelings are so deep- he cannot even discuss them. I am frustrated making excuses for Michael's behavior all the time.

I love Michael. I want to understand and help. But there are times …I feel if there is no true emotion for me any longer what… should…I do? What could be so difficult to talk about?

Everyone, I have mentioned this too- has had the same answer—time needs to pass, love needs to be felt and patience would heal. Ok, time has passed, and I do love Michael so how long will it take?"

Nora knew there was something deep inside Michael that needed to come out. The question was how to get it out.

For now, she hoped everyone was right and-she just put the feelings off, thinking

Nora thought: ***In the past, we were sole mates and transparent to each; what could have happened that would change him so drastically.***

Michael almost demands my obedience. That is not the Michael I have known for years. I will try to wait it out a little longer-but if it doesn't become known then…"

Nora decided to continue searching for ways to help him get in touch with his fears, and talk to her about, his feelings. They need to face whatever it is before… she wanted to always be there for him, to love him and help him.

All the way home, Rita felt terrible for Nora and Michael.

Chapter 23

Time Moves On

Summer was just about over, and the family decided to have a cook-out at Lilly's house for Labor Day. Everyone agreed to bring something; this always made their parties easy and was less stressful for the person hosting.

Betty made a casserole of beans and greens along with a salad mixture of a variety of different kinds of lettuce.

Lilly made her famous fried chicken.

Nora roasted corn on a grill and made a fruit dish.

Rita made stuffed baked potatoes.

It was a beautiful day; the sun was shining, and the birds were singing. There were flowers on the table from both Lilly and Betty's gardens. The meal was excellent.

Everyone was happy, full and excited about the summer, being over and getting back to a schedule. Everyone was having coffee and a treat when:

Rita spoke about Mr. Parker and the work she completed. When Rita mentioned Rev. Blitz—Michael perked up.

He mentioned that he and Nora met the Rev. and his wife Catherine, at a friend's house during the early part of the summer. They thought they were a nice couple.

They were surprised at Rita's statement about a possible separation or divorce. Rita felt she must have mis-understood.

As evening approached, they were all still together the conversation moved toward everyone's desire for the coming months and the next year.

Rita was intent on new decorations for her house and now learning to cook. Michael was saving for some new tools.

Nora wanted to get some additional teaching materials. But it was Lilly's comments that came as a surprise to everyone. She decided it was time to update the house and she was thinking about:

- A modern 22 Cubic Foot refrigerator. One she saw advertised in the Sears Roebuck Catalog.
- A bigger stove, and
- New linoleum floor in the kitchen.

Rita tried to continue with her ideas about redecorating. But Betty's next comment was a surprise. Betty lived in her mother's house forever with an aging mother, now she wanted to travel.

Their first stop was to be New York City. She especially wanted to see the Empire State Building. Kevin stated that it would be a road trip and not a plane trip as he was concerned about flying.

Betty secretly wanted to be on an airplane but yielded to a road trip. Kevin agreed to go on a plane in the future-but he was not quite ready. She also wanted to talk to Kevin about selling her house; but she decided to wait a bit longer before she told him that idea. For now, Kevin was still fixing up the house.

The day ended, with Betty playing the piano and the family's vocal choir joining in. While their voices were not trained, they did an exceptionally good job-or maybe it was Betty's playing the piano that helped.

When the party was over, and Michael and Nora were alone; Nora felt that something was bothering Michael. She thought quite possibly the others noticed it. All this talk about everybody "**wanting or desiring things that was making him uneasy.**" Nora thought.

As they were getting ready for bed Michael said "have you seen *the cost of a new 22 Cubic foot refrigerator? How about the cost of a new stove! Who around here is made of money?*" he asked. *"How could Lilly want these things?"*

Nora was getting into bed and said this was not the time to discuss money. She assured Michael that Lilly would not want things to happen overnight. She kissed Michael good night and said they should think about nicer things. She was confident there would be a better time to discuss Lilly's ideas than before bed.

She knew Lilly would not expect the two of them to pay for everything. She was confident that since all three of them were working they would be able to manage purchasing the items one at a time.

It was true that the house –the kitchen—has not been updated since when the house was built in 1908; it was functional—for now at least.

She decided to wait until Lil brought it up again.

Chapter 24

A Baby Coming

The Wilson's were becoming very compatible. They were married for almost five years and they had settled down to a routine life.

It had been over two years since Lilly mentioned updating the house. Michael handled all the small stuff around the house that needed fixing.

This school year began just like all the rest. Nora Wilson was up early and getting ready to meet the students of her now second grade class.

Normally the first day of school was her favorite time of the year. She loved getting to meet and know the new little personalities that would be challenging her. She loved watching them grow and develop.

But this morning Nora felt unusually tired-and a bit out of sorts. She could not put her finger on why. She just did not feel like herself this morning.

She shrugged it off and tried to get ready for school. After breakfast she dropped Michael off at the steel plant and proceeded to begin her day at school.

The entire day she just could not get her barring. As this strange feeling lingered Nora became a bit unsettled.

The students seemed especially active. She was a bit short with them and hoped "they would settle down in a day or two." The class was small, and she was sure it would be a good year.

Meanwhile, at home, Lilly was preparing a special dinner everyone's favorite -pot roast with roasted potato and carrots with home-made bread, and jello for dessert.

When school was finished for the day Nora felt exceptionally tired. She picked up Michael from work and once home she just wanted to relax.

Instead, she changed her clothes and went down to help Lilly with dinner. The smell of the roast had begun to turn her stomach, and nothing tasted right so she picked.

When she put a carrot in her mouth-she could hardly chew it, the same with-the bread. Nora's body just rebelled. It took all her power not to up-chuck right at the table.

She concluded she was over tired over stressed and probably caught a bit of a flu bug. There was also first day jitters to consider. It had to be some-thing silly.

After the dishes, Nora sat down to read her class list and prepare her lessons for the next day.

Lilly hesitated to ask; she did not want to disturb Nora; but she had to know *"Nora is anything wrong? Was there something wrong with the pot roast?"* Lilly noticed that Nora ate little. The meal was to be a special treat since meat was so expensive.

Nora felt bad she knows all the work Lilly puts into her meals. The fact that she was not able to eat must have upset Lilly.

"No" she answered, *"It was delicious, I am just so tired today—with first day back jitters—I guess."* Lilly understood she felt the same thing when she began teaching.

Anyway, this was only Nora's first year teaching at her new school. Lilly felt that tenseness many times in the beginning of the school year. Teaching would be "old hat" soon enough.

Michael changed departments at the plant to earn an extra fifteen cents an hour. The change necessitated a "swing shift." It necessitated him leaving the house by 11:10 PM if he was catching the bus by 11:22 PM. As he was getting ready for bed, he remembered Lilly's wish to do some remodeling. **He knew that Lilly was really a great person and if she wanted a new refrigerator and stove the extra money would help them with the cost.**

He was not sure how he would like the new shift or the new position but since it just came up, it was worth a try.

The new schedule was midnight to 7 AM for three weeks and then 3 PM to 11 PM for three weeks.

After that he would learn if he would have to "swing" the shift or he would be getting a regular schedule.

Nora planned to be up to kiss him goodbye. But she was so tired, she slept through the alarm, and never heard him leave.

Nora had been driving Michael to work for a couple of years. He forgot there was a new bus schedule. When the bus did not come by 11:30 PM he returned to the house, wrote Nora a note left it on the kitchen table where she would be sure to see it and took the car to work.

The night seemed short as the alarm went off and woke Nora at 6:50 AM. She went into the kitchen to make a pot of coffee. There on the table was the note from Michael. She knew she would have to rush to make it to class by 8:00 AM.
Taking the bus meant needing an extra twenty to twenty-five minutes travel time-plus walking to the bus and then to school.

She showered quickly; dressed and got out the door at 7:35 AM. Funny, she just could not drink the coffee this morning-the smell made her stomach upset. A glass of milk just hit the spot.

Not her normal morning drink but she would manage. Breakfast was not in the picture as Nora's stomach did not want any food. Even the thought of eating was making her ill.

Meanwhile Rita was also on her way to work. She was invited to have dinner with Nora and Michael that night.

Nora was going to be doing the cooking again.

Lilly had a dinner arrangement with an old friend. The day seemed to go by quickly for everyone. Rita's new group of students were bright, and she expected a lot of diversified talent.

Rita arrived at Nora's at 5:20 PM. Michael answered the door. As always, he leaned over, kissed Rita on the cheek; he whispered in her ear *"Nora has been acting strange these last two days, I think she is ill or concerned about something at school? And does not want me to know-see what you could find out?"*

Nora seemed happy at dinner. She made a stuffed chicken with mashed potato, green beans, and Jell-O for dessert. Everything was delicious. Right down to the coffee, and except for a statement, that the coffee smell; seemed to make her ill-Nora seemed fine.

She did mention her *"stomach has been off kilter still."* Michael and Rita just exchanged glances. After dinner as the ladies were doing the dishes, Rita mentioned her ideas for decorating her house and how she was going to re-do the whole house. She described the new paint color and the new curtains in the Kitchen. The ladies talked for a while and Nora gave Rita a few suggestions.

The next thing on her calendar was to prepare a dinner for Betty and her father at her house. Rita loved saying and even thinking "**This is my house**."

She invited the two of them for dinner and decided to make her father's favorite: corn beef with cabbage, carrots and boiled potatoes.

Thinking about the dinner she remembered she still needed to purchase some carrots. She still had time to get the carrots. Two days later, she was on the bus to the grocery for the carrots. Someone left a book on the seat of the bus. Rita was intrigued by the cover. But more so by the author's name:

Rev. Fulton J. Sheen.

She picked it up and put it in her purse, "**I'll read it later**" she thought.

The grocery was unusually crowded. She only planning on carrots, but as she walked through the aisles, she thought that some rye bread would add a nice touch.

As she extended her hand to pick up a loaf of bread suddenly a warm hand was on top of her hand. *"Excuse me miss it seem like we are both after the same loaf of bread,"* a gentleman said.

He was very tall, had good built, with broad shoulders, wide jaw, brown eyes and his hair was nicely combed.

He had on a suit and tie. To be honest, he looked like someone from the movies.

He continued, *"I am sorry, I did not mean to startle you?"* *"No"* Rita said. *"We were both going for the same loaf of bread"* he was still talking. *"I have no problem letting a little lady like you get the best of me for a loaf of bread."*

Rita did not know what to say except *"Thank you."* She picked up the rye bread and began walking away.

"No problem miss" he commented as she was going down the bread isle. **"Now that is one fine lady"** he thought as he watched her **"And very pretty if I do say so myself.**

I will have to come back to this store soon in the hopes of meeting her again."

Rita's dinner was perfect the rye bread added a great touch. After dinner Kevin asked Rita if they could talk for a moment about *"Something important to us."*

Kevin seemed quite serious *"Sure, is there a problem?"* Rita asked. *"Well yes and no."* He continued *"Betty and I love each other, and we are married, and. Well, we think it is time to –I mean—to do something most couples do after they are married."*

Rita was confused but decided to have a little fun along the way. *"Dad, I thought you knew all that and had been doing it for a long time. Did you suddenly forget? Or if you need help...* she began with a twinkle in her eye *"if you need help... we could find...*

Kevin interrupted. *"Now Rita, do not assume! Betty and I want to go on a honeymoon. We want to go* to *Niagara Falls for three days. I remember Michael and Nora went there and they loved it"*

Betty was laughing as Kevin said *"The problem is Betty's dog—Saffo. Someone needs to be responsible for the poor animal. We were hoping we could count on you to take care of him-we trust that you will walk them and adhere to his schedule. So will you help us out?"*

Rita thought **"the two of them looked so cute sitting there anxiously waiting for her decision—just so they could plan a honeymoon."**

"Of course, I will take care of the dog. The two of you have a super time." They assured Rita that they would write everything down about Saffo's feeding schedule and the vet's name.

Betty asked if they could bring him over the last week of October on a Thursday evening and pick him up on Sunday afternoon."

"Sure" she said. "So, it is all arranged?" her father said. "No problem" Rita said.

Excited and happy, Betty and Kevin left Rita's early then she sat down to a cup of hot tea. She thought how nice it must be to be in love and planning a honeymoon.

Without realizing how tired she was when she sat down, she immediately fell asleep in her chair.

When the teacup she was holding turned over and tea fell on her lap the wet woke her. With wet cloths she realized this was a sign it was time to get ready for bed. As soon as put her head on the pillow-she was fast asleep.

Meanwhile Lilly and Nora were trying to sew the ripped curtains from the front hall. Nora took this opportunity to tell Lilly about..." Once again, Lilly repeated that "T*ime and love is what Michael needs. Many men are having nightmares about the war-that is what war does to people.*" Lilly said.

Nora felt Lilly was probably right. She began to feel ill and tired again both at the same time and resting did not seem to help. Her stomach had been out of sorts for the last three weeks. She resolved to keep her annual physical appointment with Dr. Rogers. After, all it was only two days away,

She surmised some tests would need to be performed. She was worried about the possibility of an ulcer? Or **even cancer.**

Meanwhile Michael was noticing all the vomiting. He felt her vomiting brought back all the memories of his mother's illness and what cancer was like.

He prayed Nora did not have cancer.

Chapter 25

Changes

This school year was a happy time. Nora learned she was pregnant! Their first baby was due in May.

Michael's reaction was one of concern for Nora and trying to decide:

"Where are we going to put a baby?

This house has only three bedrooms and one bathroom."

Lilly has one of the bedrooms. We have one bedroom. The third is used as an office by the two of you to prepare your class work."

Lilly was so excited about the baby her only comment was that they would work it out. She had a plan and now an excuse to move on it.

The next morning, without telling anyone, Lilly searched the local paper and found an ad for a contractor that read

"Retired man loves to work. Carpentry a specialty. Free Estimates?"

She called the telephone number and asked the gentleman if he would come to the house the next morning to give her one of his "free estimates."

She chose the morning because Nora and Michael would be gone, and she was determined to keep this a secret until she learned more. The contractor agreed

The next morning a good-looking older gentleman arrived at the house. He looked around the house, making notes, for over an hour.

Lilly offered him some coffee. They sat down to talk. He presented some ideas for this beautiful old house.

1. *The pantry is huge. It could easily be an office, when I take out the cabinets, finish the walls, add a window, and put a door on it.*

2. *"The kitchen is exceptionally large. It has a number of bare walls especially on the left opposite where the telephone is located; the cupboards from the pantry could easily be moved onto that wall in the kitchen for additional storage and easy access."*

Lilly loved that idea as she hated having things in two rooms and running back and forth for cupboard items. This would solve the issue of only three bedrooms. The contractor continued

3. *"There was a large hallway leading to the second-floor staircase. I could cut open—just enough space under the high point of the stairway to add a half-bath with vanity, sink and toilet. In this way people would not have to run up-stairs all the time to use the toilet; and it would be a better use of the space while increasing the value of the house."*

4. *"The upstairs hallway wraps around the three bedrooms. There is a large deep linen closet between two of the bedrooms. The linen closet is 10*

feet wide and eleven feet long. It could easily be opened on each side of the back, to accommodate a second-floor full toilet with vanity and sink, and on the long side a tub-shower. The second bathroom could have access: from one, two or three doors. One door would be attached to each bedroom and the third door would stay from the hall. You will have to decide on the number of doors wanted.

5. *A third option is that you could just have one access to the new bathroom from the hallway for company. My recommendation is that one of the bedrooms-the one on the right have a door leading to the bathroom. That bedroom is where your son-in-law and daughter sleeps."*

Lilly was happy. This would solve everyone's issue about a bathroom and a room for the baby.

The contractor was about to continue when Lilly suggested they have a piece of home-made Blueberry Pie. He agreed. Then, he said *"getting back to the house and garage."*

6. "The back of the house there is a large lot and that gives room for a garage. And it would not take much to put in an asphalt driveway instead of stones."

7. "Finally, there is plenty of room in the basement to *put up some shelves for storage."*

The man said he could begin as soon as she was ready, and they agreed on the cost. When the man gave her his estimate Lilly froze. *"I have to talk with my daughter and son in law to see how much we can get together."*

The man told her not to worry. He was retired and on pension. He would minimize the cost as much as possible. But he just could not use cheap materials for construction. If he were doing the job-the work cost the same for cheap or good; and he wanted to work with good stuff that would last and look like it was part of the original house. Lilly agreed.

She mentioned that Michael did not like mowing all the grass. She liked the idea of adding a driveway and garage. It would fill the bill for "a change that was a true improvement to the property." Hopefully, this would excite Michael to agree to part of the cost. There was no way Lilly could do it all herself.

The cost for all the material and labor would be an issue.

The fixtures for the first and second bathrooms alone would be $360 plus the cost of the labor.

The cost of a garage would be an additional cost for labor. The driveway would have to be dirt-because blacktop would cost another $200 –plus labor.

Removing and relocating cabinets, adding a window; cutting in for the bathrooms; materials for garage shelving, and doors: *The total cost **for labor plus materials**-barring anything unforeseen that could happen would be about $3869.*

Lilly thought it was the answer to a prayer and decided to discuss it at length. Michael and Nora thought that the cost for all the work was reasonable.

But they really did not have a lot of money and they did not want to "*owe*" anyone. They suggested waiting until they had all the cash saved. When Lilly called the contractor to tell him the decision reached; he decided to stop over to discuss the situation. He arrived and stayed a couple of hours

Lilly made lunch for them all. She gave him a piece of her pineapple short cake. Talking to them, he said that the coffee, lunches and deserts was worth his taking off $100 off the bill. They all had a nice laugh and he left.

The contractor offered to make a drawing so Michael and Nora could see what the place would look like when he was finished with the work.

Lilly invited the contractor to bring the drawing to show them all on Saturday morning.

But when Lilly discussed the construction, Michael was visibly upset. He began screaming, and ranting about the cost, wondering where they would get the money. Especially since the money did not include adding a new refrigerator, stove, or linoleum floor. They did not have that kind of money in the bank.

"*All this and with the new baby and the holidays not far away-how could we afford it?*" Michael said. His behavior was something neither Nora nor Lilly had ever witnessed before.

Michael was so upset he refused to discuss anything-and left the house for a walk. He ended up at Rita's house. He explained the situation saying how expensive the whole thing was even though it would enhance the house.

At that moment Rita decided she made enough money-and was only taking care of herself-she could give her brother some of the money. After all, he signed over his interest in the house, she was living in, to her when he married.

He did not ask for or take any money. She decided it would be a gift. She did not tell Michael of her plan. In four days, the family would have a Halloween luncheon. Everyone would be there, because this was also Betty and Kevin's going away luncheon before they left for their honeymoon.

It would be a perfect time to tell Nora and Michael of her surprise. Added to the money Kevin had given her -Rita had a total expanded to $450.89 at the Clayton Savings Bank.

On Thursday Kevin came to Rita's to drop off the dog, Rita told him of her plan to give Michael the money for the construction. Kevin had a better idea. He and Betty were both working, and they could afford to give Michael and Nora the entire amount as a Christmas and new baby gift!

After all this was a first grandchild and neither Betty nor Kevin had any other children.

With their money they would have enough for everything needed to do the house and the garage. It would be a great gift.

Kevin rationalized that one-day Michael and Nora would inherit Lilly's house; it would be nice to see them all happy now and enjoying things.

Rita wanted to do something as well. She agreed that her money would go for the new stove and refrigerator.

Kevin thought it was nice of her since Michael gave her his interest in their house. It was all agreed.

So, the day of the Halloween luncheon Lilly had a luncheon all prepared and everyone was amazed at how she integrated the holiday theme to the food.

After desert Kevin, Betty and Rita told Lilly, Michael and Nora about their gifts. The ladies were all in tears.

Michael thought it was a handout-but he knew that without the money they could not afford to do anything like what was planned to the house. He gave in and thanked them all. Kevin had a check ready as did Rita. Nora and Lilly cried with tears of joy.

The house would escalate in value plus there would be a more efficient floor plan. Everyone was excited to see the results. Lilly called the contractor the next day. He agreed to start the job immediately. He worked at the house every day while Nora and Michael were at work.

Lilly had coffee ready when he arrived and a small breakfast.

As the days went on the man was there most of the day Lilly made him lunch every day and they ate together. The two people got to know each other quite well and got along very nicely.

The contractor's name was George Bellow. He was a long-time widower with no children. He lived in a home on Tanner Avenue. George's house was a two flat. It was located about eight blocks away from Lilly's house.

George lived in the lower flat and rented the upper. Michael thought that the work was taking a lot longer than the original plan of eight to ten weeks. He was concerned about the man finishing in time for the baby's arrival.

But he surmised George was soft on Lilly. To his amazement it seemed as if she felt the same toward George. He and Nora agreed to never mention it to her.

While George was at the house, he also did many other repairs without charge. It seemed like he just wanted to be with them and especially Lilly most of the time.

He did not work fast but he did do great work. The work was completed the by the end of March it took five and a half months instead of the planned eight to ten weeks.

As Mr. Bellow was packing his box of tools for that last time; the look on both his and Lilly's face —was unmistakable the two of them were feeling lost without their time "together."

They had been spending most of their days together and now they were going to miss each other.

As George finished packing, he asked Lilly if she would permit him to take her out for coffee and lunch sometime. Lilly liked the idea and the two agreed to meet for lunch in a couple of days.

Nora was shocked hearing that her aunt was considering going out for coffee with George-but she was happy that the two of them got along so well.

Things seemed to be moving along quickly because by the end of April, Lilly and George were becoming noticeably close.

They saw each other four or five times a week. They went for walks and would often visit the diner together.

George would buy the coffee and they would sit and just talk. By May, George was becoming a fixture. He was over for supper every Sunday. He was five years older than Lilly. A good-looking man with silver gray hair and blue eyes.

George and Lilly went grocery shopping together and even shopped for baby's clothes together. George and Michael seemed to have developed a good respect for each other. Michael liked the way George took care of Lilly-it was obvious to everyone that they had fallen in love.

On April 16th Nora's coworkers gave her a baby shower. On April 30th Kevin went to Rita's. *"Honey, I have to tell you something. There is a room hidden in the attic. I built a wall in front of it and unless you knew it was there you would never find it.*

did it after your mom died. Follow me." He proceeded to the attic and made a cut in the wall it opened a doorway into a room. *"I do not understand Dad."* Rita said. *"I hid things in here that would remind me of another time."* When the door opened—there in this small room was hers and Michael's crib, a small, wooded bassinette, a rocking chair and some other baby items and a sewing machine.

Kevin said, *"when your mother passed away I,* put *everything away and built the wall to forget all about those years. Now with a grandchild due soon I believe it is time to bring out the baby items and give them to Nora.*

Rita decided to help her father bring all the baby items down and load them in the car. When they arrived with all the baby furniture Nora, Michael and Lilly were in the kitchen enjoying a cup of coffee and Nora had tea. They were overjoyed to see all the baby furniture.

They had not purchased and furniture for the baby. They were planning on looking over the next weekend.

Nora especially loved the crib, but the rocker was a real hit for Michael, he could not wait to begin refinishing and cleaning each item. He was excited about putting them in the green room nursery for the baby.

He painted the room a cool green not knowing whether the baby would be a girl or boy. On one wall was a picture of an elephant and on the other was a photograph of Mother Goose. There was a stuffed elephant in one of the bags.

As they moved in some of the bags of clothes there in the last bag was a stuffed gray elephant with two ribbons-blue and pink.

Chapter 26

Greta

The 7th of May-Michael was getting prepared for the baby. He took Nora to her Dr.'s appointment. Dr. Martin suggested at least two more weeks. Nora's bags were packed, and Michael had his clothes on the chair next to their bed. On the 26th he asked Nora *"you do think the baby knows how to get out-right?"* Nora just laughed and assured him the baby will be here soon.

On May 29th shortly after mid-night Nora's water broke. They left for the hospital when her labor pains were fifteen minutes apart. Michael was so excited driving to the hospital he went through all the red lights, as he drove directly to the Clayton Memorial Hospital Emergency Room Door.

Ironically, there were no police cars available to offer an escort.

As Nora was getting out of the car Michael yelled *"Wait for me! I'll be there as soon as I park"* Nora looked back at him and did not comment. But to an observer, her look said it all.

She went directly to the Emergency Room where a kind nurse put her in a wheelchair.

Michael parked the car and went into the Emergency Room. He learned that Nora had been taken to a room. He was not able to join her until he "*filled out the paperwork.*"

He soon learned that arguing with the admitting nurse "**would get him nowhere**" so he complied.

When he finally arrived at the room, he saw her for a moment as she was on her way to the delivery room.

"*Ok honey*" Michael said, "*This is a piece of cake just breath and you will be fine.*" Nora dismissed his words and told him she "*Was going to be busy for a while and he should just try to rest.*"

Every half hour Michael was at the nurse's station arguing that something must be wrong. "*My wife is only just delivering a baby. It should not take this long.*" He called Lilly, "*The nurses will not tell me anything. I bet my child has already been born. If they keep this up, I will take Nora to another hospital.*"

All night Michael was at the nurse's station every fifteen minutes asking, "*Where is my baby?*"

The head nurse, Mrs. Pascal, finally had enough. She told Michael to "*Sit in a chair and do not move until she calls him.* She assured him "*he would be told the minute the baby was born.*"

At 10:30 AM. May 30th, Greta Jean Wilson immerged. She was pink and perfect. When the nurse told Michael, it was a girl he asked, *"Who does she look like?"* The nurse suggested he could see for himself and took him to the nursery.

The nurse asked the baby's name *"Her name will be Greta Jean. Her last name will be Wilson-like mine.*

Greta was born with a full head of curly auburn hair, big brown eyes and long fingers. Michael called Lilly and told her it was a girl and the time she was born. He then asked her to *"Please Lil will you let the rest of the family know it was a girl. I am exhausted"* she agreed.

Michael went to see Nora. The first thing he said was *"tell me the truth was she really born at 10:30 this morning?* Nora just laughed. The nurses filled her in about Michael's constant visits to the nurse's station.

The first two months with the baby home were the easiest. Nora breast fed, rested, and took care of the baby. Lilly cooked and took care of the house and Michael.

Lilly had more energy these days thanks to all those evening walks she and George took along with them being in love. In fact, Lilly had lost at least twenty pounds -feeling young and happy again.

Meanwhile as the second month ended Michael was beginning to feel left out. Nora's time was taken up with the baby. Lilly and George spent much of their free time together. Nora was cautious about anyone near the baby who was not clean. Michael played with the baby-after he cleaned up from work. Michael loved Greta

George was at the house more these days. He too loved Greta. He often said, *"I can't believe I missed all of this-she is just so precious."* George became an honorary Uncle.

George loved telling the baby *"Hi baby I am your Uncle George and I love you big time!"* Betty was thrilled as she and Kevin relished being Grandparents. Everyone was always taking pictures of the baby and to their amazement the baby always seemed to smile when her picture was taken.

Greta's Baptism was August 20th. Lilly and Rita were the Godparents. The priest called Greta a gift for everyone. The baby never cried- she appeared to be observing the whole thing except when the Holy Water was put on her head-it was cold, and she looked at the priest. After the service everyone went to Rita's for dinner. The baby did not like being startled when one of the balloons pooped or there was a loud noise.

Nora used the christening dress that was in the bassinet when Kevin brought over all the furniture. Seeing the baby in that dress brought back memories for Kevin.

He told everyone Mary Jo received the dress as a gift from a neighbor named Carol who moved away-to live with her daughter. He said Carol taught Mary Jo how to can and gave her the sewing machine that was still in the attic; they were great friends.

Rita thought it was strange to hear him talk about her mother –he rarely ever commented on their life together. Betty said she told Kevin-he did not need to forget that part of his life but to remember it and all the love that he and Mary Jo gave to each other. That is what made him the man she fell in love with and married. **How unselfish, and kind of her**, Rita thought.

Then George decided, the family was together, and he was going to make an announcement and the time was right.

The day before the Christening- George called Michael; *"Michael since Lilly does not have a father or son to give their permission for me to ask Lilly to marry me., I am asking you for Lilly's hand in marriage. Before you answer, I want to remind you that Lil and I are not getting any younger and the time is now that this should be done."* Michael was honored and told him *"George, you mean you want me to give you permission to ask **our aunt** Lilly to marry? Well, since it is **My** decision, I say: Go to it George-we already consider you family."*

With that under his belt, and his love for Lilly in his heart, George decided, he was nervous, and a bit shaken—but he was determined.

As soon as everyone was comfortable, he said: *"I want to take this opportunity to say something to all of you. This little girl has brought this whole family, including me, **a new beginning** of the love I have missed all my life. Being with all of you has shown me what a real family* *means. It has brought me together with an unbelievable person that I have become devoted to. It gave me an opportunity to find out what I have missed and needed for an awfully long time."*

George, shaking a bit walked over to Lilly and got down on one knee. Nora was amazed he could do that-at his age. But then he shocked everyone at what he did and said next.

Taking Lilly's hand in his he said: *"Lilly, I think I fell in love with you the first day we met. Being with you makes me happy and I feel alive again. Will you do me the honor of being with me for the rest of my life as my wife? I promise to be devoted to you and try every day to make you happy. Please accept me as your husband, I promise to cherish, respect and appreciate your love forever!"*

The room was so quiet you could hear a pin drop- even the baby was looking at George. The women were in tears and suddenly, Lilly was in tears. *"Oh George, I love you. I would be honored to be your wife and have you for my husband. I will cherish your love and respect you, all the days of my life. Yes, George, I will marry you."* Lilly said.

Everyone jumped up to congratulate them. No one ever dreamed Lilly would fall in love let alone get married. But, with Nora now happily married, and a mother, she was ready for some love and happiness of her own. There was no doubt in anyone's mind that she so loved George. He was indeed special.

Betty could not contain herself and blurted out *"When will there be a wedding?"* She knew everyone wanted to know. *"Well, I do not know"* Lilly said. *"George, what do you think?"* *"Lilly, I do not want to rush you but tomorrow would be fine with me. I am not getting any younger Lil-so please think fast and let's now waist too much time getting to the priest."*

Everyone laughed and charmed in…but Rita said out-loud *"We want to plan a wedding. We want to plan a wedding!"* Nora interrupted and asked Lilly, *"Aunt Lilly-needless to say we are all excited for you. But it is not what we want or would like to do. What would you like?"*

"Well since I never had a wedding, I would like a small intimate gathering with all of you there. I would like to be married by a priest and have a wedding cake." Lilly said. *"But George is right at our age, we should not wait too long."*

George said *"How about I call Father John at St Lucy's?*

He has been teasing me saying "he could be ready in an hour." Would next Friday be too soon Lilly for us to be married? We could be married at lunch time."*

"George that sounds like a plan. Next Friday is a perfect day for a wedding," said Lilly. Everyone began hugging kissing George and Lilly as love and laughter filled the room. George said he would call Father John first thing tomorrow. He kissed Lilly and the two decided they would get their marriage license the next morning.

After getting a marriage license, Lilly mentioned to George that she wanted to shop. George dropped her off at Taylor's while he took the car to have the oil changed. Lilly wanted to look for something special to wear for the service. She found a beautiful Powder Blue dress for the ceremony with ¾ sleeves "A" lined with side pockets and it stopped two inches past her knees. To her amazement she was a size 12. She found a small blue pill box hat that had a net to go over the top of her thick auburn curly hair.

She then did something that even surprised herself. Years of wearing pajamas now changed to a long satiny type of blue night gown with a matching robe and of course blue slippers. This was a beautiful set and Lilly knew that George would like her wearing this set. She also purchased a new morning robe and other house slippers. She thought it would be a good time to purchase a "wedding gift" for George. She found a navy and blue men's robe.

When George picked her up and saw all the bags he commented *"Did you buy the place out?"* She laughed and said, *"Would it bother you if I did?"* *"No way-honey you can buy and have whatever makes you happy -that is my promise to you from now on"* they kissed, and George drove her home.

On their way home they stopped at the bank where George introduced Lilly to his banker, and she added Lilly's name to all his accounts and his safe deposit box.

George planned his own surprise. Knowing that a woman does not like to live in a house with another woman's decorating; George began updating his kitchen when he and Lil started dating. He was slowly working on changing things at his house. The month before George asked Lilly to marry him, he purchased new appliances for the kitchen and put in a new Armstrong floor just like the ones Lilly had picked for her house. He knew Lilly's favorite color for a kitchen was yellow and so he found a shade of yellow that he knew she would love.

He purchased all new linen including a bed set that Lil had seen in the Sunday paper - she mentioned it was "too expensive but very beautiful." He gave Michael his carved bedroom set for Greta. George ordered a three-tier wedding cake with a man and woman on the top. The cake had one tier chocolate, one white and one marble all with white frosting and a chocolate raspberry filling.

George also ordered three dozen long stem roses to be placed all over the house on the wedding day. He carved a sign out of wood and engraved it in bold letters

"I WILL LOVE YOU FOREVER."
He hung it on the wall in his bedroom. On Thursday Michael and George moved all Lilly's things over to her new home.

When Michael saw the kitchen and the bedroom, he said "George who would have guessed that you were such an incurable romantic." George responded *"Michael do you think she will be happy-I mean as a wife—you know what I mean?* Michael responded, *"Love makes all the difference in the world George and there is no doubt that she loves you."*

On Friday morning while everyone was dressing at Lil's house Michael went to the florist and picked up an orchid for Lilly and a boutonniere for George. He also purchased a sign that said, "Just Married" and tacked it on the front door of George's house. He put a sign on George's car and strung some old shoes on the back and a bow on the front ornament hood.

The Wednesday before the wedding Lilly took George to see Mr. Frank her attorney. George told her there were things he wanted written down. He did not have an attorney.

At Mr. Frank's George wanted a will giving Lilly everything he owned should he pass away. He also wanted to place his house in both their names.

He knew that if Lilly passed away first, she left everything to Nora. Lilly already had a will. But now with getting married she wanted papers transferring the house immediately over to Michael and Nora. She knew Nora would understand that Michael was like a son to her.

The wedding took place at 1 PM Friday September 9th just as planned. Lilly looked beautiful and there was no doubt that she and George were happy.

The entire family and Father John went to the Swiss Chalet for a chicken dinner on George. At dinner Lilly wanted George to make an announcement so—he asked everyone for their attention.

He said *"You are all aware-with Lilly Bing as my wife, I am a lucky man. And as so My wife will be sharing my heart, home and everything I have from now on.*

Lilly feels, there is no need for her to own another house. She planned on Nora having it one day. But now, he paused as he handed Michael a piece of paper, *"Michael and Nora the house now belongs to both of you, this is the deed.*

It is "Lilly's gift to both of you. All the papers are official, and the new deed has already been recorded." Everyone clapped and was excited. Michael and Nora had tears in their eyes.

Nora, Michael, and Greta would live in their own home. Nora loved the house and Lilly's gift was theirs free and clear. This gift could not be measured in dollars. Michael felt truly blessed this was the best –a beautiful wife and healthy baby. He thanked God and George and Lilly for everything.

Arriving at George's house that evening they saw the sign Michael tacked on the door. A few of the neighbors left some presents and flowers. Lil had been to George's house prior but when the door opened, and she saw the new kitchen she said: "Oh George, I love you." George replied "Baby, you the greatest." Jacky Gleason had been on television that week and George used his reply from that show. They both laughed and kissed.

As George put the gifts that were left outside in the house. Lilly was a bit nervous. But, within a few minutes the doorbell rang. Three of George's friends came in bringing a huge basket fill with fruit and candy along with a beautiful plant loaded with greenery. The men stayed about ten minutes-knowing that this was a wedding evening. They teased George "be a good boy George and remember your age" as they were leaving.

When the men left Lilly and George retreated to the kitchen; Lilly looked around, she loved all the new appliances and the flowers all over the house. They looked at the beautiful picture of Michael, Nora and the baby with a note that said, *"Just in case you miss us!"* George had purchased matching chairs for each side of the sofa with the help of Rita to be sure the furniture all matched.

Their first night together George was an incurable romantic as Lilly went into the bathroom to change. George sang the song *"Let me tell you all the ways I love you!"* he made up the words as he went along and when she came out of the bathroom they kissed, and George said she looked–beautiful. With that they both knew it was time to share their love. George was ever so gentle, careful, and tender. When it was over, they slept in each-other's arms.

Before the wedding, the ladies arranged a schedule for Lilly to watch the baby at her new house. Nora only wanted Lilly to care for Greta. So, Nora had to arrange her morning schedule giving her time to drive Greta over to Lilly's, and still have time to take Michael to work while arriving on time for her teaching position.

For the two- weeks after the wedding Nora's friend Millie watched Greta, Giving Lilly and George some private time together. After, the two weeks were over Nora began dropping Greta off in the morning and picking her up on her way home for school. It all worked well until around Thanksgiving things when things began to unravel for Michael.

Nora picked up the baby at Lilly's after work. When Michael worked a swing shift, he had to take the bus home. That meant that Michael would come home to an empty house, in need of straightening without dinner being ready. He was tired from working all day. Lonely, he began drinking a beer while waiting for Nora to arrive home with the baby and cook supper.

He hated doing anything when he came home but showering and watching TV after a long shift. Instead, he needed to watch the baby, who was just waking up from a nap and wanting to play, while Nora cooked. After working in the steel plant, he just wanted to clean up and just wanted peace, rest and eat supper and watch TV

Saturdays were anything but peaceful things needed to be done and they were even more tiring. There was food shopping with the baby, helping with the laundry, paying bills, fixing things, cleaning the yard and trying to find time to see the rest of the family.

It did not take long, and the hum drum of daily existence found them seeing less and less of everyone and less time with each other. **Babies have a way of changing lives.**

George and Lilly were always busy in the evenings and even on the weekends. They went for walks, did some redecorating of their living room, and yard joined a bird watching group and found some friends where they played cards three evenings a week. It also didn't take long, and Lilly found a cooking club where there were five couples their age. One evening a month rotating cooking for the group was fun.

It was getting close to the holidays; no one wanted Nora to take the baby out in the cold weather. So, it was unanimous: that Thanksgiving, Christmas Eve, Christmas and New Year's Day would all be at Nora's. Thanksgiving worked out perfectly. All the ladies assisted with the dinner and the baby was doing well.

It was agreed that a new tradition would begin for Christmas. Normally, the adults opened their gifts on Christmas Eve. Now, with a baby, everyone agreed to open their gifts on Christmas Day. To be sure that Santa arrived.

On Thanksgiving Nora made a sixteen-pound turkey. Lilly made sweet potatoes, pork and beans, and a pumpkin pie. Rita brought a lettuce salad and broccoli;

Betty founds recipes for unusual brownies called "sand-ies" and she made ribbon Jell-O. The men were well fed.

With the women cooking and decorating, all the men needed to do was to keep little Greta occupied—easier said than done. They took turns and before anyone knew what happened there was a room of very tired people.

By Christmas Greta was seven months old. She was smart and as cute as a button, crawling everywhere and getting into everything. She began calling people by a name. Her first word was "Da" for Michael. She called Kevin "Papee" and George "Gumpa" somehow, she knew the difference. The funny part was she called Lilly-and Betty both "Me ma" and Nora was "Mom," but Rita was "Tee-ah." It was something that seemed to stick but no one figured it out. The baby babbled she could say "no no" or "tup" for yes; but doll was "doll" and everyone knew she loved her doll.

This Christmas was going to be special it was Michael's favorite time of the year he did the decorating in and out of the house. When the tree was decorated Michael turned the lights on and Greta just starred at the tree with her mouth open. It was a Kodak moment, and Michael captured it on his camera.

Everyone loved seeing the baby enjoy the decorations and gifts. Despite Michael's normal sour attitude, he did love the holidays. It was hard to understand anyone not loving Christmas or a beautiful baby.

Getting things ready for Christmas dinner meant that Rita needed to be at the grocery for some additional items. Shortly after arriving a voice from behind her- said: *"Hi rye bread—how was your dinner?"* As Rita turned, she thought:

"It is him again the man who touched her hand when she was reaching for the rye bread. She was amazed that he recognized. *"How did your dinner come out?"* he asked. Rita said, *"Have we met? Do we know each other?"* she knew perfectly well where they had met before. *"Of course, you don't recognize my hand—why we both touched a loaf of rye bread together and our hands met."* **With that he extended his hand to shake her hand**

"Hi, I am Victor Clark nice to meet you—ah, ah…" he hesitated to wait for her to answer. *"Rita Wilson"* she blurted out as she extended her hand. *"Nice to meet you Rita Wilson, what are you doing tomorrow night -will you have dinner with me?"* *"What, well I do not even know you sir"* she said. *"Ah but we have a mutual friend, Mr. Rye Bread!"* and with that Rita began to laugh and moved her head up and down. Rita's thoughts were going wild: **"He is sure handsome. I am surprised he remembered me. I wonder if I dare go out with a stranger-after all who is he where does he live why do we meet only at the grocery store."**

"I" Rita hesitated. *"Great, I take it that means, yes?"* he said. *"Well, Miss Rita Wilson where would you feel safe to meet an absolutely perfect stranger?"* Rita

thought about it for a minute she really wanted to find out more about him. She decided to choose a place very public and during the daytime.

"*Do you know Simon's restaurant on the corner of North?*" she said, "*I do.*" He answered. "*Great, I will be there for—(she hesitated)—lunch at noon tomorrow if you would like to join me*" she said. "*Noon!*" Mr. Clark said "*Noon! Noon! That is lunch time little lady and not dinner time? Ms. Wilson*" and before she could answer he continued "*But, if lunch is what will make you safe than I will see you at—noon— Miss Wilson, I will be there tomorrow at noon. Oh, and buy the way, may I buy your lunch? I mean if that is OK with you Miss. Wilson?*"

"*Sounds Fine Mr. Clark until noon tomorrow then at Simon's,*" She said. *He added, "It is a good thing to-morrow is a Saturday."*

On the way home Rita had to laugh-**he really is cute** she thought. She was also apprehensive. "**I do not know where he works. There were a lot of questions popping up that are still unanswered**" she thought. When she got home, she picked out her outfit for this luncheon. She took out her green shirt waste dress, black high heel shoes yellow hat and scarf and black gloves for the event. She needed heels as Mr. Clark was very tall and she felt little standing next to him. She had a gold tone necklace that set the outfit off perfectly. All that was left was a hot shower and a good night's sleep.

When she arrived at the restaurant on Saturday noon, Mr. Clark was waiting for her. He stood up at the booth when she arrived. He complemented Rita on how she looked. They talked for over two hours.

Come to find out he was an adjunct professor at the university. He knew Mr. Parker and Mr. Phillips. He was single and twenty-nine years old. Before coming to Clayton, he lived with his mother, sister and aunt-his mother's sister. His aunt passed away just a few months ago. His father died when he was twelve years old. Rita and Victor soon realized they had many things in common; they liked the same books, enjoyed the same movies and even had a birthday three days apart.

His mother and sister were going to Illinois to spend Christmas with another sister Ann, and his mother's brother. He would be in Clayton on Christmas Day and celebrating the day alone. On Christmas Eve a group of students that invited Victor to party and midnight mass. As they finished lunch neither of them wanted their time together to end. They seemed to be having so much fun talking and getting to know one another when Victor suggested "Would you be ok with *walking around Main Street and just looking at all the holiday window decorations.*" Rita agreed.

Soon they were playing together in the snow and laughing. At five o'clock he invited her to dinner at his favorite restaurant "China World." She hesitated at first confessing she never had Chinese food before –he was overjoyed.

"Well then, allow me to be the first to introduce you to Chinese food." **Rita agreed after all "the Chinese must eat some kind of normal food"** she thought.

They walked down main street to the restaurant still talking and laughing. The restaurant was small but quaint. He had obviously been there before as everyone greeted him by name. He ordered things called: won tong soup, egg rolls, and chicken with mixed vegetables." Everything was delicious.

Rita enjoyed the soup very much and surmised that the Chinese people finally found American type food. As Victor paid the bill Rita's thoughts were on the holidays; **"It is a shame that Victor was going to spend them alone and without family."** She thought about how they seemed to get along well and even knew some of the same people. She really enjoyed spending the day with him and did not want it to end after dinner. Just then Victor said *"Ok, this is too nice a day to just end it-lets go to the library it is only a few blocks away."* As Rita agreed, they were off again. They stayed at the Library until almost eight o'clock and then walked to the bus stop together holding hands.

They both caught the #12A bus. Victor got a transfer to the #10. While sitting on the bus Victor asked "Rita, I genuinely enjoyed today. May I see you again?" Rita laughed and said, "Victor after such a wonderful day like today, of course you could see me again." With that answer, she gave him her home telephone number. The bus stopped at her corner first and as she began to leave Victor took her hand. He held her hand for a second looking at her and then he said, *"Thank you, for such a pleasant day."* She thanked him for lunch and dinner.

And with that she was off the bus and crossing the street walking to her front door. As she turned, she saw the bus pass the house and Victor had moved to the other side of the bus to wave goodbye.

At 10:30 PM her telephone rang. "Hi," It was Victor, *"I want to thank you again for a perfect day-I really enjoyed being with you."* *"I enjoyed the day as well-thank you Victor"* Rita said. They talked until midnight. Rita surprised herself as she had invited Victor to Nora's for Christmas dinner—and what was more amazing than her boldness was the fact that he accepted the invitation. Now she just needed to explain it to everyone else—especially Michael why she invited a stranger to share their Christmas Family Holiday

Chapter 27

A Stranger

Rita's fears about telling the family she invited Victor over for Christmas were warranted. Michael, halfway serious, gave her the most grief.

"Inviting a "perfect stranger" to my house for Christmas Dinner of all things- without asking first!"

Thank goodness for Nora and Betty—they thought it was about time Rita found someone she liked. Michael gave in as she knew he would. He gave Rita a hug and said,

"Just for you sis."

Christmas Eve was freezing. The buses were behind. Rita promised herself she would own a car next year. When she got home there was an invitation in her mailbox from Mr. Phillips inviting her and a guest to a party on the 27th at the University. He noted that Mr. Parker's group was giving a reception for him. There was no RSVP on the invitation.

Rita thought it might be fun.

Christmas Dinner was at 3 PM. Rita promised to help Nora prepare everything. She arrived at Nora's around 11AM.

It was 2:30 PM when the rest of the family arrived. Everyone spokes about their personal gifts that they opened at home. Nora did not talk about the towels from

Michael. She wondered if everyone realized that there was nothing personal for her under the tree.

This year, Michael had an idea about what Rita really wanted. He was able to talk everyone in the family to pooling their funds and permitting him to purchase the gift that he knows would be the perfect one for Rita. They all agreed, and he was about to bring her gift in to the living room when Victor arrived.

Victor gave Rita flowers and a box of candy. He brought a bottle of wine to give to Michael and a stuffed animal for Greta—a cute stuffed small dog that barked. She laughed and said "Ruff." For the hostess, Nora, he purchased a Xmas Santa that lit-up. It was a hit as Nora placed it on the mantel-a great compliment to the tree.

Rita introduced Victor to everyone. Then he sat on the sofa watching as Rita's gift was brought in. Michael announced that "*This gift was something that everyone kicked in because we felt you would need this large cookbook and never misplace it.*" They all laughed.

The box was quite big as Michael and Kevin carried it in the room and placed it in front of Rita. "*Now sis, I want you to understand about this gift*" Rita interrupted and said "*Let me see this cookbook.* She took the paper off and in a second said:

"*OMG it is a Television set! A real large television-oh my goodness. How did you all know? It is perfect, thank you all it is exactly what I have wanted.*"

They all loved seeing Rita so happy. Michael knew she wanted a new TV. Her television at home was just ten inches and this was a big twenty-four in model.

Michael found it for a great price—cheaper than anything in the newspaper. They all chipped in-it was perfect surprise and Rita loved it. Victor was noticing all the love in the room and how the family interacted-it was quite different from what it was like at his family's holidays. It was almost captivating. His first thought was *"I want what they all have."*

Dinner was delicious there was so much food, cookies and laughter with everything homemade. Victor did not want to ever leave **"He thought, I really want what they have—and followed up with maybe there will be a chance?** After dinner, they played a game of BINGO. Nora made some gag prizes anticipating Bingo; and all had fun opening the prizes.

Then Lilly went over to the piano, and they all followed as Lilly played everyone sang Christmas Carols. No one guessed what a great singing voice Victor had he literally stole the show by singing a solo of "Oh Holy Night."

When the festivities were over, Victor asked Rita if he could take her home, she agreed. Michael said he and Kevin would bring over the TV in the morning and set it up.

After Victor and Rita left, Nora remarked "What a *nice couple they seemed to make. I hope this could be the start of something nice for Rita*." everyone agreed.

On the way home Victor pulled out a small box from his pocket. *"This is for you Rita"* he said handing her a beautifully wrapped box.

"Just a minute, the candy, and flowers not to mention the other gifts were more than enough-what is this?" she asked. *"Never mind-just open it"* Victor said.

She debated mentally **"It is too soon for this guy to be giving out so many gifts I'd better be careful.** But then she opened the box and inside was a slice of rye bread wrapped in a plastic with a note on top: *"I owe a lot to this rye bread!* Signed Victor Clark*"* Rita laughed and promised to keep it in the refrigerator.

She had a small gift for him in her purse. *"Here-this is for you"* she said as she handed a small package to Victor. He opened it and the two of them burst out into laughter. It was also a piece of rye bread wrapped in tin foil-with a note saying, *"Thanks to a loaf of rye bread we will spend Christmas together."*

At her door Rita felt that saying good night was difficult. She had so enjoyed his company. Victor held her hand and then gently kissed her on the cheek. *"Thank you for a great dinner, super company and a fun day. We need to do this again soon"* Rita agreed. *And with that* Victor left."

On the 27th Rita arrived at Mr. Phillips party he greeted her with the words "*Quite a gentleman that Mr. Clark.*" Since she had not spoken to Mr. Phillips about Victor, she was stunned to realize he knew she had met Victor. What was more amazing was Victor was at the party she had not seen him since Christmas Day.

He was alone and -as he said later – since the invitation allowed everyone to invite a guest Victor said he was just waiting to see if she brought a "special someone."
They spent the evening together talking.

Chapter 28

The Robbery

Mr. Parker's party was a great success. Victor took Rita home. Once again, he gave her a kiss on the cheek at the door and they agreed to meet for dinner the next evening.
Rita was feeling romantic and special. That night as she cleansed her face and applied a cream. All her thoughts centered around how good it felt to "**be special to someone.**"

The next evening, she and Victor went to a restaurant in the Anderson Hotel. Victor introduced her to something called "lamb stew." While skeptical at first Rita found she loved it.

Victor said "I am *happy this is the second time I have introduced you to something new. I hope to introduce you to many new things in the future, Rita"*

Rita blushed and he laughed. The evening ended with him kissing her cheek again as he took her to her door.

After that evening, they spent every afternoon and evening together for the next three days. On New Year's Eve Victor took Rita back to China World for dinner.

Then the couple went to a party that was given by one of Victor's students. At the stroke of midnight Victor kissed Rita passionately. Things seemed to be moving right as Rita was enjoying getting to know Victor. She was still cautious not wanting to jump to conclusion too quickly.

They saw each other every day for the next eight weeks. They talked on the telephone for hours and it seemed as if things might be getting serious. She was interested in Victor Clark and soon everyone in the family was noticing a change in Rita. She was genuinely happy for the first time that anyone of them could remember.

March 3rd Rita agreed to babysit Greta. Michael wanted to do some painting. Nora wanted to go shopping with Betty. Nora brought Greta, and her highchair over to Rita's about 10AM.

Greta and Rita played in the snow for about an hour. Then, they read a book and danced with the music before lunch. Greta loved peanut butter and jelly sandwich served with a side of chicken soup.

Just as lunch was over Greta fell asleep in her highchair. Rita put her on the sofa with a pillow tucked to the side of her to be sure she would not fall. Greta usually took a two-hour nap during the day.

With the baby asleep Rita found a book to read. She sat in a chair near the sofa to watch the baby.

A half hour later the telephone rang. There was a woman on the other end of the line crying as she spoke:

"My name is Jennifer Clark, I understand you are a friend of my son, Victor." "Yes, I am a friend of Victor may I help you Mrs. Clark?" Rita answered not sure why the lady called her or why she was crying.

Rita wondered how Mrs. Clark knew her telephone number. *"My son was shot about an hour ago-he was taken to Clayton General Hospital. "What!"* Rita was in shock!

"What happened? Is he ok?" Rita asked. *"Two kids tried to rob the cleaners while Victor was there picking up his suit. I do not know much more. Will you come with me-to the hospital? I have a cab coming."*

Rita began to cry. She told Mrs. Clark she was babysitting and would meet her at the hospital just as soon as someone came to help with Greta.

Rita called Lilly and asked if she could come over and watch Greta. Lilly agreed and George took her over it took about fifteen minutes for them to arrive.

Lilly told Rita "*There was a cab outside and the lady in the cab asked me to let you know that Jennifer Clark was waiting for you to join her.*"

Rita was a bit stunned at how fast Mrs. Clark had arrived; and at her presumption, that she would be going to the hospital with her.

But Rita decided not to debate it with the woman. As she left the house she walked toward the rear door of the cab; Mrs. Clark opened the door and said "*Please get in.*"

Getting into the cab she asked Mrs. Clark how she knew where she lived. Mrs. Clark replied, "*Let's just say, I know a lot about you.*" Her voice was so direct and firm Rita felt a bit uneasy. Mrs. Clark had white hair and looked to be in her mid 60's. She wore a blue and gray dress and had a fur type coat hanging off her shoulders. She wore leather shoes and carried a blue leather purse. She wore makeup, earring, a gold necklace and a watch. The lady looked like a woman of means and education.

They arrived at the emergency waiting area and were told Victor had been taken into surgery. The ladies were shown to a special waiting room.

While in the waiting room Rita called Kevin, Betty, Nora had just arrived home she asked for prayers for Victor then she asked them to call Lilly and George and ask for prayers.

It was four and a half hours later when the doctor returned. Unfortunately, he did not have good news. Victor's wounds were quite serious. He was now in a second surgery.

Dr. Higgins said: *"Victor was shot at close range and the bullet passed through his heart. He was also hit on the head several times with something hard and with great force.*

Victor sustained injury to both his heart and his head. While he is alive, we were able to repair the bullet hole in his heart he sustained considerable damage in both his heart and his head. His head will be swollen. He had some internal bleeding that is being taken care of in surgery as we speak. Victor has a serious concussion and damage. I am afraid that recovery for Victor will be long, and I am sorry to say but at this time uncertain."

The ladies cried together. It took two additional hours before Victor was out of the second surgery. At 1055PM they were permitted to see him. They went into Victor's room together. His face was gray and completely void of color. Bandages were everywhere and there was a drain in his head and in his chest; IV's were everywhere.

While in the waiting room they heard the 11PM news. The owner of the shop was interviewed. He said that Victor argued with the robbers; they were young boys. He tried to talk them out of the robbery. It was at that point-one the robbers shot him; the other hit him in the head with a pistol a couple of times kicking him while he lay there bleeding.

The police had both of the sixteen-year-old boys in custody. This was their first offense. They stole the gun from a relative and wanted some money to purchase cigarettes.

Mrs. Clark was obviously tired. It was a long disturbing day. She was weak as neither of them ate much in the hospital dining room. Victor was in a drug induced coma, and the Doctor suggested "*They go home and rest. We will know more tomorrow.*" He assured them he would call if there was any change; but not to expect it for at least twenty to thirty hours. It was a difficult decision, but Victor did not move. They left feeling tired and concerned about his future.

Rita could not sleep. It was 7 AM when Rita arrived at the hospital. She went into Victor's room; he was still asleep.

Several hours later he opened his eyes. He did not remember what had happened-or Rita. He asked her name.

The doctor mentioned memory was lost at times when there was a major trauma. The doctor said both surgeries were major, and Victor was under anesthesia for many hours. He suggested: "It may take a couple of days before they would know everything. Victor may or may not remember things. Rita called Mrs. Clark's residence; a lady answered and mentioned that Mrs. Clark had appointments most of the day but, Mrs. Clark was on her way to the hospital. Rita waited for her to arrive.

When Mrs. Clark arrived, Rita tried to prepare her that Victor may not even know them. However, Mrs. Clark said. *"My son will know me."* When Victor woke, he did not recognize either one of them.

She entered his room and called out to him saying *"Victor this is your loving and devoted mother."* He just looked at her and did not speak.

Leaving the hospital Rita noticed all the newspaper reporters still hanging around looking for a scoop. They wanted information on Victor-How he was? How old he is? They wanted to know if he was married; to whom and, if his wife was at the hospital?

Victor was a hero. The police arrested the robbers because of him. While the boys were arguing dealing with Victor the clerk notified the police.

Victor was going to get a reward. None of that meant anything to Rita.

She just wanted him well. She left the hospital and did talk to the press. Three weeks went by before Victor recognized Rita-not as his girlfriend but as a lady that visits him.

He had trouble breathing his memory was affected. It would be a while before they knew about his motor skills. Victor tried but he really needed time to recuperate. Her visits and numerous conversations with the medical staff suggested; Victor would never be able to lead a normal life. He needed to recoup both physically and mentally, it could take ten years or more. His heart would be weak all his life, no running, skating, boating or anything physical.

One doctor was blunt *"The Victor you knew will never be back."* Mrs. Clark was becoming difficult constantly wanting to baby him. She was usually there all day every day.

With that prognosis, Rita was not sure she could continue to be involved. Their relationship was short lived; not something she could commit to for a lifetime.

Victor only had a limited memory of their relationship. They had just begun getting to know each other—this was not her battle.

She decided to back off-tapered and shortened her visits. After two more weeks she did not visit at all. It was hard to face but she needed to be realistic and practical.

Ten weeks later Victor was going home-he did not remember about the shooting or Rita. He was going to live with his mother. He would always walk with a cane, studder, and limp and need constant time in rehabilitation.

Rita was not there when he was released; she did not see him for three months after his release. Then one Saturday afternoon there was a knock at the door.

Opening the door-there was Victor. He was thin, looked old and weak. The cab was waiting with his mother inside. All the awards, rewards and acclaim did nothing to help his struggle-he was a sick person. He asked if he could come in.

Rita's heart was heavy. He spoke quickly. His mother told him they used to be friends and he wanted to wish her well.

He missed her visits. She gave him a quick hug, wished him well and he left. He left her life just as he came in-quickly

Rita wondered why things happened the way they did and if they would ever see Victor again. Just before Easter a card came in the mail from Victor's sister their mother had passed away; Victor was feeling much better. He was going to be living another sister. Rita put the card down and thought **"It was a nice while it lasted."**

She was deeply entrenched in her class work and in working for Mr. Phillips. In fact, Nora and Rita enjoyed teaching. Even Michael was doing better with Greta.

A four-some had developed with Lilly, George, Betty and Kevin. They began doing things together-Sunday dinners, the show, playing cards and monopoly on weekends. They enjoyed each other's company very much. It was probable because they were so close in age.

Meanwhile Michael met Randy Gray at the steel plant. He, Nora, Randy and Randy's wife Karen were close friends now. The Gray's had a son Justin Cole. They called him J.C. he was four months older than Greta and named after his grandfather. The family became "regular" visitors at Michael's house.

Rita was beginning to feel left out-oh she knew it was not intentional but just the same—she felt alone. They all seemed to be paired off and busy. She was the only person without a mate.

She began donating her time to Mr. Parker at the university; hoping she would meet someone there but that did not give her the opportunity to meet anyone. All the men she worked with were either married and austerity limited the number of new interns at the university.

Rita thought she might join a church guild, but then she realized that most of the people there were married as well. She decided to investigate returning to the Red Cross. They were very understanding about her leaving, and they did offer her to return "anytime she wanted." Calling, she learned that the section she was in had merged into another area and her supervisor retired.

Chapter 29

Rape

It was a sunny Sunday afternoon the last week in May. Every-one in the family was busy with one thing or another.

Michael, George, and Kevin were on a job down-town working on one of the big hotels. Randy was gulfing. Nora took Greta over to Karen's so the children could play. Lilly and Betty were at a baby shower. Rita had no specific plans for the day.

Nora invited her to join them at Karen's, but she decided to stay home. It was a beautiful day and Rita wanted to take a walk.

The sun was shining and there were so many flowers still blooming; Rita felt that a walk is going to be beautiful and just give her some fresh air. There were a few stores open around the area; but since it was Sunday-Blue laws were in effect-and most the stores were closed.

Rita planned on what she called **"the best kind of shopping-window shopping. One saves money and still returns with ideas."** She loved the warm sun and the air smelled so fresh. There were still flowers growing in the street planters giving the walk have a spark of beauty.

She dressed casually and left the house. Walking for about a half hour, suddenly she became aware of a man walking toward her. She could not see his face because he was wearing sunglasses and he was walking toward her very quickly. She was not sure why, but she felt frightened. Rita decided to turn down a side street not to pass by him. She noticed his hands were in his pockets pushing his coat forward. Quicky, she turned down the corner to enter the next street. Then, he began moving faster toward her.

Rita became more frightened-and began to walk down the side street faster she heard footsteps getting closer and moving quickly. His shoes made a loud noise as he walked.

Out of the corner of her eye she pretended to look at a house on the opposite side of the street; that strange man turned down that same street and stopped; he was definitely watching her –but why?

He seemed tall and there was a cap on his head. He had a long beige jacket, and his hands were still in his jacket pockets, they pushed his coat toward the center of his body. His shoes were hard on the street. Her heart began racing-she wanted to get home as fast as possible, only she was still one street away.

Moving quickly-her heart began beating faster and faster. There was no one on the street-no one to talk with-she was getting more frightened, and she could not understand why.

She rushed as fast as her small frame could take her. But as fast as she was walking, she could hear his footsteps moving quickly and getting closer. When she realized, yes, he was not far behind.

Finally, four houses from home Rita picked up her pace began running toward the house. He was running-she could hear his shoes he was close by. She rushed up the front stairs of her porch—sweating and out of breath –the hair standing up on the back of her neck-she put her key in the door and was beginning to open the door—she heard his steps–OMG—he was on the porch!

Instantly, the stranger had one hand around her mouth and the other was held tightly around her waist. He was strong. She was lifted as he used her body to push her into the front door and then the hallway. He said nothing. Her hands were moving everywhere looking for the light—something to hit the man with—but she dropped her handbag and found nothing.

She tried to fight and kick, but she could not scream with his hand over her mouth. He was in control. With his foot he closed the door. A second later, she was thrown on the floor with great force. On the dark hallway floor, he began punching her face and chest until she blacked out. **Oh, it hurt so bad.**

When she came to, he was on top of her raping her. She tried to move but she was hurt and could not fight or scream –she moaned—that again brought his fists—he was strong as he hit her-punching her repeatedly. **"Oh God! God why-why me? God please, I don't want to die!"**

She blacked out again. She must have been unconscious for a while because when she woke up, she heard movement in the house—**"He must be still here! Oh no!"**

She could not move-she tried not to speak but her moan brought him back to her-she closed her eyes hoping he would think she was still blacked out. But now he was saddled on top of her pulling her hair cutting it. She passed out as he bit each of her breasts—punched her again and slapped her. She was still blacked out.

Upon wakening she realized that she was still on the dark hallway floor. Her dress was torn and open, her breasts were exposed red with blood was coming down from the front of her body. One breast had just his teeth marks the other was ripped and bleeding from where he bit her.

Now blood was coming down her face, her left eye was cut. Her nose and chin were also bleeding. She even tasted blood. She lay there for a minute checking for noise **"It appears he has gone"** she thought.

She tried to stand up from the floor—when she did there was blood gushing down her legs—e weak and in great pain. She blacked out again—and was on the hallway floor. When she woke up, she began looking for something to grab—to help her get up from the floor; unable to find anything she began to crawl to the kitchen.

The place was ransacked. Crawling at a snail's she noticed the living room was a mess and on the floor were her under pants and her slip filled with blood.

The pain of the rape and beating left her weak and she passed out again. When she came to her eyes caught the sight of a rag near the corner of the kitchen counter. She tried to lift herself up and finally grabbed the rag and put it between her legs.

Crying in pain-wondering **"Why-why-Oh please tell me-why? We have lived her forever-we were a family-I have never heard of this happening before to anyone—why me?"**

She never even saw the man's face, but the smell of his cologne was still in her nose. She remembered he was strong.

She thought there was something strange about him-but she could not remember what it was.

She was thinking of calling the police-but suddenly she became afraid. **"I have been raped; what would people think? Was it my fault? Because it went out on a Sunday alone for a walk? I did not ask for this to happen-by just going for a walk. I should not call the police. But what would I say? I grew up in this house! I need help."**

Frantically, she crawled into the kitchen-seeing the telephone she tried to reach it to dial Nora –unfortunately, she passed out. When she awoke, she stood up bracing herself against the wall and dialed Nora crying.

When Nora heard the fear, terror and tears in Rita's voice she knew something was wrong. All Rita could scream was "H*elp now, help now, now please Nora real emergency*!"

Michael was taking a nap with Greta in his chair; Nora grabbed a sweater, left Michael a note "at Rita's" will call.

It took her about ten minutes to get there. The front door was open about an inch Nora opened it slowly and took small steps in-calling for Rita. She noticed –Rita's purse was on the floor. The hallway was dark, but she could see the floor filled with blood. Slowly she began walking in further still calling Rita's name.

As she passed the living room, she noticed it was ransacked. On the floor was Rita's under pants and slip filled with blood. She turned the light on—and immediately noticed all the blood on the floor in the hallway leading toward the kitchen. She said a prayer as she walked in further. Heading toward the kitchen she became very frightened-as she continued walking, she saw some of Rita's hair and her bra on the floor. Again, she called for Rita—praying she was alive. With her last call she heard Rita moan.

She entered the kitchen and saw Rita on the floor near a corner. Rita looked like she was the loser in a boxing ring. Her nose was bleeding, her chin was cut and bleeding, her face was quite swollen her left eye had a bleeding cut. The buttons on her dress were ripped off and the dress was open exposing her breasts. Nora could see teeth marks on her breasts and blood dripping down the left one. Parts of her body had already started to turn color. Her legs were filled with blood and she was not wearing shoes. Her hair was cut on the sides! Rita was coming to and began to cry. It was obvious that she could not move from the corner. Nora saw a clean kitchen towel and whipped Rita's face. Blood was coming down her legs Nora quickly grabbed another clean towel from the drawer. She tried to help Rita to sit on a chair. But Rita slid off.

Nora went to the telephone and dialed 911. She then moved the chair and sat Rita down. When there was a voice on the other end of her call; she explained the sensitive nature for the call and asked for a police officer to come into the house as soon as possible. She requested he drive without a siren and walk into the house as she left the door open.

The man at the other end of the call said he understood the situation. He took down the address and Nora's name. He checked and said one of his men, Officer Brown, was only a couple of streets away and he would be there soon. Nora told Rita *"I called the police. Whoever did this to you cannot get away with it"*

Rita muttered *"I did not see his face—I mean—I do not know—I am afraid"* Regaining some focus she continued *"what will people think—I need a few minutes to get a hold of m-m-m?"* and with that she fainted. Nora tried to hold on to her, but Rita slipped off the chair-back to the floor.

When Officer Brown arrived, he walked slowly into the house and when he saw all the blood, he called out identifying his name. *"In the kitchen"* Nora said, *"We need help."* Seeing Rita he said, *"this lady needs immediate medical care."* He asked Nora to call for an ambulance. Rita heard the word "ambulance," and she began screaming: *"No ambulance! No ambulance! No-No! The neighbors- No-No! I can't." then she began to pass out again. The officer caught her before she fell on the floor and placed her on the sofa just off the kitchen.*

The officer told Nora he would drive them both to the Emergency Room. Rita cried –she was still bleeding, and Nora grabbed a coat to put around her shoulders and kept a towel between her legs.

Officer Brown moved his car to the side entrance then picked Rita up and carried her to his car. Nora followed. He laid Rita down on the back seat because he understood that she still had a fear of anyone seeing her in a police car and wanting to know what happened to her.

Office Brown called the station he asked for another office to secure the house, take pictures and lock it up. He said he was taking Rita to the ER and for the dispatcher to notify the hospital that he would need a stretcher immediately and have a doctor ready to administer immediate care as this was a bad situation. It only took a few minutes to get them to the emergency room. Doctors were waiting for them to arrive with a stretcher.

A lady doctor checked Rita's vitals. Gave her a mild sedative then a police photographer took pictures of her face, breasts, hair, and legs. When the photographer completed Rita was moved upstairs for x-rays, surgery to stitch her cuts and a D & C. retaining some seaman for identification. Rita had an obvious concussion. Based on the type of rape <u>with extreme force-</u>the doctor said it would be best to keep Rita in the hospital for a few days for observation.

The doctor told Nora and Officer Brown they could not see or talk with Rita during this time. Officer Brown offered to take Nora home. On their way Brown asked Nora how she ended up being at Rita's house. Nora explained Rita's telephone call. Officer Brown went into the house with Nora to see Michael. He was awake. Nora explained that Rita was brutally raped, and the house was a ransacked and is still a mess. She said that Rita was in the hospital; and would be there for a few days.

The officer asked if they knew anyone that could have done this to Rita or why? Neither one, could produce a name of a person to consider.

Before Officer Brown left asked for a key to Rita's and told them not to go into the house until further notice. *"It was now a crime scene, pictures and fingerprints needed to be taken."*

Nora explained to Michael what she saw in the house and how Rita looked. Michael was outraged. *"I hope they catch the guy. My concern is for her safety. This guy knows where she lives. I wonder if she should stay there anymore."* Then, Michael called Kevin—he wanted to go to the hospital. Nora assured him Rita was given a sedative and to wait until morning. What Rita really needed now was rest and to try to get past this terrible thing. Kevin told Betty and she could not believe this could happen. She called Lilly and told her. George tried to comfort Lil as she cried and asked *"Why? Why? Would anyone this to her?"* George told Lil that the world was changing, and more bad things just seem to be happening to good people without explanation. He promised Lil that Rita could live with them if that was what she wanted-and that he would take Lil to the hospital in the morning.

A young intern, Dr. Carl Hammer was in the emergency room when Rita arrived. He heard Nora's account. He felt sorry for Rita—she was pretty and badly hurt.

He was outraged that this happens to women. Carl's oldest sister Ellie was raped when she was fourteen years old. He was ten years old at the time and witnessed firsthand how the rape almost destroyed a beautiful young girl and their family.

Seeing Rita's face, he thought this guy was cruel? She received stitches on her lip, ear, chin, left eye, forehead, and her breasts.

Her face looked like she was boxed. The x-rays will determine if there was any internal bleeding or injuries. There would be small scares from the stitches but with a small graft in time they would fade enough to be barely noticeable.

Dr. Hammer remembered how freighted his sister was at night; he requested permission to stay in Rita's room that night and sit in the recliner just in case she needed someone.

He knew how many times his sister would wake up screaming and he wanted to be there for Rita. Rita was still under sedation.

During the night she sat up half awake and began screaming. Her eyes saw the young doctor in his white jacket sitting in a chair next to her. The room was dark and through the outside streetlight she saw Carl's face.

He immediately stood up—re-assured her he was a doctor, and she was safe—in a hospital.

"My name is Dr. Hammer I am an intern here at the hospital and you are safe here miss." He repeated it a couple of times before she seemed to understand him.

The nurses heard her scream and were in the room giving her an additional sedative in her IV.

Dr. Carl Hammer was a thirty-two-year-old young man from Philadelphia. He was six feet two inches tall with dark brown hair with natural highlights. His sister's rape was a deciding factor in his becoming a doctor.

Carl had reassured Rita over and over repeating that he was a doctor, and that she was safe in the hospital. He tried to calm her—it took about fifteen minutes. The nurses came in and gave her an additional sedative. She calmed down and went back to sleep. The nurse told Dr. Carl Hammer that Rita would most likely sleep the rest of the night. He asked the nurse to check on her every half hour and call him if she was up again. He went back to the intern quarters.

Carl felt that he needed to help this girl, so she did not go through all the pain that his sister experienced. He was determined to have one of his friends-a councilor-help Rita.

The next morning Officer Brown was at the hospital to see Rita. He hoped for a description of the man-but left without it. Rita was under heavy sedation and unable to assist him. She was not in any condition to go home. The attending physician decided she was still concerned about the concussion; they would keep her in the hospital for a few more days.

Officer Brown asked the doctor to let him know when Rita was well enough to be questioned. The doctor agreed.

Meanwhile, Officer Brown and another policeman went to Rita's to look around. They took pictures and found a pair of scissors on the floor in the hall. The officer felt the scissors must be the ones the rapist used to cut part of Rita's hair. The officer placed the scissors in a bag hoping for fingerprints and a clue; they also took her pants and slip for identification. Brown told Nora that there would be other police needing to see the house before it could be cleaned up and the key returned. The next day four men arrived and again took pictures and fingerprints. They cut the part of the rug from the hallway.

The third day Officer Brown dropped of the key off and told Nora they could clean the house.

Everyone went along to help. When they saw the house, all the blood, and part of the hall rug gone and the blood in the living room and hallway into the kitchen, they all felt sick to their stomachs. *"It was lucky Rita was not killed in the attack."* George said.

They began to work on the house straightening things up washing the floors trying to get the house back to "normal." It was difficult washing days-old-blood-that seemed to be in every room and hallway. Nora mentioned Rita was afraid people would judge her for this attach. George said, "it was just her Catholic upbringing; *any true Christian would not blame her for this terrible thing."*

Nora called Rita's principal and told him she was in the hospital with a serious concussion. She did not mention the rape-but said Rita may not be able to complete the school year. The principal agreed to get a sub but wanted more information and a doctor's medical opinion. Nora knew Rita did not want people to know about the rape. Nora understood Rita's feeling, yet she felt **"Rita was too trusting- after all -she invited Victor to a Christmas dinner after knowing him just- one day."**

Nora's thoughts continued **"There are times when you are just not sure how people would react. Rita is a Catholic she would have feelings that may be difficult to understand or deal with by some people.**

Nora wondered if Rita's-decision to go out for a walk alone on a Sunday- would- to some—be

considered as somehow opening herself up to bad thing happening.

Logically she knew that could not be the case but there are some things and people that defy logic."

It was Friday before Rita was able to leave the hospital. Dr. Hammer gave her a restrained hug. He spoke with her at great length during her stay-about his sister's rape; and the emotional scars she suffered. He warned her that she should not let this incident take over her future.

He mentioned his sister *"Became so frighten, she did not leave the house for two years. She lost weight and* **withdrew from everyone. Finally, she got some help, but it took** *several years more before she was able to be home alone. To this day, all these years later, she only goes to work and the grocery alone. She still lives with our mother"* Carl said.

Carl wanted Rita to understand some of the emotions she was going through and what those emotions do to the mind. He suggested she see his councilor friend and asked if he could arrange an appointment for her to talk about what happened. She agreed but said it was too soon and she would call him when she was ready.

Carl let her think that was ok for now, but he could not wait for her to call; so, he knew eventually he would take the lead.

Rita was apprehensive about being in the house. **"He knows where I live"** she thought. **"He could come back at any time. I do not know who he is—he may not**

leave me alive next time." Her thoughts were running wild. And her heart was racing-**what to do?**

Michael and Nora were supposed to pick up Rita from the hospital as they invited her to stay with them. She anxiously accepted. But Michael came alone to pick Rita up from the hospital.

Rita felt odd leaving with just Michael. He said Greta was sleeping. She had an ear infection and Nora did not want to leave her with anyone. **"This is my brother, and he loves me"** Rita thought. Wanting her to relax Michael did not mention the rape. The entire family had visited her in the hospital and knew that she needed time to heal.

Rita stayed with Michael and Nora; and the first week all she did was cry and stare at the walls. She did not cook, clean or help with the baby-she just sat and cried.

When the next four days were up –Nora called the school principal letting them know Rita was not well enough to return to complete the year. Her principal said she had some sick time left if she wanted to use it, but the school needed a doctor's explanation. Nora said the information would come soon.

She called the hospital and was put in touch with Dr. Hammer. Nora told him the school needed an explanation; Dr. Hammer agreed to write a letter. The letter identified Rita suffered a severe concussion, was under medical attention, and would need to stay out of work the rest of the school year. Rita was going to continue staying with Michael and Nora. Dr. Hammer agreed to bring over a letter for her school. That Sunday, he brought the letter to Nora and visited with her-but left without seeing Rita.

The next Saturday Dr. Hammer arrived at Nora's again. Carl identified Rita needed professional help. He was determined to take her to meet his councilor friend. Nora was not sure Rita would even see him; let go to a councilor. Nora spoke to Rita that Dr. Hammer was at the house and wanted to visit with her. She agreed. Carl sat with Rita in the yard, and they talked. She refused to go with Carl to the councilor. Carl was persistent.

He came over two or three times that next week meeting with Rita for at least an hour each time discussing her needs.

Rita finally agreed to go with him to the councilor. Carl came with a cab two days later and took her for that first meeting. To his surprise the meeting lasted more than hour. Carl in the waiting room the entire time.

When it was over, Rita said she was happy Carl's friend was a young lady. This happened to her when she was twenty years old and in college. She was very understanding and kind.

Rita made a second appointment. Carl dropped Rita back off at Michael's. Nora thanked him for all his kindness and Rita assured him she would keep her appointments.

Kevin and Betty came over on the weekends as did Lilly and George. Everyone rallied around Rita and tried to comfort her as much as possible. Rita ended up staying with Michael for four weeks. Then came the day when she was going back to her own home; it was difficult to say the least.

Michael changed all the locks and added dead bolts and extra lights to the front and back doors. The ladies added fresh flowers; Kevin and Michael put a new rug in the hallway.

The first night Rita could not sleep. Michael moved the television to her bedroom and Rita had it on all night. He also installed a telephone extension line and phone in her bedroom, and a bolt lock on her door.

It was the last day of school; kids would be coming to for their report cards. Rita wanted to see her students.

She planned on saying that she had an accident and was just getting better. She wanted to thank them for being so kind to the substitute teacher.

She barely made it to the bus with only about a few seconds to spare. It was then she realized, she did not want to continue taking the bus any longer. She decided to purchase a car as soon as possible; and would ask Michael's help to see what she could afford.

The principal and students were happy to see her. She looked very thin, pale and still ill. In the meeting with the principal he assured her that her position would be available next year. He asked if she would be returning to work. She assured him she planned on returning in September.

During the months of June and July, Carl stopped by about every other day to "check up on her." He stayed for about fifteen minutes to a half hour each time.

By the end of July his visits were a little longer and he would take Rita out for a short walk. Rita still was not comfortable taking walks alone. In fact, the only places she went were to family; they took her out grocery shopping. She was determined to purchase a used car and gain her independence.

In August, Michael found a car for her to look at and see if she liked. He was going to go with her to check it out, but he was called to work.

Rita called Carl and he agreed to take her to look at the car. It was good to hear that Carl worked in a garage to help pay for college. After seeing the vehicle and talking with Michael that night Carl negotiated the price that Rita would pay for the 1957 Chevy with 12,500 miles.

The owner passed away and his nephew flew in to sell the car and the house. He agreed to the price Carl mentioned which was lower than what Michael felt she would have to pay.

Rita felt she would be more comfortable driving where she needed to go. By the end of August Rita was trying to pick up the pieces of her life and begin anew.

The new school year was about to begin, and she attended the first day at school. She was overjoyed at how small her class was this year. It would be a joy to be with these students.

Carl was a regular visitor now getting to see more of Rita all the time. The last Saturday evening in September they went out to dinner. It was a first for Rita out with Carl to dinner.

After that first dinner together the two of them decided to make it a "regular" dinner every other Saturday taking turns paying. Before long they added alternate Sunday evenings for dinner as well. This went on for about eight weeks as they claimed to be just friends. Rita was comfortable with Carl. She was keeping her appointments with her councilor.

The school year was proceeding nicely. Rita was seeing the councilor every two weeks. Rita was resolved to deal with the situation. She prayed the rest of year would be calm and enjoyable-she was ready for peace. The students were beautiful. One day the third week of October there was a knock on her classroom door-normally when classes were in session no one entered. When Rita opened the door there stood her principal and Carl. Carl agreed to give her students a lecture on the new medical trends. The class loved the lecture, some asked questions and they all wanted him to come back again. Before he left, he told the class that their teacher "was so special—they were lucky to have her." He asked them to do themselves a favor and pay close attention to everything she was teaching because there was a kind of magic in her and if they did, they would all get great grades and do very well in school. They all promised him they would pay particular attention to their teacher this year. Carl promised to return before the end of the year just to check on their grades and see what they had learned. Rita had no discipline, the students seemed especially bright and attentive. During October, Rita asked Carl if he would like to accompany her to dinner at Michael's house for their annual Halloween evening. He agreed.

Everyone was surprised at how attentive Carl seemed to be; and, how relaxed and calm Rita had become with him around. During the first parent- teacher open many parents mentioned being overjoyed at learning how much their child loved their science teacher.

Just before Christmas - Carl's second sister, Ann called him. She and their mother were going on a trip to Europe for Christmas. His sister, Ellie decided on going to a religious retreat for eight days during the holidays. Ann thought that spending Christmas in Fosdick England would be a nice gift for their mother; she expected Carl to contribute to their cost. She hopped Carl would enjoy being with them when they all returned.

Their mother was born in England and lived in Fosdick until she was twenty-one years old. That was when she met her husband and moved to the states. This trip would be her third time back and possibly her final time back as she was now in her late sixties. Two of her siblings were still alive as was her niece and nephew.

Carl agreed it would be a great trip for their mother and Ann. He agreed to contribute to the cost of the trip for their mother only. He an Ann shared some unkind words-as she expected him to pay some of her cost as well. But he reiterated that she was working; and he had many school bills to pay. He mentioned how he loved spending his time in Clayton was not planning a trip in the immediate future. He had many friends and would not be alone for the holidays. She wished him well said she hoped he would see their mother on their return.

Carl did not have a good relationship with his family, and he was not eager to see them currently. He would purchase a small gift for all of them and would send the gifts to arrive there when they returned.

Carl and Rita made a nice couple. When Carl told Rita about his family's plans for the Christmas Holidays; Rita checked with Michael and he agreed to her inviting Carl to spend the holidays with her family.

When she invited Carl-he quickly accepted. He noticed that over the past few weeks Rita added more locks to the front and back doors. He knew the police had not found the rapist and that Rita was apprehensive going out or staying home alone.

Carl was her safe escort everywhere. Christmas shopping provided an opportunity for them to have fun. They played in the snow, joked and had snacks at all the stores. They loved walking around and seeing the holiday decorations-in the store windows. They shopped, wrapped gifts together, decorated Rita's house and Carl enjoyed Rita's homemade lunches and dinners.

The Saturday before Christmas the two of them shopped most of the day as Carl wanted to purchase a small gift each for his mother and sisters. Rita helped him pick the gifts out and package them so he could take them to the post office. In this way, they would receive them when they returned from their vacations. He mentioned possibly going home on the Sunday after New Year's Day.

The next day, Rita and Carl went shopping for a Christmas tree. They got together at 8 AM –Rita made breakfast, they found the tree by 11AM, stopped for lunch and went back to Rita's to decorate the tree. They cooked dinner at 7:30PM. It was 9 PM when they finished cleaning up. While Rita was putting everything away Carl fell asleep on the sofa in the living room. Rita was also very tired. She decided to let Carl stay asleep on the sofa. This would give her a chance to wrap the scarf and gloves she purchased for him.

When she finished wrapping Carl's gift, she checked on Carl-he was out for the night. Rita locked up the house, left a small light on for Carl to see his way to the bathroom and covered him with a blanket. She then proceeded to her bedroom locking the door behind her. Rita fell asleep as soon as her head hit the pillow.

The next morning, Rita woke to the smell of bacon cooking. She went downstairs in her robe. There was Carl cooking bacon, eggs, and toast. The coffee was ready, and breakfast would be in just a few minutes, he said.

He waited until she stirred before putting on the eggs. After breakfast Carl returned to the hospital. He said he would see her later in the day.

She went to school and picked up papers to work on during the holiday vacation. On her way back she stopped and purchased another gift for Carl. It was a Timex watch. The man on the television, John Cameron Swayze, said **"this watch will keep on ticking."** She thought it would be a great thing for Carl since he was always looking for a clock or asking the time. His wristwatch broke months earlier and she knew Carl would appreciate the watch.

Everyone in the family had become used to Carl being around. Rita was sure his being there for the Holidays would be no problem. Nora told Rita she purchased some pens for Carl as a Christmas gift. This way he would not feel out of place when everyone was opening their gifts. Betty said she and Kevin purchased a radio alarm clock for Carl. Lilly said George made a name plate for Carl and engraved it and layered it in gold paint. They also found a key chain that they thought he would like.

It seemed; Carl was accepted by the entire family as being "one of them." This was going to be a beautiful Christmas.

Carl met Rita and then went to Michael's for the families traditional Christmas Eve Dinner. The dinner on Christmas Eve was an all-fish dinner. This was something vastly different from what Carl was used to. One dish would not be Carl's favorite it was Linguine with

Clam sauce. When Lilly was young her family had an Italian neighbor, she called "Uncle and Aunt." This Italian tradition of fish the day before Christmas, was so nice everyone just kept it going. Betty added a shrimp cocktail, Rita fried Calamari, Nora made a salad and George fried bullhead fish. This was an adult's meal. Greta enjoyed macaroni and cheese with green beans and a glass of milk.

They finished dinner about 7:30 PM and did not open their gifts. Michael wanted Greta to get used to Santa bringing gifts. They all decided to open gifts on Christmas day after dinner. Carl and Rita left.

On their way back to Rita's they decided to play a game of monopoly. When they finished playing Carl asked if he could asleep on the sofa. It was about midnight and Rita made a joke that she wanted to see if Santa would be able to find him for his Christmas gifts? Carl didn't laugh.

She agreed to let him sleep on the sofa and gave him some covers. She left him and went upstairs to bed. Since the rape she had normally locked her bedroom door-but she forgot all about it that night.

It was 7 AM Christmas morning when she heard Carl in the kitchen. She put on a robe and opened her bed-room door to the smell of coffee perking and something on the stove. Carl was in the kitchen fixing breakfast. "Good morning sunshine, I was very tired last night, thank you for letting me stay on the sofa-again. I will try not to make it a habit. I really slept well. In fact, I have not slept that well in quite a while.

I hope you do not mind, I made us breakfast?" Rita just looked at Carl-he looked so cute with an apron tied around his waist cooking for her. It was at this time Rita realized she was falling in love with Carl. He made French toast and bacon for breakfast with a side of fresh fruit and coffee.

Rita also slept soundly that night as well she felt "safe" with Carl. Since Carl was not on call, they had planned on spending Christmas morning together anyway. After breakfast Carl said he had some things to attend to at the hospital. He also wanted to shower and change his clothes. Rita needed to finish baking and dress. They would meet back in about three hours.

Carl was back in about an hour and a half. He brought a hammer, nails and lights for the front porch. While Rita was in the kitchen cooking, he proceeded to put up the lights.

Rita made a couple of cinnamon-apple strudels to take to Michael's. The first one was out of the oven-cooling. The second one would be out in about twenty minutes. Staying home most evenings after her classes-Rita had become an excellent cook. She received both local newspapers, "The Clayton News" and in the morning "The Town Cryer." Each paper had interesting recipes- Rita tried and mastered many of them.

After the lights were on the house Carl asked Rita to come outside and *"check something out."* This was the first-time lights were on the outside of the house and they looked festive. Rita was excited she grabbed Carl and kissed him then concerned she was being too forward-she pulled back. *"I am sorry Carl-I...as she stammered for the words to say"* Carl answered, *"that kiss made all this work worthwhile—thank you let's do that again."* Rita blushed. Then Carl kissed her tenderly saying Merry Christmas.

When they arrived, Michael, was still putting together the toys for Greta. Nora was in the kitchen. Greta was out with Lilly and George. This gave Michael a chance to set up the doll house he made to surprise her. He had planned on making all the furniture for the doll house but just did not have the time. Nora picked up many of the items at the 5 & 10 cent store.

Greta's doll house looked beautiful. It looked just like their house and Michael painted one of the rooms just like Greta's bedroom. Nora opened the small pieces of doll house furniture she purchased at Grant's and filled in each of the rooms. It was a perfect surprise. The second strudel Rita made was still hot when they arrived, and the smell was driving Carl crazy. They all concluded; it was important to eat dessert first so Nora made some coffee, and everyone had a piece of cinnamon apple strudel.

It was delicious. Then Carl and Rita helped Nora wrap the "special gifts for Greta from Santa." Santa had lots of trinkets—barrettes; a necklace; a doll; and ring like Mommy's only not real. Everything came from Grant's store.

Carl added to Greta's gifts a rag doll that he purchased from the hospital gift shop just for her. It was a doll with auburn curly hair and a lovely apron dress like the one the Betty made for Greta for Christmas.

Michael promised Nora he would take pictures of Greta's first reaction to the gifts under the tree. Everyone decided to also purchase a "Santa" gift for Greta. When Greta returned from her outing with Lilly and George, she was sound asleep. Nora put her in her crib, everyone saw this as their opportunity to add their other gifts under the tree.

There were many packages under the tree for Greta. Nora knew that would happen; she hoped no-one went overboard. Greta would receive her presents when everyone was there-after dinner. She and Michael felt strongly that they did not want Greta to be spoiled and with seven gifts under the tree for Greta from Santa that was enough.

Kevin had an idea that he and Betty wanted to discuss with Rita after dinner. He was anxious to hear everyone's response. His impatience was beginning to show.

Carl was in the kitchen making his special brussels sprout and bacon dish. He brought all the ingredients. Rita brought- the strudel, stuffed brownies and homemade cranberry dressing for the salad.

Nora's ham was still in the oven as Lilly finished mixing her sweet potato casserole. Dinner was excellent and everyone was pleasantly full. Just as they finished Michael opened the two doors to the living room presenting the lit-up Christmas tree.

Greta let out a scream.

"Suntan was here! Look presents!" everyone watched as Greta opened her presents. There were Lincoln logs, a huge coloring book with crayons, two story reading books, PJ's and a pair of slippers-pink! With her name sewn on the top front! Greta was overjoyed. Then it was time for Michael to remove the screen in front of the doll house. Greta stood up *"Da Da-my house?!"* *"Yes, baby it is your doll house"* Michael answered. Greta tried but needed help opening the doors. Michael put the doll house on the table and Greta said *"fank you sunta?"* Michael corrected her *"This is not from Santa it is from Momma and Daddy."* *"Fank, you love"* she said.

The rest of the afternoon Greta was babbling about her toys. As Nora was getting her ready for bed -everyone was in the kitchen -the child came in the kitchen with her mother to give everyone a kiss goodnight; what happened next was a total shock. Greta grabbed Michael tightly around the neck-as tight as a little child of her age could do-and as she kissed him good night, she said for the first time that anyone knew or had heard before *"wuve da da wuva da da."* Michael was almost in tears as he kissed her.

Everyone was deep in conversation when Nora returned from putting Greta to bed -still in the Kitchen enjoying coffee and dessert. Carl called the hospital to check in. The nurse said a three-year-old had just come in with burns all over her body. The Christmas tree fell on the child. Carl asked Rita if he could borrow her car-she agreed. He said he would see her later.

Weeks before the holidays Betty had been discussing with Kevin her house. It was too big for just the two of them and she had been toying with the idea of downsizing. Betty mentioned she really loved the style and size of Rita's house. A second after that statement both Kevin and Betty looked at each other and both had the same idea—they could swap houses. If Rita would be ok with moving to Betty's house it would be an easy swap. It was not so much about money they felt; the houses were the same value even though; one had a fireplace and the other did not. Rita's house had a small Kitchen and a big living room and that was what Betty loved. Betty's house had a large modern kitchen, and the living quarters were equally as large. There was a lot size difference-Betty's lot size was 45 feet by 110 feet and Rita's was 35 feet by 110 feet. The smaller lot was less for Kevin to mow. Rita had a shed and Betty's lot was completely fenced.

Betty liked the quaintness of Rita's house. They decided that the "main" differences were not important the only thing that mattered was the taxes and the upkeep costs. At the table Kevin began to expose their desire to move into a smaller place. Kevin began by mentioning that Betty needed less work and stress. When Rita returned from kissing the baby good night, she took a seat at the table when Kevin began.

"Rita, Betty thinks our house is too big, and she wants to move to a smaller house. Rita said: *"So I guess you will be selling?"* Kevin continued, *"Rita, Betty loves your house. I wonder if you like Betty's house enough to swap houses?"*

Before you say anything let me say we are aware there will be an additional cost from one house to the other. Betty suggested we could establish a bank account in your name to accommodate the extra costs until your salary improves-say for three years. Would that be something you would consider? If the facts were known Betty was a bit concerned about being in Rita's house due to the rape but—with Kevin home most of the time she was not too worried. Now it was time for the family to chime in and discuss the proposition. Kevin was tactful yet he painted a good picture identifying that if Rita ever married the larger living quarters would serve her well. With the larger lot a garage could be added one-day.

Kevin ran this idea by Michael a few weeks earlier to get his thoughts. Michael felt "This was an opportunity for everyone to be happy; Rita would be in a better place emotionally if she lived in a different house." He was concerned about Rita being in her house and the rapist still not caught. Rita was in tears as she heard the idea- she was frightened in her house alone and now her family was coming to the rescue. It was an easy decision. She said "*yes,*" everyone rallied around Betty and Rita.

Kevin decided they should go to a lawyer on the next Monday morning and change ownerships. That night everyone was happy as this Christmas really brought them all together and closer than ever before-all looking out for each other. It was a great feeling.

Love shared for and cared for expands—its 'gloriousness.

There was a concert at St. Joseph's Cathedral in downtown Clayton. Everyone except Michael and Nora had planned to go. Michael wanted them to go the morning mass and take Greta. When Carl returned to Rita's he learned about the swapping of the houses. He thought it was a perfect solution for Rita, Betty, and him.

Earlier Rita asked Carl to join them at the midnight concert mass she was not sure if Carl was Catholic. She really did not think it mattered as he agreed to go. The church was beautifully decorated, and a full choir was singing. The concert mass was over in an hour.

Betty's mind was working overtime she was mentally planning the changes she wanted Kevin to do when they moved. Rita was thinking about Carl, and the fact that they had a good friendship. She did not want to presume anything else and make him uncomfortable. After all he never did or said anything to give away any other kind of feelings for her. She knew his goal was to help her get past the trauma of the rape.

Meanwhile Carl was having issues of his own. Money was tight for a resident and he hated the living quarters at the hospital. He had been contemplating taking a year's hiatus to earn some extra money.
After the mass, Kevin dropped Carl off at the hospital.

Rita felt moving to Betty's house-was a perfect solution to her worries. Unable to sleep, Rita went downstairs to look at Carl's Christmas gift. He purchased a red copper planter for Rita. It was a unique planter twenty inches long with carvings. Rita loved it.

She was going to place it where everyone could see how beautiful it is when she moves into Betty's house. But the realization was-this gift was not something personal. Carl had not given her any reason to feel as she did about him.

However, Rita was falling in love. It was a feeling she had never had before, and she did not want it to ever go away. She thought about how caring, attentive, and understanding Carl was along with being gentle and fun to be with -all the time. That was because he was older, more settled and really enjoyed her. She loved how he always called her just to chat about the day's events-either at his work or in the world. She loved when he would put his hand, on her back and move it up and down. Even now, he often, put his jacket on her shoulders—his eyes always seemed to smile at her. When he held her hand, she felt safe and warm inside.

She resolved to restrain her thinking about love and what could happen. She wanted to remain firmly grounded and not let romantic notions consumer her.

Betty was also unable to sleep. She thought of all the hours of cleaning that would be saved –and how the two of them could now have time to travel and have more romantic nights. She knew from experience that Kevin was very romantic. He was always doing little things to surprise her—bringing her flowers, making sure there was always enough gas in their car so they could go out shopping-calling and asking her for a date- so they could go to dinner together, buying her little gifts—and those kisses -well they are terrific.

What she loved most was that they would always hold hands as they window shopped looking at things. They would discuss the value of certain items or if they liked something-the sharing of thoughts and ideas found each other becoming together closer and closer. She wanted more time to be with Kevin instead of his always mowing the lawn or fixing up something in the house.

She was still a woman in love, and she loved being with Kevin 24/7. She was never bored with his company. Since their marriage Kevin repaired everything in Betty's house. She and her mother never could keep up with things that needed fixing. Now the house was in excellent shape for Rita.

Christmas week was cold and snowing but on Sunday everyone agreed to return to Nora's for dinner. The holiday bus schedule was different from the normal schedule and not available as often. Carl secured a ride from one of the other interns over to Rita's house. He arrived at noon to help her take things over to Michael's. Rita loved having a car. Rita prepared several dishes for the dinner and Carl put them into the car. Carl wanted to know when Rita found time to cook. He asked her what she made that smelled so good- Rita teased him and said he would find out soon enough.

Everyone arrived at Nora's at 1 PM. Greta was babbling about "*Santa eating her cookies.*" She was so excited about her doll house and her doll. As every person arrived, she asked them to "*coma see*" and with her little hand she ushered them to see her doll house. Michael beamed from ear to ear knowing he made his little girl so happy.

Nora and he shared a special smile as everyone commented on the doll house. Many times, Greta would say "*wuv da da.*" As Michael would comment on how "Mommie" found all the furniture and worked so hard helping daddy.

Nora loved how Michael always gave her credit for everything she did. She loved how he appreciated her efforts and how he wanted to be sure that Greta knew it was a joint effort. Michael always felt that together they could do about anything, and he wanted to be sure he and

Nora always were together on their thoughts about raising Greta.

Their Sunday dinner was perfect as usual. Rita made stuffed pork roast with sage dressing. She topped with a cranberry sauce and mashed sweet potatoes. Everyone brought a side dish. The meal was delicious as always.

Carl loved all the gifts he received and thanked everyone for being accepted as part of the family He purchased a box of candy for Lilly, Betty and Nora and a small toolbox for each of the men. He found coloring books, stencils and two pieces of doll furniture for Greta. Kevin gave Betty a pair of gloves and scarf with a pin for her coat. George gave Lilly a jewelry box that he had made. It was with ten drawers, mahogany and looked like a wedding cake with the drawers in tiers. She loved it and inside one of the drawers was a necklace. This Christmas Michael surprised Nora with a pair of pearl earrings that were just beautiful.

Rita told everyone about the copper planter she received from Carl. He perked up and said that he always knew what a decorator she had become." Betty and Lil saw the look in the man's eyes *things must be getting closer between these young people.*"

After dinner everyone rallied around the piano and sang a few Christmas Carols. By 7 PM Rita and Carl were on their way back to Rita's. Carl's friend Fred would come by later to take Carl back to the hospital. Carl had other ideas he loved Betty's house. He enjoyed being with Rita and liked her family. The family made plans for New Year's Day to be at Betty's for dinner.

Carl wanted New Year's Eve alone with Rita. Carl did not want to return to the hospital. He wanted to talk with Rita about the changing of the houses. He felt that it was a perfect solution to all her worries and his problems. Carl knew that Rita would be comfortable in Betty's kitchen. As they sat on the sofa and discussed the timing of the move; Carl leaned over and kissed Rita very passionately for the first time. *"I think we should get married"* he said.

Rita was not ready for that question-she just realized she was falling in love; they had not discussed love or marriage at all, and this was the first passionate kiss. She was not sure what prompted his sudden proposal. **Her thoughts raced through their last few days and then...God heard her in church, and he knew it was right–maybe when she was thinking about being in love with Carl-God did not want her to wait too long. Maybe...maybe but who cared about maybe Rita felt like a schoolgirl who had just gotten an "A" on a report card. She was overjoyed and excited and in love and whatever prompted his proposal –it was here, and she said** *"Yes! Yes!"* They kissed again and Carl asked, *"if Valentine Day would be too soon."* Rita was taken at how quickly he wanted the marriage to take place and yet it was wonderfully romantic. She said *"No, that would not* *be too soon."* When Fred arrived to give Carl a ride back to the hospital, Carl asked him to congratulate them-she "has just accepted my marriage proposal."

That night Rita could not sleep-she called Nora and said that "she loved the holidays. She did not want to tell her over the telephone about the proposal-she wanted to see the look on everyone's face as she told them.

New Year's Eve Carl planned for just the two of them. Rita agreed to cook, and Carl brought flowers. It was a romantic night Rita had dinner by candlelight and put on the radio. They enjoyed lasagna, with a special meet sauce, salad and homemade bread toasted with garlic. Dessert was home- made apple pie al a mode. Rita was an accomplished cook and Carl loved everything she made. Carl did not want to go back to the hospital that evening. He presented that New Year's Eve was a dangerous evening to ask someone to pick him up. He wondered if he could sleep on the sofa sleeper in Michael's old room. Rita agreed.

As he opened the bed and Rita began to put on the sheets; Carl pulled her down on the bed and kissed her. Sensing her timidness, he assured her he would do nothing to spoil their wedding night. They sat on the bed together just talking and they fell asleep fully clothed but in each other's arms. Rita woke at 3 AM and left to go to her own room. Sleeping with Carl was going to be special. Carl was so caring. Rita wanted to give him everything she could as she did not feel worthy of his love-and rallied at the idea of both being love.

Carl knew the family dinner would be the place to make the announcement. He and Rita said nothing about getting married all through dinner.

After dinner, while everyone was still at the table Carl stood up and said: "*I would like everyone's* attention." Rita was amazed at what came next. "As you *all know I have been "around" this family for some time now. Well Rita and I have decided you should all be congratulated-on the growth of your family—as it is expanding once again!*" at that moment Kevin looked at Michael and was starting to burn thinking this man might have taken advantage of his daughter. But then Carl continued "*On this Valentine Day I will not be just "around" this family any longer. I will then become a permanent member of the family as Rita has accepted my proposal of marriage. You are all invited to the wedding.*" Kevin laughed as his face changed from budding anger to joy for his daughter.

There was applause culminating with hugging and kissing by everyone. Carl picked up Greta and said as he picked her up "*Well honey I am getting a name change instead of you calling me "Doc" in the future you will be able to call me "Uncle Carl!"*" Greta liked Carl, he always tickled her and made her laugh. Carl then asked Michael to be his best man and Michael agreed.

Rita knew Carl did not have any money as she paid for many things-many times when they went out. She made sure not to expect and engagement ring from Carl. Rita presumed that for now they would look for simple wedding bands.

Kevin and Betty had a surprise for Rita and now was the perfect time to tell her about it. Kevin stood up *"Rita, this could not have been a better Christmas. Betty and I wish the two of you a long, happy life together giving us many grandchildren to play with and we wish you everlasting love. That said we have been waiting for this day to tell you something that we want you to have.*

Your mother never had any fancy diamond wedding ring but one thing she did have was a gold band; and Betty inherited her mother's wedding band. We have talked about this for quite a while—these items will now belong to you. Betty's mothers wedding band, your mother's wedding band could either be for you and Carl or you could make them into earrings, or you could sell them. They are yours now. Kevin got up from his seat and said, *"We love you very much Rita."* Then he turned to Carl and said *"please take good care of "our" daughter? You know she is special?"* Rita was in tears. Carl got up and hugged Kevin and kissed Betty. *"Thank you both so much! For everything you are doing for us."*

Betty went over to Rita and whipped her tear with her hand. She gave her a hug and said *"Rita, I do not think I could love you more if you were my own daughter. I love you very much—and I am happy for you. Congratulations –you two make such a nice couple I pray you will always be as happy as you are now."* With that she turned to Carl and said in a joking manner

"A car, house and bride all in one –you are an extremely fortunate young man."

Everyone looked at Betty as she said her statement and she faced them and said, *"Well, isn't he?"*

Michael said, *"I think Rita lucked out as well she will never have to pay a doctor's bill and we lucked out for getting free medical consults forever."*

Ever one laughed and kissing began again.

Rita said to Nora *"Please be my maid of honor?"*

Nora replied, *"I would love to."*

Betty had two boxes hidden in her dress pockets. She took them out and handed them to each woman. *"Happy New Year."* She said. Rita and Nora opened their special gifts.

Nora spoke first *"OMG they are just beautiful. Thank you so much. I love you but I do not understand."*

Then Rita said, *"Betty these are gorgeous thank you but why?"* Betty answered *"You girls are like my own daughters. These earrings were made from rings I inherited. Who better to have and enjoy? I planned on giving them to each of you yesterday and forgot where I had saved them. I found them this morning. I want you both to know that you are like the best "daughters" any woman could ask for and I love you both dearly."*

Tears of joy and hugs continued to fill the room. Kevin looked at Betty filled with eyes full of love *"My love you never cease to amaze me, and you are such a perfect addition to this family."* The two of them kissed and George said, *"Get a room!"* with that everyone laughed. He continued

"You two have been married for quite some time-I agree with you—honeymoons are great!" Lilly blushed and Betty hugged her.

The next week Kevin and Betty went to the jeweler they took Mary Jo's old band and Betty's mother's band. Carl and Rita agreed to go to the jeweler the next Saturday to be measured.

The jeweler agreed to have the wedding bands made to fit and stated that he would "filigree" the bands some so they would look like new, and he agreed to complete them in time for the wedding.

When Betty and Kevin were at the jeweler's she asked him if he could use the stones left from her rings for a pendent necklace for each of her "girl's." The jeweler had an idea how to use the extra gold; if Betty agreed he would just charge her for the chain and he would make the pendent free just for the opportunity to try out his idea. She agreed and two weeks into the New Year everyone agreed to have Sunday dinners together. This Sunday dinner was at Kevin and Betty's house. Betty made southern fried chicken dinner and as always everyone added a dish. After dinner everyone went into the living room-Betty's piano was still in great shape and Greta wanted everyone to sing "the Peck song." *They all sang "I love you a bushel and a peck."*

About a half hour of singing and Betty brought out two boxes and gave one to Rita and one to Nora. She began, *"Rita this was part of the rings, I inherited. Every girl should have a beautiful diamond necklace and you two are no different. I had these made for both of you. The setting was an idea of the jeweler-I hope you like it?"* Rita opened the box it was a single square stone diamond set with four prongs in a gold filigree background. Rita blurted out *"It is beautiful—I love it!"* Nora proceeded to take hers out of the box-as Betty said the jeweler made hers just a bit different and low and behold –it was perfect! Nora's diamond sat in the center of a heart. Another round of hugs, kisses and thank you statements went to Betty. Kevin was so proud of her he put his arms around her waist and moved her body toward him *"I cannot count all the ways I love you-you are one special lady,"* and with that they kissed.

At this point Michael stood up and turned to face Carl *"I want you to know Carl that the love of a good woman is what life is all about. Add that to joining a family who loves and respects each other, and you have found what heaven really means. Treat her well or you will have each and every one of us to answer too."* With that he first gave Rita a big hug and kiss. Then he went to Nora, Lilly and finally Betty and kissed each of them.

He added *"Carl every lady in this room is a jewel in her own right-and each man here **is incredibly lucky to call his jewel his wife and that my man-***includes you. Treat your wife like she is a precious jewel, love her, respect her and appreciate her every day for the rest of your life. And with that philosophy and our warning stuck in your mind let me be the first to welcome you to the family."* Nora was shocked but happy she turned to Michael and gave him another kiss uttering the words *"I love you Michael very much! You are my heart and soul."* Christmas had become special this year for the entire family. And with the rings and necklaces in tow the date set—it was time to shop for a wedding dress.

Rita was not a traditionalist she wanted something simple and flattering to her small frame. She went shopping and found an off white knit dress-not a wedding dress-just a simple evening dress with a beautiful design in the fabric. It was perfect. The salesgirl found a pair of pump heals to match and a small pill box hat with matching gloves. Nora said she was a picture of loveliness and the outfit was perfect.

While waiting for Rita to change Nora found a simple red evening dress, empire waste also in a knit material that would be perfect for either a maid of honor or to use for an evening out after the wedding.

Lilly and Betty met the girls for lunch at the Swiss Chalet. They were excited to hear all about the shopping trip and the new dresses. Lilly and Betty had planned to do some shopping of their own.

When they saw Nora's dress the ladies wanted to find their dresses. They hit it big at A.M & A's. Betty's dress was cream color beige slightly gathered at the waist. She decided to add a complimenting scarf as a wrap for inside the church.

Lilly wanted something more in line with her figure. She located a beige dress with an empire waist

On the way home the ladies talked about making a wedding cake and a wedding dinner.

Carl had no money for anything. He owned a suit from his college graduation and would purchase nothing new for the event. He wanted the wedding to be held at the office of the Justice of the Peace; but he agreed to the rectory of St. Joseph's Church and Father Anthony to perform the ceremony. He asked Michael to be his best man and he accepted.

On Valentine Day at 3 PM Rita and Carl were married. The ceremony took about twenty minutes. Lilly felt that Rita missed out on a real church wedding with all the pleasure of walking down a long isle. Kevin agreed. "They should have had a real church wedding" he said. He really would have liked to walk her down an aisle. But at least they were married by a priest.

Everyone felt it was strange that no one from Carl's family was at the wedding. Kevin persisted *"He is a doctor-no family here for the wedding."*

Betty just laughed and said *"You are sounding like a father, should of, could of, would of—if the young doctor had the money- which he does not a grandiose wedding would have been great. Listen silly man he will have more money than you and me one day, but they did not want to wait until one day. Do you remember what it was like to—just want to get married? Now enjoy the fact that "our daughters are now both happy and marred to good men. Have you forgotten the feelings?"* Kevin looked at her with love and said, *"Yea, I do understand the feelings of love and the desire to marry."* With that they kissed. She continued *"Let's be happy for all of them."* Kevin looked at her with love and they kissed again.

Rita did not care about anything she was in love and now she was Mrs. Carl Hammer and nothing else mattered. There were no gifts or acknowledgements of the wedding from anyone but from Rita's family.

After the ceremony Lilly had prepared a two-tier wedding cake and everyone went to Betty and Kevin's house for a Pot Roast supper that was terrific: Rita had put a pot roast in Betty's oven before the wedding, Lil made boiled carrots with green beans, Nora had mashed potatoes ready, and George made beets and a salad. Everything was well planned and delicious.

By 8:00 PM Carl and Rita were back at Rita's house. Carl forgot some of his things at the hospital, so he took Rita's car to the hospital to gather the remainder of his things.

It was almost 9:30 PM when he returned. Rita prepared a small cheese snack with a bottle of wine for them she was concerned and wanted to prolong retiring. Carl returned from the hospital with a candy heart, flowers and a beautiful card for my "Wife."

After the cheese and wine, it was time for the couple to retire now Rita was extremely nervous she asked Carl if she could change alone. She was going to put on one of her nightgowns, but she decided to just sit on the edge of the tub for a minute.

Carl called out to her and asked her to come out "*for a minute.*" When she did, he sensed her apprehension and ushered her over to sit on the bed together. Instead of their wedding night ending with a consummation of their love Carl held her in his arms kissing her gently. He sensed her nerves and told her "*we have the rest of our lives to love each other.*"

With that they both laid back on the bed talking about their life together and fully clothed they fell asleep. In the morning Carl showered and left for work before Rita was up. He left her a note that read "*I love you.*"

Rita took the day off from work. There was no money for a honeymoon and anyway the paperwork to switch homes would be completed within a few days and the move would take place in less than a month.

Betty had spent her time designing the changes she wanted Kevin to do in Rita's house. Kevin would enclose part of the front porch making it like a vestibule entrance adding a closet. He would purchase a new front door getting one with a window in the middle so you could see who was seeking to come in. He decided to put a different kind of doorbell just "*inside*" the front entrance as an alarm. The buzzer would frighten anyone not invited.

Betty loved the quaintness of the smaller home. She really loved and would enjoy the hidden room in the attic that Kevin showed her. She decided it would be her sewing room.

Carl wanted to add a garage to Betty's house but since neither he nor Rita had the money, they decided to wait a while. When the switch happened, it took about a month each for them to all be settled.

Betty's house was closer to the hospital it made Carl's travel time easier. Rita loved having a wood burning fireplace. The fireplace was about the only thing Betty missed when she moved into Rita's house.

It took Kevin about three months to find a way to add a fireplace that would not be too traumatic for the house or him financially. The living room was small, but he would remove the bay windows and change the focus of the living room to feature the yard instead the front of the house. The rear porch was grounded in concrete, so he would extend the living room and put two bay windows on each side of the new fireplace. It would be dramatic and beautiful.

George was also a mason so it really would not be all that expensive to brick up where the front windows were and prepare a platform and fireplace. Michael agreed to help him with the changes in the summer. Betty said it would be like rally having their "new" house. With Michael's and George's help they finished in three weeks. The house would have a completely new focus.

Five weeks into their marriage Carl came home and surprised Rita with the statement; that they needed to drive to Pennsylvania that weekend to meet his family.

Carl's sister Ann had been seeing Paul on and off for years. Paul was her high school sweetheart, and they had a son Josh now a year old. When Ann returned from England they decided to marry.

Carl's other sister Ellie was not married, and she still lived with and cared for their mother. Carl had called them and told them when they would arrive the next day.

Gail Hammer, Carl's mother was shocked that Carl would marry without any of them knowing or being present. She was a bit cold toward Rita when she learned that Rita was one of those "Catholic Girls." They were all raised Lutheran.

Ellie did not like to cook for a large group; after their first meal she asked if Rita would take over the kitchen. Rita did all the cooking after that for the entire week; and by the end of the week Rita felt accepted.

As Rita cooked Ellie helped do whatever was needed to help in the kitchen. The two had become friends. Ann said she was *"Happy that Carl was married and had someone to help with his expenses."* She was not thrilled with the idea of Carl married out of their faith. She told Ellie while they were all the kitchen she felt "*Carl needs someone like Rita to help him along after all Carl is a survivor.*" Rita pretended not to hear.

Gail Hammer was kind the whole week. Rita liked her. She was a woman with principle, and she was not afraid to say what was on her mind. By Sunday afternoon, as Carl and Rita were getting ready to leave, the two women were able to hug and be friendly. Carl promised they would return to Pennsylvania again in the summer.

On the way home Rita decided to ask Carl "*Why didn't you invite any member of your family to our wedding?*" He hesitated for a bit before answering and slowly began "*Rita, my family is different. They accepted you now but –if they knew about the wedding, they would have attempted to stop the marriage especially if they knew you were Catholic let alone had been raped.*"

Rita was shocked at his answer. She could not speak to him the rest of the way home. She turned her head toward her window and pretended to fall asleep all the while thinking about Carl's statement and wondering what she has gotten herself in to.

Chapter 30

Ma Cookson's

Time For Each Other

Time marches on. Greta was now two and a half years old and talking constantly. Nora miscarried in March.

Kevin and Betty had the house in Rita's name alone. Rita continued to work full time. Michael was getting tired of the Steel Plant and itching for another job.

Carl's training would be over in July. He had limited money. Carl wanted his own car. He found one but he did not have any money to put down. So, he found a dealer that accepted the sale with no money down. Rita's name was on the loan because she had established credit and employment, but the title was only in Carl's name.

Shortly after he finished his residency Carl was offered a job with a small medical group in the area. His salary was not great, but it could grow as the group established themselves.

Carl affiliation with a medical group was becoming a good choice. The group was growing and a few more doctors joined so they could offer medical specialists to their patients. Carl specialized in Dermatology.

With few referrals Carl was making only a small salary. While his salary would help with some expenses it was not enough to cover the car payments

Rita had an opportunity to move to a new school. With having two cars both Rita and Carl could each get to work on time.

Meanwhile Betty wanted to retire. She had been working at the grocery store forever and now she wanted to travel. Kevin felt she was too young to retire. He felt she still should work just part time. He promised to take her to Canada often on weekends if she agreed. The grocery store had no problem with her changing her hours to part time and they moved her to Customer Service. Three week there and Betty was—once again—happy working.

Kevin kept his promise and on the weekend he and Betty began to explore Canada. Every time they returned from a trip, they would tell Lilly and George what a great time they had and all the things they saw.

It did not take long for Lilly and George's curiosity was heightened and they joined them in Canada occasionally. Lilly learned of a vacation place called "Ma Cookson's Farm." It soon became a favorite spot to rent a cabin and really relax. Three excellent homecooked meals were prepared fresh daily by Mrs. Cookson. There were indoor games, scrabble, bingo and monopoly, plus horseshoes, shuffleboard and swimming.

It was worth the all-inclusive cost for great food and fun.

If there were two couples together each received a discount of the bill if they stayed the full week. It was a no brainer. The couples spent three weekends there during the first summer. During the next summer they stayed four weeks. They had all become super friends. Everyone at Ma Cookson's farm loved them and catered to them whenever they visited.

As the year ended, the holiday celebrations found the families close, happy and relaxed with each other.

Chapter 31

Rita's Turn

It was February when Rita announced she was pregnant. The Baby was due in September.

George announced he was going to make a special cradle. Betty found enjoyment in planning a baby shower for the happy couple.

Carl was concerned about Rita's health-she was vomiting several times during the day-looking pale and not resting. However, Rita was excited and fine. She surmised if the baby were on schedule, she would have time to meet the new group of students in September. She planned on taking the first half of the year off and then returning to work in January.

Betty would watch the baby during the school week. Betty loved the idea and so did Kevin. With the prospect of caring for the baby Kevin agreed Betty should quit her job a month before the baby arrived to get things ready. Lilly was watching Greta-and loving every minute of it.

Rita, Lilly, Nora and Betty planned the summer. They would learn more songs paint and decorate the nursery. They planned on knitting some blankets and booties. This kept all the women busy and loving every minute of their time.

Babies do not necessarily follow their due date.

Rita began labor after dinner on August 4th. Carl drove to the hospital at 8:15 PM- after checking that Rita's pains were every fifteen minutes. On August 5th at 4:08 AM Shana Marie Hammer was born. Carl's maternal grandmother's name was "Shana," and he loved the name and her—he asked Rita if she was ok with the name.

Rita chose Marie as a middle name to complement her mother's name. Thus, their beautiful baby girl was named Shana Marie Hammer she weighed five pounds two ounces with curly brownish-red hair and big brown eyes. She had long fingers and her cry identified a great set of lungs. Carl was overjoyed seeing his child. He almost missed her birth. One of the nurses saw him enter the emergency room, she asked him to handle a case-before she realized why he was there. He checked the patient and waited for another doctor to arrive then returned to Rita just in time for the birth of Shana.

Walking into the delivery room Carl took the baby from the nurses and held her talking to her telling her how much he loved her, what a beautiful girl she was and that she was going to always be special to her daddy.

Rita changed her mind and decided to take the full year off from teaching. Shana was Carl's pride and joy. He sang to her, played with her all the time and they even took naps together on weekends.

When they brought Shana home from the hospital-everyone marveled at how gentle Greta was with her.

Time has a way of moving quite rapidly as both Rita and Nora enjoyed watching their girls grow and become best friends. Nora had hoped for another baby-but Michael was against the idea of them trying he felt two miscarriages had to be a sign. Greta felt like the little mother around Shana the children were great together.

Kevin, Betty, George and Lilly had established that one night a week they would all dine together. George heard of a place in Arizona—called Scottsdale. Everything he read about it sounded great he wanted that to be their stop next summer. The two couples made plans to *"test the waters of Scottsdale."*

Their communication, likes and dislikes were bringing them closer and closer all the time and adding the memories of these trips made them really a family.

Chapter 32

Things Happen And Time Marches On

Nora was beginning to be concerned that Michael's relationship with his daughter had become too strict. Greta was now in the second grade and Michael had given her strict orders to get her chores finished before dinner. When Michael worked the second shift his schedule kept him and Greta apart for most of the day. However, when he was home for dinner, he wanted Greta to help set and clear the table and for sure she was not to chew any gum in his presence and to have her homework finished right after supper. With gum, Greta was constantly blowing bubbles and playing with her gum—out of her mouth. Michael found gum on the top of the bathroom sink, on the floor in the kitchen and in their car.

Greta loved being in school. She was a quick learner always up early and ready for school. When school was over the bus would stop at Lilly's house and Greta stayed there until Nora picked her up.

Never having children of her own-Lilly enjoyed taking care of Greta. Greta looked like a beautiful doll every day going to school. Nora would put her long auburn hair into pig tails. When the baby was asleep Betty made beautiful dresses for both the girls, dressing them like twins.

Betty loved babysitting Shana. It was a great experience never having any children. Both Lilly and Betty enjoyed taking care of "their" girls. Betty, with Lilly's help, will eventually teach Shana to read.

The men found themselves slowly entering a carpentry business together. George was teaching Kevin how to be a carpenter. George was expanding on Kevin's abilities. They worked on a couple of houses together; then expanded to add a few small jobs at businesses. The two men got along like brothers. They were good together.

Working together Kevin and George put in a fireplace in Kevin's old house. The job went so well the men then built a garage for Carl and added a sunroom to their house. The more they worked together the more they enjoyed each other's company.

The men laughed and had fun working together. It was: **A new beginning** and soon they decided it was time to form a partnership and business. and they titled it: "G & K's Carpentry." Michael did not want to leave the security of the steel plant just yet; he agreed to join them when the time was right.

Chapter 33

Change

Greta loved to watch the men work. One day she decided she wanted to work with them—as their helper. She approached George -who was fine with the idea. Then next she approached Kevin. He was a bit concerned about her abilities and if she was expecting to be paid while she was learning. He told her everyone must start from the bottom, and he wanted to know her demands.

She thought about it for a few seconds and then said; *"I don't have demands grandpa, but my cost is ten cents an hour. And when I get good then I want to get paid a quarter an hour."* Kevin said since he and George were partners, they needed to talk about hiring someone and to think it over. He told her they would get back to her.

After lunch they were ready to make a deal. Kevin began *"Since everyone starts at the bottom-we will permit you to help paint some of the lower trim with the understanding that it would be—when we needed her help. And when they called on her for assistance, she would receive ten cents an hour. If she became a good painter-she would get twenty cents an hour. In time, then they would raise her to 25 cents an hour."* Greta said, *"I like you grandpa, but you have to remember I am a little girl and I like candy. I agree to the 10 cents while I am learning but I learn fast, and I want the twenty-five cents when I do a good job.*

Holding back from chocking on laughter George chimed in *"Well Greta I own half of the company. I will pay the twenty-five cents an hour as soon as you have graduated to being good at painting the lower lever. Is it a deal" "and when I want a raise Uncle George I will come to you—first."*

Kevin burst out laughing. He told George *"If this is what she is like at nine and a half years old can you imagine what she will be like at fifteen years old?"* The men just laughed.

Greta was spending more time with Kevin and George. She did identify them as her "bosses" and that she was learning. She loved doing the baseboards and by the third baseboard she did a perfect job. George paid her twenty-five cents an hour after that. She usually worked two and a half hours a week in half-hour intervals.

One day Kevin took George into his confidence. He was concerned about Michael's patience with Greta and with Nora. Lilly remarked that the child would often cry saying that *"Daddy did not love her."*

Kevin did not know how to approach Michael-but he thought it was getting time to discuss the matter with him.

George was concerned himself about Michael's behavior he had witnessed his outbursts once or twice. But he was more concerned that Kevin would just alienate Michael if he tried to discuss that behavior with him.

Consequently, George tried something a bit different. George decided to see if Michael was ready to join their business. Maybe Michael's quick temper came from the swing shift. His felt regular working hour meant regular sleep.

Michael was a good foreman and organizer; George thought, in time Michael could not only handle a large crew; he could own the business. Michael could take on additional work and the two men-Kevin and George-would wait for an opportunity to see if the issue they were concerned about continued.

George's approach worked. Michael was ready to join them. He hired a crew. Now George and Kevin realized that it was the right time to expand their business while preparing Michael to eventually become the owner.

Chapter 34

The G-Men Are Formed

The winter in Clayton was exceptionally cold this year and shoveling driveways was hard for both Kevin and George.

George had a plan: he would hire six young boys from the neighborhood. Each boy would get a new shovel, a hat, gloves, and a pair of rubber boots then the boys could shovel, and they would get paid-like a business.

He spoke to a few boys who wanted to do the work and they found a few other boys interested. All the boys loved the idea, so, George proceeded to visit the parents. The boys were Bobby Dyer; Joe Park; Mark Jones; Billy Devine; Zack Staple and Philip Cooper. They were all in the 8th grade.

The plan was: the calls would go to George's business telephone for snow shoveling orders and George would, check-out the job, make the appointments, collect the money, and pay the boys.

Philip Cooper was 13 years old the oldest-the other boys were all 12 years old. Phil would act as the foreman.

George went to all the parents and discussed his business plan. No boy would go alone-three at a time was the best. They would only work with in a three-block radius of their house. The requirement was that each had to keep up their grades or they would not work for George.

The boys and parents signed a letter of agreement. Each driveway shoveled, gave the boys a percentage of any tip that came his way. At first the boys shoveled two driveways day; but these were young boys filled with energy and a burning desire to make money. The boys were supposed to solicit other friends to the group. Zack found four boys to add and the rest each added one. That made a total of fifteen boys to shovel.

Philip Cooper was the leader of the group. He wanted a special name for their side of the business. All the boys loved George even though he kept them on their toes and even checked with their parents if they were keeping up their grades.

Philip decided on a name for the boys

"The G-men." George loved it.

The entire winter the teams shoveled a total of four to six driveways a day.

By spring, the boy's business expanded to raking leaves and cleaning out garages. George would charge the owners for the work; he wrote a note to the owners asking them to "rate" the success of the work completed. He stated that if they wanted to "tip" it would be used for all the boys, as they worked as a group and not one individually. He told the boys they were to be judged as a team.

He also paid the boys everything they earned and took nothing for the company. The deal identified that their grades were primary and needed to be kept up, this made all the parents happy. The boys had spending money and not one got into any mischief. It was a win-win for everyone including the school.

When Michael joined George and Kevin in their Carpentry business, they got along very well-except for a few outbursts between Kevin and Michael. George saw that Michael's patience seemed to resemble his fathers. At times George felt he needed to sit both down and give them a good talking too. But as always George had another way to do something and in time, he would bring it out to both Kevin and Michael.

Chapter 35

Hair

Lilly invited the family to have Easter Dinner at her house. She asked the woman to all arrive early. She loved how all the women cooked together and helped each other. It was never a chore for the hostess to arrange for a meal. With the women cooking all day the men agreed to bring the girls later.

Carl was on call at the hospital. He decided to take Shana to the hospital with him and show everyone how beautiful she looked in her new Easter outfit designed and made by Miss. Betty.

Michael and Greta were home most of the day. Arriving at Lilly's house, Greta came in crying. Michael warned Greta several times about chewing gum and playing with it in and out of her mouth. This time she took the bubble gum out of her mouth; played with it like a ball. She had five pieces of gum in her mouth. She bounced the gum in the air and the gum came down all over her hair and clothes.

Michael could not get the gum out of her clothes or her hair. He took out a pair of scissors and cut the gum out of her hair. According to Greta he was angry that she was playing with the gum and just cut and kept cutting more hair than had gum in it. Greta's long hair was now cut short and close to her head. She told Nora that she "I *asked Daddy to stop-and promised not to play with gum anymore, but he would not listen.*"

Greta was almost hysterical in her crying and this made Nora very was upset. When Greta took off her hat and Nora saw her hair, she was shocked. Greta screamed "*Daddy did it – because he hates me, and I hate him—do you understand*

I hate him! He made me ugly! I look like a boy." Betty tried to comb the hair—it did look like someone went over it with a lawn mower. Nora tried telling Greta that her hair would grow. But that was not the only issue-she felt Michael went too far this time. Greta's hair was about three inches long all over. It did make her look like a boy.

Years later stylists would call the cut a "pixie."

But for now, it was not a good cut. Nora began arguing with Michael about his quick temper with the child. Everyone else got involved taking sides. Michael did not care "*She will learn how to chew gum and how not to play with gum or she will not have any gum to chew.*" he said.

Nora knew Michael loved her long hair-both she and Lilly had hair just past their shoulders. They were all embroiled in the discussion and were interrupted when Carl arrived with Shana.

Shana hated her thick curly hair it was so difficult to brush and to keep it neat. It always had to be put into braids or pig tails. The first thing she said when she saw Greta's short hair was "*Mommy can you cut my hair like Greta's?*"

That set off an argument between Rita and Carl. Rita did not like combing the snarls out of Shana's curly hair-the child cried every day-and any time someone combed her hair. Carl told Rita that Shana's hair should not be cut- "*women need long hair*" Carl said. That remark made Rita angry. She had long hair-and she wore it in a French twist most of the time.

Now all the women looked at each other and as if they made a "Pack" they took two girls by the hand and marched into the bathroom locking the door.

Since arguing with the men got the ladies no-where once in, and the bathroom door locked, they told Greta-her hair cut was going to set a style. On the way into the bathroom Rita put a pair of scissors in her pocket.

She took it out as Lilly took Shana's braids out. "*Ok here we go*" said Rita and she cut Shana's hair. While it was not quite as short as Greta's it had a natural wave and did look good. Then Rita looked at Nora. Nora said "*go for it*" With that look giving her the "go" Rita cut Nora's hair. Lilly cut Betty's hair and then Lilly cut Rita's. Betty cut Lilly's hair last. All this beauty shop work took one hour and a half before the women came out of the bath-room. The women felt they were making a statement to their husbands and to the girls. Each woman had her hair cut in different lengths.

When the men saw all the haircuts, they were all upset. Michael turned to Nora and said *"That looks ter-rible! I hate it!"* Nora smirked and just walked away from him.

Rita did not care-how she looked either-she wanted her hair cut close to her ears with just a wisp of hair in the front of each ear curled toward her face. Carl said, *"Oh my God you look like a young boy!"*

Kevin said nothing but gave Betty quite a look of disapproval all he said was *"why you?"* George an-nounced, *"I bet your short cuts will be easier to care for-and any way hair is not that important-it is what is inside the person that I love."* Lilly kissed him and gave him a hug. Michael just sat in a chair and fumed. George said that *"the day was still young, and a holiday let's try to enjoy the rest of the day. The food smells delicious."*

Dinner was late and the men were upset and none of them ate much except for George who was hungry. And after supper all the women were heard crying in the kitchen. It was obvious that none of them really knew how to handle the situation and they knew they would miss their hair. Michael announced to the men *"How stupid and stubborn the women were, "I am glad men are not like that."* Kevin could not hold his tongue any longer.

"You are the stupid and stubborn one! You are responsible for all this-you and your temper. How you treat that child and Nora at time is ridiculous; she is not in the army let alone the enemy. In fact, Greta is a great kid-both she and Nora are fabulous people. What has gotten into you-you just have no patience, tolerance, or kindness in your blood since you have come back from the war. What happened Michael? where is the old Michael? The old Michael he would never have cut his daughter hair!"

Kevin was shaking as he looked at Michael-and Michael was stunned. His father never spoke to him like that before. Michael's eyes went across the room as tears came down his face. Without a word he went to the closet took his coat and walked out the door. He walked home. They were all stunned. Kevin apologized for his rudeness to everyone. That night Michael slept in the guest bedroom and said nothing to Nora or Greta.

After Easter vacation it was Michael's turn to take Greta back to school. Greta cried all the way-she did not want to go into her classroom. Michael took her hand and brought her into the classroom. Now Michael was a big strong man walking with Greta's hand in his and her crying! You could hear a pin drop when Greta took off her hat and the children saw her hair.

Some of the children let out a loud gasp. Greta's teacher, Mrs. Dale asked "What happened to Greta's hair?" Michael's answer was: *"You teach children your way and I'll teach my child my way."* All the children heard Michael's comments and saw Greta's tears. No one ever mocked Greta's hair-in fact, they were more compassionate and friendly than ever before. It was as if they understood not only her hair being cut but the kind of father she had at home.

She told her teacher and the students about the incident with the chewing gum and how it happened to get in her hair. As the month's past, Greta's hair grew, and seemed as if the color was redder than it had ever been before. The children in her class thought it was so red because she was truly angry with her father and it was showing up in her hair. Who knew for sure, but Greta certainly did have much redder hair than she did before it was cut? Greta never wanted to chew gum again after her hair was cut.

The next six months things began to change. Michael was working with a new crew, and he was more mellow. For one thing he was more respectful to Kevin, he seemed more relaxed, and he even laughed at times. Kevin and George never discussed the hair cutting situation again.

One Friday while doing a roof for Mrs. McCarthy, Michael fell from the garage roof and was brought to the ER by ambulance. Carl called Nora from the hospital and told her he had a broken foot and arm. He would be fine but would be laid up six weeks—at least!

Carl said he would drive Michael home; Nora need not come to the hospital. The accident worried Nora.

Not because Michael was hurt, she knew he would heal but because school was going to be over in just a couple of weeks.

That meant Greta and Michael would be home alone—together. She was concerned about Greta's attitude toward her father, and she did not want that to grow with the two of them home alone together. She decided not to take her normal summer teaching job this year.

Michael would have limited mobility and would have to rely on Greta if she were the only one home. Greta's hair was growing in, but she had not changed her attitude when dealing with her father.

Since that haircut incident Greta repeatedly told her mother *"I do not want to ever get married-no man will ever control me! I will never have a husband!"*

Nora told her she would change her mind one day when the right man came along.

But she was a determined young girl.

The summer began quietly. Michael sat in the yard or on the porch most of the time. He really was not very demanding he was either reading or listening to the radio. He seemed lost in thought at times. This concerned Nora. Especially because she would often ask him about what he was thinking, and he would answer "just stuff nothing important." Michael still had nightmares and they were troubling her.

Michael insisted on Greta doing chores and following the suggested summer reading list. He would question her about some of the reading-but she was brief in her response.

Greta kept busy most of the time she was doing chores, reading, or out playing. If she had free time, she would call Betty or Lilly asking for them to pick her up. They always did and she would be with them for a while.

BOOK 11

Chapter 36

Explanations

The summer went well with the help of Lilly and Betty; until…one day right after the 4th of July, a man approached the porch where Michael was sitting.

It was not someone from the neighborhood or one of the men from the crew. Nora did not know who the man was, but Michael did. He said, *"Hello Michael."* Upon seeing the man Michael's face turned red, and he yelled: *"Get Out! Get away from my home-and out of my life. Did you hear me, Sergeant? Get Out!"*

Nora could not understand what else he said but she ran outside hearing Michael screaming and shouting.

"Who are you?" Nora asked as she saw the man. *"I am Sergeant Harris Ma'am I was Michael's Sergeant and Platoon Leader in Germany,"* the man said.

Michael could hardly stand but he said loudly *"Get out of here-get away from my house-out! Out I said! And do not come back Sergeant. The war is over. I am not under orders any longer."* Nora walked down the stairs of the porch toward Sergeant Harris.

"Why is my husband so upset with you Sergeant?" she asked. *"Miss being in a war is terrible. There are things some people must do, that they may have difficulty living with after the war is over.*

Your husband is a man I respect, and I believe he needs to talk with me." *"Why Sergeant? Did my husband do something wrong?"* Nora asked. *"No Ma`am he did nothing wrong. That said, I need to talk with Michael. There is something he needs to understand for himself to set the record straight. God brings me here Miss and tells me I need to do this whether Michael wants to hear it or not. Michael needs to understand."* Nora watched the Sergeant as he walked up the stair and said *"Michael, I am sorry that it happened—it was war. In war leaders need to make decisions. I did what I thought was right. Two men dead and you were in the same scenario. I had no choice but to give the order. God has been dealing with me for a long time telling me to come here and talk with you. That was not your fault Michael-it was mine. I made the decision. Michael, I lost two valuable men-I could not lose you. I made the call. It was my responsibility and job to save my men. I tell you again Michael—that it was not your fault! It was my call. War makes men and women change for many reasons. Are you listening Michael? Michael?"* and with that Michael began to cry.

Nora had never seen Michael cry like that and now he was sobbing uncontrollably. *"What happened out their Sergeant?"* Nora asked.

The Sergeant looked at Michael and turned to Nora. *"May I sit here"* he asked motioning to a chair on the porch. He began.

"When we landed in Germany-we were warned of Hitler's sympathizers. On our second day, four of my soldiers were on parole walking a street. Two were in front

and two in backup—a woman approached them with what appeared to be a baby in her arms; everyone wanted to help the people. We all knew how they were treated and what they went through in the camps. My first two men permitted her to approached them as she did, she said something in German. The men presumed she was asking for help for the child. The two back up soldiers were not as close to the woman as the first two men. When the woman got close to the first two soldiers —my men saw her pull out a gun and shoot the two soldiers.

The backup soldiers killed the woman. Hours later Michael and I were on parole. A woman began walking toward Michael-I was about fifteen feet behind Michael then a woman approached carrying a child. The picture of my two dead soldiers came into my head. I ordered Michael to shoot. He waited a few seconds. I yelled the second and then a third time —the lady was getting closer-I ordered him again to "shoot!" this time he fired.

He was ordered to shoot, and he followed orders. The woman dropped to the ground-she was dead. When Michael got close to the women there really was a baby in her arms- the bullet also went through the mother and the child they were both dead.

Michael screamed at me that "She did not have a weapon I listened to you! I killed a mother and her child!" He was angry and Michael has hated me from that moment on for making him kill the woman."

Michael screamed at me a couple of times, *"She did not have a weapon! It was a baby! A Baby! She might have been asking for help. Both are dead! I listened. I followed orders."* As the Sergeant spoke-Michael continued crying. *"This pain has been with Michael all these years since the war. He changed that day Miss-he tried to find out the lady's name, but no one knew. Michael became a totally different person that day. He did not joke with the guys, he wanted to go on his watches alone-without back-up. He barely spoke to me no matter how I tried. But now this is different. God has put it in my heart that Michael was still suffering and that I had to come."*

Nora understood what the Sergeant meant about the change in Michael's behavior. Everyone noticed something different in Michael after the war. He demanded obedience and the reason was now becoming clear. Nora told the Sergeant that Michael had been living with this alone—he never told anyone. She sensed the Sergeant and Michael needed to talk so she went in for some lemonade.

Two and a half hours later, the men were still on the porch talking. Nora told the Sergeant that this incident has left an indelible mark on Michael and created a change in his personality. She said that Michael never discussed the events of the war. Nora invited the Sergeant to join them for dinner and he agreed. After supper he played with Greta. When the Sergeant was preparing to leave, he said he would be back the next day. He felt that Michael needed to understand this situation better and then he left.

Before leaving Clayton, Sergeant Harris visited Michael three more afternoons. Each time the men talked for a couple of hours. Michael seemed to be feeling better after each visit. *"Something like this should have been talked out a long time ago"* the Sergeant told Nora *"But the army people did not understand that solders had a need to release all that bad stuff before leaving the army. They did not have enough people or systems in place to help them mentally. I have been thinking about that incident and Michael since the day it happened. He has been on my mind and a couple of months ago, God began working in me that I needed to come here in person and speak with Michael.*

Ma'am, please take care of him, I will write him- take care him. He is an exceptionally good man."

And, with that the Sergeant was gone. Michael was still dealing with somethings but after the Sergeant's visit he seemed feel a bit better. After the sergeant left, Nora was beginning to understand the kind of guilt Michael carried on his shoulders and dealt with-alone. She knew that talking was necessary to his healing.

Michael—needed to accept the change this incident created in him and understand the way it affected him and his family. Nora thought. **The army should be responsible as well but all they cared for was the physically wounded. It is too bad the people that sent theses boys to war did not understand that their heads, hearts, and emotions all went along with them.**

Five months later Michael had a terrible dream and woke up in a full body sweat it—frightening Nora. She thought:

What else could have happened in the war that would torment him to this point? Lord I –We need answers!

Michael was reluctant to talk about his dream and the war. But then he realized that after his visit with the sergeant he felt better. He decided to get it all out; and he trusted and loved her enough to expose all he had bottled up inside.

They sat at the kitchen table and over tea. Michael began:" *The two men that were killed were my friends. Since day one, we all trained together and fought together. One of the men Thomas saved my life. Shortly after we landed in Germany, he killed a sniper who would have hit me. I wrote letters to both of their families. They were married and each had one child.*"

Michael said, "*he just wanted to say the things-not necessarily in order but to get them out of his mind.*" Rita agreed.

"*As if the concentration camps were not bad enough there were many, thin dehydrated starving people. Some were deformed in the infirmary and smelled bad. They were happy we were there. They cried and tried to touch us—like proving we were real. Numbers were branded on people-like is done to animals.*

Those that touched an American soldier thank them for being there. We found clothes for some of the naked people and tried to clean them up-but they were afraid of the showers. We learned why-acid and gas was pumped into those showers to kill them in mass. The survivors of the camps told us they heard the screams. The smell near the ovens was terrible. There were some bodies still in the ovens about to be burned the smell takes a lot of time to get out of your nose.

Nora, I love you and I am sorry to tell you of these things. I see those showers in my dreams. I see me walking into one of the showers to clear out the bodies. That was not my job other troupes from other divisions did clean-outs of the barracks and showers. Our job was the medical center, the was the smell of those found in the medical center. They were mutilated used as guinea pigs for medical experiments. Many of us did not understand German and we were apprehensive as to what the people were saying. It was terrible what was done to them; cruel and sadistic. There was nothing we could do to help save a few of them. Michael was crying."

They talked for hours.

"There were Hitler sympathizers, lurking in buildings and shooting at us. We had to keep our eyes peeled everywhere and our ears open for sounds. We were frightened and apprehensive. A naked man grabbed my leg and would not let go. He was crying and kissing my

pants. Another soldier took him from me-he understood German. He gave the man some clothes and food. They had beautiful buildings half up and falling around us, we had to watch what we touched and where we walked. Nora, there were so many bodies, men women, children and babies. They suffered terribly and the survivors were so thin. The graves were heartbreaking –everyone piled on top of one another."

Nora understood; it was the observations, with the men as witness, of the reckless destruction of property and the seizing of humans, to eradicate an entire race. That changes men and it changed Michael. It was everything he held dear-home, family, people, dignity, and country. Those were experiences and events, of war.

Now Michael needed to understand and believe that HE was ONE of the liberators in the war. Michael needs to understand the kind of memorization that all the destruction and killing has on soldiers. Talking is necessary to healing and understanding how his experience in war has "affected" him. And now, how his "new" environment-of returning home from war- has been affected by that experience-it is germane to his healing.

Sometimes the shock of reality is necessary.

Nora patiently told Michael that the war had changed the way he was before he left. He came back a man demanding control: to the men on his crew; her, Greta, and the rest of the family. She mentioned how cutting Greta's hair now has given her a fear of him and of being controlled. She relayed Greta's statement that she *"never wants to marry."*

She mentioned incidents of his that identified a cavalier, controlling, demeaning attitude toward her and the things important to her. She explained how Michael behaved with the rest of the family at times.

Nora knew that healing for Michael would begin once he accepted the realities that war be-folds on men. She was determined to help him. She was confident his healing would begin now that she and the family knew what he was struggling with.

Michael—needs to accept, and understand, war tends to change personalities, visions, and feelings. He then needs to resolve, with faith and hope, that what took place since that fateful day (he shot the woman) has changed his personality, attitude, and taken from him the joy of life he once loved.

She was determined to help him she knew what his struggle.

That night, after Michael went to bed Nora called Kevin and relayed what happened in Germany. Kevin understood how this experience hurt Michael deeply and affected his attitude. Thinking and behavior with everyone. He said, *"Something like this should have been talked out a long time ago.*

The army must understand that solders need to come to grips with the effects of war if not our wonderful soldiers will suffer and so will all they encounter at home."

Talking and sharing with Nora created a deeper bond between them.

One afternoon while taking one of his medicinal walks Michael returned with Mathew Blitz in tow

Michael and Nora met Mathew at Roger Gray's picnic. "Guess who I bumped into?" he said to Rita.

"Mathew just returned from California. He and Catherine have a daughter-now Sarah is her name. They were on their way to Michigan where Mathew took a teaching position.

Chapter 37

Journals and Fear

Michael still had another week before he could return to work. Nora was pleased the summer went off without a problem between Greta and Michael. She felt his accident gave them all a chance to get closer.

The day after Labor Day school was in session and both girls enjoyed going to school. Shana and Carl now had developed a "tradition;" on the first day of school,

Carl would take Shana out for breakfast before school, and then drive her to school. It was a time for the two of them to continue bonding-Rita was never invited. That hurt Rita a lot; but she would never tell Carl. She felt as if Carl was sending a signal to Shana and to her "Mom isn't that important it's just you and me!" It is strange how some parents seem to "indoctrinate their children" on their feelings of the other parent or person, Children are very perceptive. They are sponges for learning. What a poor message both parents were sending Shana; Carl's for excluding Rita, and Rita for allowing this to happen on this special day repeatedly. Each parent has the right to be with their child alone; but not to make that privilege demean the other parent. Everyone needs to be respectful of the example they set.

Rita returned to teaching after the summer and was assigned to the seniors again. This would be a more difficult year. Many seniors had jobs with little time to study. Some would be applying for college-she needed to be sure they were all well prepared for their final exams. Senior year would be all regent exams for some. The successful results would be a great help in getting into the right college. The pressure was on the teacher as well as the student.

Betty loved sewing for the girls. One day while in the sewing room she found a lose board in the bench she was sitting on. She never thought about the board before but this day the jiggle of the board bothered her, and she got a wedge and lifted the seat. Inside hidden in the seat were several old journals. Upon viewing them, Betty learned they belonged to Mary Jo –Kevin's first wife. It was obvious Kevin had not found these journals in the past or he might have put them elsewhere or destroyed them. She began reading them and as she did the pages written by Mary Jo gave Betty more of a picture into Kevin and Mary Jo's marriage and life together. She decided to hide the journals once again and to not tell Kevin she found them. Betty decided to purchase additional journals and update the information for both Shana and Greta-one day. She told herself these updates would be her way of giving back to the next generation-an insight into their families. She would keep a secret and leave all the journals in the special place for the "someday-one day" finding.

Betty was feeling particularly good about this decision in fact it gave her some feeling of enhanced character-she had a secret to keep! Betty and Kevin did not join Lilly and George on their next vacation. Betty was tired of trips for a while.

Lilly was especially anxious for their next trip. George heard of a place in California-called Palm Springs. The brochure outlined that in October the hotel would be most affordable. George suggested they could take a week to drive there seeing the sites along the way. Lilly was the researcher and navigator. She kept everything neatly organized in a three-ring binder. George was proud her. They were compatible in the fullest sense of the word they accepted each other's diversities and their similarities. The two had become one.

Kevin had decided that while George and Lilly were away it was not time for him to slack off on the job. He lined up several some small jobs he felt would be no problem. Michael was back to work and able to handle not just one but two crews. Betty just wanted to sew and enjoy the girls.

In November she designed special Thanksgiving outfits of a beige and yellow dress with copper accents and a copper coat for the girls. The colors were perfect for fall. To "pull it off" she needed the right kind of material. There was an advertised sale in the paper. She took the bus to the store and found the perfect material at a fifty percent discount. Betty was sure her design and the colors would be a hit.

Chapter 38

Fear

Betty caught the bus home arriving around 4:30PM her shopping was a success. Getting off the bus, she noticed a strange man standing across the street from her house looking directly at the house.

The man was pacing back and for then touching his head and putting his hands in his pockets.

Kevin was not home and for some reason Betty did not want to go toward the house. She watched for a few minutes as the man continued pacing back and forth while looking directly at the house.

Betty decided to try and see if Mrs. Miller was at home. She walked to her house and knocked on the door. There was no answer. As Betty moved toward the end of the porch, she glanced toward the young man. He was looking right at her and had a strange look on his face. Betty was not normally a nervous woman-but there was something about this person that gave her an uneasy feeling.

Just as she turned on to the sidewalk in front of Mrs. Miller's, Kevin drove up. He pulled up next to her and rolled down the window: "*Lift little Lady?*" Betty was very relieved.

She got in and asked Kevin not to stop at their house. She told him to drive by and watch the man.

The man must have seen Betty get into Kevin's car. He turned and started to walk down another street. Kevin decided to follow him and as soon as he turned the car the man began to run.

Kevin drove quickly but the man ducked into a yard and was gone. Betty felt sure it was the man that raped Rita. This changed everything because until he was caught Betty felt she was at risk in the house.

They called the police and Officer Brown came to the house to talk with Betty.

After he left Betty called Rita. Betty explained what she saw and what happened when Kevin tried to follow him.

Rita then asked Betty *"if the man was wearing a beige colored coat and if his hands were in his pocket."* *"Yes"* said Betty. *"I am pretty sure that was him."* The men decided the man must live near the house or have someone he knows living in this neighborhood.

Betty and Kevin stayed with Lilly and George that weekend. Betty told Kevin she felt uncomfortable living there until the man was caught. Kevin understood.

George's apartment was to be vacant the first of March-it was not as nice as Kevin's house-but it was far enough away to be safe. They would move into the apartment and sell the house-if the man was not caught by the New Year.

They stayed with them until a week before Thanksgiving when Betty decided she needed to finish the clothes for the girls.

She and Kevin returned to the house and Betty kept the door locked during the day while Kevin was at work. She was literally confined to the house until Kevin returned.

Thanksgiving Dinner was still to be at Kevin and Betty's house. All the ladies would be arriving early to help. Rita and Shana arrived first then Nora and Greta arrived. The two girls wanted to play in the yard. Kevin had the "G-Men" rake the leaves the day before. Two girls from the neighborhood Judy Veda who was not quite eight years old and Mrs. Miller's granddaughter and Donna Louis who was nine years old came over to play.

Kevin told the girls not to leave the yard. Everyone was busy helping decorate the table and getting the dinner ready. Carl and George arrived after picking up some bread from the bakers. About a half hour after the girls went outside to play Shana came in screaming.

"Mama mama…" she cried. *"I listened, I listened"* she was hysterical. *"What-what? What do you mean you listened? Shana honey, please talk to Ma-ma what is the matter?"*

Rita said as she tried to calm down Shana to understand what happened. Hearing Shana cry Betty and Lilly ran outside with George and Kevin on their heels to see the other girls. When the door opened, they saw Judy on the ground she had blood all over the front of her clothes.

Lilly was screaming for Greta and Donna- Betty ran in the house for Carl who was in the bathroom. Pounding on the bathroom door Betty yelled, "Carl come quick Judy is hurt she has blood all over the front of her clothes."

Carl ran outside. The other girls were not in the yard.

Kevin began calling them frantically. Then, suddenly, he heard crying –the girls were hiding in the back of the garage-too frightened to move.

George went into the house to call the police and Mrs. Miller's daughter Karen.

Carl approached Judy she was on the ground very still with blood on the front of her clothes. The child was Stunned -unable to talk and then passed out. Karen and Mrs. Miller ran into the yard. Karen screamed when she saw Judy on the ground and the blood on her clothes *"Oh no! No!"* Carl was checking Judy's vital signs.

Carl spoke quietly, "Hello Judy, you remember me I am Dr. Carl. I am checking your pulse and soon I will pick you up and take you to the hospital, He whispered to Rita *"she is still alive.* "He began searching for the wound. Karen was screaming *"Judy-Judy—who did this—who would do this."*

A police car was there in minutes.it was Officer Brown, Carl said, *"no time to wait for the ambulance-I am a doctor let's go."* and with that—Carl lifted Judy into the police car. He told Rita to get in with them, and then they were off siren blasting. *"Thank God, Carl was here,"* said Betty. *"Come on Karen, I will drive you to the hospital."*

Judy and Karen's four-month-old son Philip were visiting Karen's mother alone this Thanksgiving. Karen's husband Steve had just gotten over a bad flu; he was still weak and stayed at home. Karen called him, told him what happened. They picked him up on their way to the Hospital Emergency Room.

Betty, Michael and Kevin were all in the emergency room waiting area with Karen. Lilly and George stayed back at the house with Nora and the girls trying to calm the children.

The first officer had no time to talk to the girls; he radioed dispatch asking them to send someone to the house to speak with the children.

Carl went directly into an examining room with Judy; Rita helped him remove her clothes. Carl told Rita it was a knife wound. Then Rita went into the waiting room looking for the others. Everyone waited about 30 minutes; then Carl came out of the examining room. He said *"Judy will be fine-she was on her way to surgery. The knife did not hit any major artery."* Karen screamed, *"Knife! Why would anyone want to knife a child?"* She was very distraught. Carl ordered a mild sedative for her.

"Look Karen this surgery will take a couple of hours she is going to fully recover-she will need you to be calm." Everyone stayed until Judy was out of surgery. Karen and her husband stayed at the hospital all night.

Meanwhile, Officer McKenna was at the house and wanted to talk with three girls: Shana, Greta and Donna. Nora stayed in the room as he questioned each child.

Greta said *"A tall man came in the yard and we were playing in the leaves-he stood there a minute and looked at us. Then, he looked directly at Judy. He told her "to come to him" and as she did. The man then hurt her-and blood came from her. Donna and I ran-he did not come to us"*

The officer asked the girls if the man said anything to them. *"Yes"* said Greta-he said, *"He was sorry, but it had to stop and then he ran away."* The officer asked what the man was wearing. Greta said, *"He had on a light color jacket and when he came in the yard his hands were in his pocket-he was tall and big."*

Donna agreed with the description from Greta and everything she said. Nora called Kay Louis and she listened to the account of the attack. Donna was still shaking and crying when her mother walked in. The Louis's were visiting from No. Carolina. Mrs. Louis was Mrs. Wrigley's niece. She gave the officer her name, their address in No Carolina and Mrs. Wrigley's telephone number. She gave Donna a hug and motioned for her to sit near her. *"Who would want to hurt children?"* said Kay. Officer McKenna remarked *"I just do not know. But I promise we will find him—somehow."* The officer asked if any of the children remembered something else to call him. Now more than ever Betty wanted out of that house. She was not going to spend even one more night there. They all waited until Judy was out of surgery and when they returned, they gathered all the food and things they might need and left the house and went to stay at Michael's.

Chapter 39

Moving

Judy was back with her family in a week. She talked about the fact that—the man said to her "*this must stop now and then he put something into her chest and blood came out.*"

It made no sense to anyone. The doctor said that in a month the child would be fine, but she needed to be careful for a while-especially until the stitches were out.

With the stabbing fresh in her mind-Betty decided they needed to sell the house Kevin and Michael agreed. Christmas was a short time away and Betty could not see being in that house any longer let alone doing anything there for a holiday. Michael insisted they stay with them until they could find another place. So, furniture still inside their house—Kevin and Michael closed the house. They took more personal things out and went to stay with Michael. Kevin called a real estate man, and he came to list the house. He put a "FOR SALE" sign on the front of the house. He was a nice man. He told Kevin what he thought the house would sell for. Kevin was shocked-it was $23,000 more he had figured.

The agent was concerned about the winter. He suggested the heat and water stay on. Kevin and Betty liked the salesman and they told him what they were looking for in another house. He said he would keep and "eye out."

He asked them where they would to be. They both wanted to stay near everyone.

Betty said she loved quaint little houses. But this time they for sure wanted a house with a fireplace. The salesman told them of a house that was just vacated as the owners were transferred. It ended up around the corner from George and Lilly's house. It was a great neighborhood, so they all decided just "**to look at it**." The appointment was made for that Saturday. The agent said he thought the company would let them move in until their house was sold if they were under contract. When they arrived at the house it was smaller than Kevin's house, but this house had an over-sized wood burning fireplace, a shed with a work area and electricity, as well as a garage, full basement and room for - four bedrooms. The bus stop was right in front of the house. The first floor had a kitchen, a small dining room, a bath and two small bedrooms. The house had style. To the side of the dining room were nine stairs leading to a second floor with a huge un-finished attic that went across the entire house. The second-floor ceiling was eight feet-so no dormer was needed. Kevin decided that he and George could make that attic into two bedrooms and even put a bathroom up there between the two rooms. George talked about opening the dining room to the kitchen. Betty wanted the two bedrooms in the downstairs to be made into one large bedroom and the bath to have an adjoining door from the bedroom.

When the agent told them the asking price, Kevin and Betty looked at each other with amazement. Not only was it a perfect location-but the asking price was $8,000 less than they were asking for Kevin's house.

The agent suggested they could "*put in an offer.*" He stated that the current owner's company was paying the real estate commission-and it was winter-their company might take less not to hold the house through the snow season. "*These were all things in favor of a buyer*" the agent said. Kevin and Betty did not want to wait another minute. They went back to the agent's office and put in an offer that evening for $5,000 less than the asking price. That was the amount Kevin felt would be the cost of the improvements to the house if a new owner were to hire it being done. As of right now it was just a small two bedroom expandable. The offer called for a closing in four weeks with permission to begin the renovation immediately. Two days later their offer was accepted. Kevin and Betty were greatly relieved. Their plan was to do the work and move in by the first of February.

The day after Christmas, with the permission given, Kevin, Michael and George went over to the house to begin work. They began at six am and in one day they had the walls between the two bedrooms down, the wall between the hallway and the kitchen removed and finally the wall between the kitchen and the dining room taken out.

Everything was supported and wow did that place look different and nice. Betty decided that the floor in the kitchen and bath needed to be changed to the new Armstrong style shown on television. When the rugs were removed in the living room and bedrooms downstairs, they found hard wood floors underneath the carpet.

Kevin took the wood floor from the floors they opened and was with a little creativeness was able to make it work for the area between the bedrooms where the wall was down.

Now the dining room was gone since it opened to the hall-the men were cutting walls to make a large beautiful bar in kitchen with a full dining area. It was beautiful.

The kitchen cabinets had wallpaper or shelf paper in the center. Michael took one door off and when he took the paper off-when he began, he noticed that the doors were cathedral style made of Burch wood. *It would be nothing to take these down to the natural wood and stain them in walnut or cherry"* he said.

They all agreed on him doing that and Betty wanted the stain to be walnut. It took him six days to have them all stripped and sanded. George wanted to stain them and put the finish on himself. Three days later the floor in the kitchen and bath was installed. It was an Armstrong cushion tone one –just like advertised on the new television that Kevin bought Betty for Christmas. Betty loved the floor it looked like a beautiful marble. Kevin worked on finishing the downstairs while Michael and-George brought the heat and water to the second floor. Their new house closed on January 30th. Betty and Kevin moved almost everything from their old house into their new place. What did not fit went into the basement. They did not mind that work on the upstairs would not be ready for another month. There was going to be two bedrooms and a bathroom upstairs. It would be perfect for when the girls stayed over. Betty and Kevin's bedroom was a dream with a large window and window seat facing the rear yard and a door was put in to open to the outside. Eventually there would be built a small terrace just for the two of them facing the yard-for their private nights. The company patio would be built behind the living room. George's idea was that he would open the current fireplace to the back yard and put a steel divider from the rear of the fireplace giving them a fireplace in the back yard for late evenings.

Everything in the house was new and beautiful. Their first night there they lit a fire in the fireplace and sat near it just hugging and kissing each other so much in love with each other and with their new home.

February 22nd. became their lucky day that was the day an offer to purchase their old house came in. Two brothers who put in the offer worked construction they were from Rochester the offer was cash and for the full asking price. It was immediately accepted. When the men met Kevin and George, they all liked each other. Both brothers were looking for work. After they helped George with a couple of projects, they joined the company.

It was a great match all around. John and Charlie Winston were in their forty's. Charlie was the oldest at forty-three years old, divorced with two children living in Rochester with their mother. John was forty-one years old- never married -lived with his mother until her death a year ago.

Charlie's wife had an affair and Charlie caught them. He filed for divorce and left. Charlie's divorce happened about the time their mother died. The two brothers decided to live together. John sold the house he and their mother were living in. He used that money to purchase Kevin's house without a mortgage. Charlie's children were about to finished high school, and each drove a car. They would be able to see him whenever they wanted. In fact, young Charlie might even live with them one day. His daughter Charlotte was thinking of coming to Clayton for grad school except she had a boyfriend and his family, had their business in Rochester.

There was a man the men knew and worked with in Rochester named Marcus Banes. Marcus moved to Clayton when he married Darlene a year earlier. The men kept in touch. Marcus saw John at his mother's wake and mentioned there was a house for sale only five minutes from his new place. The joke for him was that if the brothers moved there the men could continue their Friday night poker game. He mentioned that according to all accounts the house was *"haunted"*

John and Charlie's decision to move was predicated on the idea of **a new beginning.** The brothers thought that a "haunted house" sounded like an intriguing place to begin.

Things changed when they saw the house and later when they were friendly with Kevin and George. Living in the house, they want to make something it theirs. The brothers decided to change some things. John was an electrical engineer. He loved to design new things. He found a way to hide a buzzer under the porch. In this way as soon as someone stepped on a stair a bell would ring in the house. He did that same thing with the back entrance with a different bell ring for each entrance. He called it an "alarm system." He then wired the two front porch windows and the doors. They each had a different kind of a buzzer. John said, this would identify if there was a break in where it was coming from—giving them a heads up. Betty, Lilly, and Nora loved the system. They asked him to install a similar system at their houses. John promised to and he did that for each of them in no time.

The alarm system worked great. John was developing new ideas for this alarm system all the time and, he had another system designed for and homeowner interested.

Betty and Lilly's houses were in walking distance to each other, and the ladies got along like sisters. Kevin and George were very close-not just like business partners but like brothers.

The foursome had their Thursday night scrabble and there Monday monopoly games. They alternated houses just to keep things lively. Kevin and Georges business was growing leaps and bounds. Michael hired a few more men to help with the number of jobs they were landing.

The boys in the "G- man" group were getting older, and George felt comfortable turning over the kid's business to one of the boys-in the group. Everyone was settling into their roles.

Chapter 40

It All Becomes Clear

Two days before Easter, Kevin asked the ladies about taking a trip to Canada. The men wanted to see all the excitement near Niagara Falls. They read in "The Town Cryer" all about a "fright house" that opened there for kids. The ladies did not want to travel to Canada-specially to see a fright house and not with the little girls. They were not going to let the girls go there with them for fear of nightmares while the men were acting like little boys.

Nora, Rita, Lilly and Betty needed to bake their pies, color Easter eggs and decide on what the Easter Bunny had in mind to include in a basket. The men decided to go by themselves. They told the ladies not to worry about getting supper for them they would stop. The men left after breakfast and expected to be home around seven pm. Michael decided to go with them. Carl was on duty at the hospital and could not go. Shana and Greta were learning how to make cookies, Easter Bread and coloring Easter eggs.

Midafternoon the telephone rang. It was Officer McKenna *"I wonder if I could stop over, I would like to ask a few questions-may I drop by?"* *"Sure"* said Betty *"I will put on the coffee you will be just in time the first batch of Easter bread and cookies coming out of the oven."*

When the officer arrived, he saw Rita, Nora Lilly and Betty. He asked to speak with Rita and Betty. Lilly stayed with the girls.

"Do you think-either of you-would recognize the man that you each saw?" Neither of the ladies saw enough of the man enough to pick him out of a picture. And they thought it was the same man that hurt both Judy and Rita. Neither woman said they could give a sold identification of the man.

The girls were listening to the policeman they ran into the kitchen Greta said, *"I know what the man's face looked like do you have some pictures for me to look at?"* Nora said Greta had been watching television and saw that policemen showed pictures of suspects. Shana was not far behind her and she said she saw the man's face as well. The girls wanted to help.

The office asked if the mothers would allow him to show the girls three pictures of suspects. They agreed. The officer asked if he could show the pictures to each girl separately. The mothers agreed, Rita took Shana out of the room.

Moments later Officer McKenna pulled out three different pictures of suspects and put the pictures on the table. Greta was first; the officer told her to touch the picture she thought was the man *"That is the man I remember him"* she said.

Shana was then brought into the kitchen; Greta was taken to a different part of the house.

Shana looked at the pictures and said, *"That is him-that is the man that hurt Judy."* Both made a positive identification of Dell Frig.

Then the officer asked for the children to be both in the kitchen. He assured the ladies and the children that the man would not be hurting anyone any longer. That man was dead. His name was Dell Frig.

The girls were happy and decided to return to their room on the second floor and play. The officer told the women that the man was thirty-eight years old and let out of a mental hospital about the time Rita was hurt. He did not use the word "rape" out of respect. He continued *"Frig was supposed to be taking a drug called lithium to help him control his bi-polar problem. Yesterday, in the home he was staying at since he came out of the mental hospital, he killed himself and the owners called the police. The* man was dead. There were all kinds of notes and letters. In one of the notes, he said he wanted forgiveness for hurting the little girl.

He wrote that he *"had a fear that she might have been a child from when he did something bad."* The note said he *"did not want her to suffer like he had with the illness she might have gotten from him."*

Shock and emotional relief rang out among the women. Rita's primary concern was *"what affect this situation could have on all four of the girls as they grew up."*

That is when Lilly asked to see the photo; she repeated the man's name out loud- and after a moment, she said, *"Officer has anyone else seen this photo?" "No why?"* Lilly was apprehensive,

"Well, you see-I think this man used to live on Rita's street—when he was a teenager. His father was married to Mrs. Miller many years ago. In fact, the boy was one of her reasons for divorce. The father did not want to put the boy in a home.

"What a small world" the officer said. *"No wonder he was in the neighborhood-but why the rape?"*

Lilly hesitated, "I think it had to do with Rita's mother Mary Jo. This was talked about after the wake for Mary Jo. A lady said that she was kind to a strange child and even invited him into the house giving him milk and cookies. She did this mostly when Michael and Rita were in school. Then one day, she stopped. It made the boy incredibly angry.

Mary Jo thought the boy stole something from the house. But he refused to admit it or return it. The boy was terribly upset when Mary Jo would not let him visit her anymore."

Rita "Do you remember him the young boy with the funny nose? "Robert, the boy's father hit him when he was young, and the boy's nose was always moved to one side. He was laughed at all the time in school and Robert refused to have that nose fixed"

"Yes" Rita said "I do remember a boy at the house with Mom-I only saw him once or twice. "Could that be the same person-that raped me?" Lilly continued

"Since Mary Jo only let him come at certain times. She did not want you kids involved as the boy had a bad temper. After the item was stolen Mary Jo would not even talk with the kid. The lady telling the story said that Mary Jo's cancer progressed rapidly about that time. Mary Jo was hospitalized many times. The boy would sit on your porch crying trying the door a few times looking for Mary Jo. You and Michael were in school and Kevin at work. Mary Jo died shortly thereafter and Mr. Frig, and Mrs. Miller divorced."

Lilly said, "I wonder what he stole?" Officer McKenna said, "I think I know, when they found him dead this picture was in his pocket." and with that he handed the picture to Rita. "This is a picture of me and my mother." Rita said. Lilly continued "Mrs. Miller divorced Robert Frig when Dell was about thirteen years *old. They had been married about three years when Dell began hitting Mrs. Miller; then the father became very abusive to now Mrs. Miller—l Karen's mother. The father refused to even let a councilor see the boy. Robert Frig died two years after their divorce. His car was someplace on South Avenue; the paper said he had a massive Heart attack on his way to work. When he died the boy's, mother put him in an institution another sad story."*

Officer McKenna replied *"I am afraid that the story is not over yet. I still must talk with Judy's mom— Karen. She must have been just five or seven years old when Robert married her mother."* Lilly Said *"Karen's real father died when she was an infant, another horrible story. Karen's father was at work at the Steel Plant. He had been working extra shifts to pay for the things for the baby. One day while leaving his apartment he slipped and fell on the ice he hit his head on something. At the hospital he received twenty stitches. He went to work that day; but came home just a few hours later, saying he was tired. He lay down on the bed and died. It was devastating. At the time Mrs. Miller was just nineteen years old and the baby was due in less than a month. She stayed single until Karen was five years old and then married Robert Frig. After they divorced, she married her divorce lawyer- Mitchell Miller."*

The officer left, he said he would call and go over to Mrs. Miller's on the Monday after Easter and talk with them.

When the men returned from Canada that evening and heard the story about Dell Frig, they were astounded. Michael asked Kevin if he remembered mentioning many years ago there was a man on the porch at Mrs. Miller's. At the time Kevin and Michael presumed was Mrs. Miller's husband.

Michael continued *"One day after Mom died, the man stopped him as he was coming home from school. He told me he was sorry to hear about my mother's death."* Michael said he never saw the man after that day. *"Well, it is all over now-we will definitely have a celebration this year"* Kevin said.

Chapter 44

John Fitzgerald Kennedy

John Fitzgerald Kennedy was elected as President of the United States. John, a Catholic married to Jackie Kennedy. They had a beautiful daughter named Caroline and a son John.

This was a "Camelot" romance for the country and the world was enjoying the young family in the White House. Every move they made, or event hosted was highly published. Dignitaries from all over the world admired the young family.

Mrs. Kennedy became a fashion icon with her pill box hats and three strand pearl necklace. She spoke a couple of languages and shortly after the election became pregnant. The wife of the President of the United State was going to give birth while living in the white house! Now, the whole world waited with excitement for the birth of their child.

August 1963, headlines identified Mrs. Kennedy was rushed to the hospital. Her husband flew to be at her side, but he missed the birth of their son, Patrick. The child was premature and unfortunately passed away. A physically weak and distraught Mrs. Kennedy retreats from the public view to gain her emotional and physical strength.

Greta is now twelve years old, and Shana is nine years old. The girls are more than merely cousins-they are best friends and as close as sisters. Neither child had a sibling of their own to play with, so they considered each other as siblings.

Rita and Nora continued teaching. George and Kevin were enjoying the success of their firm. Kevin added a new group of finish carpenters. Michael's crews doubled in size. John was foreman of two crews of his own and had developed a great alarm system. Charles was working on a monitoring system for John's alarms. All things for everyone were great.

Philip Cooper was once one of the G-Men; now in his first year of college. He still loved George and Kevin.

Phil kept a crew of young boys working for him still calling them the "G-men."

Greta and her father had a sort of love-distant relationship these days as Michael was very demanding of her obedience. Greta had many chores, little time for television or friends. Michael wanted her to be with her mother or family most of the time-no time frivolity or friends. Shana loved having Greta as her best friend and referring to her as her "Big Sister."

Unbeknown to anyone, Rita and Carl were having issues. Carl was frustrated feeling there was not enough opportunity or money for him in Clayton for his burn theories and research. While he enjoyed the family, he felt passionately about his research. To Carl—Rita appeared to have no interest in his theories or research. Carl's days became humdrum as he felt unable to discuss and fulfill his dreams.

Carl had a feeling his ideas about burn creams would be a success, but he needed a bigger lab and more funds for research. Without telling Rita, he began sending out resumes and letters to different hospitals around the country to see what was available. It took a while, but Carl's field was dermatology with research on Burns; it was a highly sought-after field.

In less than a month Carl received a call from a Dr. Ross at a Hospital in Chicago, Illinois. Dr. Ross requested a personal interview and suggested Carl come to Chicago on the twentieth of November, all expenses paid. Carl accepted telling Rita it was a business trip. Carl landed at O'Hare Airport and took a Shuttle to downtown Chicago. The hospital was putting him up at the Edison Plaza Hotel located on Chicago's magnificent mile.

Carl met with Drs. Ross, Mathew's, Field's, Weiss, and Ms. Powers from Personnel on November 21, 1963, at 10 AM.

The interview lasted six hours. They took him to lunch and discussed the current technology along with the surgery ideas for burn patients. Carl discussed his theories and his research. He also stated that with the creams his research was developing there would be better results even in surgery. The response was terrific. This was exactly what Carl hoped for and it excited him. He wanted this position and was going to get it.

Carl returned to the hotel about 4:30 PM exhausted, elated and excited thinking **"This has to be it. They followed the whole idea and were excited for me to continue my research at their hospital"**

He laid down on the bed to think and fell asleep. At 6:45 PM a call came to the room. It was Ms. Powers inviting him to dinner. He accepted. She met him in the lobby and suggested they go to the hotel restaurant-it was well known.

Carl wanted a steak and to see more of Chicago. On the plane Carl read about a steak place called George Diamond's. Ms. Powers agreed to take him there for dinner.

They took a cab and Ms. Powers asked the driver to give them a bird's eye view tour of downtown Chicago. He drove down Oak and State Streets and passed the Marina Towers.

When they reached George Diamonds Carl ordered an *"eighteen-ounce rib eye man cut with baked potato and corn on the cob"* he was starved, Ms. Powers had a *"six-ounce Ladies cut rib eye with a small dinner salad."* Their conversation was directed to the workings of the Hospital. Carl could not help but notice Ms. Powers was an attractive blond.

She was about five feet four inches tall with curly blond hair and quite petite. She wore a navy and blue business jacket and navy skirt with a blouse that sort of tied to the left hip and crossed in front. She had a necklace of blue and gold beads and gold earrings. She did not wear a wedding ring. During dinner Carl asked if her if he was to continue calling her Ms. Powers. She laughed and said, *"No call me Margaret." "Well Margaret or does anyone call you Maggie?"* he asked and before she could answer he continued *"Are you married?"*

Margaret Powers did not like having the tables turned on her with all kinds of personal questions. She rarely answered questions about her life but hesitantly she said *"I am a widow, and no one calls me Maggie. I have a four-year-old son named Joseph."*

"I am sorry about your husband Margaret" Carl said. Margaret immediately said: *"Let's get back to why*

we are having dinner; you are leaving in the morning and there is much to discuss. I have been requested to make you an offer."

Carl was stunned as she said: *"I am requested to offer you the chairman's position, all moving expenses, and a stipend for Rita"* When she said the salary it was a terrific increase from his current salary—Carl almost choked!

Margaret continued: "This offer gives you p*aid commission on the sale of your residence, and a full moving package with an-allowance that includes packing and unpacking. There is a stipend for Rita since she is currently employed until she locates a suitable teaching position. The stipend would be equal to six months of her current salary. We will aid in your finding a house in Chicago along with helping Rita locate a position."*

Carl was stunned the salary represented a twenty-five percent increase over what he was currently earning in Clayton.

As a bonus there was an opportunity to publish and teach at the University of Chicago as an adjunct.

On November 22, 1963 at noon Carl was on a plane back to Clayton. This position was a great opportunity. Carl was deep in thought when the pilot interrupted, he announced that the President of the United States- John Fitzgerald Kennedy had been shot in Dallas.

When the plane landed Rita was at the airport to pick him up in tears. The President of the United Stated-Kennedy was dead. Everyone was wrapped up in the emotions for the President, his wife and his family.

Carl wanted to talk to Rita about his offer and he did not want to wait. It was not an easy discussion since he had never mentioned to Rita he was looking or wanted another job.

Rita, and half the world, was caught up in the funeral of President Kennedy and the installation of Mr. Johnson as president. Carl decided to wait before talking with Rita until later in the day when she calmed down.

Chapter 42

Planning

Later that day, Carl tried again to tell Rita all about his trip and the appointment at the hospital along with his fabulous offer—she was not in the mood. She felt this idea of moving and his dissatisfaction with his group was just to quickly sprung on her. She told Carl he should have *"discussed this issue with his medical group and her prior to sending out resumes and going for an interview."* **Privately she felt that sneaky.**

She remarked that there were *"Other groups in Clayton he could and should have tried first before uprooting the family. He knew Clayton-was her home-and her family all lived there.*" None of that carried any weight with Carl. Everything about the offer was fabulous. It truly was the best he could ever have hoped for, and it would never have come in Clayton.

Carl was quite upset with her attitude, saying she "Was selfish and inconsiderate of him. This was his career, everything he had struggled, worked for and tried to discuss with her from the beginning." He promised to put it off until later giving her time to think about the move and what it would mean to his career and their family.

Carl's mind was made up he was going to take the offer. Rita began discussing Carl's trip and his offer-with Lilly. Carl spoke to Kevin about the terms of the offer and that "He did not want to turn down the "*Opportunity of a lifetime.*" Carl was not going to let this opportunity pass him by. Two days later he went to the hospital and faxed an acceptance of the offer to Margaret Powers. He agreed to begin work February fifteenth. He reasoned that if he gave Rita the Christmas holidays, she would agree to move.

The hospital agreed to fly them into Chicago four times so they could work with a Real Estate Agent and purchase a house. Ms. Powers asked Carl to notify her when they chose their dates. Carl said nothing about the position for three days, giving Rita time to adjust. Meanwhile he was on the telephone with Margaret Powers two to three times a day. He learned they liked the same music; and they had seen some of the same shows. Margaret lived with her father as well as her son.

On November 28th, Carl approached Rita again about the move. Despite not wanting to move, she agreed to go with Carl to Chicago and look around. Carl arranged the trip for December third preparing to be there four days. Lilly agreed to take care of Shana.

Carl felt sure that Rita would fall in love with Chicago. He called the Real Estate agent and asked him for an opinion as to what Rita's house would sell for. He dropped off a key before they left without telling Rita his plan.

Rita thought this trip more like the honeymoon they never had when they married. She felt this was her chance to talk with him alone. Rita had never been on an airplane before and loved the plane ride.

The hospital had a limo waiting at the airport to take them to the Edison Plaza Hotel. The hotel was just the most beautiful place Rita had even seen. She commented "it was like something you would see in a magazine or movie." Carl said *"Wait until you really get to see some things. Hurry and get settled I want to show you around. There is Michigan Avenue, State Street, Lakeshore Drive and more-more —more! Chicago is just a great place— let's get going I want to show it to you!"*

They left the hotel and Carl hailed a cab. He asked the driver *to "Hit the spots" go down Michigan Avenue, then hit Oak and State Streets so I could show my bride how great it is- in Chicago."* Rita did not think this was going to be necessary they were only going to be in Chicago four days. Still Carl insisted and they drove around for an hour at least.

Finally, Carl showed her the hospital and the lab where he would be working. It was vastly different from the facilities in his group, extremely modern and advanced with all the latest equipment. Rita felt Carl's mind was made up and she sensed he was pushing her to move. She also realized that this was something he really needed to be successful with his theories.

They returned to the hotel when Carl mentioned that *"Ms. Powers would be meeting them for a late lunch."* Rita asked Carl *"Why?"* Carl answered, *"She has arranged a few places for us to look with the real estate person the hospital uses."* Rita had no idea they were going to look at houses. She tried to discuss her feelings, but Carl said, *"Please Humor me."* They looked at houses in suburbs of LaGrange Park, Oak Brook, and Lake Zurich.

Rita said it *"seems silly for people to take a train everywhere let alone travel so much to get to work. Were there no houses near or in the city's downtown?"* She really was not interested in purchasing a house in Chicago she was just commentating because taking trains everywhere seemed a waste of time. The agent identified that there was a house on Oak Street-that was close everything and off the "Magnificent Mile." It needed work-but there was a fenced yard and four bedrooms. He said most people living on the "Magnificent Mile" in Chicago did not need a car it was so convenient to everything by cab or bus.

Ms. Powers called the agent about the Oak Street house. They had an appointment to see it at ten am the next morning. Late evening Carl took Rita to George Diamond's for dinner, the city was all lit up and beautiful as they drove to the restaurant. They had coffee and dessert in the hotel. They were both tired and when they were back in the room Carl thanked Rita for her patience and understanding and then fell asleep. Rita saw the righting on the wall-but how this was all handled was still giving her problems.

Ms. Powers met them for breakfast, another surprise for Rita. After breakfast they went to see the house on Oak Street. It was close to the curb unlike houses in Clayton and narrow with big, long rooms. On the first floor, there was a room that would make a great office; there was also a rear sitting room, a large kitchen with a huge dining room and living room.

Upstairs were four-bedroom rooms; master bedroom with full a bath, one bath in the hall between two of the bedrooms. The last bedroom had a half bath inside-it was used as the owner's painting room. There were four large windows in that-making it a bright room and a triple closet. The basement was finished with a place for a television, a built-in stereo system was in the wall. The lot was fenced and there was security system. Carl was only blocks from the hospital; he could walk.

In front of Ms. Powers and the Real Estate Agent- Carl said, *"Without having to own a car they would save money."* The agent said the school bus would pick up Shana at the door and return her right there. Carl pushed Rita *"I love it-It would be easy to get to work and you would walk for shopping there are terrific stores and restaurants on Michigan Avenue-it is perfect! Let's buy it?"* Rita had not reconciled with even the idea of moving. Rita kept silent.

Carl kept talking about the house. Ms. Powers said she would call them later to see how they felt about the house.

When they returned to the hotel Carl asked Rita if she liked anything about the house. Rita replied that there were some things she liked but she felt rushed. Carl asked, *"Would you like being so close to a fantastic shopping area?"* she said *"Yes, but Carl we have many things to discuss regarding this move. Ok Carl said, "could we have an early lunch and put this aside for a few hours. We have tickets for an afternoon show-and I would like us to go. Ok? Rita agreed. After the show they returned to the hotel. Carl wanted to talk about the house and the move.* He said, *"I think it is perfect and I feel we should buy it before we lose the chance."* Rita tried to continue discussing the idea of leaving her family and Carl's handling of this move when the telephone rang.

It was Ms. Powers she was there to take them to dinner. Rita did not want to discuss her personal feelings in front of either the agent or Ms. Powers. She was torn about moving and she felt pushed. She recognized this was a great opportunity for Carl, but communication in their marriage was changing-she was seeing a side of Carl that concerned her. She was still thinking about their marriage and Carl's way of going about getting this job offer when Ms. Powers arrived.

While Rita was talking at the table with Ms. Powers about her teaching position; Carl left the dinner table and called the real estate agent "We would like to submit an offer," he said. When he returned Carl said nothing about his call. Ms. Powers identified that the Oak Street location was an extra special opportunity because the owners had already moved to another state.

After dinner while waiting for coffee and ice cream; the Real Estate Agent came to the table. He had the purchase offer for the house with him and he needed Rita's and Carl's signatures. Carl announced he had called the agent and asked him to bring the papers over. He signed the papers and then asked Rita to sign allowing him this opportunity.

Rita felt trapped, with Ms. Powers sitting across from her, and the agent in the chair next to Carl. Carl was handing her the pen; the contract was on the table. They were all waiting for her to sign. Two cups of coffee later she signed the offer. The contract was for $7,500 less than his asking price. There was work to be done on the property it also asked for early occupancy for repairs. Rita signed the contract.

Rita had enjoyed the steak at George Diamonds. She did not like the way things were manipulated by Carl. Dinner over and back at the hotel; Rita confronted Carl. She spoke about his behavior, presumptions, the way he went along soliciting a new position and his not considering her and her family in this move. As they were talking the agent called their room and told Carl *"They now owned a home in Chicago!"*

All this was happening too fast for Rita-she was in tears. She had not come to terms with even the move let alone owning a home in Chicago. But deep down she knew the writing was on the wall and she was moving to Chicago.

She called home to check on Shana. Lilly was shocked when Rita told her what happened. Kevin said *"He definitively understood Carl's impatience. This was a wonderful opportunity for all of them and he agreed with Carl that they all had a new place to visit."*

Neither Shana nor Greta was told about the move to Chicago. The rest of the trip Carl told Rita about how this move would broaden their horizons and give them greater financial opportunities. Carl felt sure Shana would understand. He thought about how to make this discussion a win-win. As soon as they were home and settled,

He told Shana they purchased a house and were moving to Chicago. He created an image of the magnificent mile. She would be able to be within walking distance to "*tons of fashionable named label stores.*" He told her about Sax Fifth Avenue, Carson's, and Montgomery Wards to mention just a few. He told her about live performances every weekend and movie stars walking the streets. He outlined the beautiful buildings and the many interesting restaurants and places to see-plus there were trains to ride.

He mentioned that Chicago had a China town and a Greek Area let alone a fabulous zoo. But, for all his efforts-he guessed wrong Shana's reaction was tears and screaming "*I want to stay here-I do not want to leave everybody. You are selfish to take us away from all the people we love. I hate that you would do that to us. Don't you love us? Don't you love all the family?*" Carl would have none of it-"*Stop this right now young lady-this is my opportunity and in fact it is the opportunity of a lifetime for me to exceed in something great and that success would help my family. It is a new beginning for all of us. I promise we will fly back to Clayton often; everyone will also come to Chicago-you will see. It is not like we are moving off the face of the earth. Besides your mother and I have purchased a house and this one is going to be sold.*"

Rita asked Carl about timing "*all this will take time to organize and get ready-besides we have not even sold this house*" Rita said. Carl then told her "*that it –the sale –and the move was all arranged.*"

Both Rita and Shana went to bed that night in tears. Rita thoughts were not just about the move—but what Carl had exhibited-

He was blindly inconsiderate of her and Shana's feelings. He was very deceitful in the way he went about sending out resumes- without telling her or trying other groups. He lied to her about why he was going to Chicago. He did not communicate his frustrations with his position. This gave her a new feeling about his integrity and character. He was selfish, self-serving and cunning. She was thinking about their marriage and how he had proposed just at the time when she was swapping houses. He hated staying at the hospital, he needed a car, and his money was tight. With her salary and a paid place to live he had a wife who loved him and served him like he was her king. The problem was he did not see her, treat, or love her like his queen." Just then Rita heard Shana crying she went into her bedroom. "*How could you let him do this to us—you love Aunt Nora; she is your best friend. Greta is my best friend. How could you buy a house Mom?*" Rita hugged Shana at that point and told her that "*there are times that a family had to stick together, and, in this case, it was her job to consider her husband and what was best for his career and that also meant what was best for all* *involved and that this was one of those times."* The ladies fell asleep in each-other's arms.

When Nora and Michael told Greta about Shana's family moving it was the same story. *"How could Uncle Carl be so mean? Did he ever really love us? Isn't love all about "giving" why did he decide to "take the job?"* They tried to explain to Greta *"this was an opportunity for Carl to see his burn theory and cream brought to fruition. He has worked for this for years."* It did not work—Greta persisted: *"All he ever thinks about is what he wants. Shana tells me how he jokes about Aunt Rita—why? Why? Did Aunt Rita marry a man that just thinks of himself? I am never getting married do you hear me——Never! Never! I do not want a man to take me away from the people I love and to boss me around and manipulate me to what he wanted only. If I need a boss, it will be me! "ME-ME and No One but Me."*

Michael and Nora tried to explain to Greta the great opportunity Carl had; but Greta was sure she would be *"alone forever without my cousin and best friend Shana— we are blood sisters."* Christmas was more important this year than ever before for the girls.

Greta and Shana spent most of the day in tears. Carl won the support of every male in the group. Men are so supportive of men! The way Carl presented his new position was that he would oversee all the new and upcoming methods of treating burn patients. He could make a name for himself as being there from the ground up. With that in mind the men all agreed it was a great opportunity for him and the money would be good for their future and available if Shana wanted to go to college.

They knew Rita-would be able to get a teaching position in no time. Everyone in the family agreed to visit. Carl assured them that they would be traveling back to Clayton often. *"Chicago is not that far"* he said, and it is *"only a one-hour plane ride."* Betty's ears perked up; she has been wanting to go on a plane for years.

Carl decided that waiting until February would be foolish just prolonging the agony of the move for everyone. The house in Chicago was vacant and movers would handle packing and unpacking everything. Carl felt that Shana needed to be in school at the start of the second semester and he did not think she should come in late.

On December 12th Carl called Margaret Powers and told her the family would move by January eleventh. The day before the second semester of school was to begin in Chicago.

Margaret agreed to seek permission for them to move in early. She agreed to discuss it with the Real Estate salesman and the seller's attorney. Carl asked her permission to obtain an agreement for the hospital to pay the mortgage payment for the house in Clayton until it was sold. He did not want to have to pay two mortgages.

Ms. Powers stated his contract identified the hospital would pay both mortgages and the Real Estate Commission along with the movers if he accepted the offer and arranged to move within forty-five days-he was overjoyed and agreed.

Now all he had to do was tell Rita and Shana. Carl and Margaret Powers went over everything in the new contract and Carl was amazed at what was provided. Along with a stipend arranged for Rita there was a tutor for Shana to help her adjust to the new school; as well as locating a music teacher for her to continue her lessons.

Carl knew the house in Chicago needed work; he did not want Rita to stress over it. He decided to see if Margaret Powers could handle the work. He wanted this move to be perfect without worry for Rita. He asked Margaret if she could have the house ready for occupancy by handling the redecorating. She agreed and mentioned that the hospital had a crew that could paint and do minor work on the house.

Carl was great with people. Margaret agreed to handle the small changes Carl needed to make the move more enjoyable. Margaret Power fell into the task of handling all the repairs and purchasers.

The hospital permitted their painters to paint the entire house. Carl wanted new wall to wall carpeting put in; as well as all drapes purchased.

Margaret set up a running tab for costs of the paint, rugs, appliance, construction costs, and drapes. The hospital agreed to pay for the painter's time; but the cost of the paint would be on their tab. Margaret Powers was a star. She handled everything. Carl wanted new washer and dryer and the back hall made into a laundry room. That necessitated putting a better enclosure to the room and extending it to the side by adding a half wall over the concrete walkway. No problem the finished construction looked as if the laundry room was always part of the house.

Ms. Powers arranged for the hospital gift shop to give her some flowers for the family on the day they arrived. They permitted her to use their discount in purchasing things for Shana's room.

Meanwhile at their New Year's Day dinner Carl announced the arrangements he made for the move. He made it sound like it was his gift to both Rita and Shana. Both cried and so did everyone-at the dinner table. It was over the realization that they were finally going to move was now facing them all. Carl told everyone that January eighth was the day that they would fly out. Carl felt he had enough of all the crying and wining. His plan was to have everything done in the house by the time they would move to Chicago. He thought Shana would begin school without losing time and she would be so busy making new friends that being homesick would not fly.

Ms. Powers arranged for the movers to pack them on the fifth of January. everything brought to Chicago and settled in the new house when they arrived. Margaret loved the challenge, and she knew she could handle it. She and Carl were on the telephone every day going through things and arranging how furniture should be placed and what should be purchased.

Carl had already given his notice at work. He made it sound as if the hospital in Chicago had pursued him because of his ideas on how to handle burn patients.

Since they were not going to need a car in Chicago Carl, without Rita knowing, put an ad in the Cryer to sell both of their cars. Rita argued that they needed a car to travel back and forth but Carl said they could fly.

Rita's principal was not overjoyed when Rita called him on News Years Day and told him about the move. He had to hire a new teacher immediately and would have to pay a substitute teacher for the first couple of weeks of school. When teachers are changed mid semester-it is sometime difficult for the students to adjust. Rita sympathized with his position but stated that this was short notice for them as well. In Clayton, the students returned to school on January second. Shana's teacher arranged for a party and Rita sent in cupcakes for all the children. The kids in Shana's class all said they would miss her and for her to always remember her school.

On January fourth Carl sold both cars. Kevin agreed to drive them to the airport. The Movers arrived and began packing they agreed to stay with Nora and Michael for their last few days in Clayton.

Meanwhile Carl arranged for the Real Estate salesman to visit so Rita could sign a listing contract to sell the house that was in her name alone. The list price increased with the addition and all the decorating that Rita was so handy at doing. The difference in cost between the two homes was less than $15,000.

Of course, the new place was in both Carl and Rita's names. With Carl's additional salary and the fact that Rita's house had no mortgage they were approved for a mortgage on the house in Chicago.

It would be a small mortgage as Carl told the bank that they were putting down sixty-five percent the funds they would receive from the sale of their home in Clayton. The remainder of the money paid for all the renovation being completed in Chicago and what was left would pay for the new siding, and windows in the summer. Rita was again seeing a side of Carl that seems strange. On the morning they were getting ready for the plane everyone was saying goodbye.

Tears, good wishes, promises to come back to Clayton were exchanged and finally it was time to go.

The original plan was for Kevin to drive them to the airport-but Carl had a last-minute surprise he hired a Limo to take them to the airport. He felt it would be less stressful for everyone. Parting was especially difficult for Rita and Shana. They cried all the way to the airport.

Once up in the airplane Shana loved flying. She especially loved the stewardess. One gave Shana a pair of "wings" and a deck of card with an "American Airlines" logo.

Shana said that when she grew up, she might want to be a stewardess.

Rita was thinking about Carl and the way all this was handled. She was not aware that the work was done in the new house. Carl told her he still had another surprise for her. He was anxious to get his family **"into the grove"** as he called it.

And unbeknown to Rita and Shana, Carl and Margaret Powers had arranged for everything in the new house to be completed.

Chapter 43

Chicago

Margaret Powers hired a contractor, handled the painting, purchasing of the rugs and other items. Carl suggested the front two windows be replaced with a large picture window and in the fenced yard he wanted a small shed to be put in the back for storage.

The contractors were working ten hours days. The inside of the house was completely painted. The outside would have to wait until summer. Ms. Powers had Shana's room painted pink. All the other rooms were in an eggshell except for the master bedroom it was painted a cream blue-Carl's favorite color.

Carl asked for all the new rugs to be a beige color. In the living room he wanted a twenty-four-inch boarder of hardwood floors. Carl had style and Ms. Powers was great at making his ideas look professional.

Since Margaret did not have a little girl-Margaret moved Shana into the room with the half bath. She opened the hall closed and added thirty-six inches to the bedroom giving Shana her own shower. This made three full bathrooms on the second floor-one in the master, hall between the two bedrooms and one in Shana's room. There was a half bath on the first floor on the first floor next to the laundry room. All these changes increased the value of the house. Margaret loved purchasing curtains and a matching bedspread for Shana along with an off pink rug in her room. Margaret had a full-length mirror installed on the closet doors in both Shana's room and the master bedroom. She accented Shana's room in purple. It was beautiful.

When the furniture arrived, Margaret had the men place most of the furniture where she thought things might best be. She picked out a linen bed set for Rita and Carl from Marshall Field's magazine according to Carl's directions.

When the family arrived in Chicago a stretch limo was at the airport to bring them to their new home. Margaret had flowers on all the tables, music playing from the new intercom radio, and a bowl of fresh fruit in the kitchen.

The refrigerator was stocked with eggs, milk, and a pound of butter, bacon and fresh bread. In the cupboard were salt and pepper shakers-filled, oatmeal and two cereals, Oreo cookies, peanut butter and a variety of jellies. The Laundry room had a detergent, Clorox, White vinegar, fabric softener, and a few hangers.

All the bathrooms had toilet paper, toothbrushes, toothpaste, a hair dryer with the closets in the bathroom having wash cloths and towels. Everything was neat, clean and acceptable. There was a plant in every room. Shana let out a scream when she opened the door to her bedroom-she loved it especially the full-length mirror on her closet door and her private bathroom. She told Margaret: *"I love seeing my drapes and spread match. And having a bathroom all to myself-makes me one lucky girl!"* Margaret also found a quaint dressing table to add to the room. The table was painted pink with a pink and purple skirt added for a twist of youth.

Just as Margaret Powers began to greet everyone else Shana thanked her again for a *"perfect bedroom."*

With Shana happy it was now time for Margaret to help Rita feel settled. She asked Rita if she felt everything was satisfactory? Rita was in awe at how everything looked she thanked Ms. Powers and Carl; stating they did an excellent job renovating the place it looks terrific!

Margaret said Carl ordered each change and color. Rita was surprised.

Margaret told Rita arrangements were made for her to see a personal banker at the Harris Bank. Margaret said, "Her name is Connie Blair, and she is expecting you any time within the week to open all their accounts." With that Margaret gave her a brochure with the phone numbers and location of the Bank. Next Margaret gave Rita a map and a book with the number of all the buses to all directions around the Chicago area. She identified which bus number for the bank, state street, and the zoo. There was a gift package for Rita and Shana it contained a shopping pass worth $200 for Rita and $100 for Shana courtesy of the hospital gift shop.

Shana's school bus #34 will be at the house at 7:35 AM the driver's name is Elaine. Elaine will be expecting Shana. Rita felt that things seemed to be moving quickly, efficiently and just perfectly. Noting that Carl wanted there to be no stress for Rita.

Rita noticed all their clothes were placed in the closets. Their drawers which were originally covered with plastic during the packing so there was no need to do anything but place them back into their original place-nothing needed to be done. Carl commented that Margaret was a jewel having arranged for everything about the move. Shana took and immediate like to Margaret-meanwhile Rita was not so fast.

Their first night in Chicago, Margaret Powers arranged for Chef Andrew to come to the home and cook dinner. He prepared: a shrimp cocktail appetizer, roasted chicken, garlic spiced mashed potatoes, and cooked mixed veggies. The meal was topped off with homemade peanut butter chocolate pie.

It was accompanied with red wine for Rita and Carl and for Shana a special chocolate milkshake. It was like

"Being Queen for a day!" Rita said. Shana said she loved the special treatment. Her question was *"Does The chef come every day?* Everyone laughed and Carl announced, "Just *for today."* Margaret had four extension phones put in; one in the master bedroom, one in Shana's room-that was pink to match her accessories, one in Carl's office, and finally one telephone in the kitchen.

That night they called the family in Clayton and spoke to everyone telling them all about their day and their new home. When Shana was able to talk with Greta, they talked about their feelings being apart. Shana was excited about her room and how coordinated it was Greta felt envious but was happy to hear from her.

The next day Shana arrived at her new school she was told to see a lady named Lori who would be waiting to take her around and introduce her to all her teachers and show her the schedules. Shana loved the school and there were some students who were excited to *"show her the ropes."*

It did not take long for Rita's house to sell in Clayton. The amazing part was that they had received three offers and ended up selling the house for $2200 over the asking price.

While the family was keeping busy in Chicago learning their way around. The first Sunday in Clayton without Rita, Carl and Shana was a lonely day for everyone.

Michael and George found themselves in a situation where they had to work on a Sunday to finish the job. Lilly and Betty went over to Nora's the women cooked dinner.

Greta just sat and read a book most of the day. She was lonely and needed to find a hobby or worse yet some other friends.

Everyone missed Rita and Shana they reminisced about things from the past when everyone was together. The men arrived home about 4:30 M for supper. They missed Carl telling them stories about situations in the hospital or having him check out their minor aches and pains.

Nothing seemed the same without Rita and Shana everyone missed the family being together just as they had done for years. Greta was frustrated and lonely. After supper she went to her room and lay on the bed crying. Nora came to console her but unfortunately Greta did not want to be comforted-she just wanted Shana. Betty did not like how the day went and so the next morning she went shopping. That Sunday was the same as the Sunday before.

Betty left a package in the trunk of her car and when everyone seemed sad, she decided the time was ripe for her surprise. On Saturday she purchased a recording camera so the family could take videos of them together and send those reals of the family to Rita and Shana. Betty brought the box from the car into the house and announced her surprise.

A new air of happiness entered the room. Now the ladies went into the bathroom to freshen up they wanted to look good for the camera they even put on a little make-up. Betty talked the men into combing their hair (those that still had some hair-Kevin was losing his) and washing up as well. When they were ready, they all proceeded to "talk" into the camera to Rita, Carl and Shana.

Betty also purchased a camera and screen for Rita-this way both sides could send things back and forth. She would send this first gift out on Monday. They all spent about twenty-five minutes getting ready and rehearsing for what they would do in front of the camera. It really was a challenge to act normally. They figured that all this new stuff takes time to get used to.

Rita and Carl received their present on February 1st. They were as excited as children to see how this new equipment worked. When the tape arrived, it was quite a trip down memory lane of the Sundays spent with family. Both Rita and Shana ended up with tears.

This transfer of tapes continued for the next to nine months. Things began to taper off by August. Carl was working about fifty hours a week; he was stressed and short tempered much of the time.

Rita was really looking forward to traveling home over the summer. Rita had not searched for a teaching position she wanted to get acclimated to Chicago. She mentioned to Carl that she would like to drive to Clayton rather than fly. Carl would not be able to justify the two days of drive time each way. So, they planned to fly; Carl would stay for the weekend and the ladies could spend two weeks. At the last-minute Carl had an emergency and was going to miss the trip. Rita and Shana were disappointed but did not want to forgo the opportunity to see everyone. They got the airport shuttle at the Edison Plaza and left Chicago Tuesday evening.

When Kevin picked them up from the airport, he told them that George was feeling ill. He hurt his back the beginning of June and was still not back to work. Michael was a bit stressed taking care of both crews. Lilly recently had about with the flu and was just recuperating. Things seemed a bit different Greta made a new friend at school her name was Nancy. They had known each other from kindergarten and now Nancy was at Greta's house just about every day. They were becoming best friends. Shana and Rita felt a bit left out. After all they moved away, and nothing stood still everyone moved on with their lives. But it was home-and they loved being there and enjoyed their stay.

Their next trip to Clayton was for Thanksgiving. The dinner was especially good this year. But there was not the same festivity that always accompanied a family dinner. The men retreated to the living room and the television set. The women cleaned up the dishes and all enjoyed a cup of coffee and cake at the kitchen table. Shana, Greta and Nancy played monopoly in Greta's bedroom. Despite the uneasy beginning –Shana really missed going back to Chicago. She told everyone about Chicago shopping, their new home, all the different restaurants, the fabulous zoo, and the shows along with her school. Rita mentioned she was hoping to get pregnant wishing the old saying of new house new baby would come true. Meanwhile Carl was at the hospital until about 4 pm. Margaret Powers invited him to have Thanksgiving dinner with her family. Margaret did not want him to spend the day alone. He enjoyed meeting her son Joseph, and her father Richard.

All these past months Margaret never mentioned that her son was blind. It was a totally new experience for Carl.

Richard, Margaret's father mentioned that it was a rare when Margaret would bring someone home from work. Carl enjoyed time with Margaret's family. He learned Margaret was just finishing up her nursing degree. She had one semester to go. The hospital promised she could ease out of personnel and into the nursing department making the transition within four months after graduation.

When Carl arrived home after dinner at Margaret's he immediately called Rita. He told her all about his dinner and about Margaret's father and son Joseph's blindness. He missed her and for some reason-he just could not tell her.

Rita talked about everyone in Clayton and told him how much they missed seeing him. Carl decided Christmas would be a better time-for all of them to be together in Clayton. Carl promised to join them this year in Clayton over Christmas. He made arrangement immediately to take the time off not to disappoint Rita. Carl felt strange these last few days going home without Shana and Rita. He enjoyed Thanksgiving with Margaret's family; but felt empty inside. He decided not to give it much thought-anyway Christmas will be here in no time.

Chapter 44

Christmas

Carl, Rita and Shana went to Clayton for Christmas. Carl joked around with the men and Rita enjoyed cooking with the ladies.

Shana and Greta had a great time in the snow building a snowman and having snow angels in the yard. Greta's friend Nancy was visiting relatives in Canada. So, it was just the two of them again.

Leaving was once again difficult. But this time they were getting homesick for Chicago. When the family returned from their holiday and went back to their routine; Rita invited Margaret and her family for dinner. Rita had come too really like Margaret over these past months. Margaret and Rita had lunch and shopped together many times. Margaret's son Joseph and her father were joined the family for dinner often.

Then in March one of the nurses came into Carl's lab and suggested he meet his new assistant. Low and behold it was Margaret Powers! With only two months left in training the hospital felt she should get used to her new environment and the staff. She requested to work in the lab with Carl's group.

Carl felt that this could not be better for his group as Margaret's work was always top notch. Rita was happy that Margaret and Carl would be working together. She had a good personality and was liked by everyone.

Rita felt Carl would enjoy her being part of his staff and she might be able to alleviate some of his stress.

In April, George had a mild heart attack and was taken to the Clayton City Hospital. When Lilly called, she seemed frantic. Rita agreed to get a flight to Clayton. on holidays Rita loved sending in a special meal for Carl's research group. This was something she began doing when they moved to Chicago. Rita wanted to help Carl bond with his staff, and she knew that sending in food always made for a team environment.

Rita hoped to leave the third week of April. She needed to find someone to take care of Shana and a substitute for the two classes she was teaching.

Carl said he "was too busy to be responsible for Shana." He had been involved in the brink of his research for the last four months and *"far too busy to return to Clayton. He was putting in ten-hour days."* Rita had a doctor's appointment for a repeated ear infection; that she did not want to cancel especially with taking a plane to Clayton.

Four days before she was to leave, she learned she was pregnant. She called Lilly and postponed the trip until June.

It would be easier to leave after school was over and take Shana with her. She wanted a baby more than she wanted to travel to Clayton. Lilly said George would be laid up for six weeks. Betty and Nora would help.

A few days later Carl came home early. He had been called into his boss's office. Carl was "<u>officially reprimanded</u>" for being a "<u>know it all and trying to tell senior doctors how to conduct their research</u>." He was devastated. *"They just do not understand what I am trying to do"* he said. *"There is no excuse for what was done today,"* he continued *"those Dr.'s knew I could handle this research it was just jealousy that initiated this problem. There was no reasoning with any of them. They just did not believe I could develop the cream the way I predicted it would come out."* There was nothing Rita or anyone could say or do. Time needed to pass for this problem to be solved. Rita just listened. Carl always felt his way was right. He stayed downstairs in his office that evening trying to understand what he needed to add to the cream to get the results he anticipated.

Meanwhile Rita was having problems she was vomiting constantly and had a terrible pain in her stomach. After Carl left for work on a Friday, Rita called her OB doctor and made an appointment for later in the day. At 1:30 PM she was in the Dr.'s office. After examining her he assured her this was all normal. It had been years since she was pregnant, and her stomach needed to get used to what was about to happen.

The next month was the same as the last-Rita was vomiting about fifteen times a day and always tired. She had begun substitute teaching at a local school and was determined to finish the school year. There were days the class worked at their desks the entire period and Rita just sat and monitored. Rita figured it would not be long and school would be out. There was less than three weeks left.

On June 1st-it was over. Rita miscarried. Carl took her to the hospital for the D&C and brought her home. Rita went to bed, and Carl went back to work. He said, Shana was old enough to care for herself and her mother. Carl never missed a day at work, Rita moved around the house slowly trying to heal physically and emotionally.

Carl did not want the emotions and he refused to listen to crying. Nora was on the telephone with Rita every day she understood the feelings Rita had and the loss she felt.

In July, Rita and Shana decided they needed to go back to Clayton for a couple of days. Carl could not leave—his project it demanded all his time.

So, Rita decided to drive. It really was a great trip-she and Shana took their time and split the drive into two days. They stayed at a motel for the night-ate in restaurants and had a great time making up songs and singing in the car all the way.

When they arrived in Clayton, Shana was surprised at how tall Greta had grown since Christmas, and how she had physically developed. Shana had not started to develop but, Greta was already fully developed.

She was over a head taller than Shana and appeared quite well endowed. Greta was in the tenth grade now. In fact, she had a boyfriend! His name is Peter, Greta told Shana *"I really do not want a boyfriend. But he is smart and not pushy. He calls only once or twice a week. He just wants me to hang out with him at school a bit. To tell the truth I think he is a "bit different" and doesn't know it yet."* Greta had to explain that last sentence in detail to Shana. The facts of life were still new to her.

Greta's experiences with Nancy and her family seemed to change Greta in many ways. Nancy was into fashion and wanted to be a designer. Her influence saw Greta dressing more maturely and "in style." Nancy's mother was a reporter and told stories about the life of a reporter. Her father was a chemist-and boring. He was into ingredients *"what is in this-let's check it out."* Not something young girls paid much attention to.

Betty was not feeling herself these days. Nora lamented about her second miscarriage she said, *"It just wasn't in the cards and Michael says it was a sign that we should just leave well enough alone."* When Lilly and Betty came over to Nora's it was like old home week for Rita. She mentioned to them how Chicago had seemed to change Carl. *"He had no interest in what Shana or I did or do let alone the things we care about. All he wants is for us to have food on the table for dinner and for us to order the food for Birthdays. He likes a clean and in order house. When he is home the television is all that interests him and the telephone. He could be on the phone for hours talking to doctors from other research centers all around the country about their findings. He is Ok with taking us out to dinner-but he was not especially crazy about any of my friends.*

He rarely attended any of Shana's school functions because he is always busy. Research is all he likes and talked about. He is on the brink of a miracle burn cream." She said.

Carl loved Shana-whatever she wanted her father would see to it he bought it for her. He would talk about his research with her and his feelings, but he was limited in not wanting to do many things together.

Nora talked about Michael and Greta and their relationship being almost non-existent. *"He is there for what fathers had to be-but otherwise-she wants nothing from him. Michael loves Greta and tries to reach her but she seems to have shut down doing things with him."*

As the girls talked, Betty listened and was attentive. She did not want to share with the women her situation. **She was embarrassed, frustrated and hurt. It had been over six months since Kevin asked her to sleep in another bedroom.**

The love Betty so cherished from Kevin was different now as Kevin claimed impotency. Betty "knew" that was not the case. She felt that all those years of handling his personal needs by himself-made him just not want to take the time to do anything else.

In reality**, the** only time he was attentive or responsive to her was when other people were around like Lilly, George or Nora and Michael. He just went to work, ate, watched television and then went to bed. Occasionally, they went out for Chinese food-but nothing was the same. She missed traveling together, talking things over and most important the tenderness and love they shared together in the past.

She missed the attention and kindness they gave each other in the beginning. She missed his smiling at her and touching her back when they were together. It is true she has gained fifteen pounds since their marriage and her hair had thinned a bit; but Kevin was twenty-two pounds heavier, and almost bald; wasn't love supposed to overlook stuff like that?

Betty never dreamed that this would be her situation-she felt young enough for romance. She wanted Kevin's love and attention desperately. Many people complemented on how Betty looked-despite her weight gain she kept herself looking very well. She always had her hair styled at a beauty shop and her clothes were attractive. Despite how Betty looked Kevin had gotten to the point of not even kissing her when he left the house. She tried to show him love hoping to reach him, but she could not identify what were his issues with her. All she knew was that she loved Kevin, and this was a lonely feeling.

Betty thought **that they went through just to be together –their love should have lasted forever.**

Meanwhile, Lilly also just sat she had a secret of her own. She could never tell anyone not even George.

Chapter 45 A

It Happens To George

Rita and Shana were staying with Nora and Michael for their visit. Michael's construction crews had grown to a total of twenty-five men each. Having a mild heart attack George wanted to take life easier and just spend his time with Lilly. He was thinking about possibly: **retiring or selling his share of the business to Michael and John.**

John had taken over George's crew-when he had the heart attack. John's efforts of developing a security system increased the business as well. Charlie formed a company that monitored this system-24/7. It too was a great money builder and Charlie was always working to make it better.

George and Lilly's house did not have a mortgage. Their cars were only two-years old, and they were paid for in cash. There was a life insurance policy for Lilly to help her should anything happen to George. And there was money in the bank; added to Social Security. George felt they both would be comfortable if he decided to retire. Previously, George and Michael discussed the settlement they would reach just in case George retired. Michael just did not know how John would feel working for him and not George.

George had not told Michael that the company should be divided between both men. Each should be own-ers of their sections: John would have the security system and Charlie's group; and Michael the construction group. George felt the "security" system and monitoring was part of the business should belong to the brothers-since they developed it.

He decided to approach the subject a little at a time planting the seed first with Michael.

The Sunday just before Rita and Shana were getting ready to return to Chicago—John came to the house. He was invited to have dinner with everyone. That was the first time he and Rita met in person. He told her how much he loved her mother's house. She asked him if they found the hidden room in the attic. John said: *"attics are for storage-we have about four items up there and are never there; Betty still uses it as her sewing room. She still cleans for us –although I think Kevin is quite jealous of that, but he never comments."*

George saw the look on Kevin's face when he mentioned Betty cleaning for John and his brother-it was a strange and unfriendly look. Michael caught that look as well.

It told George that **there was more going on with Kevin than he was willing to share. He felt sorry that Betty was probably dealing with his anger and jealousy. It was written all over Kevin's face.**

John immediately liked Rita-no one had ever seen John joke with anyone like he did that day with Rita that day. Rita liked him as well-she flirted back. John was sorry she was leaving but even sorrier to hear she was married. *"That is one fine lady"* he said.

Shana was getting anxious to return home she missed her friends. While she enjoyed being with everyone-Chicago was far more exciting. Her relationship with Greta seemed to have changed. The girls were still friends, but that certain closeness seemed gone. When they returned to Chicago Rita noticed another change in Carl. He wanted to go on a diet. Margaret's father mentioned that he "seemed to be a bit heavier.

Rita knew it was all the snacks, candy bars, and company dinners along with birthday celebrations at the office that was responsible for his weight gain. Carl had also been a smoker-and Margaret mentioned that he was now smoking much more, and she was concerned about him.

In October, Carl was awarded another research grant. He was thrilled. Then all that was needed for his burn cream was the FDA approval. Once he had that approval, his cream now will be used in all hospitals across the United State. Doing things his way was about to make him famous and the family would be in a better financial situation. It worked this time because he had the leeway, the funds and was in control. It became a challenge to show the other doctors what he was made of; Carl loved challenges because most of the time he wins.

It consumed all his days and most of his evenings. Videos were made about the cream and leaflets were now being sent with the cream to the hospitals and to doctors all over the world. Carl was a success. They never needed to worry about money again. As Carl had a 99-year patten on this cream.

Rita kept busy with different projects on the house. She crocheted at night and began reading novels. Shana loved sports, and she also had a boyfriend. She met Tom

Sweet at a baseball game. His father was transferring to Chicago after the holidays. Tom was five feet nine inches. Tom's family was moving to an apartment located at the beginning of Lake Shore Dive. The apartment would be in walking distance to Shana's house.

They would be on the same bus for school and because they were friends, they would be able to see each other even after school. Tom had hazel eyes and blond hair loved sports and was a good student. He was going to be in Shana's school beginning in January. Tom thought it was strange that she was two years younger than he was and only in one grade lower.

She told him she began in first grade at age five because she was very smart; and, because her mother was a great teacher. Tom, like many boys, did not begin school until six due to a late birthday. His home state had something called "pre-primmer" adding another year before beginning first grade. He began first grade at seven years old. Shana thought it was a match made in heaven. Tom played the piano and the guitar. Shana played the piano and the flute. Music was big to each of them, and they would both be in the band at school.

Meanwhile, Carl was spending less time at home. He was happy both found things and people to keep them busy. When he was around the house physically-he was not there mentally or emotionally. He was either on the telephone or working his creative juices doing whatever it took to keep his success alive. If he was not working, he was too engrossed in the television to have more than a passive interest in what they were doing. Rita made sure she always had a project-that kept her busy and kept her sanity. She felt confident that someday-one day Carl would know that she was there: be more attentive, appreciative and caring along with hopefully loving. It just may take a little longer than she hoped it would.

The first half of the New Year went by very quickly and so did the summer. Unfortunately, Rita and Shana did not get to Clayton that summer-there were just too many things happening on both sides. Michael and Nora had decided to do some renovation of the house building a patio and basement recreation room for Greta to bring her friends. Lilly and George went to Palm Springs for the winter-they would be gone three months. Kevin put on a new crew. Betty took a part time job.

The week before Christmas this year, Rita's marriage had become even more difficult if that was possible. Carl became more critical of anything she said or did. He used humor as his means of exposing her or the things she said and did. Someone suggested a marriage counselor and they agreed.

At counseling Carl said Rita was *"controlling, that she "knew" what was best for Shana and he did not like her parenting style. He continued "Rita talks and really does not know much, she comes out with stuff that I do not understand."*

Still the counselor agreed some with Rita and some with Carl. He was furious-arguing with the man. The counselor said, *"Carl, you may say you love your wife, but do you **like** your wife?"* with that statement Carl left the meeting and demanded that they never return.

For some reason Carl changed everyone's plans and again agreed to go to Clayton for Christmas. This time he made all the arrangements for the family to fly, and he even called Michael to give him all the flight arrangements. Rita was a bit taken as Carl also helped her get things ready ordering the limo and assisting in the packing.

After they arrived, Carl took the bags upstairs to their room. He even occupied Shana and Greta so the ladies could get re-acquainted. Later in the evening Nora said to Michael *"Now, they seem like a happy couple."*

Rita overheard that remark -she thought **"How little Nora knew or realized-because it was all a facade. No one would be able to guess their true or how uncaring and indifferent Carl was at home. No one really cares about the truth. The Bible mentions that "Love always covers."** Rita knew all about covering.

The reality was she was ashamed of how her marriage had evolved. She failed him but most of all she failed herself. Rita remembered how Carl was so attentive and caring when they first married; now Carl had become a loaner. He was so engrossed in becoming a success that he dismissed her.

Early in their marriage they communicated about everything –but could it be that she was the one who communicated? She wondered **"Was that all an act and if so, why? Why did he want to marry me? What was it that attracted him?"** She pondered in thought— **the fact that I was a teacher –or owned a house— maybe it was the closeness of a larger family—what was it that attracted him?** Rita never considered herself attractive in fact she had low self-esteem.

Michael, Nora and Greta mentioned visiting them in Chicago for Easter. Rita was not quite sure how that would even play out with guests on their home turf-but if it happened Carl's posture would be everything as "usual."

The entire holiday season went off perfectly. Lilly hoped they would return to Scottsdale for the next winter as they had been doing of a couple of years. They would close their house and drive there. When in Scottsdale

George seemed anxious wanting to return home or find something, he enjoyed keeping busy. Kevin and Betty usually checked their house regularly when they were gone. When they returned, they were both very rested?

Kevin was relieved Betty found a job she liked working at the rectory of St. John's church. She would work Monday through Friday from 9 AM to Noon as a secretary to the pastor. The church paid her minimum wage but at least it got her out of the house. Kevin thought **"it keeps her away from John and Charlie."** But Kevin was wrong. He became more upset and resentful when Betty continued to clean house for John and Charlie. She had offered to do their cleaning right from the time they purchased the house. Kevin could not understand just why she would do such a thing. He thought **she might just love the company of two men who appreciated her. It seemed to me she likes men and I do not like that in her and I am done**. He became more as time went on.

But Betty did have a secret that she would not share. She loved cleaning John and Charlie's house-the men were not dirty, but it gave her an opportunity to be in the hidden room now her sewing and reading room. She was adding to the diaries she found for the sake of Rita and Michael's children. It was a long cold and hard winter.

But spring was in the air. Lilly and George had gone to Arizona for a short trip. When they returned George was even more bored. He decided to help manage the books of the construction company. He hoped to keep his hand in it and have something that he enjoyed. The first couple of weeks he went to the office and worked a total of thirty hours.

It was not long before he realized he really was no help to the accountant. Michael and John hired stellar accountants' months before George decided to retire.

George found himself with nothing to do and bored. Lilly asked him to plant a garden in the back yard and do some landscaping. That kept his hand in things. He was happy to do it. He enjoyed planning everything needed to build a small garden. He would enclose it with wood and put a mesh net on top three foot high to keep the critters out.

By the first of May the area was built, the ground had been rototilled and some of the plants had routed the flowers were already growing. But George missed the crews and working with the men.

Occasionally, he drove over to one of the sites where the crews were working just to "inspect" how things were. By July-that was no longer viable either.

They hired so many new people that George was slowing things down trying to talk with them.

Tending the garden hurt George's back. Lilly did what she could to help; Nora came over a couple of times to help pick the ready vegetables. As the summer went by quickly George was not happy. He needed something to give him a feeling of being useful and productive. As the summer ended George became weak and tired sitting around the house.

November rolled along only to find George with about of the flu. After Thanksgiving George had another heart attack and spent nine days in the hospital. His ability was limited.

The doctor said he would need at least six months to recuperate. It was going to be a long winter, but Lilly was determined to keep George well and happy.

She made homemade soup all the time and watched his diet. She purchased some long under-ware to keep him warm—because for some reason he was always cold.

Lilly wanted to take George back to Scottsdale-and stay there until March. But George would not miss Christmas with the family. He said they would go to Scottsdale after New Year's Day like always.

George had his own reasons for wanted to stay in Clayton on Christmas. He wanted to have a talk with all the men, especially Carl. The year before everyone noted something different in Rita's marriage. George wanted to talk to Carl.

Chapter 45 B

Christmas George/Carl

December 25th was a much warmer day there was a light snow fall, no wind and it was clear. The air smelled fresh and clean. Carl, Rita and Shana arrived two days before Christmas.

Nora was an exceptional cook; she made stuffed pork roll with yams cooked in sauce and green beans with almonds. Nora made great pies. This time it was coconut custard with mounds of whipped cream on the top. Dinner was terrific.

The house was beautifully decorated as it was always Michael's love to decorate for Christmas. Everyone exchanged presents and Shana and Greta each received a record player.

Kevin purchased a box of candy-for Betty; a strange gift for a diabetic; everyone knew there were issues between them. Betty gave Kevin slippers, a robe and some ties. George gave Lilly a broach. He said, *"It would complement her winter coat."*

Michael purchased a bottle of Nora's favorite perfume. He also gave her some beautiful flowers-their relationship was remarkably close and loving. Carl did not have a gift for Rita. His answer was always the same. *"She knows how much there is in the bank and if she wants something she will buy it."*

After the gifts Carl agreed to bring up the tray of cookies from the basement refrigerator; George found this his opportunity to talk privately with Carl.

George wanted and felt a need to take a liberty with him. He followed Carl down the basement.

George began by saying that Carl should not to be upset with what he was about to say to him. He confessed that he was taking a liberty, but he felt it was something he needed to do.

Carl said,
"It is OK George, just say what is on your mind." George said, "I am *an old man and I wanted to share a lesson I learned very late in life."* The two men sat in the basement of Michael's home and George spoke. *"Love and family, Carl are the best things to happen to and for a*

person" he said. *Since I married Lilly, my happiness was in loving her—doing for her—giving to her, being proud of her, and appreciating having her as my wife and respecting her. We are really two different people. But we allowed our love to grow together. It took conversation, understanding, exposing our inner selves, weaknesses and strengths, and compromises to become what we have today. Lilly's loving me in return has given me an inner strength and a kind of courage and peace difficult to explain. Her love and caring gave me my life. Being with her, I feel invigorated and confident enough to do whatever I have to do-more like a man should feel.* He continued to say *"As I mentioned, we are two different people; but her love lifted me Carl to an unbelievable level inside my heart and soul. My life completely changed.*

Carl love is a choice not merely a feeling. It is the feelings that we chose to allow, follow and explore. We must be careful not to throw it all away for something that appears important now. There is rarely a perfect match but choosing to give love—and to receive love- is what makes a match perfect."

One more thing Carl—*"Love involves truth, forgiveness, growing together and not being afraid to make mistakes. It means accepting the diversifications in your personalities and enjoying them for what they bring to the table.*

Real love is never being afraid to make those mistakes or say something out of the question. Love -genuine love goes beyond all that to come to a togetherness of the soul for an unconditional love. Carl do not to let anything, or anyone destroy the years you and Rita have had together. Cherish your time and continue to build happiness. Children come and grow but Rita has been there –and-will be there after the children leave home.

The Bible says in marriage you "become one." Carl it is the "becoming one" that really makes love work. Yes, you will have differences of opinions but one either agrees to disagree or there is a compromise. I hate to preach Carl, but real true love is extremely hard to find. Michael had to find out-that the war created a burrier to his love. Kevin refuses to see love. You escape it by being so busy and closing your eyes. It –love is too valuable to treat cavalierly.

I am sorry, I had to say my piece—please forgive my intrusion. But I am an old man who just wishes to see -love concur all." Carl answered, *"I know, and I understand your concern thank you for caring so much-I love you man."*

George felt he did the best he could but somehow, he felt sad. He did not feel Carl's answer indicated he really understood, cared or got the message he was trying to convey. George felt his answer was just geared to hummer him. So, George added *"It is up to you Carl to recognize what you have and appreciate it and make the most of your time together. Life is short and once time is lost it can never be returned it becomes wasted.*" George appreciated his attention.

This time Carl said, "*thank you*" and with that the men returned to the family. When they came upstairs Carl used his eyes to express to Rita his frustration with George. Rita wondered just what took place in the basement, but Carl only said George had become "*some kind of a Philosopher.*" Every night the family all had dinner together. The night of December 29th at Michael's house was different. Everyone was especially happy and in a terrific mood, joking, kidding around and laughing they teased the girls and sang some songs and they all played Bingo. Suddenly the mood changed when George stood up and walked over to Lilly, he took her hand and knelt in front of her and said: "*Lil, you are the heart of my heart and the soul of my soul, my best friend. Lilly, I love you completely. I thank you for being my wife and making me the luckiest man in the world. My life has been happy since we met. Your love has made me grow and become a better person. I thank you for loving me so unquestionably and unconditionally.*"

Lilly at first thought it was just for this light holiday mood that George was talking; but she soon realized George was serious. His face told her something was wrong she answered "*George you are the love of my life my heart my soul. I thank you for being my husband you have helped me grow and become incredibly happy. I am indeed a lucky woman.*"

Moments later George touched his chest—he suffered a massive heart attack. As he fell to the floor Carl attended to him. Nora called for an ambulance. The ambulance took him to the Clayton City Hospital where his cardiologist worked.

Carl spoke to the doctors-it did not look good for George. In fact, George never regained consciousness and did not live through the night. Rita and Carl went back to the house to attend to the children. Nora and Michael never left the hospital that night they stayed in the room with Lil as she was holding George's hand telling him that she did not want him to leave her. But God had other plans and shortly before four PM George opened his eyes, smiled at Lilly and then he closed them. He was now with the Lord. Lilly did not leave the room until a short time after he passed away. She stayed in George's room giving him a kiss—telling him *"They would someday meet again; and, that she could never love anyone else."* Michael got the car and pick up the ladies. George prepared for his death from the time he and Lilly married. When notice of George's death appeared in the newspaper; Mr. Frank, contacted Lilly. George had a special safe deposit box at the Bank. Mr. Frank went over to Michael's and gave Lilly the key. He said George had planned everything to care for her. Michael felt Lilly should go to the bank and open the box- just in case- George had directions and last wishes outlined. Michael wanted to be sure to follow them. So, he went to the bank with Lilly and together they open the safe deposit. There in the box was a notebook, five envelopes and a small jewelry box. Inside one of the envelopes were two insurance policies. George purchased a total of $50,000 of life insurance with Lilly the beneficiary. They were purchased two days after their marriage years ago.

In another envelope there was $5,000 in cash. A third envelop had a bank book. There was $50,000 in the bank in Lilly's name. He had been depositing over $150 a month from his Social Security and all the rent from upstairs tenant at their home. Included was the interest on his accounts put into her name since they married.

The fourth envelope had some special dollar bills with a note. *"Lilly these are Gold and Silver certificates-not to be used as cash they will be worth more than their face value someday."* The small box held eight gold coins and five troy ounces of silver that George had accepted one time as payment for a small job he completed.

The last envelope had a card in words expressing love and praise for Lilly. Inside the card was a paper telling Lilly where to look in their house for important papers about his funeral-it was all paid for and arranged.

Lilly was not up to going to the house, so Michael went alone and located the papers. Michael made all the funeral arrangements as George had outlined on those papers. He had come to love and respect George; and he felt his loss just as deeply as they all would.

Michael handled everything for the funeral in a solemn and loving manner. He asked everyone in the family to speak during the service and tell of their experiences knowing George.

Some of the workmen and the boys that George had hired and worked with over the years wanted to speak as well. Overall, there were seventeen speakers. The service was longer than anyone dreamed.

Everyone remarked how kind, appreciative and fair George was to them. He was also a great friend to all of them caring about their safety and their families. He often gave them gifts when they either married, had a child or for a holiday.

One man talked about how George helped him on a Saturday to find his missing dog. There were 300 people that came to the wake. George was buried at St. Ann's Cemetery. George's first wife was cremated, and her remains were given to her brother.

George's parents purchased four plots at St. Ann's many years ago. George was their only son and they wanted to be sure he would be buried near them. They figured he would marry one day. Lilly would eventually be buried next to George and his family. After the service, Michael arranged for the family and some of the guests to have lunch at the Swiss Chalet. Everyone enjoyed their lunch.

Shana and Greta had never been to a funeral before. This was exceedingly difficult for both girls they loved George-he was like a second grandfather to the girls.

Kevin was proud of Michael he really did a terrific job handling all the arrangements and greeting everyone as they entered and left the funeral.

When they returned home after the luncheon Greta was especially upset. *"Life is so unfair...I will never get married or fall in love. Who wants all this pain? Why does God allow all this pain?"* she asked.

Rita answered *"Life is living a journey by going through the darkness, bringing out, and appreciating the stars when they appear. You will fall in love one day- and you will see what I mean."*

That was not the answer that Greta wanted but somehow it quieted her down.

Carl was so taken with the closeness of the family he felt their sorrow. He felt the love that George's death brought out of everyone and the emotions soon hit him.

As he and Rita were in bed that night he turned to Rita and began with a passionate embrace. He had not made love to Rita in over a year, but that night he was ready to be with her.

Rita did not know what hit him but suddenly, he was kissing her, holding her and gently moving his hands everywhere up and down her body. His kisses were tender, sincere and so loving that Rita was sure no one could fake that behavior.

They made love twice that night and Rita fell in love with him all over again as the two fell asleep in each other's arms.

Chapter 46

It Happens

It was the middle of January when Rita learned she was pregnant again. The baby was due late September. Things had been calmer with Carl since the night of the funeral and when they returned to Chicago…they made love often.

Rita felt everything in their marriage would be fine. She was sure that whatever Carl had said in the past was to be forgotten it was a fluke in their past that meant nothing.

Like her other two pregnancies Rita began vomiting every day many times. This time she took no chances. She notified the school that she would be on leave from the middle of February and would take the next year off. The doctor suggested that after her miscarriages rest would be the best for both her and the baby.

Shana was so excited. She began helping around the house doing the laundry and everyday asking Rita how to cook something. She was doing so well cooking that Carl purchased a special cookbook from Marshall Fields for her. She loved it and began preparing all sorts of dishes.

Lilly planned on flying to Chicago when the baby was born to help Rita for a week or two. She wanted to feel useful again and a baby always makes a woman feel useful and good.

Nora called Rita every Sunday to check on her. She and Betty began sewing clothes for the baby. A baby coming seemed to bring new life to all in the family.

Rita said the baby was moving around a lot and she was really getting big. In fact, by the beginning of the third month she had gained nine pounds! By the end of the fourth month a visit to doctor brought something else no one had thought of-but the doctor suggested there could be more than one child. He went so far as to suggest that there could even be more than twins. He wanted to take a test.

On the day of the test Carl kept repeating—*"think one-just one or two-no more!"* Carl seemed happy and excited about having a baby, but multiple births seemed to be a bit much for him at this time. Still even that seemed to continue bringing new life into their marriage. The test did not prove conclusively that there was more than one baby, so they still had to wait.

Names were the next issue. Shana wanted "Megan" if it was a girl. There was a girl named Megan on a television program and since we associate names with people-the girl was beautiful. Shana thought a simple name like Megan was easier for people to spell and remember. Carl suggested the name "Olivia." Neither Rita nor Shana liked the name it sounded...old.

Rita had been thinking about an unusual name it was the name of one of her students...it was "Taylor." Immediately Shana was against it, *"There are no Shana's anywhere- in the world why did you name me that name? Why would you give another child a stupid name? I hate being Shana-why couldn't you call me some nice name like Ann or Sandy?"* Carl refused to entertain Shana's wrath he said, *"What do we call it if it is a boy?"* They had no boy's names.**" If the truth be told he did not like his name either, but he would not tell Shana especially since it was, he who gave her the name Shana**.

He asked, "And what if there are twins?" he said, *"that would pose real problems."* The conversation ended with everyone resolving to give it some thought. It was the June before they actually settled on names. If there was one child and it was a girl, it would be "Katherine Ann" If it is a boy, it would be "Joseph Carl." If there are twins' girls, the second girl would be named: "Taylor Marie" and if there were two boys the second one would be "Michael George." Shana was not happy with the name "Taylor," but it was a name she felt the chance of it being used was small. She really liked "Marie."

Rita was really gaining-she was not sure if it was Shana's great cooking or if indeed there were two babies but either way, she put on forty-three pounds.

On August 10th while Rita was walking upstairs, she felt a cramp in her back and her water broke. She was in labor and this delivery was coming early and fast. She told Shana to call her father and tell him there was no time to waste. Carl came home as soon as got the call and was shocked.

Rita's pains were about a minute apart her water continued to flow. The baby was crowning when Carl came in the room. He told Shana to call Powers and ask her to bring the OB/GYN or get a standby OB/GYN that was in the hospital for an emergency and bring him over to the house.

Carl had no choice but to deliver Joseph and four minutes later he delivered Katherine. It was a tremendous rush to deliver his own children and Carl felt it. He had not delivered a baby since his inter-ship days.

When Margaret and the young OB arrived at the house -Carl had completed the delivery of both babies. The babies were beautiful and doing fine. But Carl said he needed to rest. The babies were still premature and needed to be checked out by a pediatrician.

An ambulance was waiting to take Rita and the babies to the hospital for a checkup. When the children were weighed Joseph was nineteen inches long and weighed five pounds four ounces; Katherine was seventeen inches long and weighed four pounds eleven ounces.

Both were in excellent health. Not so for Rita-she hemorrhaged for eleven hours. The doctor finally tested the drug they were giving her to stop the bleeding-she was allergic to it! Three hours after the new drug was given an emergency D & C was performed. Rita was now resting quietly. Carl was tired, in shock and yet elated at the idea of delivering their twins.

After he spoke with the doctor he checked on Rita and then called Nora *"I delivered my twins earlier today. I have a son-Joseph Carl and another daughter-Katherine Marie. I delivered both! Rita is in the hospital with the children they are all doing well."*

Nora was excited all she could say was *"two of them-two of them a boy and a girl!"* *"Thank you, Carl, for the call I will let everyone know. Did you take any pictures yet?"* Carl thanked her for calling the rest of the family. He agreed to take pictures tomorrow. He told Nora that Rita should be home in a few days. He mentioned she had caught a cold, but he did not want to tell them about her hemorrhaging not wanting to worry them unnecessarily.

That night Shana did not cook-she went to the hospital to visit her mother and siblings. **"They are just beautiful, and they look like me!"** She said as she held both at the same time. Rita thought she looked like a little mother holding the twins. She asked Rita to please consider "Katherine Marie and Joseph Carl" Rita had already given those names to the nurse. She looked at looked at Shana and said, *"My dear wonderful daughter those were the names I gave the nurse when I arrived."* Shana was in tears *"Thank you Mom"* she said.

Everyone in Clayton was excited at the idea of twins! The ladies were deciding on the schedule for them to fly to Chicago as soon as Rita was home to help. They would alternate their time. Five days later everything was arranged: Lilly and Betty would be the first ones to fly into Chicago and help. Nora would go next. Carl did not care what the names where he was just happy it was all over, and they could get back to a normal life again. The time in the hospital went by quickly and five days later everyone was home.

Shana made a new creation-instead of having a two-layer cake with the layers on top of each other she put the layers side by side and put the names Katherine Marie and Joseph Carl on each. When Lilly and Betty arrived, they commented on only one crib. No one really had planned on twins even the doctor wasn't quite sure.

A friend of Carl's loaned him a bassinette. Joseph was put in the crib because he was the biggest and Katherine was in the bassinette. Rita breast fed both children. As Rita was putting Katherine to bed one night, she told Betty *"I feel like a milk machine."* Joseph is always hungry.

Two weeks later Rita took the twins to the doctor she was exhausted the doctor suggested Joseph be given a bit of rice cereal in the morning and evening preferably with breast milk.

It worked like a charm and Rita was relieved! Her breasts were sore. Lilly and Betty stayed a total of four weeks. Their being in Chicago and helping gave Rita time to get the children on a schedule; and for Rita and Shana time to bond with them. When they left Rita was feeling so much better.

Carl went back to work the day after the children were born. He was back working late again and invigorated at the next challenge.

When the ladies left both children were now sleeping in the one crib *"This situation cannot last for much longer"* Rita said. Carl posted a note on the hospital billboard. In two days, he had the option of three cribs. He chose a white Jenny Lyn Crib for Katherine- it was beautiful. Shana was like a little mother hen shopping for pink sheets to use in the crib. She not only helped with the twins, but she continued her love of cooking.

Shana concluded she would be a chef and someday own a restaurant. She began talking to Rita about cooking schools, but she did not mention that the one she liked most because it was in New York. She hid that information feeling that when she graduated from high school it would be the better time to discuss the location of the school.

Rita was exhausted she hired a lady to help her during the day when Shana was in school; and someone to clean every two weeks. She also joined a class for "mothers with twins" to keep up on the latest way to handle all the schedules and issues that may arise.

Nora paid a visit around the beginning of October. She stayed for a long weekend. She really loved taking care of the babies her day for having another child was gone for good and a sad realization.

Shana continued to cook. Nora was shocked at all exotic and delicious meals she prepared. Rita and Carl were used to Shana doing all the cooking they felt it kept her focused on her education and her future goals.

Initially Rita was going to take a year off from teaching; but she loved being with the twins so much she decided to stay home until the twins went to kindergarten. Carl was not happy with that decision. Carl's salary as an adjunct researcher was not great and Rita's salary was quite some help; but after all there were two of them, he accepted her decision.

Everyone agreed that the holidays would be in Chicago that year, but no one wanted to drive there during the winter.

So, they did the next best thing and flew. Carl purchased a sofa sleeper for the downstairs office and Shana slept on the sofa in the living room. Lilly, Nora and Michael got to sleep in the twin's room, and everyone pitched in to help decorate and cook. It was tight but they made do. By New Year's Eve everyone was back home, and plans were made for visits in the summer.

The babies were a real excitement and a joy for everyone. Nora felt the pain of her miscarriages and the longing for a baby. Michael was not interested.

Greta-was in her Senior Year at high school and planned to enter the State University when she graduated. Michael said this was not a time for a baby.

Greta wanted to work in television as a writer or to be a reporter. She was not exactly sure which one would be best-so she decided to try both.

The year was going by quickly and the twins were growing nicely. When the family came for Christmas Rita talked about how the twins would be old enough for the family to travel next Christmas.

In November, Lilly fell on the ice and broke her hip. She moved in with Nora and Michael. Michael and his crew built a room with a bathroom on the first floor for her. Lilly had private quarters. It did not take more than a week of being there for Lilly to decide to sell her house and stay with Nora and Michael. Michael called the Real Estate agent and in a few days the house was listed for sale. Lilly asked Nora to sell most of the furniture. Lilly was tired of the upkeep and of tenants. Since George died, she went through renting the upstairs twice and she did not like going through that exercise. Her hip was having trouble healing and she was in a wheelchair to minimize her stress.

Christmas was hard for Nora without much help. Lilly could not lift the twins. Lilly did not enjoy the holiday festivity without George. Nora and Michael just finished the decorations as Rita and family arrived for the Christmas festivities. Carl checked over Lilly; her face seemed flushed, and she had high blood pressure. Her heart was a concern if she did not get moving. Carl suggested her internist check her heart on a regular basis. He told Nora that sitting all the time and not exercising was not the best idea for her heart and blood pressure. Nora assured Carl that she and Michael would both work with Lil on exercising after the holidays and things settled down.

The twins had no problem flying. When they left Clayton, they were each sitting near a window on the plane. Katherine wanted to be with Shana, so she sat on her lap and Joseph was on Carl's lap. There were only three seats across, and Shana was able to have a window seat right in front of her parents. The entire first year with the babies went by without a problem.

Both children were walking early. By the time of their next trip to Clayton the twins would be two years old.

Chapter 47

Marriage

The next two years passed peacefully Carl and Rita did not have many passionate evenings again but there were nights when love making did take place.

Greta loved college she was determined to finish early just like her mother. She talked her school into permitting her to take courses in a local community college for credit. This was something new. She also was able to attend an evening course for college credit.

Greta was an exceptional student always a 4.0 status. She had Nora's determination. She planned on taking an internship working at both television and journalism-the newspaper was slowly becoming her passion. She also loved to travel, and she was super at writing.

The next September Lilly was still in a wheelchair she had no desire to move around and was not in the best mood many days. There were days she would just lay in bed and asked Nora to bring her meals. Her major problem was depression. Her physical body just needed a push but unfortunately, she did not have the motivation to push.

George had really changed her life. As soul mates they loved each other very much and did everything together. Lilly was lost without him wondering how she ever did things before they met. George was so attentive, caring and kind. He thought of her needs before she even exhibited the need. George was appreciative of everything she did-even a simple meal.

She missed that kind of caring and love. She missed George and the love they shared. Now she needed a reason to go on—something to give her purpose-but what? Nothing anyone said or did entice her.

Packing up the family and traveling to Clayton was getting more difficult. Now, there was four to pack and the twins wanted all their stuff. They decided to drive in the summer they skipped the holidays.

The twins loved every minute of going to school. Shana never changed from her desire to be a chef. After high school, she enrolled in a famous cooking school in New York City. She planned on owning her own restaurant one day.

Carl was at the Hospital or traveling giving lectures most of the time these days. It seems he was more involved than ever before. He and Rita were still together.

Rita went back to teaching full time to give herself strength. There were things she needed help with at home. She kept a housekeeper, with Shana away, she now did the cooking.

Rita felt the push of being lonely, working taking care of the twins and still doing things to help Carl as he traveled. When he received government approval for his burn cream it was in every hospital and burn center in the world.

This Christmas she was looking forward to going to Clayton for the holidays. Carl did not think they needed to go. It seemed to him as if they were falling further and further away from the Clayton family. Carl remarked:

"The girls —Greta and Shana-are not going to be there; remember Shana is doing an internship in a famous NY Restaurant during the Christmas Holiday.

Greta accepted an assignment in England. Not to mention the fact that, Lilly is still not well. I'll bet not even Lil would want to put on a "face" for the holidays. She probably would not enjoy having the twins there making a ruckus or any company at all, for that matter. Probably, no one would like the excitement of preparing the house; with a tree and everything. Let alone having to do all that special cooking for the holiday. Nora's been stressed; with teaching, taking care of Lilly, and taking care of the home.

Remember that Nora put all the furniture from Lilly's that was not sold in her basement; well Michael said, she still had ads in the paper, meets people all the time, and it trying to sell the left-over pieces.

It was great that she gave the Goodwill all the linen and George's clothes. It would be a shame for her to have to get the house ready just for our coming to Clayton. You know how hard it is to prepare everything for a holiday-and this would be just for our coming.

I bet Kevin and Betty are still busy during the day. Let's stay here this Christmas-with the twins. There visits here are getting shorter all the time. Let's give everyone a break. What do you say? How about just being with us? Do our family a favor and have Christmas at home okay?" The twins heard their father's suggestion and they chimed in; yea Mom lets 'stay home this Christmas. With all three against the trip Rita decided to call Nora to discuss the situation.

Nora agreed-this was a tough time. She told Rita Kevin was ailing and his stomach seemed to always be a problem. Rita called Betty and she confirmed that Kevin had an ulcer. *"He listens to no one and does whatever he wants to do"* she said. "He has medication—*if he decides to take it. He argues when I remind him to take his pills, or I give him some vitamins- that-I am "mothering him." He definitely does what he wants and no one-not even the doctor can change his mind"* she said.

Betty did not tell Rita that it had been years since her father acted like a husband to her. Or that he sleeps in another room and hardly talks with her or finds time for her. Rita did not want to mention to Betty that her father told her a year ago that he felt committed to Betty-but tired of marriage. There appeared no rhyme or reason for his behavior. Everyone knew he loved Betty. So, why he was rejecting her was hard to understand.

But then, Rita had something similar to deal with and she did not understand why. After her calls home, Rita agreed with Carl-this Christmas would be just for the four of them. Rita wanted the house to look especially nice.

She purchased a large artificial tree and some sparkly ornaments. She learned from years past that Carl would not take the children to see Santa. Years ago, she forced him to go with her to take Shana to see Santa. When he saw the line-he said, *"no way am I standing in this line for forty minutes so she could see Santa for a minute and spend $5.00 for one picture."*

Consequently, Rita always took the children to see Santa alone. Carl never liked to shop; he would argue "that what happened was-they would go to a store and he would end up just *"following her around."* He had no interest and was no help in determining which gift to purchase either, let alone purchasing something for Rita.

For years he gave her nothing-if she was lucky, she might receive a birthday card. She missed those beginning years **"when Carl would bring her flowers and cards or call her his "bride." All that was short lived. She wondered if it was really sincere. Well, it was past and, there was no point thinking about it again."**

Rita hated doing things alone but to minimize "discussion" she began doing most things alone. She purchases all gifts, handled decorations mostly alone, decides on the food, makes and ordered the food for his office parties, get the house ready for holidays, cleans up after and put things away. All while still holding down a full-time job, taking care of the twins and managing the house. Well, there is no point in thinking about it. It was just a mixed bag of issues.

Carl takes the gifts to the post office; helps with the tree or the wrapping, take packages to the post, and helps with the heavy stuff when I shop. That is a blessing. At time, he also watches the twins so she could accomplish what needs to be done. This year the twins wanted to go to the grocery. They decided they were going to help make a special dessert-jello!

Carl's office always had a Christmas party for his group. Everyone, including Rita, would bake and send different dishes. This year Carl wanted his staff to come to their house. He felt the house would be more personable.

"Everyone will bring something, and Rita should not have to put herself out. It would be just 25-30 coming and no real problem." He said. Rita loved company and parties. She did not try to talk Carl out of his idea. But his famous last words "there should be no problem you should not have to put yourself out. It would just be twenty or thirty people, no real problem."

For years Rita cooked and ordered food for his group, she did this for her teaching group, the PTA, and the church women's group. What really happens when there is a party there is loads of sweets and just a few appetizers. Now his group was going to have a party at her house. Rita thought: **Just wait, I am going to give this group a great party like never before, everything will be home-made and delicious!"**

Years earlier, she found a stand-up freezer at Montgomery Ward's; it was a "steal." The twenty-five-cubic foot freezer stands in the basement and is always in use. For this party Rita decided to bake tons of cookies and breads, lots of different appetizers along with some unusual dishes. She worked for days on cookies, and breads. Everything was packaged and ready to go. Then, a week before the party, Carl announced he had "invited another "group" that usually works with his staff-maybe just twenty-five or thirty more people."

Rita was at the grocery early the next morning. She prepared to cook thirty-nine special appetizers and twenty main dishes. Two days before the party everything was cut and packaged ready to cook the day of the party.

Carl hired a band to play at the party and rented some chairs and tables. He and a few friends moved most of the furniture out into storage unit. Carl wanted the party to be held on December 18th

Rita prepared the food. It really was easy for her-she called it a "Labor of love" because she really enjoyed doing the work. Rita and the children decorated the house perfectly.; it looked beautiful. Everything was set by 6:30pm.

The invitation was for 7-11PM. By 8 PM there were ninety-five people in the house. Some brought an appetizer many brought a sweet. Rita was so happy she had that freezer filled with appetizers in reserve.

All her homemade appetizers were eaten including those from the reserve group. There were a few different punches-liquor, pop, coffee, and tea – all gone when the last three people were leaving. A few people asked for recipes others wanted to take home some cookies. Rita anticipated a few wanting recipes; she placed copies of the recipes next to each appetizer. There were small bags for anyone wanting a few cookies.

Rita danced with a few of the doctors and visited with many of the wives. The party was a success.

Carl spent much of the time with his group-or just milling around. He and Rita were busy the entire evening. When the party was over Carl said, *"I am glad you had a good time I am going to bed."* He left Rita in the living room.

He never said thank you for all the work—or for how beautiful the house looked or how great the food was–he did not comment at all. Rita was frustrated. Carl knows the work such a party requires; how could he just go to bed? He was rude, unappreciative and insensitive to her efforts and all the work involved to make his party a success.

Rita could not let all the clean-up sit until morning. She worked most of the night putting things away, organizing, cleaning and vacuuming. Finished and exhausted she fell asleep, still in her party clothes-on the sofa. When she woke, she showered and dressed. Carl had gone to work.

Carl actions were a careless disregard for her. Did he think she was there just to provide a service? At this point, after all these years Rita wanted to know *"what about me?"* Rita felt hurt, deflated and rejected and-she felt there was no respect, caring, or appreciation for her.

Christmas was just a few days away and there was still so much to do to get ready for the morning gift giving and preparing a special meal for the family.

Carl did not plan on taking any time off. He was leaving for five days after new year's-he had accepted another speaking opportunity and he needed to prepare. Rita continued to get things organized. The twins wanted to go Christmas shopping. The telephone rang just as she was getting ready to leave.

It was Nora, Rita told her all about the party, the food and how great everything came out. Then Nora said that Kevin was over the night before and Rita was the topic of discussion. "Why?" Rita asked

Nora blurted out sarcastically *"Carl must feel that you are wonder woman. He certainly keeps you hopping, and you do and agree with just about everything he asks. You are a wife washing, ironing, cooking, cleaning, taking care of two children, grocery shopping, preparing lunches for him and at times his group, taking care of his clothes, sewing, planning parties, and cooking: all while holding down a full-time job.*

You stay up with the twins when they are sick-because Carl needs his sleep, even though you work the next morning.

What does Carl do specifically for you Rita? Is he kind and considerate of you? Do you realize that all

Carl is responsible for, or care about, is his work in research and selling his cream, along with whatever else that makes him look like a success?

This has happened in many marriages; some resulting in divorce. Rita -where is his love for you? Does he ever have your back? You allow his success by assuming all the other things, which should be important in his life, giving him free time to research, travel and promote his creams.

How does he take care of you? We are the ones that always take care of you-even in Chicago. What does he do to show you how important you and the twins are to him? Has he set things in motion should something happens to him on one of those trips around the world? Will you and the children be taken care of, or will you be working forever? What gives Rita?"

Rita was shocked no-one had never spoken to her in this manner before. Everything she did was out of her heart and with love and understanding. Many men feel work and paying the bills is all they need. Women often have a great deal more energy, love projects, and have no problem multi-tasking especially when there are children.

In Carl's defense, *"he is focused on his research, and he is phenomenally successful, respected and admired. His creams are now in every hospital in the United States and soon they will be in every hospital in the world. Giving us financial security."*

Nora replied *"And how about a woman's energy-how much do you have-is it an unlimited supply?*

I still ask you Rita when, and what does Carl, do to take care of you? There is always one of us there when you need help. It seems that way with most women-someone always comes to help. How does Carl specifically care for you? Is Carl your soul mate? What recognition or praise does he give you outside of you being a good cook? Do you understand what I am saying Rita? Some men forget to admire us as wives. We know that you thrust yourself into this marriage whole heartedly, but has he thrust himself into the marriage or just into burn creams?"

"Carl is a good man. *He helps with the children, takes out the garbage and even helps with the laundry at times. Excuse me, Nora the doorbell is ringing,"* Rita said, *"I bet it is,"* said Nora. She added *"You will not listen you love your Carl so much that you trusted him with all your time, thoughts, fears and money just like Betty did with your father and what did that get her? I have four mothers in my class that do the same thing and they are always stressed."* Rita did not like the way Nora was talking-she seemed to always be on a soapbox. So, Rita said, *"I have to go,"* and she hung up.

Nora was in one of her moods. But what she said made sense. It is so important for men to understand that there are many things a wife does to make a marriage successful, and for that. she should be loved, respected, appreciated, and cared for in all ways. Men and women seem to be looking for that romantic time of dating, infatuation and newness. In the past when married, it was the man that usually had a job and was the breadwinner; but now, women work as well, and many make decent salaries. When people come home for working all day and they are faced with too much responsibility it gets frustrating. Before marriage, they each put on their best clothes, and behavior—but marriage means working together on everything and really becoming a team. That team job is difficult when you are both tired, have a family to care for, cook, clean and do all the things necessary to run a home.

Chapter 48

Change Again

Rita often asked herself **"Why does Carl act like he does? She does help him; and she has given him everything."**

Frustration, and the desire to please; along with the hope of being recognized keeps people working harder and trying at everything.

Fighting with Carl was not the answer—she was no match for him. He was superb at turning the tables. It always ended up her fault in one way or another. Carl went to the councilors to *"Fix"* Rita. He would call her *"controlling and is not interested in my creams or how I do things, she is a know it all when it comes to the children and after all we have been married a long time."*

Rita felt **Carl has many good qualities: he is a good provider and a great doctor-establishing creams that will save embarrassment for people all over the world. I am confident he genuinely loves me.**

Meanwhile, Carl was wondering, "What happened to Rita she looks so tired all the time? She hardly ever dresses like she did when we were first married, and she has gained weight?

On his last trip the buyer was a woman, Carl took her to dinner and the subject of marriage came up. The lady said she was divorced without children. There was no romance in her marriage and no appreciation from her husband for her bringing in as much money as he did. Back at the hotel he thought about what the lady said and decided he would talk with Rita when he returned.

Rita wondered about all the things Nora said: Are people really changing? Do we all show less emotion and run from commitment? Why are there so many divorces? What is happening? Now there is a birth control pill, it gives women liberation and the freedom of choice; but what is it doing to families and marriage? Everything is a two-sided sword.

Back in Clayton, Lilly was still in the wheelchair. She had no desire not to get better depression had set in and she was ready to give up this world. Michael made it easier for her to manipulate with the wheelchair from room to room. But when all was said and done Nora and Michael recognized that Lilly had no interest in anything without George. Michael realized that Nora did not want to leave Lilly alone. She told Michael she did not want to teach full time for a while.

Nora brough in a lot of money for all the extras that they liked and for help with Lilly's special needs. He did understand and he appreciated all Lilly did for them-giving them the house; but her care was not cheap. They now needed two cars and one that is like a van just to help her go to the doctor. Then we need to be sure to pick up her drugs and renew her prescriptions. She was doing nothing to help the situation.

Nora decided to teach part time for now. Teaching was no longer as rewarding. It seems young children are more unsettled than ever before, and it is difficult to talk with parents-so many people are divorced. Many parents have a hard time disciplining or setting up standards for their children. If the truth be known some parents have little time with their children to teach values seeing them only a couple of days a week.

No one recognizes the effect of a divorce on a family not only does it divide the parents, but the children are divided with who and how to love. That takes its toll on relationships of every kind. All this happening not to mention I fear someday Prayer will

be taken out of the schools as will the teaching of religion. Where will children get their values? How will they develop a conscience? Normally, that takes place as a child grows from birth through adolescence experiencing identification with parents, grand-parents, aunts, uncles, and associations.

"The world is changing-and the changes are genuinely concerning. Greta had changed. There was a time when she and I could talk but now with my taking care of Lilly there was little time, for heart-felt communication.

Greta is always busy; all she wants to talk about is how much she loves her job and being on her own. Greta continual comment has been that she "never wants to have any man boss her or have to get his approval for anything." Lately even her telephone calls home is like a duty. She and Michael have not really become close again since the hair cutting incident. It seems to have left an indelible mark on Greta's mind and heart. What is happening?"

Nora does her best to keep the doors of communication open she calls Greta every Saturday or Sunday. Unfortunately, most conversation never last more than two minutes leaving Nora feeling lost. She tries to discuss a variety of things with Michael, but nothing seems too important. He will not discuss anything about Greta and the hair cutting that seems to have made a mark on her desire to get married.

Nora told her principal *"Parents do a lot for their children. Some children do not even honor them with sharing their lives. It is a terrible slap in the face leaving parents with a feeling of loss. Many ask themselves— why—why all the years, love, time, money, worry, and training?"*

Rita was having a similar issue with Shana. Shana also had a grudge against marriage. She watched her father and mother's love change as they went their separate ways. That really made a mark on her. That is the behavior and influence she saw and has in her heart as to whether to trust or love men.

She continues with words like: *"It is not going to happen to her. I made a rule to be "out for Shana" to fulfill my own needs and goals."* She has often commented to others *"I resent my mother; my father tried to make her happy. She just had no interest in his burn cream."*

Shana moved to New York for a cooking school, and it was the best thing for Shana. Things really changed for her when she met David Stein at the school. She was determined to work for him when she graduated cooking school.

He seemed so accomplished, determined to make a go of his deli, and she liked that in him. So, when she needed a job, his deli was her first stop.

David hired her instantly and it seemed to some of the workers that they immediately had a "different kind of relationship." It was true. David noticed her at the school as their eyes met several times during the sessions. Shana liked him from the start. He was ten years older than Shana. His family's deli was in downtown Manhattan. Shana needed to find another apartment as her place was going condo. David invited her to live in his extra bedroom. She agreed. Shana never told her parents about their living arrangement.

Knowing nothing about Shana's living arrangement; Rita would call and ask if she was seeing anyone. Like most mothers she wanted to see her daughter happy and fulfilled as a woman. Always hoping she would fall in love and settle down with a good man; and love life giving her many grandchildren. Shana would not tell her mother about David. Trusting a man was still a major issue for Shana.

Shana was cautious with David never giving him any reason to think there was something more to their relationship than his being just a landlord

At first when David offered her the bedroom, he said she could live there "*until an apartment opened up.*" But the deli kept them busy most of the time. Shana did not have time to look for better accommodations. It was about six months into their living arrangements when things began to change.

David would have meals ready for her. He would bring her flowers. They would share a drink together after work and soon David fell in love with Shana. Slowly, he talked his way into her heart.

The two were in a difficult situation Shana had never been with a man in the past; the idea of becoming lovers was difficult for her to accept. Shana refused to trust David.

Despite his desire to marry her. By the end of the first year living in the same apartment things changed again.

One-night things happened to progress to the point that stopping was not what either of them wanted. Shana refused to consider it as an "affair" or as being in love." She was resolved that it was only "physical." She was a mature woman who could handle this—but not "LOVE."

After living together for two years David had enough. He gave her an ultimatum "marriage or separate." He was in love and he knew Shana was in love with him. Her fears were not founded, and he would not allow her to run away from life because she was afraid to trust.

He was serious when he said he had enough "*marry him or leave*" and Shana knew it was true. She was frightened but David was so kind and loving she did not want to lose him—but—marriage? It was a Thursday when David gave her no time to argue. He had tickets for Las Vegas leaving the next day and he was ready to get married.

David Stein was a good man who genuinely loved Shana and promised to love her forever. So, tickets in hand he said the time was now. Shana cried she was did not have time to really think she had fallen in love with David and did not want to leave him.?

David promised to never leave her and to love her forever...three hours of fighting and she finally agreed. The next morning, they were on a plane to be married. Neither Rita nor Carl was told about the wedding or asked to attend.

Two days later they were to be married at a small chapel in the hotel. Before the wedding David gave Shana a gift, a massage, hair appointment and he purchased a beautiful dress with pearls, a purse and shoes to match. Shana was excited. The facial was her first and she was very relaxed with the massage. The hairdresser was incredibly talented, and years of indifference were tinted away, and she looked beautiful.

When she came out of the bedroom all dressed for the wedding David fell in love all over again. He said, *"You are my Queen, and I will always try to make you feel like one-I love you, Shana."* The ceremony was short, but they were both in love and their marriage began with deep emotions they made love three times that night.

Unexpectedly three months later Shana called and announced to Rita and Carl that she was married. They had mixed emotions of shock, disappointment and yet relief and joy. They only knew that David was Jewish and the owner of the small diner where Shana worked.

Shana said he was a hard worker, a bit older than she was, and had a different religion. She had never given her parents any other information.

Rita began reading about the Jewish faith. She did not want to do something that would offend David Stein should they ever meet. Shana said he was not orthodox-but still there were some things that he followed.

She told Rita and Carl they could look forward to meeting him on the 4th of July. Shana promised they would be home for that holiday for a week. She said they would have some pictures of the wedding for them. Rita told Shana that the twins were graduating high school and it would be nice to have some members of the family invited. Unfortunately, that did not happen-everyone in Clayton had legitimate reasons for not coming.

Shana could not wait to tell them how he proposed. But there would never a mention they lived together. They would say that they were in the same apartment building, and he was her boss at work.

Chapter 49

Secrets

June was hot. Nora was happy school was over. The time had come when Nora really wanted to retire but Michael thought dropping to part time and only substituting would be the best.

On June 16th, a strange letter was delivered to Michael's house. It was registered mail and Nora signed for it.

It was addressed to Lilly only her maiden name "Lilly Bing." There was a New York return address. When she gave the letter to Lilly –Lilly opened it and as she read it and began crying.

"*What is it Aunt Lil?*" Nora asked. Lilly did not answer she just wheeled her chair into her bedroom and closed the door.

When Michael came home Nora told him of the letter and of Lilly's strange behavior. He knocked on Lilly's door,

"*Aunt Lil-are you coming out for dinner? I brought you a peanut donut from Freddie's?*" Lilly did not answer so Michael opened the door. He found her with the letter in her hand in her wheelchair just staring at the ceiling. It was obvious she was upset-but Michael could not figure what it could be. He knew all her friends and family there was nothing bad or terrible had happened recently. There were no bills that she could not handle. He was concerned about her.

The letter is bad news from some test she took. He went into her room and as he walked closer toward her, he asked her *'what was wrong."* She still did not answer him. He asked her again-no answer, so he walked up to her.

He took the letter from her hand and said *"I am going to read this Lil do you understand I am concerned about you. I hope this is not from your doctor. I am going to read the letter. Do you want me to read it Lil?"* Lilly was crying she looked up at him with tears in her eyes and said, *"It is time. I cannot keep this to myself any longer. Please, Michael read the letter."*

It read:
"Dear Ms. Lilly Bing,

My name is Christopher Stone. I believe I may be your son. I was adopted by Judy and Max Stone when I was less than two weeks old. Is it possible that you are the Lilly Bing L am looking for?

Please contact me at:

101 Corel Blvd
New York City, NY 15034
537 345 8790

Thank you,"
It was signed Christopher Stone.

"Lilly" Michael tried to get her attention: *"Lilly could this be your son? Did you have a child, Lilly? Lilly, please answer me?"* **He said her name a couple of times, but she did not answer she just cried. Michael left the room and told Nora about the letter they were truly baffled.** *"Is it possible that Lilly had a secret-and told no one?"* **They were not sure what to do with the letter-Nora went into Lilly's room.**

"Aunt Lil is this possible? Did you have a child? Did you put it up for adoption? Could this be your son? When and how Aunt Lil did this happen?" Lilly looked up there were tears in her eyes. Nora said *"Lilly, you must answer me?* Lilly began

"In those days, a woman not married did not have children. They were called bad names. It was a stigma that passed not – just to her but also to her family. We were in love-and he was going off on a planned trip to Germany to visit some family. It was only supposed to be for a month and then we would be married. The war broke out-I never saw him again. My mother told me we would be ridiculed and so would the child. It would be that the child would forever be known as a "bastard." I had to give him away; there was no other way. She told everyone we were going on a sort of vacation. Your mother knew how painful this was for me. She cried with me. And our mother let her come with me. I would never have been able to go alone I did not want to give the child away-I didn't. Our Mom told people we were going to live

with Grandma Bing for a year to take care of her-no one would ever have to know. This way it would be less obvious to anyone. When the boy was born-he looked just like his father-very handsome. I wanted to keep him-but there was no way. Christian Services said they would find him a good home. I had to give him up when he was just two weeks old. It was hard-very hard. When your mother and I returned we agreed never to speak of it again."

Nora was stunned. *"What are you going to do now Lil? Do you want to see him or answer the letter?"* Nora said.

Michael was standing in the doorway listening to everything. He walked into the room and knelt down. He put his hand on Lilly's knee and said: *"Lilly that was a different time-no one today will say anything about what you did but now he is reaching out to you. Nora and I feel terrible that you had to keep this secret alone all these years."* Lilly cried and asked *"Michael to please call him"*-she wanted to see him.

She was not sure she could do it herself. She felt ashamed and she said *"he may just want to know why I gave him away. How could I answer him? Would he understand all that I went through? He may even want money. What can I do? What should I do Michael?"* she asked. Michael said, *"I will call him."*

Michael called the number on the letter and a man answered. They talked for a long time. Then Michael returned to Lilly's room and he said:

"He is coming to Clayton next week. Aunt Lilly he never married. He lives in a trailer. Both his parents are dead. He does not have any siblings or other relatives. He has a blood disease—Lil - he has been dealing with for a long time and he is ill. For the last eighteen months he has been in and out of the hospital's taking treatments."

Lilly cried as Michael spoke. *"He is not upset with anything-he just wants to see you because he does not think he has long to live."*

When Michael was finished telling Lilly the arrangements for Christopher to come to Clayton; Nora called Rita, then Betty.

It was sad and everyone felt bad for both Lilly and Christopher, but they really wanted to meet him and to let Lil know they did not feel anything but sad that she kept this secret alone all these years.

Chapter 50

He Is Home

The day finally arrived when Lilly was to meet her son. Michael picked Christopher up at the airport. They had set a place where they would meet and how they would each be recognized.

Michael was shocked. Christopher was about six foot tall and very thin. He had blondish brown hair and brown eyes. The men exchanged pleasantries and proceeded to walk to the car. In the car Christopher told Michael about his parents. They were kind church people—good people who had suffered terrible losses of their own children.

By the time they adopted Christopher they were in their forty's. Their son died and later a daughter of an inherited disease. The lady in the adoption center was the sister-in-law of a friend of his mother. His parents really doted on him.

"They died about five-and six years ago" Christopher said. *"Both were ill for about five years. They died one year apart."* He had been looking for his real mother for over four years. Based on information and in the adoption file that his was provided alone with his birth certificate Christopher was able to locate his father's name on the death list of German soldiers.

"It was harder to locate Lilly-I guessed she was married or remarried, and she did not live in New York any longer. The address given for her at the time of my birth was now a parking lot. The old name that was listed for the address was "E. Knight." So, initially I looked for Knight and then "Bing." Then "I tried looking for just any person named "Bing" in the State of New York. I sent out a dozen or so letters no one replied but you Michael." At first, I did locate a *"Bing but she was married and died."*

Michael explained that it must have been Lilly's sister. Michael explained that after Nora's parent's death

Lilly adopted her. Christopher commented on the irony of that situation.

At home Lilly was anxious. She felt ill for a while until Nora brought her some tea. She sat in her wheelchair in the sitting room next to her bedroom waiting for Christopher to walk into her room.

When the men arrived, Michael sent Christopher in to see Lil alone. He was in Lilly's room over two hours. The two of them came out looking happy they all sat down and had dinner together. Christopher was holding Lilly's hand and pushing her wheelchair. After dinner Nora and Michael left them and went to a movie theater. Christopher would stay at the house during his visit. The sitting sofa in Lilly's room was a sleeper. The bathroom could be shared and there was a closet and television. Christopher stayed for three days. All they did was talk and talk. Lilly wanted him to make an appointment at the Clayton Research Hospital. Lilly hoped to be a match for a bone marrow transplant. Nora offered to be also tested.

Christopher would return in three weeks. This time he would drive his small trailer in and park it in their back yard. Christopher had been living in a trailer for the last year unfortunately his parent did not have much money and with being ill he lost his job. Now that he found Lilly, he wanted to be near her. Nora and Lilly were his only family. Since he was ill Lilly was confident that the doctors could make Christopher well. She was determined to help Christopher and she wanted him near her. Lilly had a picture of Christopher's father- hidden and to everyone's surprise Christopher looked just like his father. He filled in the information about his father that Lil did not know. She had feared that Christopher's father died in the war.

Upon Christopher's return, he went to the Clayton Research Hospital for tests. Lilly and Nora were tested as well to see if they were a bone marrow match for Christopher's transplant. Unfortunately, neither Lilly nor Nora where a match for the experimental bone marrow transplant still Christopher liked the hospital and doctors so, he was anxious to let them treat his leukemia.

The doctors at the hospital identified they would work on locating a match. Christopher would receive radiation therapy beginning in a couple of months. He needed to put on some weight and get a bit stronger and healthier for chemotherapy. Christopher's life did not turn out the way it was supposed to when Lilly permitted the adoption.

During the next month Christopher took care of Lilly. They sat together in her sitting area watching television, talking, playing chess every now and then he took her to Bingo. Because Christopher was there, Lilly—now concentrated on leaving her wheelchair and focusing on the family.

In a while, Christopher took Lilly out for walks, to church and to the grocery store. They were helping each other get well. Lilly found renewed strength with the love of her son. At times, Lilly and Christopher would cook dinner together for the four of them.

After dinner, the four of them would play cards or monopoly. The relationship between Christopher and Lilly was filed with love and devotion.

Eight weeks of Christopher being there, and Lilly was walking again. She had a reason to live and to be happy.

Christopher had a good in relationship with Michael and Nora. Christopher also had a good relationship with the men on Michaels' crew. He would often visit Michael on the job to bring him lunch. The crew men seemed to really like Chris. The guys joked with him and he asked them questions about their jobs. When Christopher left the house to go to the trailer at night-Lilly looked sad. She did not want him to leave the house. Michael had an idea. He first wanted to discuss with Nora. Both Nora and Michael agreed that Christopher should live in the house, so he brought his idea to Lilly and Christopher.

Michael's crew was just about finished with their current job. He thought

"Why not keep them working and have them enclose the back patio. They could make it into a room that was attached to Lilly's sitting area. It would be a big enough room to be used as a bedroom room combination sitting room by Christopher. The room was near the bathroom. There might even be enough room to add a shower. It would give Lilly and Christopher

better opportunity to be together like an apartment for the two of them. When Michael brought it to Lilly and Nora, they loved the idea.

Christopher was grateful he offered to do some of the work. Michael showed him his plan and while Christopher liked it. Privately, he had another idea. No one knew how handy Christopher was or if he under understood construction. He never discussed his abilities. Michael said any changes to the house had to increase the value. Everyone agreed that was the most important thing.

Knowing Christopher was taking care of Lilly; Michael and Nora asked him if they could plan a trip to see Rita and then go to California. Christopher agreed. Michael said *"Any changes to the house would have to wait as they were scheduled to leave in a few days.* Michael said *he would keep thinking about the possibilities.*

Michael had an idea that from California "they would rent a car and drive to that gambling town, what was is called Las Vegas. From Vegas we could take a plane back to Clayton." Everyone thought it was a cool idea, so the entire trip was now going to be twenty-seven days long.

Nora was excited as they had not had a vacation since their honeymoon. She called Rita. The ladies talked about Las Vegas and all the things there would be to do live shows, gambling, night clubs, and us going to a grand hotel and sleeping there-that was what Nora was looking for—it was their first real vacation.

They were confident and comfortable with Christopher taking care of the house and of Lilly. The two of them really needed and wanted the time alone they were very much in love.

For now, Christopher could use the extra bedroom downstairs so he would be near Lilly while they were gone—just in case she needed him. Michael assured Christopher they would discuss all the possibilities about the house on his return.

Christopher agreed but again he had other ideas regarding how things should get done. Christopher never mentioned he had a degree in architecture. He asked Lilly if he could begin drawing some ideas he had, about how the house could look. She agreed. She was not sure that he had in mind-but wanting her son to stay close to her; she said "*yes*." Christopher re-designed the entire house. When he showed his design to Lilly she was amazed and proud but did not think it possible. Christopher confessed to her that he was a certified architect. He was now going to put his plan into motion.

The first job he tackled was preparing to move the detached garage—he planned on moving the garage up closer to the entrance of the house. In its current location everyone was always running to the back of the lot. Christopher's plan was to move the garage forward and run blacktop twenty feet from the back of the moved garage. Christopher staked things out and did all the measurements and then prepared to run the blacktop. Next, he marked the three walls of the garage and planned on moving them around to the front of where he would black-top. He would leave the back of the garage off for now. Before moving the garage, he ran blacktop from where he extended it to the rear of the garage—right through to the side of the front of the house. He planned on a breezeway.

There was going to be a fire wall on the back of the garage. The fire wall would be between the garage and the two rooms he planned on adding to the back of the "new" garage. He figured the garage door would be a problem both from the noise and the air coming in, so he laid the foundation for the bedroom sitting room leaving some space to be insulated between the rear of the garage and the rooms. He prepared to move the garage as soon as the black top was settled, and he rented the equipment. Everything would have to be set in place piece by piece carefully.

At the rental place he met Sam Rooney-one of Michael's workers. The two men talked for about a half hour and Sam felt intrigued by Chris. He decided to help Chris and not to tell Michael. Sam was still on Michael's payroll and even though Chris wanted to pay him, he would not accept any money from Christopher. He knew Michael would appreciate his helping wherever possible.

Chris was happy to have Sam on board. He knew together things would go much faster. The two men did not rest until they moved the sides of the garage. Then, they put up the back of the garage and finally they put up the door. It was something to see. They moved the garage forward approximately twenty feet and cut in for the walls Lilly bedroom and sitting area. They marked all the pieces like a puzzle when they moved the garage walls.

Behind the back of the garage, they "spaced in" for two different rooms with nine inches of insulation and a fire wall between the garage and the other rooms.

It took the two men five and a half-14-hour days total to move the garage, frame and enclose the exterior of the extended sunroom into Lilly's two new rooms. After they began work, they only took a break for a sandwich or to go to the bathroom. Christopher was amazed at Sam he was the best worker. Then, Christopher purchased eight new windows. One of the new windows was installed, to give Lil a view of the back yard. Another was put in the sunroom.

Later, the men framed an enclosed the breezeway between the garage and the house-so Nora would not have to go outside with groceries. Next the men finished the inside walls of the breezeway, garage and Lil's two rooms, added heat and electrical.

Next came something that was amazing. Christopher was not interested in getting a permit to expand the whole house-but he was an architect, and he had an idea how to make it larger and more modern.

Knowing time was short and Chris wanted everything finished before Michael and Nora arrived home Sam brought over Steve to help. The three men worked long hours exhibiting real teamwork. They were going to cantilever off the foundation on the entire back of the current sunroom. Chris purchased lumber to enclose the sunroom and attach the new room to Lilly's sitting room and bedroom. Then they added the bay window between Chris's bedroom and the old sunroom.

The men removed all the siding from the back of the house to later be used on the back of the new room they framed to be in for Christopher's bedroom.

"Nora will love it" Lilly said. The next few days Christopher worked alone. He put up insulation and dry wall to close the walls in the back of the house. There was a gas line to the grill close the house, so Chris cut the line, extended the gas, and expanded it adding a heat ducks to the new enclosed rooms.

The next four days they with Sam and Steve, they worked finishing the interior moving all kinds of pipes and electrical wires.

> *Michael's gas line also now worked for the oven and range from the trailer that Chris added in the bay. He took the cupboards from the trailer and put them in the bay area as well leaving room for a new stainless-steel sink he purchased. He used the refrigerator from the trailer by setting it up on two drawers he constructed for under the refrigerator. The finish product was a full Kitchen*

making the space look like a perfect small apartment.

It was something to see the men were shocked at how it all fit together. Lilly could not believe her eyes. In no time the It all fell into place and looked like it had always been there as part of the house.

Next, was the big job according to Christopher. Three things needed to be done and they were going to have to work fast. There was a closet on the side of the current bathroom and another closet used for junk. They knocked down the walls and put in a vanity a three-way mirror and full walk-in shower and tub. The new full bathroom was ten times better and larger than before.

Christopher gave Lilly a real shock when he told her they were going to take the stairs to the second floor out. With a minor adjustment and turn the stairs so they were facing the front of the now enclosed breezeway. The stairs to the basement were also moved making it much easier to move things to the basement from the kitchen.

The men took down the walls of the old dining and kitchen areas. Sam was not sure about what was happening. He thought Nora and Michael should be asked. But it opened the living room and made a nice big room on the first floor. While Chris was out getting supplies, Sam put in a separate door from the enclosed breezeway into Lilly's apartment.

The next eight days they moved the kitchen cupboards, the appliances and everything else from the kitchen as they put in a new bar and seating area using the furniture from the trailer making a full dinette with buffet and cabinet. Sam thought this whole thing impossible. Lilly could not believe what was happening, but it was coming together and looking fantastic.

Christopher worked with the building inspector; they agreed to his coming over-when everything was finished but he liked and approved of the plans. Chris was upfront with the inspector and after reviewing the drawings the inspector was also a fan.

When Nora called at night, to check on things Lilly had promised Christopher she would not divulge anything as it was going to be a big surprise! The entire kitchen was moved it was larger, more efficient and beautiful the cabinets from the trailer made a nice pantry. The new dining area had a beautiful oak breakfast nook -that came from the trailer and looked fabulous. The dining room furniture was moved into a new dining area. It was unbelievable. Sam thought Christopher was a genius.

The house was being totally transformed and made more modern and larger. The next project was going to be difficult. Chris redesigned the front of the house moving the entrance, stairs and windows. He purchased new windows for the front of the house. Installing the new windows made the living room look beautiful. The finish work took another three days, but time was running short.

Christopher was getting anxious with only a few days left until Nora and Michael coming home and many things' miscellaneous items still to finish. Christopher heard Michael promise Nora a new rug for the living room. Christopher purchased a huge beige area rug and pad then the men put in hard wood floors around the perimeter of the living room and in the dining areas. Then they put in a new floor in the kitchen and moved the half bath to the side of the pantry.

No one would believe these things could be done to this old house, but it looked fabulous like a new house.

Then men still had to move the front entrance for a better balance to the house. The concrete stairs had never been directly attached to the house they just sat in dirt-they still needed to be moved. Not a problem Sam and Steve borrowed a piece of equipment, and the stairs were moved in an hour. The door was next. Chris had figured the siding perfectly adding windows on each side of the door and the windows to the living room he had enough siding to make an unusual design on the outside of the house, so it did not look like things were moved.

The final job was the entrance to Lilly's place. There was stone and concrete needed to finish the enclosed breezeway. Christopher was determined it would all be completed before Michael and Nora returned from their trip. He kept saying he just wanted to see the expression on their faces when they walked in their new place.

Unfortunately, all this time Christopher's health was getting worse. He was so excited doing all the changes to the house and working with the men that he missed two doctor's appointments for his radiation treatment. They men could not believe how Chris was driven. Sam and Steve put in the stone and finished the concrete-just as Christopher had directed, they knew that Chris needed care.

Lilly called the hospital and made another appointment for the next day. Christopher needed to catch up on his treatments. Lilly was concerned about his health.

Christopher was now dragging his body. Kevin had been following the renovation and doing some of the work- also sworn to secrecy. He was shocked at the design and the job Christopher and the guys had completed in such a short period of time. It was a tremendous upgrade to the house and beautiful.

Kevin was more concerned about Christopher's health. In just two days Michael and Nora would be home. The men completed everything about three hours before Nora and Michael were to be picked up from the airport. Kevin and Betty went to the airport to pick them up and prepare them for what they were about to see.

But Christopher was not doing well he had been vomiting all night and Lilly called the doctor who sent an ambulance for Christopher to the house an hour before Michael and Nora were to arrive.

Christopher was running a temperature and needed care- he would be in the hospital a week. It would have been nice to have a picture of Nora's and Michael faces as they saw what the men and Christopher did to their home.

When they drove up and saw the garage moved it was a surprise.

Nora walked in, she took a quick look around and loved it all she was like a child-joyously admiring everything.

Michael could not believe what was accomplished in such a short time. Their excitement was cut short by the note Lilly had left on the table.

"Called an ambulance for Christopher he is not well we will be at the Hospital. Everyone proceeded to the Hospital.

They arrived and learned Christopher was in critical condition. Lilly was there supporting him. She was using a walker and met them in the waiting room.

Chapter 51

Christopher

It was three weeks before Christopher was able to return to the house. This time he slept in his own bedroom and shared the apartment with his mother. It was like a dream for Lil. He needed to get stronger to withstand the treatment needed for his illness; but he was very weak.

He did a wonderful job building the apartment and updating the house. Everyone sang his praises. Michael tried to pay him, but Christopher would not accept any money from them.

When Christopher was in the hospital Lilly just wanted to be near him. She called him several times a day to check on him. She and Nora visited him every day.

When Christopher came home-he could not seem to rest. He insisted on planting some flowers for Lilly to see from her window he put in lilac bush near the front of the house something Nora loved.

He ordered some trees and helped Michael plant the trees around the property. All this man wanted to do was to work and pay back the kindness shown him and how happy he was to finally locate his mother.

The property looked terrific, and the value was increasing but Christopher was pale. He loved Lilly more with every passing day. They were always talking and being together they played board games and cards and went for walks.

The first year of Christopher living there went quickly. It was in the fall of the second year Michael noticed that Christopher was not really improving. They had called an ambulance for him a couple of times as the chemotherapy made him weaker.

Christopher wanted to help with the Christmas Cookies. He and Lil decided to also do some holiday breads. They worked every day for a week. When he and Michael returned from purchasing the Thanksgiving Turkey- Christopher began vomiting. It lasted all through the night. They called an ambulance again. On November 20th, the ambulance came to the house for the last time

Christopher did not make it through the weekend. Lilly was beside herself. She was now seventy-six years old, and she was going to miss her son very much. The time they were together was all she would have out of his lifetime.

Before he died, he thanked everyone *"You will never know just how happy you all made me. You all have really been my family and I love you all."* It was devastating for Michael and Nora as well, really loved Christopher with him at the house, he livened up the place. He introduced them to so many foods-he was such a good cook, a great carpenter, and the best friend to all the family. Everyone will miss him, especially Lilly.

With Michael's help Lilly purchased a cemetery lot that was just below her and George's. Christopher would be there. They would all be together –like a family should be. The funeral was taken care of by Michael— he wrote a beautiful eulogy about family and how true love given honestly to one another is the greatest gift in life. Unfortunately, Rita and Carl were not there it was Katherine Ann's wedding day.

A week after Christopher's death a man called for Nora. He was an attorney, and his name was Howard Prichard. He asked if he could come over to the house and see the three of them. She asked his business and he stated he would tell her when he came over. Michael agreed he could come over in a couple of days. Everyone wondered what he wanted. The attorney said he needed to see them all to read Christopher's will. None of them even knew Christopher had a will let alone an attorney. When Mr. Prichard came, he stayed for over an hour.

Everyone was baffled because no one was aware Christopher had any money, but he left Nora and Michael $42,000 in cash and 100 shares of a stock. The attorney said the stock was a company called IBM and that they should hold on to it. The attorney said that Christopher had put the stock in both their names when he moved to Clayton. There was a letter-asking them to use the money to *"Please take care of my mother-I love her and feel so lucky to have found her and you both. I love all my extended family."*

The irony of it all was that he was given away-adopted and yet he loved them all.

There was also a letter from an agency in Germany that arrived about two months after Christopher died forwarded by Mr. Prichard. Michael answered the letter advising that Christopher had passed away. The answer was shocking-they had been looking for Lilly and Christopher for years.

Harold Von Beck had set up a trust fund for her and an unborn child. When Christopher contacted them looking for his father, they were excited thinking they finally found the heirs—but the address he originally gave was no longer his and they lost track of him. He must have not set up a forwarding address when he moved to Clayton.

The trust had a letter written by Lilly Bing to Harold about the child. It now had interest from all these many years and the total amount came to just under $98,000 American dollars.

The man wanted a copy of Lilly's Birth certificate and of Christopher's death certificate and then they wanted to know which bank to send the money too.

OMG Lilly could not believe what she was reading. Michael and Nora felt that Lilly was truly fortunate that she had written Harold about the child. They surmised that Harold and Lilly must have really been very much in love.

She wondered what Christopher's life would have been like if Harold had returned from the war and he and Lilly married.

Chapter 52

Change Happens

Time passes slowly when you miss someone. Lilly passed away six months after Christopher died. She died of a broken heart.

As was planned she left everything to Nora and Michael.

They returned from JC's wedding and decided that the house brought back too many memories after Lilly's death.

Michael and Nora decided it should be sold. The realtor billed it as having an in-law apartment and that increased its value. Michael and Nora moved into a two-bedroom apartment. They two of them had begun to mellow and rarely was there ever a cross word between them. It was obvious to anyone they had become the "one" the two of them being sole mates had a good marriage.

Greta and her father were communicating better. There were times they even joked. Still Greta did not call often and in fact it had been over five years since she was home.

It was a great real estate market that year and Kevin decided it was time to sell their house as well. Betty was not able to bring back the love they once shared and the two of them decided that the sale of their house allowed them to separate. Kevin wanted to live on his own in a senior living residence.

Betty took a small apartment not too far from where Nora and Michael were now living. In the beginning, Betty went to see Kevin three times a week. He was still distant and non-responsive to her caring, but she was used to him. Kevin spent most of his time working puzzles, reading the newspaper and watching television many times he would sit by other women and even flirt. He was getting colder, more callus and indifferent with each visit. Betty did not want the stress of the situation to continue more than was necessary she cut her visits down. She took the opportunity to continue a life on her own-and she became involved in a few charities and with her church friends and joined a book club. She would not divorce Kevin-she remembered loving him for all the good times and memories.

She needed to take the bus to visit him, but he really did not appear to care if she was there. He ignored her, spoke to others while she was there; or he would just walk away.

The other residents felt he was a funny man, entertaining and a great person—but they observed it changed when Betty was there to visit. He was cold toward her; the other tenants of the home said nothing as most felt it was not any of their business. Eventually Betty stopped going.

Greta was now calling her mother a couple of times a month. She was the managing editor of a travel section in a local paper with a car and great apartment in

Mid-Manhattan. She loved her life. There was no man in her life-because she did not want one.

The twins both married. Rita and Carl were still having problems. It had been years, and nothing had changed. All she liked was to read books and she talked too much.

The councilor told Rita "Things did not look promising for Carl to ever change after all it had been 35 years married.

Carl felt Rita did not understand or care anything about his burn theories or his creams, and she lacked his finesse with people. Carl felt every decision he made was always correct. Carl traveled alone. He did not see the need to "take care of her." She was working still and had a pension and Kevin was still alive. No one ever gets used to rejection and Rita was no different. But she wondered if hope ever dies.

Rita appreciated and recognized the life that their marriage provided. It was better than she ever dreamed –a beautiful house, three children-not to mention living in beautiful-Chicago. Carl allowed her the freedom to do whatever she wanted. Rita was no longer a fearful young girl she was a developed accomplished woman. She reasoned with her feelings; Carl was a good man in many ways. He always said that together they would be better off financially and for the children. He liked the idea of companionship. He was always one step ahead of her.

As the years went by Carl was indifferent and did not discuss their marriage just his burn theories or the children. Carl had become well-known and received many awards. He still gave speeches. Rita was never with him. Rita missed and needed love, but she found other ways to deal with loneliness.

When a position with Cook County came up to develop a training program. She jumped at it. She was required to attend a few seminars out of town; Carl did not get up to say goodbye or to help her put the suitcases in the car. He told her he treated her *"as she deserved."* Rita was resolved not to pay any attention to his indifference. It was hard, she cried alone, hoping for the man she fell in love with-but to no avail. Her survival was her job, their children and her friends.

Love is a monumental part of life

Rita knew the children recognized their marriage was not very loving. She answered that statement by saying *"People stay married for many reasons- divorce, is easy to get-but a good mate is hard to find."* Rita said, *"Your father and I understand each other, and we accept each other."*

Rita told Nora that she *"understood Carl and his drive and desire to be a success."* But Nora did not buy it. Nora realized that even with all the things a spouse may say or do or even how that a spouse makes his/her significant other feel-when there is love there is no argument. Who can really understand why someone loves? Carl may be a great doctor; but as a husband that loves his wife he failed terribly.

Rita was always there to help Carl and she always had his back. Rita says she loved him and learned a lot about love. Kevin says, *"He believes her. But "strongly feels Rita, needs to take care of herself!"*

Kevin died still upset and resentful of Betty. He never called her when she stopped coming to visit him, he never mentioned being married after that as well. But that said, he still provided for her after his death and Rita. He hated her continued allegiance to Charlie always helping him. He felt she must be attracted to other men-and that bred his resentment, indifference and lack of caring.

He was totally wrong, but no one could change his mind. Kevin was stubborn even after John married and moved away. Betty was hurt and deflated-he was the love she had waited so long for and even though his behavior was terrible she put it in perspective:

"What if he had a disease or an illness-would I hate him or leave him? No, so this is the same thing-I will love him for all the good times we had and for the fact that he really is a good man in many ways. This situation made him "closed to reality." Nora felt, **Maybe Betty's assessment is what Rita holds on too—all the yesterdays?"** Still Kevin did set up a small trust fund for Rita-feeling Carl would just leave his money to their children.

Now, Charlie was getting up in age and being alone with his lung cancer was difficult. A couple of months after Kevin passed away, he asked Betty to move into his house. There were three bedrooms, and she could live-rent free instead of paying for an apartment. All she had to do was cook, keep the house up, and be there for him. The visiting nurses would take care of his personal and medical needs most of the time. Charlie said, she" could even purchase new furniture if she wanted-just do not change his bedroom."

Charlie had lung cancer he was not able to work. The aids came in to give him his meds and clean him so all she really had to do was cook and bring him the newspaper.

Betty discussed it with Nora and Michael and eventually they all agreed. Betty liked the idea it had been a house she always loved and there was still her sewing room in the attic.

On October 1st with the help of Michael and some friends she moved in with Charlie. He was kind and not demanding but his lung cancer had progressed. Charlie lasted just six months-going in and out of the hospital. He never told Betty but, with John's permission, before he died, he gave Betty the house and some cash to help-with expenses and updating. He gave his daughter's son Griffin $2000 and gave his daughter $25.00. The rest of his money went to John.

In his last letter to his daughter Charlie lied saying he had married Betty and was leaving everything to his wife. She never questioned his will or answered his letters.

Betty was getting older and not sure about living in the house all alone. She loved Nora and Michael they were still living in a rental-she asked them to move in with her. Charlie's money-would help with all the expenses for quite a while, the house was in good condition, so all they had to do was help with food and minor chores.

On April 1ˢᵗ Nora and Michael moved in with Betty. Those that knew them envied how close they were-and how much they loved each other. Living in a home verse an apartment brought Nora and Michael back to life. They all cooked and cleaned together, watched television and played cards.

Betty just requested—that she be able to keep the "sewing room in the attic to herself" both agreed.

Their relationship was one of envy. The three of them went to picture shows together; went to church and even grocery shopping together-they were a family always loving and caring for each other. They even went for walks and had a couple of parties for their friends during the holidays.

It seemed that all this activity was keeping them young. Now Greta was even interested in how they were living. Nora wrote her a card about how healthy and happy they all were, and she decided to visit.

Chapter 53

Something New

When Greta read that her parents had moved in with Betty —she changed her thinking and decided to come home more often beginning with Thanksgiving. It would be the first time in years that she would be home for a visit. She arrived on the Tuesday before Thanksgiving and left the Sunday after. She loved seeing them all together and they had a great visit.

Greta told them all about New York, her job and her beautiful apartment in Manhattan. To look at Greta one would have thought she was a model. She was dressed in Christian Dior clothes her hair and makeup were perfect. Greta was petite with beautiful auburn hair down to the middle of her back. Greta was perfect and Nora and Michael were proud of her.

Occasionally, Rita would ask Greta if there was a "man" in her life. Greta made up her mind not to fall in love. Her rule was to never date anyone more than three times. Her love was her job. She had no time for men! She resolved "Not to Ever Marry!"

Greta told Nora she would not be home for Christmas. The company was giving a Christmas party and she should be in attendance. With having to be at the party it would be hard to travel but she promised to call.

Her boss was sending her to Chicago on New Year's Day. She promised to come home again by St. Patrick's Day and have more time to spend with the family at least a week.

BOOK 111

Chapter 54

By Chance

On the plane back to New York Greta felt amazingly comfortable with her visit home. She and Michael seemed to have reached a good place where for some reason she enjoyed their time together. For a moment she even felt a pang that everyone was getting older.

Life has a strange way of awakening us to a crude reality

When Greta returned to her office, her boss was waiting for her. He had a new assignment for her. The competing paper decided to have a traveling European Correspondent. That person would be going to thirty different countries and sending back pictures and stories. Mr. Gardner decided that Greta should travel the US going to all states and their major cities for six to eight months and do the same thing that the European Correspondent was doing-on the paper's expense account—of course.

Greta was not at all anxious to travel she traveled for years and now all she wanted was to be in New York and work at the paper's travel section. All the traveling she did in the past was just to get to this position. She hated living out of suitcase. She told Mr. Gardner she would think about it and give him an answer after he returned from his vacation.

He was not pleased but agreed. Greta had an assistant in her travel area that would be perfect for the assignment.

She wanted to discuss it with her assistant Lucy Crain first before mentioning it to Mr. Gardner. She planned on announcing it at the Christmas party if Lucy agreed to the assignment. Lucy was out for a couple of days to visit her parents in Michigan but due back from vacation on the tenth of December. There was a note on her desk to see Greta asap. Lucy Crain was twenty-five years old, and single. She graduated from the University of Chicago three years earlier while living with her divorced father. She was hired as an assistant, but she was waiting for her "break" as a reporter. She submitted many articles in the last year and only one printed and by-lined.

She was eager to prove herself and make her mark in the business. She was a seasoned traveler thanks to her father; she was thrilled with the possibility of traveling all over the US on the paper.

Greta discussed everything that she would have to include in her articles giving her almost an outline of what the paper expected. Lucy was rooming with her cousin in New York and Greta was sure the paper would pay her half of the rent if there would be no problem with her cousin with her gone for the full six months.

Lucy was sure her cousin would love the opportunity of being alone. Lucy was excited to have the opportunity to prove herself she gave Greta a hug promising not to disappoint her or the paper. With Lucy on board Greta now had to sell Mr. Gardner on the idea of letting her intern handle the assignment. He would be returning from his Florida on the twelfth of December. Greta made an appointment to see him that morning with his secretary.

The office party was later that month and Greta wanted to announce Lucy's special assignment at that time.

Martin Gardner was not really pleased with the idea. He felt Lucy was flighty, too young, and far too inexperienced. Greta agreed that if Lucy could not handle the assignment in a professionally written manner after a month on the road, she would take over the spot herself. Lucy promised to focus on all the things Greta had discussed and do a "great job."

Greta ordered Lucy to send her articles directly to her for approval. Lucy could leave the 27th of December.

Gardner said it was a deal and Greta was overjoyed. To make sure he did not change his mind she announced Lucy's assignment at the Christmas party. Greta was assigned to be in Chicago for a meeting on the January 6th. Gardner was still upset with her not taking his assignment-so-he arranged for her to be to California on January 10th to interview someone in Palm Springs who was opening a new motel. The paper will be doing a center fold on the Motel and he wanted Greta to handle the spread.

She hated the idea, but she was not able to talk him out of her going. She would think of something after the Christmas party.

The party was being held at a restaurant outside of Manhattan. It was an area Greta was not familiar with-but she had a map and directions. She originally planned to take a company car but that was not allowed for recreational purposes. She decided to take her own car. Since the weather, this time of year was uncertain, she felt more comfortable in her own car. She asked one of her co-workers *who picked this place- it is fifteen miles from the city?* She was told that the owner was one of Mr. Gardner's friends.

On the night of the party Greta was alone as she went to the parking garage and got in her car. She did not like driving people home late at night especially after a drinking party where she may get stuck with a drunk. She had been that route before and wanted nothing to do with it.

Anyway, she planned on leaving the party early and coming home to a nice hot bath and some coco. Greta called Nora, Betty and Michael early in the evening telling them these were her busiest months especially with Lucy gone on assignment.

Nora told her Michael was not feeling well and asked her to think about coming home in February rather than in March. Greta promised to work something out-but it may not be the long visit. Nora agreed but was grateful for the consideration Greta showed about her father's condition.

When Greta arrived at the party, she was pleasantly surprised. The food was fantastic, the music great and the decorations-were outstanding. There was even a Santa giving everyone a gift. Her boss gave her a bottle of expensive wine and a silk scarf. After her announcement all the young interns congratulated Lucy. A few mentioned they would like to interview for Lucy's spot.

Greta felt that the announcement went over well, and the party was a great success. To her surprise she really had a good time, but Christmas Parties give many people the opportunity to drink too much and misbehave in ways that they would not normally consider appropriate—this party was no different.

Greta saw it coming and decided to leave the party at 10:30 PM she was tired, and a few people were a little happy for her peace of mind. One of the young interns made trays of assorted sweets insisted Greta take home a tray and let her know how she liked them. Greta knew this girl hoped to be noted as a columnist on the cooking page of the paper, so she promised to critique the deserts.

Leaving the party, Greta noticed that it had snowed quite a bit. It was very cold and the roads where slick as black ice was everywhere. Driving slowly was not a problem as she kept thinking about her nice warm bath to come-her slippers and a good cup of warm coco. It was dark, windy and there were few streetlights on the road.

She had the radio with Christmas music playing and began singing with the music on the radio and felt satisfied that everything at the party went well. Lucy now had her chance to show herself as a reporter. She had to admit she did think the girl would do well.

Greta was singing and—not thinking about driving on an unfamiliar road and as she approached a turn, she misjudged the black ice on the road and ended up nearly killing herself as she swerved attempting to make the turn. Her singing stopped and the car was now nose down in a storm sewer.

The horn was blowing, the car stalled, and the items in the car: her coffee, wine, and the tray of sweets were open and all over her and the car.

Greta hit her head on the stirring wheel and was out cold. The driver in the car behind her witnessed the swerve and saw her car nosed down in the ditch. He stopped and went over to Greta to see if she was alright.

He checked her wrist-and her legs and arms. She had a bad bump on her head, and she was still out cold.

The man lifted Greta out of her car carefully. He noticed the bottle of liquor had exploded. It was all over her clothes, he commented out loud,

"Lady you are a mess, and you sure do smell."

Chapter 55

Slade West

When Greta awoke, all she saw was the beamed walls of a cabin. It took her a couple of minutes to realize she was in a bed-in a strange a room and she was naked.

A tall handsome gray-haired man entered the room a moment later. He had some clothes on his arm and a tray. *"I was hoping you would be awake"* he said. Greta asked about her clothes. *"You see miss- your clothes were sure wet and if you will pardon the expression-they stunk. You had a bottle of some kind of wine in the car and when you went into the ditch-the bottle broke and what was inside, and the broken glass was all over you and your car.*

You also had some coffee in the front and a tray of deserts that covered you. The sweets found their way into your hair, your shoes and your dress. Your clothes and you were a mess. I had no choice but to remove them." He said, *"Your clothes are ready."*

Greta asked, *"And did you clean me as well?"* *"Mam` you have been out cold; I had no choice but to rinse your hair and give you a sponge bat*h. Grateful to be alive she wanted to put her clothes on and get home. As she began to move her head it felt like it was hit by a boulder. *"You have quite a lump on your forehead"* th*e* man said. He continued, *"Yesterday the doc said you should rest for at least a week-you had a concussion."* *"A week, yesterday—uh what day is this?"* she asked, as she *was trying to put time together. "Well miss, your accident was on Saturday evening and this is 4 PM Monday after-noon." "OMG Greta said I lost two days—and I cannot remember anything."*

Greta began asking the man some questions. *"What is your name?"* sounded like a good place to begin. *"Slade West Miss,"* the man answered. She continued, *"How did I get here?" "I pulled you out of your car-checked you carefully for broken bones and blood-when I found none of that I brought you here in my car"* he said.

"Miss Wilson, I am a trained paramedic who worked in a hospital for sixteen years. I retired when my wife died five years ago."

Greta checked the man over with her eyes. He was well over six feet tall around 240 pounds thin, with salt and pepper hair and deep blue attractive eyes. She guessed he was in his mid to late 50's.

He was handsome, but she would not allow herself to think that- he did have a nice smile. *"How do you know my name?"* Greta asked. *"From your car registration"* he answered. *"How old are you?"* she asked. Slade smiled. *"Well miss—I am not really sure. The town where I was born did have all the records, but they were destroyed many years ago. I think I may be 56 years old.* Greta asked, *"Does anyone else live here—a woman maybe?" "Nope just me"* Slade answered.

"I-we had a daughter, but she died twenty years before my wife and when that happened my wife never

wanted another child. When our daughter Abby died, my wife said we could not replace her."

Greta was intrigued by the man for some reason—and it did not seem to bother her that he had seen her naked. *"If your questions are over for now, I have our dinner ready. There is a robe over there on the chair. I will give you a moment to get ready. The rest of your clothes will be ready in just a little while I still have to finish ironing one piece."*

Greta could not believe her ears—the man cooks, washes clothes, irons, and is a paramedic! Her father would be turning blue. Dinner was delicious. Slade made Irish Lamb stew with hot popovers and topped it off with coffee and home-made apple cobbler.

After dinner Greta felt tired and just about made it back to the bedroom before collapsing on the bed. Slade came in the room—thinking she was asleep he said, *"Miss please excuse my lust but as I undressed you, I noticed you are beautiful; I noticed a gentle face and beautiful hands. I have but one prayer and that is that you will visit me when you are well"* and with that he left the room. Greta thought *"**What strange comments but even more strange to find such a gentleman**"* then she fell fast asleep.

It was 8:30 Tuesday morning when she finally woke up again. It must have been the smell of fresh coffee that commanded her attention. Her clothes were all clean and pressed and hanging on the closet door. Her under clothes were folded nicely on the dresser. There was a knock on the door:

"Miss its morning I have coffee and breakfast ready" the voice on the other side of the door said. *"I'll be there in a moment"* Greta assured. Greta dressed as quickly as she could. She looked for a comb and it was on the dresser. The bump on her head was really quite big and sore.

Greta felt herself get dizzy every time she moved her head. It took her fifteen minutes before she left the bedroom and joined Slade in the kitchen.

As she entered the kitchen this time she looked around. The cupboards were attractive with a huge "W" brilliantly carved into the center of the two primary doors. There were cove moldings all around the kitchen and the appliances were stainless steel. The stove had six burners with a double oven.

He was obviously a cook. There was even an indoor grill to the left of the burners. A large overhead fan was near the stove and grill. The table was set beautifully with fresh flowers in the winter. The table had carved legs and a carved skirt joining the top of the table. Each leg had a "W' at the top.

It was obvious Slade had left his mark on the entire room and quite possibly he built the house. *"I have some French feta; homemade apple butter and my homemade biscuits are just coming out of the oven"* Slade was calm and reserved. The food was nicely arranged on a Burch table and eating breakfast was quiet, good and nice. Greta said:

"I need to be at work as I am supposed to go out of town today where is my car parked?" *"Miss, the axel is broken –the car is still in the ditch. I was going to have it winched out-but your insurance company may have to see it first. I called them –you had that information in the glove compartment of the car. I also notified the police and made a police report. Here is a copy."*

Wow he has taken care of everything thought Greta. *"How do I thank you Slade West?" Greta asked. Slade told Greta he would drive her where she wanted to go as soon as she was ready to leave."* It took her about twenty minutes after breakfast to be ready and Slade then drove to her Perry Street apartment in Manhattan. The drive took about forty-five minutes, but the time went quickly as there was never a lag for conversation. Greta was not sure but there was something about Slade West she liked maybe more than she should.

Slade was sorry to see Greta leave and as she said goodbye, he gave her his telephone number and asked if she would let him know how she was doing. Greta agreed.

Greta called in to work letting Mr. Gardner know of her accident. He agreed to send someone to Chicago and California in her place. It took Greta a couple of days to decide to have her car towed and to pick up the loaner that the insurance company arranged. Returning to work Greta still had quite a bump on her head and since the accident Greta was more tired than usual with a headache much of the time.

She was able to get an appointment on Friday with Dr. Lisa Cantor. Dr. Cantor was a lovely lady with salt and pepper hair that blended nicely with her brown hair. She always had a big smile to match her big brown eyes.

When Dr. Cantor walked in the examining room Greta began telling her of the car accident and the bump on her head. As she mentioned Slade West's name Dr. Cantor said "*Slade West was a great paramedic he really should not have left, too bad about his wife. Did Slade tell you he called me about your accident?*" Greta said that Slade did mention he called a doctor *or that the doc said*" but she did not know the name of the doctor he called. Dr. Cantor said Slade not only called but she saw Greta while she was at Slade's house on Saturday.

Dr. Cantor seemed quite taken with Slade she mentioned that he built all the desks for her office group and for the dental group on the fourth floor in that building. Greta said that Slade did not mention much about himself.

As she left Dr. Cantor, Greta felt this Slade West must be quite an unusual man indeed. She felt her curiosity heighted and suddenly she found herself wanting to give Slade a call. That evening after finishing her dinner Greta sat down to review her mail. It had been piling up and this was the first opportunity to actually go through the holiday cards and mail. There in the mail was a get-well card from Slade. When she opened the card, she recognized the New Psalm 23rd prayer:

"The Lord is my Shepard, there is nothing I lack. In green pastures you let me graze; to safe waters you lead me; you restore my strength.

You guide me along the right path for the sake of your name. Even when I walk through a dark valley, I fear no harm for you are at my side; your rod and staff give me courage.

You set a table before me as my enemies watch.
You anoint my head with oil, my cup overflows.
Only goodness and love will pursue me all the days of my life.
I will dwell in the house of the Lord for years and years to come."

The card had a beautiful picture of a dove and the words "Be Well" were written in silver print. The handwritten note said:
"I pray for your health.
Please let me know how you are doing?"

It was signed just "Slade" and his telephone number was under his name.

For some reason Greta could not wait to dial his number.

She immediately picked up the telephone and he answered on the first ring *"Hello"* said Greta, *"Thank you for the lovely get-well card. Thank you for taking such good care of me."* He answered

"You are most welcome beautiful lady." "I wanted you to know that I am fine. I understand you are a friend of my doctor-Dr. Cantor?" "Of course, I am she is my "niece"-of sorts." "Well –what—no?" Greta was taken back. Slade continued: *"You see her parents were neighbors of mine at one time. Her father and I became friends from the start.*

Since, I was about the same age as her father-and Lisa was five years old when they moved in as my neighbor her father insisted Lisa call me "uncle" out of respect. Her father is my attorney. I have had the pleasure of watching her grow into a beautiful young woman and finally a doctor." He continued: *"I knew she was your doctor- when I called to ask about the bump on your head. Did she tell you I worked with her as a paramedic?"*

Greta was taken back but answered: *"She did mention that she knew you."* Greta found herself quite at home talking with Slade. They made a date for coffee the next day at 2 PM across the street from Dr. Cantor's office at the new coffee shop. All Greta could think about was how kind Slade was and that Dr. Cantor had known him for most of her life.

Greta made up her mind before going: *"This is only a coffee. I will not allow myself to get involved."* The rest of the evening went by slowly. Greta reviewed the rest of her mail and then proceeded to check her closet to see what to wear for her meeting with Slade tomorrow.

She decided on a Kelly-Green pant suit with a Pink blouse and navy shoes and purse. The pants were low cut, and the legs were slightly flared. The jacket was green with ¾ sleeves and six brass buttons-three on each side. The blouse had a large man-type collar and no sleeves-just pearl buttons. It would be perfect. She would pull her hair back with a rubber band. For some reason she wanted to look beautiful. At 10 PM she was exhausted but still showered and settled into bed.

She had a book on Communication that she wanted to review. Being editor of the travel section on a major paper she wanted to keep abreast of new trends in communication. She began to read but ended up thinking about her coffee date and the recent events. Even the accident kept going through her mind. Before long she was fast asleep.

Greta was startled by her alarm at 7:30 AM and found it hard to believe the night had gone by so quickly. Breakfast did not appeal to her-all she wanted was coffee. Greta loved black strong coffee. Her father would always comment that *"Only those that do not like coffee added milk or sugar."*

For some reason, this morning her coffee did not taste right. She tried orange juice, but she was in the bathroom vomiting. Still feeling uneasy she decided to lay down *"for just a moment."* As she turned over for what seemed like just a few minutes she awoke with a startle—her clock had to be wrong—it was 11 AM. She chastised herself for falling back to sleep.

"I must have been more tired than I thought" she rationalized. A bowl of cereal just hit the spot and for some reason with a glass of milk. Milk was something Greta rarely had except with cereal-but this morning it was just what she needed to settle her stomach. She dressed and checked herself a several times—*"gee I look good"* she thought.

She applied her lipstick and coco butter to her face. She rarely used any other make-up

She was about ten minutes late arriving at the coffee shop. Slade was sitting calmly at a table he stood up politely to greet her. Greta ordered a coffee cappuccino and sat down. The two talked for about an hour. Greta took only a sip of her coffee.

Slade asked if she would join him for a late lunch or early dinner. He so wanted to spend as much time with her as possible. Greta forgot all about her stomach and the coffee and suddenly she was starved. *"I'd love to"* she said, *"but my treat."* *"No way"* said Slade *"When I ask a lady out, I pay!"*

Greta agreed and as they both got up to leave, she found herself suddenly getting tired again. She asked Slade if he minded cooking for her at her apartment. He said he would love the opportunity. They two stopped at the commissary in her building for some supplies which

Slade insisted on paying for *"Great idea—I do like to cook"*

Slade suggested she take a little nap while he cooked. Mostly to keep her out of his way as he had some ideas of how he wanted things to look. It was close to 7 PM when Greta came out of the bedroom *"What happened to lunch?"* she asked walking into the kitchen. *"You slept through it"* he answered. *"This is your dinner little lady."* Slade thought of everything. While she was napping, he called a florist shop and had flowers delivered.

Slade prepared chicken soup; stuffed roasted chicken with sage dressing; mashed potatoes and peas with a cup of hot tea with honey. The entire meal was delicious, and the soup really hit the spot. She was happy that he had made a large pot full of soup. She knew she would enjoy it later.

At the table, their conversation went to Slade's wife and what happened. She had been ill for five years and he alone cared for her. The turmoil of their daughter's death affected them both but -she lost her will to live. She became a diabetic and that was her downfall. They finished the dishes at 9:30 PM and Slade was leaving. It was so nice to have him there-Greta liked him more than she wanted to admit.

Before he left, he put one hand on each of Greta's shoulders and leaned down and gave her a kiss on the forehead.

As he left, he told her he had something important to tell her-but that he could not bring himself to tell her—just yet. Greta wondered what it could be about-but was resolved to just wait. She thought they made a nice couple.

As she slipped into bed the telephone rang. She picked up the receiver and said *"Hello."* It was Slade, *"Thank you, beautiful lady for gracing me with your time, attention and company. I had a terrific day; may I see you tomorrow?"* Greta said *"Yes"* without hesitation and before she could say anything else Slade said:

"Thank you, get a good night's sleep little lady. I will see your tomorrow evening at six." He left. Greta could not understand how tired she was, she turned over and went too directly to sleep.

In the morning she kept hitting the snooze button. When she looked at the clock it was 8:30AM—OMG she did not want to be late for work. She dressed quickly, grabbed a glass of milk and out she went.

Chapter 56

It Happened

The doorman hailed a cab and as always Greta was sitting at her desk by 9:30 AM. There was a message on her calendar "Tyler's Birthday in two days!" Cora wrote the message. Cora was and Greta's secretary for the last four years.

As Tyler's Godmother she knew she needed to pick up a gift for his birthday she loved the boy dearly. Cora had purchased two tickets to "Jesus Christ Superstar" for Greta as a Christmas gift. Greta decided to ask Slade if he would join her on Saturday as well. She called but there was no answer.

She was shopping for Tyler and called again-this time Slade answered and said he would love to go. There was one condition he wanted to drive and suggested he pick her up for dinner before the theater. She agreed.

They were still meeting that evening and since she still was not feeling quite right, she went home early to nap. She felt the bump on her head must have done some damage someplace. She decided to call the doctor in a week if she was not better.

That night Slade was there at six pm sharp. He brought dinner in a *"hot bag"* and he came with a monopoly game. The each had a stuffed Cornish hen, baked potato with sour cream, salad and broccoli. He even thought of bringing his Chi tea and an apple turnover for dessert. Everything hot and delicious and after dinner they played monopoly and talked, he left at 10 PM and said he would see her in two days. He called again just as she was in bed and thanked her for allowing him to enjoy her company. Greta fell fast asleep after the call.

Slade picked her up at three pm Saturday afternoon. She asked where they were having dinner and he laughed *"Well at the West Cafe` of course!"* They drove back to his place.

He made a fabulous dinner.

It began with chicken rice soup, stuffed pork roast with boiled potato and carrots and fresh fruit cocktail.

Later for dessert there was Angel Cake with strawberries and powdered sugar. Everything set well with Greta's stomach except for the glass of wine and the coffee. During the show she excused herself. In the lady's room she vomited thinking the wine had upset her stomach.

The next five weeks Greta and Slade saw each other every night. Greta did not want to take advantage of his kindness by having him cook for her all the time. So, she planned other events to be at.

They went for a lecture one night; then for a walk in the park; a movie show; some shopping and another night they just sat and watched the television. A couple of nights they played scrabble in her apartment or cooked together or even did a puzzle. Greta was amazingly comfortable with Slade.

She thought it a bit strange that except for a kiss on her forehead Slade never pushed her for more. She decided not to give their relationship too much thought as she was becoming comfortable and did not want to break it off.

Their sixth week together was spent much like all the rest. Then on their seventh Saturday, Slade invited Greta to an indoor cookout at his place.

Greta normally did not work on Saturday—but this week it was different. Lucy had a great centerfold and Greta wanted to make sure it was ready for the Sunday edition of the paper.

When she arrived home, she took a warm bath. And as she began dressing to go over to Slade's house, she felt sick to her stomach.

She called Slade: *"I think I have caught a flu virus. I would not like to be responsible for giving it to you. May I bow out of our picnic for just today?"* Slade was very understanding-he asked if she wanted him to bring over some soup-but Greta declined.

Greta felt terrible but she was not up to company. She hated disappointing Slade-but decided she would make it up to him. After she hung up the telephone she began vomiting again and could barely put herself to bed. She was ill all the rest of the weekend and even called in sick on Monday but went to work on Tuesday only to have to leave because of feeling ill. She was out of work the rest of the week still not feeling well.

She called Slade's telephone several times but there was never an answer. When the whole week went by and she was still unable to reach Slade she surmised that he might have gone on vacation. Any way Greta was still not feeling well and her appointment with the doctor was the next day. Dr. Cantor was on time. On a Tuesday after-noon, Greta had to wait only five minutes before going in to see the doctor. But with being sick Greta, it felt it was an eternity.

She wanted to find out what was causing her vom-iting and feeling of being so tired-she feared the bump on her heard was the beginning of brain cancer, or maybe there was a tumor. Greta always thought the worst when she was ill because she was rarely ill. As a child she was dramatic when sick. Dr. Cantor examined her carefully. She also reviewed her chart and took a blood and urine sample. This was in addition to the blood and urine that Greta was asked to do the Friday before her appointment. Dr. Cantor asked Greta to come into her office after she dressed. Both ladies sat down together when Dr. Cantor said:

"Greta, may I ask you about your relationship with Slade West?" Greta and asked, *"Yes you can but, why doctor this has nothing to do with my physical situation are you check on my intentions with your uncle?"*

Greta thought she was being funny, but the Doctor did not laugh. Dr. Cantor continued: *"I asked you this Greta because Slade West passed away three days ago."* **Greta felt as if someone hit her with a ton of bricks.**

That was why there was no answer when she called. Greta wondered if he was sick and all alone, maybe she had given him the virus she had? Greta began to cry and shake.

She asked Dr. Cantor: *"How did he die—was he very ill?"* *"No, Greta he was not ill at all"* Dr. Cantor said.

Greta was puzzled and answered, *"Well-doctor was there an accident?"* Greta felt **She must have liked Slade more than she was willing to admit to herself-his death was really bothering her. It just did not seem right-especially since he looked so fit and well in fact, he looked the picture of health. She was holding back tears.**

Dr. Cantor continued: *"Greta did you have a date with Slade and then cancel it?"* *"Yes, I had the flu"* she answered. *"When you called and cancelled your dinner and told him you had the flu—he called my father."* *"Your Father why?"* now Greta was getting confused. **What did Dr. Cantor's father have to do with her cancelling a dinner with Slade?**

Dr. Cantor continued: *"Did you know Greta that my father was Slade's attorney?* She said Slade did mention it. Greta was getting perturbed *"what is going on? And why did Slade call his attorney when I cancelled a date?"* The doctor continued

"Well Slade wrote a will that day—Greta he left everything he had or owned to YOU!"

Stunned Greta said *"What? Me!? Why!?"* **She did not understand why he would leave things to a stranger. She was baffled.** *"Why would he leave me* *anything? Why and how did he die? I do not understand what is happening?"* she said.

Dr. Cantor took two envelops out from her drawer and placed them on her desk.

"Slade gave my father two letters for you." "For me?" said Greta. *"Yes"* said the Doctor. Then Dr. Cantor began: *"Greta, there is no easy way to say this-Greta we think Slade West killed himself and we hope it was by accident." "What? How, Why"*

Greta could not believe her ears. *"Why-why-why would he do a thing like that we were just getting to know each other? We liked each other. What information did he give your father? Why would he do something like that-why? And why leave everything to me?"*

Now Greta was becoming hysterical and crying. Dr. Cantor continued: *"Greta when you had your accident Slade had to undress you. He had been a widower for many years and seeing your naked body was just too much for him. He knew you were out cold. He also knew he could not help himself. When he found out were a virgin, he still could not help himself."*

Greta was now in shock *"You mean he raped me?! He raped me!" "I am afraid he did."* Said Dr. Cantor and then she continued,

"Slade confessed to my father that he raped you a couple of times. Slade left these two letters with my father and we will talk about them in a minute." Dr. Cantor said.

"When you told Slade, you had the flu-he felt sure he had gotten you pregnant. I confirmed it to him with my original tests. In the letter, he gave to my father he asked that we take good care of you—but that he could not face you again knowing what he did."

Then Dr. Cantor gave Greta two #10 envelopes that were sealed. Dr. Cantor said she would leave the room for a bit so Greta could read the letters in private.
Greta was still crying and trying to grasp what had just happened in the last ten minutes. As Dr. Cantor left the room Greta opened the first envelope and took out the note. It began:

"My Dear Wonderful Greta,

Oh, how I love you- you are the kindest most perfect person I know. How could you ever forgive me for what I did to you, when I am not even able to forgive my own actions?

You are beautiful inside and out—I had no right to take advantage of the situation. I fear you will never want to see me again. I just cannot take another loss or failure.

You see, I have fallen deeply in love with you. I so wanted to tell you but could never bring myself to say the words. When you were ill and could not come to dinner, I had mixed emotions.

One of them was that you may be having second thought about spending so much time with this man as there was no doubt you and I were falling in love. It took me a while to realize the timing of things. I then suspected

447

what was happening and I could not face telling you how I invaded your privacy.

Lisa confirmed my fears –my love—you are pregnant! I decided that my telling you this way would be the best. I could have gone to prison-for what I did but now the prison lies forever in my heart.

Greta, I have no other family. I know you will carry my child. Therefore, I leave you everything I own to help you care for our child.

Our time together was the happiest I can ever remember. I want you to know that I love you more than anything in the world. I would have loved to marry you and watch our child grow.

I hope there will be a time you can think of me without hate for the situation I have put you in.

Know that I value love and I hope you keep the child and the two of you will live in love forever.
Sincerely, and with deep regret, but with love in my heart for you and our child, I am,
Slade West"

The second letter was an acknowledgement of paternity and a confession identifying the days, dates, times and place of his intercourse with her. The last words were "I am so sorry but the sentence you could impose upon me is nothing to how I feel for my violation of this lovely lady's life."

Signed
"Slade West"

Greta sat still for a while in shock she was unable to move trying to understand everything what just happened and what she read. Tears were flowing as she realized she was now pregnant.

Within a minute Dr. Cantor entered the room. *"Greta my father has just arrived. May I bring him in to meet you he has something to tell you?"*

Eric Cantor waited for a moment just outside his daughter's office. When the door opened, he went in alone.

"Greta Wilson?" he asked. *"Yes"* she said. *"I am Eric Cantor, Slade West's attorney. I want to read you something. And with that he proceeded to read what was obviously Slade West's last will and testament: "I Slade West give to Greta Wilson from this day forward all my worldly possessions real and personal."* Greta interrupted and asked, *"What does that mean?"*

Mr. Cantor stated, *"I have not had enough time to arrive at a total figure for everything in his estate but without the land the house is on the rest of his land, if sold, should total a little over three to four million dollars. The value of the house, its contents and the adjoining land has not been appraised yet but that should be two to three million dollars!"*—*"But how? I mean—what?"*

Greta could barely speak. Mr. Cantor continued: *"Slade's wife inherited much from her family plus together they purchased quite a bit of land.*

Slade sold many acres after his wife died. There are no other heirs or family. The money from the sale was put in the Bank. After Slade left me, he said he was going to that bank to put all the money in trust for you.

He also signed a deed giving you his residence, car, boat, and equipment." Mr. Cantor looked distraught. "*The only thing he did not leave you fully but gave Lisa was a term lease for this building. Did you know he owned the medical center?*"

"*The Medical Center—No!*" Greta answered still in shock. "*He owned this center?*" Greta asked. "*Yes*" said Mr. Cantor. *I have recorded all the papers as Slade wished and everything is legal. This building belongs in trust to Lisa until...*"

Now Dr. Cantor entered the room and interrupted. "Greta, the results are in and final. You are pregnant" she said. Mr. Cantor interrupted, "*Greta there is another part of this will, if you were pregnant—Lisa's rent for her unit all goes in a trust for the child. The other rents are Lisa's to keep until the child is 18 years of age at that time the building is put in the child's name.*

It is Lisa's responsibility to hold it as if she were the owner-for 18 years. After which Lisa may purchase it with two appraisals with the money for the purchase going to the child you are carrying should the child survive and be alive. If the child is not alive the building is Lisa's free and clear." Mr. Cantor said it was Slade's way of giving the child money her own money for college.

Greta was mute—all she could do was to cry and stare while continuing to read Slade's confession over.

She asked where the body of Slade West was located. Mr. Cantor said "*Slade ordered an immediate cremation. He requested that his ashes be flown across his land within 24 hours. That was completed this morning.*"

"*What, so I have nothing with his picture or any other information?*" Greta said. Mr. Cantor handed Greta the keys he was given and said "*There may be something in the house? One key is for the safe deposit box another for the house and a third if for the new car he purchased for you. I have an envelope here with more keys for the buildings on the land. "Everything Slade had Miss Wilson is now yours. We are here if you need us-Lisa and I, everything has been recorded, is legal, and official.*"

Greta left the Dr.'s office in a daze. As she reached her hand for a cab-she was crying uncontrollably. Instead of going into the office she went back to her apartment and called in sick. She was out of the office - for the next two weeks.

Two days after her meeting at the doctor's office Greta drove the loaner car from the insurance company over to Slade's house. She wanted to look around.

Everything in the house was just as it was the last time, she was there except her new car was in the driveway. It was a beautiful white Lincoln on the dash—"*Be safe always, Love Slade*" There was a note on the refrigerator: "*Greta coming: Dinner—Lamb, roasted potatoes, lettuce salad, homemade apple pie."* The entire meal was wrapped and in the refrigerator. Suddenly, and for the first time Greta felt a butterfly flutter on the inside of her body.

It was at that moment Greta decided—this is a child inside of me—a life—and it is all mine.

She called Mr. Gardner and quit her job effective immediately. At first, he did not believe her and asked if she was fishing for a raise.

He was stunned when she said she was pregnant. Cora began boxing everything. Gardner told her she could free- lance writing for them anytime and that he would miss her. He wished her well. Cora cried and they agreed to talk soon.

Greta called her mother and said she was flying to Clayton and would be there in three days. This was something she wanted to tell her parents in person.

Michael was now feeling the pains of working with his back all these years and Nora was tired. Time was marching on and Greta knew the feeling but now there was a new life. They talked about selling the house-but they did not know where to go.

Chapter 57

Decisions

When Greta arrived in Clayton, Michael picked her up. Arriving home, dinner was ready. Nora was surprised. *"I am so happy you could spend some time with us,* she said.

After dinner Greta said she wanted to speak with the three of them.

Betty chimed in *"She is in Love!"* Nora asked, *"Is that true?"* Greta wanted to be truthful with her parents. she began telling them about Slade West saying she was in love. She then said—but Slade passed away. She went through everything ending with the size of Slade's estate.

Nora and Michael understood but found the situation difficult. *"What about the child? What will you say to the child?* Nora asked. *"I will say that we were very much in love; and he died before we could marry"* Greta said. Then she continued:

*"**Mom, Dad, Grandma Betty, we must all agree on what is to be told to the child. We must never again discuss the rape or his accidental death-are we all agreed?**"*

A child-not married-from the lust of a dead man! The size of Slade's estate left them shocked, amazed and speechless. Obviously, he loved you both-but why? Greta said: *"**That word must never be used again-I need each of you to give me a solemn promise**"* They all agreed.

Grete returned to her New York apartment two weeks later deciding to sell everything and live in Slade

West's house until their baby was born. Greta hired a company to move certain items to Slade's house. Once she moved in, she found all sorts of antiques, letters, albums, pictures all about Slade's life. It was quite a discovery.

Everything in the house was all hers-and the babies! She put her condo on the market for sale. There was a couple in her building wanting to downsize from their two-bedroom condo to Greta's one bedroom with a patio. They did not need to make the deal contingent to the sale of their condo. They purchased it "as is" just five days after it was listed by the building.

Greta gave her old car to Cora knowing that she and her husband could never afford a second car. She put up a trust fund for Tyler-so he would have enough money for college. Cora was overjoyed and appreciative the ladies would always stay connected.

It took a little over a week before Greta was able to get to the safe deposit box. To her amazement there was stocks, bonds, gold and silver bullion, and over $100,000 in cash and papers representing CD's becoming due over the next five years. She was rich beyond her wildest dreams.

The land in the back of the house was twelve acres. It appraised for over 4.6 million dollars five years ago-without the house and its land—there was no appraisal for that in the box.

The land that went with the house consisted of about eight acres. There was a note that there would be no problem separating the house and the land should she decide to sell some of the property. Slade had surveys completed both ways.

In each room of the house there were a several antiques and the attic and, in the basement, had some as well. Greta asked an auctioneer to give her an idea of their value. They antiques were valued at 2.8 million dollars and more at auction.

Greta would never have to work again. Slade West saw to everything. All this will more than take care of our unborn child. *"OMG-I used the words—Our Child."*

Who would have ever guessed that this nice man would have so much money and such a big estate and be guilty of... she could not say the word?

Greta checked the house. She loved the house. It consisted of four large bedrooms, a living room, dining room, office, two and a half bathrooms downstairs and two full bathrooms upstairs. Greta decided to live there at least until the baby was born. She saw three envelopes on the desk. The first was the name of the company that takes care of the land for Slade; there were the names of the owner and the cost-per year. Slade paid them for the next year. The second was the company that handles the windows in the house-they were paid for a year as well. Finally, the third envelop was the combination to the house safe-where it was located and how much money was available for daily use. Greta was shocked-there was $75,000 in small bills. The man thought of every detail to make her comfortable. Greta realized she really loved Slade and would have loved to be with him when their child was born.

Greta put an ad in the paper. She wanted to hire a woman to help her care for the house while she was pregnant; and be there helping her when the baby was born. She advertised in two papers and interviewed all twenty-four applicants in three weeks.

She settled on a fifty-nine-year-old Italian widow named Concetta DiBeliso. Connie married a gentleman who was adopted as a child; he passed away eleven years earlier. They had two sons: Antonio and Vincenzo.

After Connie's husband died, she took the boys to her brother's farm just north of Naples. They are still living in Italy with Connie's brother Franco. It was too difficult to raise them in the states alone. Manalo, Connie's husband, owned a sewing business with a partner. Before the business could be sold, they each needed to pay off all the debts. She was responsible for half and that took her five years. By then the partner had to sell the business. It sold to another Italian, but her share was not enough money to bring the boys back to America.

By then it did matter as the boys wanted to stay with their Uncle Frank and Aunt Anna. They loved the farm, and she visits them every other year for a month. They write and call every so often. Frank and his wife Anna could not have children, so this was a benefit for all concerned. Frank never asked her to give her any money. He said she gave them a gift.

Hiring Connie worked out perfectly. She moved in with some clothes, five boxes of personal items, and a sewing machine. She sewed most of Greta's maternity clothes and much of the baby clothes besides being an excellent cook.

She painted the nursery, and the two women purchased a crib and rocker for the nursery. Rita called often she was happy for Greta-but Nora felt this was not the way that she should live her life or raise a child. She wanted her to come home and let them take care of her. But Greta needed her space; and she needed to live in Slade West's home.

Nora did not want to tell Greta that Michael's ulcer was acting up again. She did not want to trouble her while she was pregnant. Nora felt that a baby and no husband—no father—all alone in a strange house with a housekeeper-away from family –was a difficult enough without adding to Michael's problems!

Rita promised to come when the baby was born, she knew Nora had her hands full with Michael and she did not want Greta to be alone. Rita was healthy could help with the baby for a week. The twins were married. Carl's schedule had him out of town when the baby was born. His schedule was booked for the next year and a half. Carl and Rita were still living in the house on Oak Street in Chicago.

On October 2nd, at 7 PM Ava Marie Wilson West was born. She was born in Slade West's bed. Dr. Cantor warned Greta against birthing at home-but Connie assisted and there was not a problem. Put on the scale at home; the child weighed 6 pounds 10 ounces and was 18 inches long with dark red hair and blue eyes like her father. Nora hoped to fly in around Thanksgiving, but an unexpected snowstorm grounded all planes. Michael was also still having ulcer issues-he forgets his medicine and eats out with the guys at work often for lunch.

Greta told her no worry she and the baby were fine. She suggested she would come home after Christmas with the baby. Greta sent pictures of the baby to everyone, and she received clothes, toys and good wishes from family and people at work. Greta thought Slade would be so proud of his daughter.

She was truly a beautiful baby. Greta knew she made the right decision she just wished Slade were here to enjoy his child with her. Seeing their daughter Ava for the first time, she forgave Slade completely and vowed never to think or say the word rape again.

Such a gift this man has given me Greta thought; and he paid for her with everything he had—including his life. She was resolved that Ava would know her father was a "*great*" man. she would tell the child about her father identifying that it was truly a love story.

Chapter 58

It Happened

Shana and Greta had a few conversations over the years since they both lived in New York but nothing like a real friendship. Shana visited Greta when she was pregnant a couple of times. Rita postponed going as Katherine-just moved into a new house and she was helping her.

Shana hoped to visit Greta when the baby was born but with looking for a new restaurant job to work; along with a new place to live-things were difficult. She was planning on getting a divorce from David. Shana loved her husband but wanted to have a life. David was a work-aholic and they had little time or much else. The deli had doubled in size during their marriage.

After Shana's past visit the two women talked on the telephone about Shana's situation several times -she just wanted to wait to tell David until after the holidays

Sometimes the plans of mice and men must yield to those of God.

The week before Christmas Shana called Greta. She told her that after eight years of trying to have a baby; she was now pregnant. She did not understand how come now—just as they are talking about a divorce. David asked for a chance to reconcile their differences. Greta asked her if she loved David "*Of course!*" Shana answered. "Then this divorce makes no sense."

Greta found it hard pressed to understand why Shana could even think of separating. This was Shana's first pregnancy, and she loved her husband; why would anything else matter to her but David and the baby? Greta suggested Shana get a good doctor and stay married to the man she loved.

Greta called Nora that night. The two women talked for a while and Greta said she would bring Ava to Clayton as soon as the snow cleared.

Greta told Nora about Shana and the women decide how strange that it would happen after all these years.

Chapter 59

New Life

As luck would have it, Shana delivered twin girls with her first pregnancy and twin boys with the second pregnancy sixteen months later. Shana really had her hands full.

Greta sent Connie to give her a hand when the girls were born thinking that Connie would help her for a short while- just to give Shana a chance to get on her feet.

But Greta did not understand how much Connie loved New York City. Shana and David lived near the deli and Connie stayed with them. Connie met and fell in love with Pasquale one of the cooks at the deli.

Now this was a dilemma, if Connie and Pasquale fell in love and moved back to Chicago- David and Shana would lose two helpers. Pasquale was a great cook; Connie helped with the four children.

David did not want to lose either one of them-

But as things between Connie and Pasquale got serious and they married; David gave them a vacant apartment free for a year.

Greta felt it was of no consequence losing Connie. Ava was a beautiful child and the two of them were like two peas in a pot doing everything together. When the weather broke in Clayton, she took Ava home to see the family. They all loved Ava and tried to tell Greta how nice it would be if she lived closer to home.

Greta said she would think about it when Ava was ready for Kindergarten because by then Greta hoped to be free lancing again.

Time flies when you are having fun-and that is just what Greta and Ava -were having-fun. Greta traveled to Disney, London and Paris. When home she and Ava played games Ave took dance, piano, art. She enjoyed the theater and often went to concerts and shows.

Chapter 60A

Ava

They travelled to Clayton about five times a year and stayed a week each time. But now, Ava was going to begin first grade. Greta held her from kindergarten-they were too busy; and Ava was too well advance for even the first grade. Still Greta recognized that-Ava needed to be near other children.

Greta decided it was time to sell everything and move back to Clayton so Ava could be near the family. Leaving the sale to Mr. Cantor to handle Greta purchased a house in Clayton.

It took the entire year to sell all the land and the house. Everything sold for much more than the appraisals. She really would never have to work again Slade's holding were enough.

Coming to Clayton Greta decided to give everyone there a vacation. It would be one they would all remember. She took them to Disney Land. Nora and Betty really enjoy the calmer rides.

Michael just loved being with his Granddaughter and taking pictures. Ava wanted to take everyone on a trip to Paris one day as she showed them all a picture of the Eiffel Tower and felt it an exciting trip.

Everyone agreed they would all take the trip when Ava was eight years old. Ava inherited her mother's travel lust.

Financially the women were set for life; Greta did not feel Ava needed to be told just how much money was available. She set up a life estate for herself and a trust fund for Ava. The fund would provide a decent living for both, Greta, Ava, and Ava's children—should she ever marry and have children. They would even be able to live on the interest alone.

Greta's house was two blocks from where Nora, Michael, and Betty lived. It was currently 1980 square feet on the first floor with three bedrooms, two full baths and two half baths. The owner had an eight-foot attic on the second floor with windows on all sides. The original owner planned on expanding in the future. There was a two-car garage, a carport and a recreation room in the basement. The first floor had a living room with a wood burning fireplace, and a dining room that opened to a sunroom. Greta made two of the first-floor bedrooms into one large television room leaving the other bedroom as an office. There was a front and a rear porch that gave the property a homey feeling. With one and a half acres of land it was great for a swing set and pool. The original owner of the house purchased three houses and knocked them all down to build this house. She learned that the owners originally planned to take in foster children. When the construction was completed, they moved to Florida. Clayton's winters were not what they were used to coming from California. In Florida they built again, and this time had nine foster children living with them with room for nine more. The wife was a teacher, and the husband was a minister.

Ava loved the house. She loved living close to her grandparents and Betty. Ava surmised she could go to grandma's every day whenever she wanted.

Greta hired a contractor and expanded the upstairs into four bedrooms, a playroom and two full baths and two half baths. When the construction was over, she and Ava re-decorated the entire house together. It really became a big house, but Greta knew there would be room for all the family to visit. She and Ava slept on the second floor.

Greta was lonely when Ava was in school. She took a job with a wire service and floated articles occasionally. Ava had friends from school over every day. Greta wondered if the children had parents. Her life was ordering pizzas, having snacks, taking several girls to the picture show, birthday parties and baking cookies for the always starving group of kids that hung around with Ava. She was there just in case of any kind of emergency.

The next eight years went by so quickly Greta was stunned when "ALL OF A SUDDEN AVA became a young lady!"

Now Michael was not doing well-he was approaching 68 years old, and his legs were not as strong as they once were. Nora had her hand filled taking care of both Michael and Betty. Betty was now 84 years old.

Age has a strange way of bringing a reality to life.

No one lives forever. Accepting the limitations of her family Greta agreed to take Ava back to Paris after high school graduation as a gift. For now, she would just love being with all the family. Shana brought the girls to Clayton more often and when she did Rita would join her. Greta had plenty of room for all of them at the house.

David kept the twin boys busy close to him in the new restaurant. Carl was always traveling giving lectures or attending conferences; so, Rita was free to do as she pleased.

When Ava turned sixteen years old Greta decided Ava should get a part time job after school. Ava began working at a local grocery store three days a week from 3-7 PM. When Ava was in senior year in high school, she told her mother that she wanted to be a reporter.

Greta laughed and remembered her discussion with her parents—when she informed them, she was going to be a reporter. History has a way of repeating itself she thought.

But as Ava was talking about her future.

Greta thought how the years had gone by so quickly. Soon Betty would be gone, and she would be alone the writing was on the wall.

Chapter 60 B

History

This Christmas Shana, David and all four children and Rita were coming to Clayton for Christmas.

They agreed to stay with Greta and Ava. Rita was getting up in age and she loved that her daughter was still close to Greta and visiting her more often.

Shana's family was growing up nicely. Shana named the girls Rita-Marie and Lillian Carol; the boys are David Allen and Joshua Ryan. They had become a close loving family.

Ava was excited to have them visit and stay with them. She wanted to decorate the house in a special way.

She and Greta went shopping for a real tree. While they were out shopping Ava introduced her mother to her widowed Biology teacher Mr. Charles Blitz. Mr. Blitz was out with his nephew Kurt also shopping for a Christmas tree.

"Mr. Blitz was the brother of Mathew Blitz a former minister who knew Aunt Rita" Ava told Greta. "The minister and his wife Catherine were Kurt's parents. The minister, his wife and daughter all passed away about seven years earlier in an auto accident. As they talked it was getting close to supper time and Greta invited them to dinner.

Low and behold they accepted. Charles helped set up the tree while Kurt and Ava decorated it. Kurt and Ava really hit it off.

As time went on Greta noticed that Kurt and Ava seemed to be calling and seeing each other often and dating. Kurt was in an all-boys high school and would graduate one year before Ava. During the rest of her senior year Kurt was her steady boyfriend and her date for all parties and the proms.

It was end of August that year when Betty passed away. She had left the house to Ava.

Kurt took a job after high school. He wanted to wait for Ava to graduate from high school so they could enroll at the State University together. It was obvious by then that the two had become a pair.

The last year of Ava's college education she and Kurt decided to marry. The old homestead was vacant as Michael and Nora went into an apartment after Betty passed away. Ava rented it for years to a nice family. Ava and Kurt like it and decided to make it their first home.

Their wedding was beautiful; Ava planned a reception at the hotel for 125 people. All the family from Chicago came. The couple went to Niagara Falls for their Honeymoon.

Greta loved seeing her daughter so happy and so much in love. She decided to go back to school and find some ways to entertain herself. Her first course brought someone new and interesting into her life.

Upon visiting the old house Kurt decided it was solid but too small.

Within six months Kurt had a dormer put on and expanded the first floor.

When he went to expand the attic, he found not only the hidden room but several boxes with journals. Nora continued them after Betty passed away.

With the advent of learning a family history Ava began reading. When she read about Rita and Carl, she began wondering what ever did happen to their marriage. Then she found the journal with all the answers.

To be continued in…
A NEW BEGINNING…See you there…

Made in the USA
Middletown, DE
09 November 2022

14509984R00269